DOMITIA

DOMITIA

A TALE OF ROME

SABINE BARING-GOULD

WILDSIDE PRESS

Published by Wildside Press LLC.
www.wildsidebooks.com

BOOK I

CHAPTER I

THE PORT OF CENCHRÆA

Flashes as of lightning shot from each side of a galley as she was being rowed into port. She was a bireme, that is to say, had two tiers of oars; and as simultaneously the double sets were lifted, held for a moment suspended, wet with brine, feathered, and again dipped, every single blade gleamed, reflecting the declining western sun, and together formed a flash from each side of the vessel of a sheaf of rays.

The bireme was approaching the entrance to the harbor of Cenchræa.

The one white sail was filled with what little wind breathed, and it shone against a sapphire sea like a moon.

Now, at a signal the oars ceased to plunge. The sail was furled, and the galley was carried into the harbor between the temple that stood on the northern horn of the mole, and the great brazen statue of Poseidon that occupied a rock in the midst of the entrance, driven forward by the impulse already given her by the muscles of the rowers and the east wind in the sail.

This Cenchræan harbor into which she swept was one of the busiest in the world. Through it as through a tidal sluice rushed the current of trade from the East to the West, and from the Occident to the Orient. It was planted on a bay of the Saronic Gulf, and on the Isthmus of Corinth, at the foot of that lovely range of mountains thrown up by the hand of God to wall off the Peloponnesus as the shrine of intellectual culture and the sanctuary of Liberty.

And a furrow—like an artificial dyke—ran between this range and Hellas proper, a furrow nearly wholly invaded by the sea, but still leaving a strip of land, the Corinthian isthmus, to form a barrier between the Eastern and the Western worlds.

On the platform at the head of a flight of marble steps before a temple of Poseidon, in her open litter, lounged a lady, with the bloom of youth gone from her face, but artificially restored.

She was handsome, with finely moulded features and a delicate white hand, the fingers studded with rings, and a beautiful arm which was exposed whenever any one drew near whose admiration was worth the acquisition. Its charm was enhanced by armlets of gold adorned with cameos.

Her arched brows, dark in color, possibly owed their perfection of turn and their depth of color to dye and the skill of the artist who decorated her every day, but not so the violet-blue of her large eyes, although these also were enhanced in effect by the tinting of the lashes, and a touch of paint applied to their roots.

The lady, whose name was Longa Duilia, was attended by female slaves, who stood behind the litter, and by a freedman, Plancus, who was at her side with a set smile on his waxen face, and who bowed towards the lady every moment to hear her remarks, uttered in a languid tone, and without her troubling to turn her head to address him.

"He will soon be here," said the lady; "the bireme is in the port. I can see the ruffle before her bows as she cuts the water."

"Like the wave in my lady's hair," sighed Plancus.

"Abominable!" exclaimed Duilia, "when the ripple in my hair is natural and abiding, and that in the water is made and disappears."

"Because, Mistress, the wavelets look up, see, and fall back in despair."

"That is better," said the lady.

"And the swelling sail, like your divine bosom, has fallen, as when—"

"Ugh! I should hope the texture of my skin was not like coarse sailcloth; get behind me, Plancus. Here, Lucilla, how am I looking? I would have my lord see me to the best advantage."

"Madam," said the female slave, advancing, "the envious sun is about to hide his head in the west. He cannot endure, after having feasted on your beauty, to surrender it to a mortal."

"Is not one eyebrow a trifle higher than the other?" asked Duilia, looking at herself in a hand mirror of polished metal.

"It is indeed so, lady, but has not the Paphian Goddess in the statue of Phidias the same characteristic? Defect it is not, but a token of divinity."

"Ah," said Duilia, "it is hereditary. The Julian race descends from Venus Genetrix, and I have the blood of the immortal ancestress in me."

"Much diluted," muttered Plancus into the breast of his tunic; he was out of humor at the failure of his little simile of the sail.

"By the way," said the lady; "the stay in this place Cenchræa is positively intolerable. No society, only a set of merchants—rich and all that sort of thing—but nobodies. The villa we occupy is undignified and uncomfortable. The noise of the port, the caterwauling of sailors, and the smell of pitch are most distasteful to me. My lord will hardly tarry here?"

"My lord," said the freedman, pushing forward, "he who subdued the Parthians, and chained the Armenians, to whom all Syria bowed, arrives to cast himself at your ladyship's feet, and be led by you as a captive in your triumphal entry into the capital of the world."

"You think so, Plancus." She shook her head, "He is an obstinate man—pig-headed—I—I mean resolute in his own line."

"Madam, I know you to be irresistible."

"Well, I desire to leave this odious place. I have yawned here through three entire months."

"And during these months, the temple of Aphrodite has been deserted, and the approaches grass-grown."

"How would my Lady like to remove to Corinth?"said Lucilla. "The vessel will be taken to Diolcus, and there placed on rollers, to be drawn across the isthmus."

"Oh! Corinth will be noisier than this place, and more vulgar, because more pretentious. Only money-lending Jews there. Besides, I have taken an aversion to the place since the death of my physician. As the Gods love me, I not see the good of a medical attendant who is so ignorant as to allow himself to die, and that at such an inconvenient moment as the present. By the Great Goddess! what impostors there be. To think that for years I committed the care of my precious health to his bungling hands! Plancus, have you secured another? I suffer frightfully at sea."

"A sure token of your divine origin," said the steward. "The Foamborn (Venus) rose out of and left the waves because the motion of them disagreed with her."

"There is a good deal in that," observed Longa Duilia. "Plancus, have you secured another? I positively cannot across Adria without one to hold my head and supply anti—anti—what do you call them?"

"Madam," said the freedman, rubbing his hands together, "I have devoted my energies to your service. I have gone about with a lantern seeking an honest physician. I may not have been as successful as I desired, but I have done my utmost."

"I prithee—have done with this rodomontade and to the point. Have you secured one? As the Gods love me! it is not only one's insides that get upset at sea, but one's outside also becomes so tousled and tumbled—that the repairs—but never mind about them. Have you engaged a man?"

"Yes, my Lady, I have lighted on one Luke, a physician of Troas; he is desirous of proceeding to Rome, and is willing to undertake the charge of your health, in return for being conveyed to the capital of the world at your charges."

"I make you responsible for his suitability,"said Longa Duilia.

"Body of Bacchus!" she exclaimed suddenly, after a pause, "Where is the child?"

"Where is the lady Domitia Longina?" asked Plancus, as he looked about him.

"The lady Domitia, where is she?" asked Lucilla.

"The lady Domitia?"—passed from one to another.

"Where is she? What has become of her? As the Gods love me—you are a pack of fools. The more of you there are, so much the more of folly. You have let her gallop off among the odious sailors, and she will come back rank with pitch. Lucilla, Favonia, Syra, where is she?"

Duilia sat upright on her seat, and her eyes roamed searchingly in every direction.

"I never met with such a child anywhere, it is the Corbulo blood in her, not mine. The Gods forbid! O Morals!"

"Madam," said a slave-girl coming up. "I saw her with Eboracus."

"Well, and where is Eboracus. They are always together. He spoils the child, and she pays him too much consideration. Where are they?"

The slaves, male and female, looked perplexedly in every direction.

"Perhaps," said Plancus, "she has gone to the altar of Poseidon to offer there thanks for the return of her father."

"Poseidon, nonsense! That is not her way. She has been in a fever ever since the vessel has been sighted, her cheeks flaming and in a fidget as if covered with flying ants. Find the girl. If any harm shall have come to her through your neglect, I will have you all flayed—and hang the cost!"

She plucked a bodkin from her dress, and ran it into the shoulder of the slave-woman, Favonia, who stood near her, and made her cry out with pain.

"You are a parcel of idle, empty-headed fools,"exclaimed the alarmed and irritated mother, "I will have the child found, and that instantly. You girls, you have been gaping, watching the sailors, and have not had an eye on your young mistress, and no concern for my feelings. There is no more putting anything into your heads than of filling the sieves of the Danaides."

"Madam," said Plancus, for once without a smile on his unctuous face, "you may rest satisfied that no harm has befallen the young lady. So long as Eboracus is with her, she is safe. That Briton worships her. He would suffer himself to be torn limb from limb rather than allow the least ill to come to her."

"Well, well," said the lady impatiently, "we expect all that sort of thing of our slaves."

"Madam, but do we always get it?"

"We! The Gods save me! How you talk. We! We, indeed. Pray what are you to expect anything?"

"The other day, lady," hastily continued the steward eager to allay the ebullition he had provoked. "The other day, Eboracus nigh on killed a man who looked with an insolent leer at his young mistress. He is like a faithful Molossus."

"I do not ask what he is like," retorted the still ruffled lady, "I ask where she is."

Then one of the porters of the palanquin came forward respectfully and said to the steward:—"If it may please you, sir, will you graciously report to my Lady that I observed the young mistress draw Eboracus aside, and whisper to him, as though urging somewhat, and he seemed to demur, but he finally appeared to yield to her persuasions, and they strolled together along the mole."

Longa Duilia overheard this. It was not the etiquette for an underling to address his master or mistress directly unless spoken to.

She said sharply:—"Why did not the fellow mention this before? Give him thirty lashes. Where did they go, did he say?"

"Along the mole."

"Which mole?"

"Madam, Carpentarius is afraid of extending his communication lest he increase the number of his lashes."

"Well, well!" exclaimed the mistress, "We may remit the lashes—let him answer."

"Carpentarius," said the steward, "Her ladyship, out of the super-abundance of her compassion, will let you off the thirty lashes, if you say where be Eboracus and the young lady, your mistress Domitia Longina."

"Sir," answered the porter, "that I cannot answer positively; but—unless my eyes deceive me, I see a small boat on the water, within it a rower and a young girl."

"By the Immortal Brothers! he is right,"exclaimed Plancus. "See, lady, yonder is a cockle boat, that has been unmoored from the mole, and there be in it a rower, burly, broadbacked, who is certainly the Briton, and in the bow is as it were a silver dove—and that can be none other than your daughter."

"As the Gods love me," gasped Duilia, throwing herself back in the litter; "what indelicacy! It is even so, the child is besotted. She dotes on her father, whom she has not seen since we left Antioch. And she has actually gone to meet him. O Venus Kalypyge! What are we coming to, when children act in this independent, indecent manner. O Times! O Morals!"

CHAPTER II

AN ILL-OMEN

It was even so.

The young girl had coaxed the big Briton to take her in a boat to the galley, so as to meet and embrace her father, before he came on shore.

She was a peculiarly affectionate child, and jealous to boot. She knew that, so soon as he landed, his whole attention would be engrossed by her very exacting mother, who moreover would keep her in the background, and would chide should the father divert his notice from herself to his child.

She was therefore determined to be the first to salute him, and to receive his endearments, and to lavish on him her affection, unchecked by her mother.

As for the slave, he knew that he would get into trouble if he complied with the girl's request, but he was unable to resist her blandishments.

And now Domitia reached the side of the galley, and a rope was cast to the boat, caught by Eboracus, who shipped his oars, and the little skiff was made fast to the side of the vessel.

The eyes of the father had already recognized his child. Domitia stood in the bows and extended her arms, poised on tiptoe, as if, like a bird about to leap into the air and fly to his embrace.

And now he caught her hand, looked into her dancing, twinkling eyes, as drops of the very Ægean itself, set in her sweet face, and in another moment she was clinging round his neck, and sobbing as though her heart would break, yet not with sorrow, but through excess of otherwise inexpressible joy.

For an hour she had him to herself—all to herself—the dear father whom she had not seen for half a year, to tell him how she loved him, to hear about himself, to pour into his ear her story of pleasures and pains, great pleasures and trifling pains.

And yet—no, not wholly uninterrupted was the meeting and sweet converse, for the father said:

"My darling, hast thou no word for Lucius?"

"Lamia! He is here?"

The father, Cnæus Domitius Corbulo, with a smile turned and beckoned.

Then a young man, with pleasant, frank face, came up. He had remained at a distance, when father and daughter met, but had been unable to withdraw his eyes from the happy group.

"Domitia, you have not forgotten your old playmate, have you?"

With a light blush like the tint on the petal of the rose of June, the girl extended her hand.

"Nay, nay!" said Corbulo. "A gentler, kinder greeting, after so long a separation."

Then she held up her modest cheek, and the young man lightly touched it with his lips.

She drew herself away and said:

"You will not be angry if I give all my thoughts and words and looks to my father now. When we come on shore, he will be swallowed up by others."

Lamia stepped back.

"Do not be offended," she said with a smile, and the loveliest, most bewitching dimples came into her cheeks. "I have not indeed been without thought of you, Lucius, but have spun and spun and weaved too, enough to make you a tunic, all with my own hands, and a purple clavus—it nigh ruined me, the dyed Tyrian wool cost[1]—I will not say; but I wove little crossed L's into the texture."

"What," said Corbulo. "For Lucius and Longina?"

The girl became crimson.

Lamia came to her succor. "That could not be," said he, "for Longina and Lucius are never across, but alack! Lucius is often so with Lamia, when he has done some stupid thing and he sees a frown on his all but father's face, but hears no word of reproach."

"My boy," said Corbulo, "when a man knows his own faults, then a reprimand is unnecessary, and what is unnecessary is wrong."

Lamia bowed and retired.

And now again father and daughter were alone together in the prow observing the arc of the harbor in which the ship was gliding smoothly.

And now the sailors had out their poles and hooks, and they ran the vessel beside the wharf, and cast out ropes that were made fast to bronze rings in the marble breasting of the quay.

Domitia would at once have drawn her father on shore, but he restrained her.

"Not yet, my daughter," he said; "the goddess must precede thee."

---

1   Double-dyed Tyrian wool cost over £40 in English money per lb.

And now ensued a singular formality.

From the bows of the vessel, the captain and steerer took a statuette of Artemis, in bronze, the Ephesian goddess, with female head and numerous breasts, but with the lower limbs swaddled, and the swaddling bands decorated with representations of all kinds of beasts, birds, and fishes.

This image was now conveyed on shore, followed by the passengers and crew.

On the quay stood an altar, upon which charcoal ever burnt, under the charge of a priest who attended to it continuously, and whenever a ship entered the port or was about to leave, added fuel, and raked and blew up the fire.

Simultaneously from a small temple on the quay issued a priest with veiled head, and his attendants came to the altar, cast some grains of incense on the embers, and as the blue fragrant smoke arose and was dissipated by the sea breeze, he said:—

"The Goddess Aphrodite of Corinth salutes her divine sister, the Many-Breasted Artemis of Ephesus, and welcomes her. And she further prays that she may not smite the city or the port with fire, pestilence or earthquake."

Then captain, steerman, pilot and the rest of the company advanced in procession to the temple, and on reaching it offered a handful of sweet gums on an altar there, before the image of the foam-born goddess of Beauty, and said:—

"We who come from the sea, having safely traversed the Ægean, escaped rocks and sand-banks, whirlpools and storms, under the protection of the great goddess of Ephesus, salute in her name the goddess of Beauty, and receive her welcome with thankfulness. And great Artemis beseeches her sister to suffer her and the vessel with passengers and goods and crew, that she conducts and protects, to pass across the isthmus, without let and molestation; and she for her part undertakes to pay the accustomed toll, and the due to the temple of Aphrodite, and that neither the passengers nor the crew shall in any way injure or disturb the inhabitants of Corinth or of the Isthmus."

This ceremony concluded, all were at liberty to disperse; the sailors to attend to the vessel, the slaves of Corbulo to look to and land such of his luggage as he was likely to want, and Corbulo to go to his wife, who had placed herself in an attitude to receive him.

The captain, at the same time, entered the harbor-master's office to arrange about the crossing of the isthmus, and to settle tolls.

For the vessel was not to make more stay than a few days at the port of Cenchræa. After Longa Duilia was ready, then she and her husband and family were to proceed to Lechæum, the port on the Corinthian Gulf, there to embark for Italy. The vessel would leave the harbor and go to Diolchus, that point of the Isthmus on the east where the neck of land was narrowest. There the ships would be hauled out of the water, placed on rollers, and by means of oxen, assisted by gangs of slaves, would convey the vessel over the land for six miles to the Gulf of Corinth, where again she would be floated.

Immediately behind the Roman general, Corbulo, the father of Domitia, walked two individuals, both wearing long beards, and draped to the feet.

One of these had a characteristically Oriental head. His eyes were set very close together, his nose was aquiline, his tint sallow, his eyebrows heavy and bushy, and his general expression one of cunning and subtlety. His movements were stately.

The other was not so tall. He was clumsy in movement, rugged in feature, with a broken nose, his features distinctly Occidental, as was his bullet head. His hair was sandy, and scant on his crown. He wore a smug, self-complacent expression on his pursed-up lips and had a certain "I am Sir Oracle, let no dog bark"look in his pale eyes.

These two men, walking side by side, eyed each other with ill-concealed dislike and disdain.

The former was a Chaldæan, who was usually called Elymas, but affected in Greek to be named Ascletarion.

The latter was an Italian philosopher who had received his training in Greece at a period when all systems of philosophy were broken up and jostled each other in their common ruin.

No sooner was the ceremony at an end, and Corbulo had hastened from the wharf to meet and embrace his wife, and Lamia had drawn off Domitia for a few words, than these two men left to themselves instinctively turned to launch their venom at each other.

The philosopher, with a toss of his beard, and a lifting of his light eyebrows, and the protrusion of his lower lip said:

"And pray, what has the profundity of Ascletarion alias Elymas beheld in the bottom of that well he terms his soul?"

"He has been able to see what is hidden from the shallowness of Claudius Senecio alias Spermologos[2] over the surface of which shallowness his soul careers like a water spider."

"And that is, O muddiness?"

"Ill-luck, O insipidity."

---

2   The term used of St. Paul by the wise men of Athens. It means a picker up of unconsidered trifles which he strings together into an unintelligible system.

"Why so?—not, the Gods forfend, that I lay any weight on anything you may say. But I like to hear your vaticinations that I may laugh over them."

"Hear, then. Because a daughter of Earth dared to set foot on the vessel consecrated to and conducted by Artemis before that the tutelary goddess had been welcomed by and had saluted the tutelary deity of the land."

"I despise your prophecies of evil, thou crow."

"Not more than do I thy platitudes, O owl!"

"Hearken to the words of the poet," said the philosopher, and he started quoting the Œdipus Tyrannus: "The Gods know the affairs of mortals. But among men, it is by no means certain that a soothsayer is of more account than myself!" And Senecio snapped his fingers in the face of the Magus.

"Conclude thy quotation," retorted Elymas. "'A man's wisdom may surpass Wisdom itself. Therefore never will I condemn the seer, lest his words prove true.' How like you that?" and he snapped his fingers under the nose of the philosopher.

CHAPTER III

CORBULO

Cnæus Domitius Corbulo was the greatest general of his time, and he had splendidly served the State.

His sister Cæsonia had been the wife of the mad prince Caligula. She was not beautiful, but her flexible mouth, her tender eyes, the dimples in her cheeks, her exquisite grace of manner and sweetness of expression had not only won the heart of the tyrant, but had enabled her to maintain it.

Once, in an outburst of surprise at himself for loving her, he threatened to put her to the torture to wring from Cæsonia the secret of her hold on his affections. Once, as he caressed her, he broke into hideous laughter, and when asked the reason, said, "I have but to speak the word, and this lovely throat would be cut."

Yet this woman loved the maniac, and when he had been murdered in the subterranean gallery leading from the palace to the theatre, she crept to the spot, and was found kneeling by her dead husband with their babe in her arms, sobbing and wiping the blood from his face. The assassins did not spare her. They cut her down and dashed out the brains of the infant against the marble walls.

Corbulo was not only able, he was successful. Under Nero he was engaged in the East against the Parthians, the most redoubted enemies of the empire. He broke their power and sent their king, Tiridates, a suppliant to Rome.

His headquarters had been at Antioch, and there for a while his wife and daughter had resided with him. But after a while, they were sent part way homewards, as Corbulo himself expected his recall.

They had been separated from him for over six months, and had been awaiting his arrival in a villa at Cenchræa, that had been placed at their disposal by a Greek client.

It was customary for those who did not live in Rome but belonged to a province, to place themselves under the patronage of a Roman noble; whereupon ensued an exchange of "cards" as we should say, but actually of engraved plates or metal fishes on which the date of the agreement was entered as well as the names of the contracting parties. Then, when a provincial desired assistance at the capital, in obtaining redress for a grievance in a lawsuit, or in recovering a debt, his patron attended to his client's interests, and should he visit Rome received him into his house as an honored guest.

On the other hand, if the patron were on a journey and came to the place where his client could serve him, the latter threw his house open to him, treated him with the most profound respect and accorded to him the largest hospitality. So now the villa of a client had been placed at the disposal of Corbulo and his family, and he occupied it with as little hesitation as though it were his own.

It was a matter of pride to a Roman noble to have a large number of silver engraved plates and fishes suspended in his atrium, announcing to all visitors what an extensive clientèle he had, and the provincial was not less proud to be able to flourish the name of his distinguished patron at the capital.

On the evening following the disembarkation, Corbulo and his wife were seated on a bench enjoying the pleasant air that fanned from the sea; and looking over the terraced garden at their daughter, who was gambolling with a long silky-haired kid from Cilicia, that her father had brought as a present to his child.

She was a lovely girl, aged sixteen, with a remarkably intelligent face, and large, clear, shrewd eyes.

Yet, though lovely, none could say that she was beautiful. Her charm was like that of her aunt, Cæsonia, in grace of form, in changefulness and sweetness of expression, and in the brimming intellect that flashed out of her violet eyes. And now as she played with the kid, her every movement formed an artist's study, and the simple joy that shone out of her face, and the affection wherewith she glanced at intervals at her father, invested her with a spiritual charm, impossible to be achieved by sculptor with his chisel or by painter with his brush.

The eyes of Domitius Corbulo followed his child, wherever she went, whatever she did. He was a man of somewhat advanced age, shaven, with short shorn hair, marked features, the brow somewhat retreating, but with a firm mouth and strong jaw. Though not handsome, there was refinement in his countenance which gave it a character of nobleness, and the brilliant eye and decision in the countenance inspired universal respect. Every one could see that he was not merely a commander of men in war, but a man of culture in the forum and the academy.

"Wife," said he, "I pray you desist. It was for this that I sent you back from Antioch. You ever twanged one string, and I felt that your words, if overheard, might endanger us all."

"I speak but into thine ear."

"A brimming vessel overflows on all sides," said Corbulo.

"Ah well! some men make themselves by grasping at what the Gods offer them. Others lose themselves by disregarding the favors extended by the Immortals."

"I deny that any such offer was made me," said the general in a tone of annoyance.

"What!" exclaimed Longa Duilia, "art thou so blind as not to see what is obvious to every other eye, that the Roman people are impatient at having a buffoon, a mimic, a fiddler wearing the purple?"

"Nevertheless, he wears it, by favor of the gods."

"For how long? Domitius, believe me. In the heart of every Roman citizen rage is simmering, and the wound of injured pride rankles. He has insulted the majesty of eternal Rome. After having acted the buffoon in Italy, running up and down it like a jester on a tight-rope mouthing at the people, and with his assassins scattered about below to cut them down if they do not applaud—then he comes here also into Greece, to act on stages, race chariots, before Greeks—Greeks of all people! To me this is nothing, for all princes are tyrants more or less, and so long as they do not prick me, I care not. But here it does come close. In every army, in the breast of every soldier, rebellion springs up. Every general is uneasy and looks at the face of every other and asks, Who will draw the sword and make an end of this? O Morals! it makes me mad to see you alone quiescent."

"When the Gods will a change, then the change will be granted."

"You speak like a philosopher and not a man of action. If you do not draw, others will forestall you, and then—instead of my being up at the top—I shall be down in Nowhere."

"Never will I be a traitor to Rome, and go against my oath."

"Pshaw! They all do it, so why not you?"

"Because my conscience will not suffer me."

"Conscience! The haruspices have never found it yet. They can discover and read the liver and the kidneys, but no knife has yet laid bare a conscience as big as a bean. You were the darling of the soldiery in Germany. You are still the idol of those who have fought under you in Parthia and Armenia. I am sure I did my best to push your cause. I was gracious to the soldiery—sent tit-bits from the table to the guard. I tipped right and left, till I spent all my pocket-money, and smiled benignantly on all military men till I got a horrible crumple here in my cheek, do you see?"

"Yes, shocking," said Corbulo, indifferently.

"How can you be so provoking!" exclaimed Duilia pettishly. "Of course there is no wrinkle, there might have been, I did so much smiling. Really, Corbulo, one has to do all the picking—as boys get winkles out of their shells with a pin—to extract a compliment from you. And out comes the pin with nothing at the end. Plancus would not have let that pass."

"Do you say that Nero is here?"

"Yes, here, in Greece; here at our elbow, at Corinth. He has for once got a clever idea into his head and has begun to cut a canal through the isthmus. It has begun with a flourish of trumpets and a dinner and a dramatic exhibition—and then I warrant you it will end."

"The Prince at Corinth!"

"Yes, at Corinth; and you are here with all the wide sea between you and your troops. And docile as a lamb you have come here, and left your vantage ground. What it all means, the Gods know. It is no doing of mine. I warned and exhorted at Antioch, but you might have been born deaf for all the attention you paid to my words."

"Never would I raise my sacrilegious hand against Rome—my mother."

"Nay—it is Rome that cries out to be rid of a man that makes her the scorn of the world."

"She has not spoken. She has not released me of my oath."

"Because her mouth is gagged. As the Gods love me, they say that the god Caius (Caligula) named his horse Consul. Rome may have a monkey as her prince and Augustus for aught I care, were it not that by such a chance the handle is offered for you to upset him and seat yourself and me at the head of the universe."

"No more of this," said the general. "A good soldier obeys his commander. And I have an imperator," he touched his breast; "a good conscience, and I go nowhere, undertake nothing which is not ordered by my master there."

"Then I wash my hands of the result."

"Come hither!" Corbulo called, and signed to his daughter who, with a flush of pleasure, left her kid and ran to him.

He took both her hands by the wrists, and holding her before him, panting from play, and with light dancing in her blue eyes, he said, "Domitia, I have not said one grave word to thee since we have been together. Yet now will I do this. None can tell what may be the next turn up of the die. And this that I am about to say comes warm and salt from my heart, like the spring hard by, at the Bath of Helene."

"And strong, father," said the girl, with flashes in her speaking eyes. "So strong is the spring that at once it turns a mill, ere rushing down to find its rest in the sea."

"Well, and so may what I say so turn and make thee active, dear child,—active for good, though homely the work may be as that of grinding flour. When you have done a good work, and not wasted the volume of life in froth and cascade, then find rest in the wide sea of—"

"Of what?" sneered Duilia, "say it out—of nobody knows what."

"That which thou sayest, dearest father, will not sleep in my heart."

"Domitia, when we sail at sea, we direct our course by the stars. Without the stars we should not know whither to steer. And the steering of the vessel by the stars, that is seamanship. So in life. There are principles of right and wrong set in the firmament—"

"Where?" asked Duilia. "As the Gods love me, I never saw them."

"By them," continued Corbulo, disregarding the interruption, "we must shape our course, and this true shaping of our course, and not drifting with tides, or blown hither and thither by winds—this is the seamanship of life."

"By the Gods!" said Duilia. "You must first find your stars. I hold what you say to be rank nonsense. Where are your stars? Principles! You keep your constellations in the hold of your vessel. My good Corbulo, our own interest, that we can always see, and by that we ought ever to steer."

"Father," said the girl, "I see a centurion and a handful of soldiers coming this way—and, if I mistake not, Lamia is speeding ahead of them."

"Well, go then, and play with the kid. Hear how the little creature bleats after thee."

She obeyed, and the old soldier watched his darling, with his heart in his eyes.

Presently, when she was beyond hearing, he said:—

"Now about the future of Domitia. I wish her no better fortune than to become the wife of Lucius Ælius Lamia, whom I love as my son. He has been in and out among us at Antioch. He returns with me to Rome. In these evil times, for a girl there is one only chance—to be given a good husband. This I hold, that a woman is never bad unless man shows her the way. If, as you say, there be no stars in the sky—there is love in the heart. By Hercules! here comes Lamia, and something ails him."

Lucius was seen approaching through the garden. His face was ashen-gray, and he was evidently a prey to the liveliest distress.

He hastened to Corbulo, but although his lips moved, he could not utter a word.

"You would speak with me," said the old general rising, and looking steadily in the young man's face.

Something he saw there made him divine his errand.

Then Corbulo turned, kissed his wife, and said—

"Farewell. I am rightly served."

He took a step from her, looked towards Domitia, who was dancing to her kid, above whose reach she held a bunch of parsley.

He hesitated for a moment. His inclination drew him towards her; but a second thought served to make him abandon so doing, and instead, he bent back to his wife, and said to her, with suppressed emotion—

"Bid her from me—as my last command—Follow the Light where and when she sees it."

CHAPTER IV

THERE IS NO STAR

A quarter of an hour had elapsed since Corbulo entered the peristyle of the villa, when the young man Lamia came out.

He was still pale as death, and his muscles twitched with strong emotion.

He glanced about him in quest of Longa Duilia, but that lady had retired precipitately to the gynaikonitis, or Lady's hall, where she had summoned to her a bevy of female slaves and had accumulated about her an apothecary's shop of restoratives.

Domitia was still in the garden, playing with the kid, and Lamia at once went to her, not speedily, but with repugnance.

She immediately desisted from her play, and smiled at his approach. They were old acquaintances, and had seen much of each other in Syria.

Corbulo had not been proconsul, but legate in the East, and had made Antioch his headquarters. He had been engaged against the Parthians and Armenians for eight years, but the war had been intermittent, and between the campaigns he had returned to Antioch, to the society of his wife and little daughter.

The former, a dashing, vain and ambitious woman, had made a salon there which was frequented by the best society of the province. Corbulo, a quiet, thoughtful and modest man, shrunk from the stir and emptiness of such life, and had found rest and enjoyment in the company of his daughter.

Lamia had served as his secretary and aide-de-camp. He was a youth of much promise, and of singular integrity of mind and purity of morals in a society that was self-seeking, voluptuous, and corrupt.

He belonged to the Ælian gens or clan, but he had been adopted by a Lamia, a member of a family in the same clan, that claimed descent from Lamius, a son of Poseidon, or Neptune, by one of those fictions so dear to the Roman noble houses, and which caused the fabrication of mythical origins, just as the ambition of certain honorable families in England led to the falsification of the Roll of Battle Abbey.

Pliny tells a horrible story of the first Lamia of importance, known to authentic history. He had been an adherent of Cæsar and a friend of Cicero. He was supposed to be dead in the year in which he had been elected prætor, and was placed on the funeral pyre, when consciousness returned, but too late for him to be saved. The flames rose and enveloped him, and he died shrieking and struggling to escape from the bandages that bound him to the bier on which he lay.

Lucius Lamia had been kindly treated by Corbulo, and the young man's heart had gone out to the venerated general, to whom he looked up as a model of all the old Roman virtues, as well as a man of commanding military genius. The simplicity of the old soldier's manner and the freshness of his mind had acted as a healthful and bracing breeze upon the youth's moral character.

And now he took the young girl by the hand, and walked with her up and down the pleached avenues for some moments without speaking.

His breast heaved. His head swam. His hand that held hers worked convulsively.

All at once Domitia stood still.

She had looked up wondering at his manner, into his eyes, and had seen that they were full.

"What ails you, Lucius?"

"Come, sit by me on the margin of the basin,"said he. "By the Gods! I conjure thee to summon all thy fortitude. I have news to communicate, and they of the saddest—"

"What! are we not to return to Rome? O Lamia, I was a child when I left it, but I love our house at Gabii, and the lake there, and the garden."

"It is worse than that, Domitia." He seated himself on the margin of a basin, and nervously, not knowing what he did, drew his finger in the water, describing letters, and chasing the darting fish.

"Domitia, you belong to an ancient race. You are a Roman, and have the blood of the Gods in your veins. So nerve thy heroic soul to hear the worst."

And still he thrust after the frightened fish with his finger, and she looked down, and saw them dart like shadows in the pool, and her own frightened thoughts darted as nimbly and as blindly about in her head.

"Why, how now, Lamia? Thou art descended by adoption from the Earth-shakes, and tremblest as a girl! See—a tear fell into the basin. Oh, Lucius! My very kid rears in surprise."

"Do not mock. Prepare for the worst. Think what would be the sorest ill that could befall thee."

Domitia withdrew her eyes from the fish and the water surface rippled by his finger, and looked now with real terror in his face.

"My father?"

Then Lamia raised his dripping finger and pointed to the house.

She looked, and saw that the gardener had torn down boughs of cypress, and therewith was decorating the doorway.

At the same moment rose a long-drawn, desolate wail, rising, falling, ebbing, flowing—a sea of sound infinitely sad, heart-thrilling, blood-congealing.

For one awful moment, one of those moments that seems an eternity, Domitia remained motionless.

She could hear articulate words, voices now.

"Come back! O Cnæus! Come, thou mighty warrior! Come, thou pillar of thy race! Come back, thou shadow! Return, O fleeted soul! See, see! thy tabernacle is still warm. Return, O soul! return!"

She knew it—the conclamatio; that cry uttered about the dead in the hopes of bringing back the spirit that has fled.

Then, before Lamia could stop her, Domitia started from the margin of the pool, startling the fish again and sending them flying as rays from where she had been seated, and ran to the house.

The gardener, with the timidity of a slave, did not venture to forbid passage.

A soldier who was withdrawing extended his arm to bar the doorway. Quick as thought she dived below this barrier, and next moment with a cry that cut through the wail of the mourners, she cast herself on the body of her father, that lay extended on the mosaic floor, with a blood-stained sword at his side, and a dark rill running from his breast over the enamelled pavement.

Next moment Lamia entered.

Around the hall were mourners, slaves of the house, as also some of those of Longa Duilia, raising their arms and lowering them, uttering their cries of lamentation and invocations to the departed soul, some rending their garments, others making believe to tear their hair and scratch their faces.

In the midst lay the dead general, and his child clung to him, kissed him, chafed his hands, endeavored to stanch his wound, and addressed him with endearments.

But all was in vain. The spirit was beyond recall, and were it to return would again be expelled. Corbulo was dead.

The poor child clasped him, convulsed with tears; her copious chestnut hair had become unbound, and was strewed about her, and even dipped in her father's blood. She was as though frantic with despair; her gestures, her cry very different from the formal expressions and utterances of the servile mourners.

But Lamia at length touched her, and said—

"Come away, Domitia. You cannot prevent Fate."

Suddenly she reared herself on her knees, and put back the burnished rain of hair that shrouded her face, and said in harsh tones:—

"Who slew him?"

"He fell on his own sword."

"Why! He was happy?"

Before an answer was given, she reeled and fell unconscious across her father's body.

Then Lamia stooped, gathered her up tenderly, pitifully, in his arms, and bore her forth into the garden to the fountain, where he could bathe her face, and where the cool air might revive her.

Why was Corbulo dead? and why had he died by his own hand?

The Emperor Nero was, as Duilia had told her husband, at this very time in Greece, and further, hard by at Corinth, where he was engaged in superintending the cutting of a canal, that was to remove the difficulty of a passage from the Saronic to the Corinthian Gulf.

Nero had come to Greece attended by his Augustal band of five thousand youths with flowing locks, and gold bangles on their wrists, divided into three companies, whose duty it was to applaud the imperial mountebank, and rouse or lead enthusiasm, the Hummers by buzzing approval, the Clappers by beating their hands together, and the Clashers by kicking pots about so as to produce a contagious uproar.

Nero was possessed with the delusion that he had a fine voice, and that he was an incomparable actor. Yet his range was so small, that when striving to sink to a bass note, his voice became a gurgle, and when he attempted to soar to a high note, he raised himself on his toes, became purple in face, and emitted a screech like a peacock.

Not satisfied with the obsequious applause of the Roman and Neapolitan citizens who crowded the theatre to hear the imperial buffoon twitter, he resolved to contest for prizes in the games of Greece.

A fleet attended him, crowded with actors, singers, dancers, heaped up with theatrical properties, masks, costumes, wigs, and fiddles.

He would show the Greeks that he could drive a chariot, sing and strut the stage now in male and then in female costume, and adapt his voice to the sex he personated, now grumbling in masculine tones, then squeaking in falsetto, and incomparable in each.

But with the cunning of a madman, he took with him, as his court, the wealthiest nobles of Rome, whom he had marked out for death, either because he coveted their fortunes or suspected their loyalty.

Wherever he went, into whatsoever city he entered, his artistic eye noted the finest statues and paintings, and he carried them off, from temple as from marketplace, to decorate Rome or enrich his Golden House, the palace he had erected for himself.

Tortured by envy of every one who made himself conspicuous; hating, fearing such as were in all men's mouths, through their achievements, or notable for virtue, his suspicion had for some time rested on Domitius Corbulo, who had won laurels first in Germany and afterwards in Syria.

He had summoned him to Rome, with the promise of preferments, his purpose being to withdraw him from the army that adored him, and to destroy him.

No sooner did the tidings reach the tyrant at Corinth, that the veteran hero was arrived at Cenchræa, than he sent him a message to commit suicide. A gracious condescension that, for the property of the man who was executed was forfeit and his wife and children reduced to beggary, whereas the will of the testator who destroyed himself was allowed to remain in force.

Lamia washed the stains from the hands and locks of the girl, and bathed her face with water till she came round.

Then, when he saw that she had recovered full consciousness, he asked to be allowed to hasten for assistance. She bowed her head, as she could not speak, and he entered the women's portion of the villa to summon some of the female slaves. These were, however, in no condition to answer his call and be of use. Duilia had monopolized the attentions of almost all such as had not been commissioned to raise the funeral wail. Some, indeed, there were, scattered in all directions, running against each other, doing nothing save add to the general confusion, but precisely these were useless for Lamia's purpose.

Unwilling to leave the child longer alone, Lucius returned to the garden, and saw Domitia seated on the breastwork of the fountain.

Ten years seemed to have passed over her head, so altered was she.

She was not now weeping. The rigidity of the fainting fit seemed not to have left her face, nor relaxed the stony appearance it had assumed. Her eyes were lustreless, and her lips without color.

The young man was startled at her look.

"Domitia!" said he.

She raised her eyes to him, and said in reply,

"Lucius!" Then letting them fall, she added in hard, colorless tones, "There is one thing I desire of thee. By some means or other, I care not what, bring me into the presence of the monster. I know how my father has come by his death—as have so many others, the best and the noblest. I have but one ambition on earth, I see but a single duty before me—to drive if it be but a silver bodkin into his heart."

"Domitia!"

"Lucius, the last words my father used to me were to bid me look to the stars and to sail by them. I look and I see one only star. I feel but one only duty on earth—to revenge his death."

"My friend!" said Lamia, in a low tone. "Be careful of thy words. If overheard, they might cause your blood to be mingled with his."

"I care not."

"But to me it matters sovereignly."

"Why? Dost thou care for me?"

"Above all in the world."

"Then revenge me."

"Domitia, my grief is little less than thine. If you would revenge the loss, so would I. But what can be done? He, the coward, is carefully guarded. None are suffered to approach him who have not first been searched, and even then are not allowed within arm's length. Nothing can be done, save invoke the Gods."

"The Gods!" laughed the girl hoarsely. "The Gods! They set up the base, the foul, and crown him with roses, and trample the noble and good into the earth. The Gods! see you now! They set a star in heaven, they grave a duty in my heart, and the star is unattainable, and the duty, they make impossible of achievement. Bah! There is no star. There are no duties on earth, and no Gods in heaven."

CHAPTER V

THE SHIP OF THE DEAD

"It is of no use in the world, Plancus, your attempting to reason me out of a fixed resolve," said the lady Longa Duilia, peevishly. "My Corbulo shall not have a shabby funeral."

"Madam, I do not suggest that," said the steward humbly, rubbing his hands.

"Yes, you do. It is of no good your standing on one leg like a stork. Shabby it must be—no ancestors present. As the Gods love me, you would not have me borrow ancestors of Asclepiades, our client, who has lent us this villa! He may have them or not, that is no concern of mine. Will you have done preening yourself like an old cockroach. I say it would be an indignity to have a funeral for my Corbulo without ancestors. O Times! O Morals! What is the good of having ancestors if you do not use them?"

"But, Madam, they are in your palace at Rome in the Carinæ—or at the Gabian villa."

"And for that reason they are not here. Without the attendance of his forbears, my Corbulo shall not be buried. Besides, who is there to impress here with the solemnity? Only a lot of wretched sailors, ship sutlers, Jew pedlers and petty officials, not worth considering. I have said it."

"But, Lady, Lucius Lamia agrees with me—"

"Lucius Ælius Lamia—it will not exhaust your lungs to give him his name more fully—is not as yet one of the family."

"Madam, consider how Agrippina did with Germanicus—she had his pyre at Antioch, and conveyed his ashes to Rome."

"Agrippina was able to have the funeral conducted with solemn pomp at Antioch. There were the soldiers, the lictors, great officers and all that sort of thing. Here—nothing at all. By the Immortals—consider the expenses, and none to look on gaping but tarry sailors and Jew rag-and-bone men."

"Madam!"

"Silence. Without ancestors!—as impossible as without wood."

To understand the point made so much of by the widow, the Roman funeral custom must be understood.

On the death of a noble or high official, his face was immediately moulded in wax, into a mask, or rather, into two masks, that were colored and supplied with glass eyes. One was placed over the dead face, when the corpse lay in state, and when he was conveyed to his funeral pyre, and the first effect of the rising flames was to dissolve the mask and disclose the dead features.

The ancient Greeks before they burned their dead laid gold-leaf masks on their faces, and in a still earlier time the face of the corpse was rouged with oxide of iron, to give it a false appearance of life.

But the second mask was preserved for the family portrait gallery.

When a Roman gentleman or lady was carried forth to his funeral pyre, he was preceded by a procession of actors dressed up in the togas and military or municipal insignia of departed ancestors, each wearing the wax mask of him he personified. For these masks were preserved with great care in the atrium of the house.

Now as Longa Duilia saw, to have her husband burned at Cenchræa, without a procession of imitation ancestors, would be to deprive the funeral of its most impressive feature.

Plancus had advised the burning at the port, with shorn rites, and that the ashes should be placed in the family mausoleum at Gabii, and that the utmost dignity should be accorded to this latter ceremony sufficient to content the most punctilious widow.

But this did not please the lady. The notion of a funeral with maimed pomp was distasteful to her; moreover, as she argued, it was illegal to have two funerals for the same man.

"That," said Plancus, "hardly applies to one who has died out of Italy."

"It is against the law," replied Duilia. "I will give no occasion to objection, offer no handle to informers. Besides, I won't have it. The respect I owe to Corbulo forbids the entertainment of such an idea. Really, and on my word, Plancus, I am not a child to be amused with shadow pictures, and unless you are making a rabbit, a fish, or a pig eating out of a trough, I cannot conceive what you are about with your hands, fumbling one over the other."

"Madam, I had no thought—"

"I know you have none. Be pleased another time when addressing me to keep your hands quiet, it is irritating. One never knows where they are or will be, sometimes folding and unfolding them, then—they disappear up your sleeves and project none can guess where—like snails' horns. Be pleased,—and now pawing your face like a cat washing itself. Please in future hold them in front of you like a dog when sitting up, begging. But as to the funeral—I will not have it cheap and nasty. Without ancestors a funeral is not worth having."

"Then," said the harassed freedman, "there is nothing for it but to engage an embalmer."

"Of course—one can be obtained at Corinth. Everything can be had for money."

As Plancus was retiring, the lady recalled him.

"Here," said she, "do not act like a fool, and let the man charge a fancy price. Say that I have an idea of pickling Corbulo in brine, and have brought an amphora large enough for the purpose. Don't close with his terms at once."

When the steward was gone, then Longa Duilia turned her head languidly and summoned a slave-girl.

"Lucilla! The unfortunate feature of the situation is that I must not have my hair combed till we reach Gabii. It is customary, and for a bracelet of pearls I would not transgress custom. You can give my head a tousled look, without being dishevelled, I would wish to appear interesting, not untidy."

"Lady! Nothing could make you other than fascinating. A widow in tears—some stray locks—it would melt marble."

"And I think I shall outdo Agrippina," said Duilia, "she carried her husband's cinders in an urn at the head of her berth and on appropriate occasions howled in the most tragic and charming manner. But I shall convey the unconsumed body of my Corbulo in state exposed on his bier, in his military accoutrements all the way to Rhegium, then up the coast to Ostia and so to Gabii. There will be talk!"

"You will be cited in history as a widow the like of which the world has never seen. As for Agrippina, in your superior blaze she will be eclipsed forever."

"I should prefer doing what Agrippina did—make a land journey from Brindisium, but—but—one must consider. It would be vastly expensive, and—"

But the lady did not finish the sentence. She considered that Nero might resent such a demonstration, as exciting indignation against himself, in having obliged Corbulo to put an end to his life. But she did not dare to breathe her thought even into the ear of a slave.

"No," she said; "it would come too expensive. I will do what I can to honor my husband, but not ruin myself."

When Longa Duilia had resolved to have her own way, and that was always, then all the entire family of slaves and retainers, freedmen and clients knew it must be done.

The vessel after a brief stay at Cenchræa had left for Diolcus where it had been placed on rollers and conveyed across the isthmus, and was launched in the Corinthian Gulf.

Nero had been engaged for some days in excavating a canal between the two seas. He had himself turned the first sod, but after getting some little way, rock was encountered of so hard a quality that to cut through it would cost time, toil and money.

He speedily tired of the scheme, wanted the money it would have cost for some dramatic exhibition, and was urged by Helios, a freedman whom he had left in Rome, to return to Italy, to prevent an insurrection that was simmering. Nero did not much believe in danger, but he had laden his fleet with the plunder of Greece, he had strutted and twittered on every stage, carried off every prize in every contest, and was desirous of being applauded in Italy and at Rome for what he had achieved, and exhibit there the chaplets he had won.

Accordingly he started, and hardly had he done so before the Artemis with spread sail swept down the Corinthian Gulf.

The ship, a Liburnian, of two banks of oars, was constructed very differently from a modern vessel. The prow was armed above water-mark with three strong and sharp blades, called the rostra, the beaks, which when driven into the side of an enemy would tear her open and sink her.

The quarter-deck was midships, and served a double purpose, being raised as high as the bulwarks it served as an elevated place where the captain could stand and survey the horizon and watch the course of the vessel, and it also served to strengthen the mast.

On this quarter-deck, on a bed of state, lay the body of Cnæus Domitius Corbulo, with his sword at his side, and the wax mask over his face. At his feet was a tripod with glowing coals on which occasionally incense and Cilician crocus were sprinkled, and on each side of his head blazed torches of pinewood dipped in pitch.

The poop had a covered place, called the aplaustre, in which sat the steerer. The hinged rudder had not then been invented, it was a discovery of the Middle Ages, and the head of the vessel was given its direction by the helmsman, gubernator, who worked a pair of broad flat paddles, one on each side.

The rowers, under the deck, were slaves, but the sailors were freemen. The rowers were kept in stroke by a piper, who played continually when the vessel was being propelled; and the rowers were under the direction and command of a hortator, so called because his voice was incessantly heard, urging, reprimanding, praising, threatening.

The captain of a Roman vessel was not supreme in authority on board ship as with us, but if the vessel contained military, he was subject to the control of the superior military officer.

The passage down the Corinthian Bay was effected without difficulty, before a favorable wind, but as the vessel was about to pass out of it, the wind suddenly changed and blew a squall from the west. And at this moment an accident occurred that was seriously embarrassing. Whilst the captain was standing near the steersman giving him directions relative to the passage of the straits, a wave rolling in caught the paddle, and caused it by the blow to snap the bronze bolt of the eye in which it worked, and the handle flying up and forward, struck the captain on the forehead, threw him down, and he fell against the bulwark so as to cut open his head. He had to be carried below insensible.

The Artemis lay under shelter till the gale abated, and then consultation arose as to what was to be done.

Lucius Lamia took the command, he was competent to manage the vessel, with the advice, if needed, of the mate. He and all were reluctant to put back to Lechæum, the port of Corinth, on the Gulf, and the broken eye in which the paddle worked was repaired with a stout thong, which, as the steersman said, would hold till Adria was crossed and Rhegium was reached.

The squall had passed, and the look of the sky was promising; moreover the wind was again favorable.

"Sir," said the mate, "my opinion is that we should make all speed across Adria. This is a bad season of the year. It is a month in which sailing is overpassed. We must take advantage of our chances. While the wind blows, let us spread sail. The rowers can ship their oars; should the wind fail, or prove contrary, they will be required, and they may have a hard time of it. Therefore let them husband their strength."

"So be it," answered Lucius Lamia.

And now the Artemis, with sail spread, leaning on one side, drave through the rippling water, passed the Straits into the Adriatic, with the mountains of Ætolia to the north, and the island of Cephalonia in the blue west before her; and as she flew, she left behind her a trail of foam in the water, and a waft of smoke in the air from the torches that glowed about the dead general on the quarter-deck.

CHAPTER VI

"I DO NOT KNOW."

The day was in decline, and although the season was winter yet the air was not cold. The mountains of Greece lay in the wake like a bank of purple cloud tinged with gold.

On the quarter-deck reposed the corpse, with the feet turned in the direction of the prow; the torches spluttered, and cast off sparks that flew away with the smoke.

On each side were three slave women, detailed to wail, but Longa Duilia had issued instructions that they were not to be noisy in their demonstration so as to disturb or swamp conversation aft.

The undulating lament swerving through semi-tones and demi-semitones, formed a low and sad background to the play of voices on the lower deck, where, sheltered from the wind, the widow reclined on cushions, and her daughter Domitia sat at her side in conversation.

A change had come over the girl, so complete, so radical, that she seemed hardly to be the same person as before her father's death. This was noticeable as being in appearance and manner,—noticeable even to the slaves, not the most observant in matters that did not particularly concern their comfort and interests. She had been transmuted from a playful child into a sad and serious woman.

The sparkle had left her eyes to make way for an eager, searching fire. The color had left her cheek; and her face had assumed a gloomy expression. The change, in fact, was much like that in a landscape when a sunny May day makes place for one that is overcast and threatening. The natural features are unaltered, but the aspect is wholly different in quality and character.

A mighty sorrow contracting, bruising, oppressing the heart some-times melts it into a sweetness of patient endurance that inspires pity and love. But grief seemed to have frozen Domitia and not to have dissolved her into tears.

The philosopher approached with solemn stalk, walking on the flat of his soles.

Such men were retained in noble households as family chaplains, to advise, comfort, and exhort. And this man at intervals approached the widow, who on such occasions assumed a woe-begone expression, beat her brow and emitted at intervals long-drawn sighs.

At such times, the Magus, standing near, curled his lip contemptuously, and endeavored by shrugs and sniffs to let the bystanders perceive how little he valued the words of the stoic.

The philosopher Senecio now in formal style addressed the widow, and then turned to harangue the daughter, on the excellence of moderation in grief as in joy, on the beauty of self-control so as to suffer the storms of life to roll over the head with indifference. In this consisted the Highest Good, and to attain to such stolidity was the goal of all virtuous endeavor.

Then he thrust his hand into the folds of his toga, and withdrew, to be at once attacked and wrangled with by the Chaldæan.

Domitia, who had listened with indifference, turned to her mother as soon as he was gone, and said—

"The Summum Bonum, the crown and glory of Philosophy is to become in mind what the slave becomes after many bastinadoes, as callous in soul as he is on the soles of his feet. The lesson of life is not worth the acquisition."

"I think he put it all very well."

"Why are the strokes applied? Why should we bear them without crying out? After all, what profit is there in this philosophy?"

"Really, my dear, I cannot tell. But it is the correct thing to listen to and to talk philosophy, and good families keep their tame stoics,—even quite new and vulgar people, wretched knights who have become rich in trade—in a word, they all do it."

"But, mother, what is this Highest Good?"

"You must inquire of Claudius Senecio himself. It is, I am sure something very suitable to talk about, on such solemn occasions as this."

"But what is it? A runner in the course knows what is the prize for which he contends, a singer at the games sees the crown he hopes to earn—but this Highest Good, is it nothing but not to squeal when kicked?"

"I really do not know."

"Mother, would to the Gods I did know! My sorrow is eating out my heart. I am miserable. I am in darkness, like Theseus in the labyrinth, but without a clue. And the Highest Good preached by philosophy is to sit down in the darkness and despair of the light. I want to know. Has my father's life gone out forever, like an extinguished torch cast into the sea? or is it a smouldering ember that may be blown again into flame?"

"Have you not heard, Domitia, how Senecio has assured you that your father will live."

"Where?"

"On the page of history."

"First assure me that the page will be written, and that impartially. What I know of historians is that they scribble all the scurrility they can against the great and noble, in the hope of thereby advancing the credit of their own mean selves. Has a man no other hope of life than one built on the complaisance of the most malignant of men?"

"My dear,—positively, I do not know. You turn my head with your questions. Call Plancus that I may scold him, to ease my overwrought nerves. The fellow has been stopping up his wrinkles with a composition of wax, lard and flour, and really, at his age, and in his social position—it is absurd."

"But, mother, I want to know."

"Bless me, you make me squeamish. Of course we want to know a vast number of things; and the Highest Good, I take it, is to learn to be satisfied to know nothing. Cats, dogs, donkeys, don't worry themselves to know—and are happy. They have, then, the Summum Bonum. If you want to know more, ask the philosopher. He is paid for the purpose, and eats at our expense, and ye gods! how he eats. I believe he finds the Highest Good in the platter."

The lady made signs, and a slave, ever on the watch, hastened to learn her desire, and at her command summoned the Stoic.

The philosopher paced the deck with his chin in the air, and came aft.

"My daughter," said the widow, "is splitting my suffering head with questions. Pray answer her satisfactorily. Here Felicula, Procula, Lucilla, help me to the cabin."

When the lady had withdrawn, the philosopher said:

"Lady, you will propound difficulties, and I shall be pleased to solve them."

"I ask plain answers to plain questions," said Domitia. "At death—what then?"

"Death, young lady, is the full stop at the end of the sentence, it is the closing of the diptychs of life, on which its story is inscribed."

"I asked not what death is—but to what it leads?"

"Leads!—it—leads! ahem! Death encountered with stoic equanimity is the highest point to which—"

"I do not ask how to meet death, but what it leads to. You seem unable or unwilling to answer a plain question. My dear father, does he live still—as a star that for a while sets below the horizon but returns again?"

"He lives, most assuredly. In all men's mouths—on the snowy plains of Germany, on the arid wastes of Syria, the fame of Cnæus Domitius Corbulo—"

"I asked naught about his fame, but about himself. Does he still exist, can he still think of, care for, love me—as I still think of, care for, love him—"

Her voice quivered and broke.

"Young lady—Socrates could say no more of the future than that it is a brilliant hope which one may run the risk of entertaining. And our own Immortal Cicero declared that the hope of the soul living after death is a dream, and not a doctrine. The Immortals have seen fit to cut the thread of his life—"

"The Immortals had no scissors wherewith to do it. He fell on his own sword. Is there a soul? And after death where does it go? Is it a mere shadow?"

"My dear lady, philosophy teaches us to hope—"

"Natural instinct does that without the cumbrous assistance of philosophy—but what is that hope built on?"

"I cannot tell."

"Then of what avail is it to lead a good life?"

"On the page of history—"

"That is where the great man lives—but the poor girl or the mechanic? Of what avail is a good life? What motive have we to induce us to lead it?"

"The approval of the conscience."

"But why should it approve? What is good? Where is it written that this is good and that is evil?"

"I cannot tell."

"So," said the girl, and she signed to Elymas to approach. He came up with a sneer at the philosopher, who retired in discomfiture.

"You, Chaldæan, answer me that which confounds the Stoic. You have learning in the East which we have not in the West. Tell me—what is the human soul? and has it an existence after death?"

"Certainly, lady. The soul is a ray of Divine light, an æon out of infinite perfection. This ray is projected into space and enters into and is entangled in matter, and that is life, in the plant, in the fish, in the bird, in the beast, in man."

"And what after death?"

"Death is the disengagement of this ray from its envelope. It returns to the source, to the pleroma or fulness of being and light whence it emanated, and loses itself in the one urn of splendor!"

"But when Pactolus and Styx run into the sea, the waters are mingled and lost, as to their individuality."

"And so with the spirits of men."

"What!" exclaimed Domitia. "When I die my little ray re-enters the sun and is lost in the general glory—and my father's ray is also sucked in and disappears! There is no comfort in a thought where individuality is extinguished. But say. How know you that what you have propounded is the truth?"

The Magus hesitated and became confused.

"It is," said he, "a solution at which the minds of the great thinkers of the East have arrived."

"I see," said Domitia, "it is no more than a guess. You and all alike are stagnant pools, whose muddy bottoms ferment and generate and throw up guesswork bubbles. One bubble looks more substantial than another, yet are all only the disguise of equal emptiness."

The Chaldæan withdrew muttering in his beard. Domitia looked after him and noticed the physician Luke standing near, leaning over the bulwarks.

He was an elderly man, with kindly soft eyes, and a short beard in which some strands of gray appeared. A modest man, ready when called on to advise, but never self-assertive.

Domitia had noticed him already and had taken a liking to him, though she had not spoken to him. An unaccountable impulse induced her to address him.

"They are all quacks," she said.

"They must needs be seekers, and the best they can produce, is out of themselves, and that conjecture. From the depths of the intellect what can be brought up than a more or less plausible guess?"

"And on these guesses we must live, like those who float across the Tigris and Euphrates—on rafts supported by inflated bladders. There is then no solid ground?"

"Man inflates the bladders—God lays the rocky basis."

"What mean you?"

"No certainty can be attained, in all these things man desires to know, the basis of hope, the foundation of morality, that cannot be brought out of man. It can only be known by revelation of God."

"And till he reveals we must drift on wind-bags. Good lack!"

"Do you think, Lady, that He who made man, and planted in man's heart a desire for a future life, and made it necessary for his welfare that he should know to discern between good and evil, should leave him forever in the dark—like as you said Theseus in the labyrinth, without a clue?"

"But where is the clue?"

"Or think you that He who launched the vessel of man, having carefully laid the keel and framed the ribs, and set in her a pilot, should send her forth into unknown seas to certain wreckage—to be wafted up and down by every wind—to be carried along by every current—to fall on reefs, or be engulfed by quicksands, and not to reach a port, and He not to set lights whereby her course may be directed?"

"But where are the lights?"

At that moment, before Luke could answer, Lamia, who had been in the fore part of the vessel, came hastily aft, and disregarding the physician, heedless of the conversation on which he broke in, said hurriedly and in agitated tone:—

"The Imperial galley!"

CHAPTER VII

THE FACE OF THE DEAD

The Imperial galley!

Domitia leaped to her feet. Everything was forgotten in the one thought that before her, on the sea, floated the man who had caused the death of her father.

"Lucius I must see—"

He drew her forward, but at the same time checked her speech.

"Every word dropped is fraught with danger," he said. "What know you but that yon physician be a spy?"

"He is not that," she answered, "show him to me—him—"

They walked together to the bows.

With the declining of the sun, the light wind had died away, and, although the sea heaved after the recent storm, like the bosom of a sleeping girl, in the stillness of the air, the sail drooped and the ship made no way.

Accordingly the sail was furled, and, by the advice of the mate, the rowers, who had rested during the day, were summoned to their benches and bidden work the oars during the night.

The sky was clear, and the stars were beginning to twinkle. No part of the voyage in calm weather would be less dangerous than this, which might be performed at night, across open sea, unbroken by rocks and sand-banks.

So long as the vessel had to thread her way between the headland of Araxus and the Echinades, and then betwixt the isles of Cephalonia and Zacynthus, an experienced navigator was necessary, and caution had to be exercised both in the management of the sail and in the manipulation of the helm. But now all was plain, and the mate had retired below to rest. During the time he reposed Lamia took charge of the vessel, assisted by the second mate.

"You take your meridian by Polaris, Castor and Pollux, steer due west; if there be a slight deviation from the right course, that is a trifle. I will set it right when my watch comes."

Such was the mate's injunction as he retired below.

"The steersman is done up," said Lamia; "he shall rest now, and no better man can be found to replace him than Eboracus, who has been accustomed to the stormy seas of Britain, and whose nerves are of iron."

Indeed, the gubernator or helmsman had hard work for his arms. The two enormous paddles had short cross-pieces let into them, like the handles of a scythe, and the clumsy and heavy mechanism for giving direction to the head of the vessel was worked by leverage in this manner.

The sailors managed everything on deck, the cordage, the anchors, the sail and the boats. In rough weather they undergirded the ship; that is to say, passed horizontal cords round her to brace the spars together so as to facilitate resistance to the strain when laboring against the waves. The sailors were under the direction of the captain or trierarch, so called whether he commanded a trireme or a Liburnian of two benches.

On deck the steersman occupied a sort of sentry-box in the stern, and beside him sat the mate, the second mate, and often also the captain, forming a sort of council for the direction of the vessel.

It was a favorite figure in the early Church to represent the Bishop as the helmsman of the sacred vessel, and the presbyters who sat about him as the mates occupying the stern bench. As already said, in a Roman vessel, there was a lack of that unity in direction under the captain to which we are accustomed. A military officer was always supreme everywhere on sea as on land.

When the sailors were engaged in sailing, then the rowers rested or caroused, and when they in turn bowed over the oars, the sailors had leisure.

The sun went down in the west, lighting up the sky above where he set with a rainbow or halo of copper light fading into green.

The night fell rapidly, and the stars looked out above and around, and formed broken reflections in the sea.

In winter the foam that broke and was swept to right and left had none of the flash and luminosity it displayed in summer, when the water was warm.

Already in the wake the Greek isles and mountain ridges had faded into night.

The oars dipped evenly, and the vessel sped forward at a speed equal to that of a modern Channel steamer.

At a signal from Lamia the mourners on the quarter-deck ceased to intone their wail.

He and Domitia stood in the bows and looked directly before them. They could see a large vessel ahead, of three banks of oars, but she floated immovable on the gently heaving, glassy sea. The oars were all shipped and she was making no way.

The deck sparkled with lights. Torches threw up red flames, lamps gave out a fainter yellow gleam. To the cordage lights had been suspended, and braziers burning on the quarter-deck, fed with aromatic woods, turned the water around to molten fire, and sent wafts of fragrance over the sea.

The twang of a lyre and the chirp of a feeble voice were faintly audible; and then, after a lull, ensued a musical shout of applause in rhythmic note.

"It is the Augustus singing," said Lamia in a tone of smothered rage and mortification. "And he has his band of adulators about him."

"But why do not the rowers urge on the vessel?"asked Domitia.

"Because the piper giving the stroke would be committing high treason in drowning the song of the princely performer. By the Gods! the grinding of the oars in the rowlocks and the plash in the water would drown even his most supreme trills."

"Hast thou seen him on the stage, Lamia?"

"The Gods forbid," answered the young man passionately, "this fancy to be the first of singers and mimes had not come on him before I left Rome for Syria. To think of it, that he—the head of the magistracy, of the army, of the senate, of the priesthood, should figure as Apollo, half naked, in a gold-powdered wig, and with painted cheeks before sniggering Greeks! The Gods deliver me from such a sight!"

"But you will behold it now. As we speed along we shall overtake this floating dramatic booth."

"I will give her a wide berth, and stop my ears with wax, though, by the Gods! this is no siren song."

Domitia leaned over the side of the vessel.

"Are they sharp, Lucius?"

"Are what sharp, Domitia?"

"The beaks."

"Sharp as lancets."

"And strong?"

"Strong as rams."

"Then, Lucius, we will not give her wide berth. You loved my father. You regard me. You will do what I desire, for his sake and for mine."

"What would you have of me?"

"Ram her!"

Lucius Lamia started, and looked at the girl.

She laid her hand on his arm, and gripped it as with an iron vice.

"Run her down, Lucius! Sink the accursed murderer and mountebank in the depths of the Ionian sea."

Lamia gasped for breath.

She looked up into his face.

"Can it be done?"

"By Hercules! we could rip up her side."

"Then do so."

He stood undecided.

"Hearken to me. None will suspect our intention as we swiftly shoot up—no, none in this vessel, only Eboracus must be in it. Suddenly we will round and ram and welt her; and send the new Orion with his fiddle to the fishes. By the Furies! We shall hear him scream. We shall see him beat the waves. Lucius, let me have a marline-spike to dash at him as he swims and split his skull and let out his brains for the fishes to banquet on them."

"We risk all our lives."

"What care I? My father, your friend, will be avenged."

Still Lamia stood in unresolve.

"Lucius! I will twine my white arms about your neck, and will kiss you with my red lips, the moment his last scream has rung in my ears."

"In the name of Vengeance—then," said Lamia.

"Eboracus I can count on," said Domitia.

"There is the under-mate. If any one on board suspect our purpose, we are undone."

"None need suspect," said the girl. "Say that the prince is holding festival on board the trireme, and that it behoves us to salute. None will think other than that we are befooling ourselves like the rest. At the right moment, before any has a thought of thy purpose, call for the double-stroke, and trust Eboracus—he will put the helm about, and in a moment we run her down."

Lamia walked to the quarter-deck, bade the mourning women go below. He extinguished the funeral torches, and threw the ashes from the tripod into the sea. Then the Artemis was no longer distinguishable by any light she bore.

Next Lamia walked aft, and in a restrained voice said:

"The vessel of Cæsar is before us. We dare not pass without leave asked and granted."

"All right, sir," said the second mate. "Any orders below?"

"Keep on at present speed. When I call Slack, then let them slacken. When I call Double, then at once with full force double."

"Right, sir. I will carry down instructions."

The mate went to the ladder and descended into the hold.

There were now left on deck only Lamia, Domitia, the steersman, Eboracus, one sailor and the physician, who was leaning over the bulwarks looking north at the glittering constellation of Cassiopea's Chair.

He was near the quarter-deck, in the fore part of the vessel, and had been unobserved in the darkness by Lamia and Domitia, till they returned aft.

Then the young man started as he observed him.

Was it possible that the man had overheard the words spoken? There was nothing in the attitude or manner of the physician to show that he entertained alarm. Lamia resolved on keeping an eye upon him that he did not communicate with the crew.

Luke returned aft when the young people came in that direction, and seated himself quietly on a bench.

Eboracus was rapidly communicated with and gained.

The Artemis flew forward, noiselessly, save for the plunge of the oars and the hiss of the foam, as it rushed by like milk, and from the hold sounded the muffled note of the symphonicius or piper.

Every moment the vessel neared the imperial galley, and sounds of revelry became audible. Nothing showed that any on board were aware of the approach of a Liburnian.

It was now seen that tables were spread on the deck of the Imperial vessel, and that the prince and his attendants, and indeed the entire crew were engaged in revelry.

Between the courses which were served, Nero ascended the quarter-deck, and sang or else delivered a recitation from a Greek tragedian, or a piece of his own composition.

If the approach of the bireme was observed, which did not seem to be the case, it caused no uneasiness. The Emperor's vessel had been accompanied by a convoy, but the ships had been dispersed by the storm; and the bireme, if perceived, was doubtless held to be one of the fleet.

And now Helios, the confidant of Nero, had ascended the quarter-deck to his master, and began to declaim the speech of the attendant in the Electra descriptive of the conquests of Orestes—applying the words, by significant indications to the prince returning a victor from the Grecian games.

"He, having come to the glorious pageantry of the sports in Greece, entered the lists to win the Delphic prizes, he, the admired of every eye. And having started from his goal in wondrous whirls he sped along the course, and bore away the of all coveted prize of victory. But that I may tell thee in few words amidst superfluity I have never known such a man of might and deeds as he—" and he bowed and waved his hands towards Nero.

A roar of applause broke out, interrupted by a cry from Nero who suddenly beheld a dark ship plunge out of the night and come within the radiance of the lights on board his vessel.

Meanwhile, on the Artemis, with set face sat Eboracus, guiding the head of the Liburnian as directed. He could see the twinkling lights, and hear the sounds of rejoicing.

"Slack speed," called Lamia.

"Slack your oars," down into the hold.

There was a pause—all oars held poised for a moment.

"Double!" shouted Lamia.

"Double your oars!" down the ladder.

Instantly the water hissed about the bows, and the oars plunged.

Eboracus by a violent movement threw himself and his entire weight on the handle of one paddle, so as to turn the bireme about, and ram her midships into the Imperial trireme, when suddenly, without a word, Luke had drawn a knife through the thong that restrained the paddle, and instantly the pedalion leaped out of place, and would have gone overboard, had not the physician caught and retained it.

Immediately the direction of the Artemis was altered and in place of running into the trireme, she swerved and swung past the Imperial galley without touching her.

Nero, white with alarm and rage shrieked from the quarter-deck,

"Who commands?"

Then to those by him, "Pour oil on the flames."

At once from the braziers, tongues of brilliant light leaped high into the air.

"The name!" yelled the furious prince.

Then came the reply:—

"Cnæus Domitius Corbulo."

And by the glare he saw, standing by the mast, distinct against the darkness of the night behind, the form of a man—and the face was the face of the murdered general.

Nero staggered back—and would have fallen unless caught by Helios.

"The dead pursue me," he gasped. "Wife, mother, brother, and now, Corbulo!"

CHAPTER VIII

THE SWORD OF THE DEAD

"It is well done," said Eboracus in an undertone to the physician; "Otherwise there had been the cross for you and me. The thong broke."

"I severed it," said Luke.

"That I saw," said the slave, "I shall report that it yielded. One must obey a master even to the risk of the cross. Did'st see the noble Lamia, how ready he was? He assumed the mask of my dead master and we have slipped by and sent a shiver through the whole company of the Trireme, and the August too, I trow,—for they have thought us the Ship of the Dead."

After a pause he said,—"In my home we hold that all souls go to sea in a phantom vessel; and sail away to the West, to the Isles of the Blessed. At night a dark ship with a sail as a thundercloud comes to the shore, and those near can hear the dead in trains go over the beach and enter the ghostly vessel, till she is laden, and then she departs."

The Artemis made her way without disaster to Rhegium, and thence coasted up Italy to the port of Rome. She had gained on the Imperial vessel, that was delayed at Brundusium to collect the scattered fleet. Nero would not land until he reached Neapolis, and then not till all his wreaths and golden apples, as well as his entire wardrobe of costumes and properties had arrived.

Then only did he come ashore, and he did so to commence a triumphal progress through the Peninsula, the like of which was never seen before nor will be seen again.

This was on the 19th March, the anniversary of the murder of his mother. On the same day a letter was put into his hands announcing the revolt of the legions in Gaul and the proclamation of Galba, at that time Governor of Spain.

So engrossed, however, was his mind with preparation for his theatrical procession, that he paid no heed to the news, nor was he roused till he read the address of Vindex, who led the revolt, denouncing him as a "miserable fiddler."

This touched him to the quick, and he addressed an indignant despatch to the Senate, demanding that Vindex should be chastised, and appealed to the prizes he had gained as testimony to his musical abilities.

So he started for Rome.

Eighteen hundred and eight heralds strutted before him, bearing in their hands the crowns that had been awarded him and announcing when and how he had succeeded in winning the award.

He entered Rome in this leisurely manner, in a triumphal chariot, wearing a purple robe, embroidered with gold, an olive garland about his head. Beside him a harper struck his instrument and chanted his praises.

The houses were decorated with festoons, the streets were strewn with saffron; singing birds, comfits, flowers were scattered by the people before him. If the Senate expected that now the prince was in Rome, he would attend to business, it was vastly mistaken. His first concern was to arrange for a splendid exhibition in which he might gratify the public with a finished study of his acting and singing.

Solicitude about his triumph, his voice, his reception, had so completely filled the shallow mind of Nero, that he gave no further thought to the vessel that had shot out of the darkness, nearly fouled his galley, and which had been apparently commanded by one of his noblest victims.

Longa Duilia arrived on the Gabian estate, with the corpse of her husband, her daughter, Lucius Lamia, and her entire "family," as the company of household slaves was termed, without accident and without deter.

Gabii lay eleven miles from Rome at the foot of one of the spurs of the Alban mountains. The town stood on a small knoll rising out of the Campagna. The stone of which it was built was dark, being a volcanic peperino; it was perhaps one of the least attractive sites for a country residence, which a Roman noble could have selected; but this was not without its advantage, when Emperors acted as did Ahab, and cut off those whose villas and vineyards attracted their covetous eyes.

A lake occupied the crater of an extinct volcano; the water was dark as ink, but this was due rather to the character of the bottom, than to depth, which was inconsiderable.

The villa and its gardens lay by the water's edge. The old city not flourishing, but maintaining a languid existence, was famous for nothing but a peculiarity in girding the toga adopted by the men, by the dinginess of its building stone, and by its temple of Juno, an object of pilgrimage when the deities of other shrines had proved unwilling or unable to help, a sort of pis-aller of devotion.

Longa Duilia hated the place; it was dull, and she would never have frequented it, had it not been the fashion at the period for all people of good family to affect a love of retirement into the country, and to pretend a taste for simplicity of rural life. Some fine fops had their "chambers of poverty" to which on occasions they retired, to lie on mats upon the ground, and eat pulse out of common earthenware. Such periods of self-denial added zest to luxury.

Domitia, on the other hand, was attached to the place. It was associated with the innocent pleasures of earliest childhood. Its spring flowers were the loveliest she had ever culled, its June strawberries the most delicious she had ever eaten. And the lake teeming with char gave opportunities for boating and fishing.

Here was the family burial-place; and here Corbulo was to be burnt, and then his ashes collected and consigned to the mausoleum.

Messengers had been sent forth to invite the attendance of all relations, acquaintances and dependents.

The invitation was couched, according to unalterable custom, in antiquated terms, hardly intelligible. When on the day appointed for the ceremony, vast numbers were collected, the funeral procession started.

First went the musicians under the conduct of a Master of the Ceremonies. By law, the number of flautists was limited to ten.

Then followed the professional mourners, hired for the occasion from the temple of Libitina, the priests of which were the licensed undertakers. These mourners chanted the nænia, a lament composed for the purpose of lauding the acts of the deceased and of reciting his honors. When they paused at the conclusion of a strophe, horns and trumpets brayed. Immediately after the wailers walked a train of actors, one of whom was dressed in the insignia of the deceased and wore a mask representing him. He endeavored to mimic each peculiarity of the man he personated, and buffoons around by their antics and jests provoked the spectators to laughter. This farcical exhibition was calculated to moderate the excessive grief superinduced by the lament of the wailers.

Then came the grand procession of the ancestors, especially dear to the heart of the widow. Not only did the effigies of the direct forefathers appear, but all related families trotted out their ancestors, to attend the illustrious dead, so that there cannot have been less than a hundred present.

As already mentioned, the wax masks of the dead of a family ornamented every nobleman's hall, usually enclosed in boxes with the titles of the defunct inscribed on them in gold characters. These were now produced. The mimes were costumed appropriately, as senators, generals, magistrates, with their attendants, wearing the wax masks, and artificial heads of hair.

The idea represented was that of the ancestors having returned from the land of Shadows to fetch their descendant and accompany him to the nether world. The corpse, that lay on a bier in the hall, was now taken up, and carried forth to a loud cry from all in the house of "Vale! Farewell! Fare thee well!"Between the lips of the dead man was a coin, placed there as payment of the toll across the River of Death in the ferry-boat of Charon. On each side of the bier walked attendants carrying lighted torches. In ancient times all funerals had been conducted at night. Now the only reminiscence of this custom was in the bearing of lights; but the torches served as well a practical purpose, as they were employed to kindle the pyre.

Before the dead were carried the insignia of his offices, pictures of the battles he had won and statues of the kings and chiefs he had conquered. The corpse was followed by a number of manumitted slaves, all wearing the cap of liberty, in token of their freedom. Finally came the members of the family, friends, retainers, and the sympathizing public.

Longa Duilia and Domitia Longina walked in their proper place, with dishevelled hair, unveiled heads, and in the ricinium or black garment thrown over their tunics; the men all wore the pænula, or short travelling cloak.

The procession advanced into the marketplace of Gabii, where Lucius Lamia ascended the rostrum to pronounce the funeral oration.

Immediately, ivory chairs and inlaid stools were ranged in a crescent before him, and on these the ancestors seated themselves, the bier being placed before them.

The panegyric was addressed to the crowd outside the circle of mimes with wax faces. Lamia had a gift of natural eloquence, his feelings were engaged, but his freedom of speech was hampered by necessity of caution in allusion to the death of Corbulo, lest some word should be let slip which might be caught up and tortured into a treasonable reference to Nero.

The Laudation ended, the entire assembly arose and re-formed in procession to the place of burning, which by law must be sixty feet from any building. There a pit had been excavated and a grating placed above it. On this grating the pyre was erected, consisting of precious woods, sprinkled with gums and spices.

To this the corpse was conveyed. But, previous to its being placed on the fagots, a surgeon amputated one of the fingers, which was preserved for burial, and then a handful of earth was thrown over the face of the deceased.

Anciently the Roman dead had been buried, and when the fashion for incineration came in, a trace of the earlier usage remained in the burial of a member and the covering of the face with soil.

And now ensued a repulsive scene, one without which no great man's funeral would have been considered as properly performed.

Through the crowd pushed two small parties of gladiators, three in each, hired for the occasion of a company that let them out. Then ensued a fight—not mimic, but very real, in front and round the pyre. Now a hard-pressed gladiator ran and was pursued, turned sharply and hacked at his follower. This was continued till three men had fallen and had been stabbed in the breast. Whereupon, the survivors sheathed their swords, bowed and withdrew.

The torches were now put into the hands of Duilia and Domitia, and with averted faces they applied the fire to the fagot, and a sheet of flame roared up and enveloped the dead man.

And now the mourners raised their loudest cries, tore their hair, scarified their cheeks with their nails; pipes, flutes, horns were blown. In a paroxysm of distress, partly real, partly feigned, a rush was made to the pyre, and all who got near cast some offering into the flames—cakes, flowers, precious stuffs, rings, bracelets, and coins.

Duilia, in tragic woe, disengaged a mass of artificial hair from her head, and cast it into the fire. Then rang out the sacramental cry:—"I, licet! You are permitted to retire," and gladly, sick at heart and faint, Domitia was supported rather than walked home.

Some hours later, when the ashes of the defunct had been collected and deposited in an urn, which was conveyed to the mausoleum, Lucius Lamia came to the house and inquired for the ladies.

He was informed that the widow was too much overcome by her feelings to see any one, but that Domitia was in the tablinum and would receive him.

He at once entered the hall and stepped up into the apartment where she was seated, looking pale and worn, with tear-reddened eyes.

She rose, and with a sweet sad smile, extended her hand to Lamia.

"No, Domitia," said he gently, "as your dear father gave me permission on the wharf at Cenchræa, I will claim the same privilege now."

She held her cold, tear-stained cheek to him without a word, then returned to and sank on her stool.

"I thank you, dear friend, and almost brother,"she said. "You spoke nobly of my father, though not more nobly than he deserved. Here, my Lucius, is a present for you, I intrust it to you—his sword, which he used so gallantly, on which he fell, and still marked with his blood."

CHAPTER IX

SHEATHED

According to an Oriental legend, the dominion of Solomon over the spirits resided in the power of his staff on which he stayed himself. So long as he wielded that, none might disobey.

But the Jins sent a white ant up through the floor, that ate out the heart of the rod, so that when he leaned on it, it gave way and resolved itself into a cloud of fine powder. Solomon fell, and his authority was at an end forever.

The termites that consumed the core of the sceptre of Nero were his own vices and follies. Its power was at an end and his fall as sudden as in the case of Solomon, and as unexpected.

In March he was possessed of dominion over the world, and was at the head of incalculable forces. In June all was dissolved in the dust of decay; he was prostrate, helpless, bereft of the shadow of authority, unable to command a single slave. The first token of what was about to take place was this.

In Rome the rabble was kept in good humor by the Cæsars distributing among them bread gratis, and entertaining them with shows free of charge.

During the winter, contrary winds had delayed the corn-ships from Egypt, and the amount of bread distributed was accordingly curtailed. Games were, indeed, promised, but these would serve as condiments to the bread and not as substitutes. Then a vessel arrived in port, and the hungry people believed that she was laden with the wished-for corn. When, however, they learned that her cargo was white sand for strewing the arena at the sports, they broke into a storm of discontent and swept, howling insulting words, under Nero's windows.

Next day all Rome heard that Galba, at the head of the legions of Spain and Gaul, was marching into Italy, and that none of the troops of Nero sent to guard the frontier of the Alps would draw a sword in his defence.

The prince, now only seriously alarmed, bade his household guard conduct him to Ostia, where he would mount the vessel that had discharged its load of sand, and escape to Egypt. They contemptuously refused, and disbanded. Then, in an agony of fear, Nero left the Palatine, and fled across the river to the Servilian mansion that adjoined the race-course, to light which he had burned Christians swathed in tarred wraps.

There he found none save his secretary Epaphroditus, whom he had sent there to be chained at the door, and to act as porter because he had offended him. Guards, freedmen, courtiers, actors, all had taken to their heels, but not before they had pillaged the palace.

He wandered about the house, knocking at every door, and nowhere meeting with an answer.

Night by this time had settled in, murk and close, but at intervals electric flashes shivered overhead.

Then suddenly the earth reeled, and there passed a sound as of chariot wheels rolling heavily through the streets; yet the streets were deserted. Trembling, despairing, Nero crouched on his bed, bit his nails till he had gnawed them to the quick, then started up and hunted for his jewel case. He would fly on foot, carrying that, hide in some hovel, till danger was past. But a thievish slave had stolen it.

Sick at heart, picking, then biting at his nails, shrinking with apprehension at the least noise, wrapping a kerchief about a finger where blood came, he looked with dazed eyes at the red flare of the heavenly fires pulsating through his open door.

He heard a step and ran out, to encounter a freedman, Phaon by name, who was coming along the passage, holding aloft a torch, attended by two slaves.

The wretched prince clung to him, and entreated that he might not be left alone; that Phaon would protect him, and contrive a means of escape.

"Augustus!" answered the freedman, "I am not ungrateful for favors shown me, but my assistance at this hour is unavailing. I am but one man, a stranger, a Greek, and all Rome, all Italy, the entire world, have risen against you."

"I must fly. They will allow me to earn my livelihood on the stage. Of what value to any man is my life?"

"My lord, in what value have you held the lives of the thousands that you have taken? Each life cut off has raised against you a hundred enemies. All will pursue, like a pack of hounds baying for the blood of him who murdered their kinsfolk. Even now I passed one—Lucius Ælius Lamia,—and he stayed me to inquire where you might be found. In his hand he held an unsheathed sword."

Nero shrieked out; then looked timidly about him, terrified at the sound of his own voice.

"Let us hide. Disguise me. Get me a horse. I cannot run, I am too fat; besides, I have on my felt slippers only."

Phaon spoke to one of his slaves, and the man left.

"Master," said the freedman, "Do not deceive yourself. There is no escape. Prepare to die as a man. Slay yourself. It is not hard to die. Better so fall than get into the hands of implacable enemies."

"I cannot. I have not the courage. I will do it only when everything fails. I have many theatrical wigs. I can paint my face."

"Sire! the people are so wont to see your face besmeared with color, that they are less likely to recognize a face bleached to tallow."

"I have a broad-brimmed fisherman's hat. I wear it against becoming freckled. That will shade my face. Find me an ample cloak. Here, at length, comes Sporus."

An eunuch appeared in the doorway.

Breathless, in short, broken sentences, Nero entreated him to look out in his wardrobe for a sorry mantle, and to bring it him.

"But whither will—can you go?" asked Phaon. "The Senate has been assembled—it has been convoked for midnight to vote your deposition and death."

"I will go before it. Nay! I will haste to the Forum, I will mount the Tribune. I will ask to be given the government of Egypt. That at least will not be refused me."

"My lord, the streets are filling with people. They will tear you to pieces ere you reach the Forum."

"Think you so! Why so? I have amused the people so well. Good Phaon, hire me a swift galley, and I will take refuge with Tiridates. I restored to him the crown of Armenia. He will not be ungrateful."

"My lord, it will not be possible for you to leave Italy."

"Then I will retire to a farm. I will grow cabbages and turnips. The god Tiberius was fond of turnips. O Divine Powers that rule the fate of men! shall I ever eat turnips again? Phaon, hide me for a season. Men's minds are changeable. They are heated now. They will cool to-morrow. They cannot kill such a superlative artist as myself."

"I have a villa between the Salarian and the Nomentane Roads. If it please you to go thither—"

"At once. I think I hear horse-hoofs. O Phaon, save me!"

Sporus came up, offering an old moth-eaten cloak. The wardrobe had been plundered, only the refuse had been abandoned.

A voice was heard pealing through the empty corridors: "Horses! horses at the door!"

"Who calls so loud? Silence him. He will betray us!" said Nero. "Hah! It is Epaphroditus."

At the entrance, chained to a cumbrous log, was the Greek, Epaphroditus, formerly a pampered favorite. But two days previously he had ventured to correct a false quantity in some verses by his master, and Nero, in a burst of resentment and mortified vanity, had ordered him to be fastened to a beam as doorkeeper to the Servilian Palace.

"The horses are here," shouted the freedman. "May it please my lord to mount. Sporus and the slaves can run afoot."

Nero unwound the kerchief from his hand and wrapped it about his throat, drew the broad-brimmed hat over his head, enveloped himself in the blanket cloak, and shuffled in his slippers to the door.

The chained Greek at once cried out: "Master! my chain has become entangled and is so knotted that I cannot stir. I have been thus since noon, and none have regarded me. I pray thee, let me go."

"Thou fool! cease hallooing!" retorted Nero angrily. "Dost think I carry about with me the key of thy shackles?" Then to those who followed, "Smite him on the mouth and silence him, or he will call attention to me."

"The gods smite thee!" yelled the scribe, striving to reach an upright posture, but falling again, owing to the tangle in the links. "May they blight thee as they have stricken Livia's laurel!"[3]

Mounted on an old gray horse, Nero rode to the Ælian Bridge, where stands now that of St. Angelo, crossed it and began to traverse the Campus Martius.

Electric flashes quivered across the sky. Then again an earthquake made the city rock as if drunk; the buildings were rent, and masses of cornice fell down.

A glare of white lightning illumined the whole field and lighted up the mausoleum of Augustus, and the blank faces of such men as were abroad.

The horse trembled and refused to move. It was some time before the alarm of the brute could be allayed, and it could be coaxed to go forward and begin the ascent of the Quirinal. The advance was slow; and Nero's fears became greater as the road approached the Prætorian Camp, and he expected recognition by the sentinels. Yet in the midst of his fear wild flashes of hope shot, and he said to Phaon:

"What think you, if I were to enter the camp? Surely the Prætorians would rally about me, and I might dissolve the Senate."

"Sire, they have destroyed your images, and have proclaimed Galba. They would take off your head and set it on a pike."

---

3   A laurel on the Palatine, planted by the wife of Augustus. It died suddenly just before the end of Nero.

Nero uttered a groan, and kicked the flanks of his steed. At that moment a passer-by saluted him.

"By the Immortals! I am recognized."

"We have but to go a little further."

"Phaon, what if the Senate declare me an enemy of the State?"

"Then you will fare in the customary manner."

"How is that?"

The prince put his trembling hand to his brow and in his agitation knocked off his hat.

The freedman picked it up.

"The customary manner, sire! your neck will be put in the cleft of a forked stick and you will be beaten, lashed, kicked to death. Better take the sword and fall on it."

"Oh, Phaon! not yet! I cannot endure pain. I have a spring nail now— and it hurts! it hurts!"

"Ride on, my lord; at the cypress hedge we will turn our horses loose, and by a path through the fields reach my villa."

Half an hour after Nero had left the Servilian palace, where now stands the Lateran, Lamia arrived followed by two servants. He found the secretary in a heap at the door, vainly writhing in his knotted chains. Lamia at once asked him about the prince, whether he was there.

"I will both answer and show you whither he is fled," said Epaphroditus, "if you will release me. Otherwise my tongue is tied like my limbs."

"Is he here?"

"Nay, he has been here, but is gone. Whither I alone can say. The price of the information is release."

"Tell me where I can find tools."

Epaphroditus gave the required information and Lamia despatched a servant to bring hammer and chisel. They were speedily produced; but some time was taken up in cutting through the links.

This, however, was finally effected, and the secretary gathered up a handful of the broken chain and clenched it in his fist.

"Now I will lead the way," said he, stretching himself.

The wretched, fallen emperor had in the meanwhile scrambled through hedges and waded through a marsh, and had at last found a temporary shelter in a garden tool-house of the villa. Phaon feared to introduce him into his house.

Wearied out, he cast himself on a sort of bier on which the gardeners carried citron trees to and from the conservatory. The cloak had fallen from him and lay on the soil.

His feet were muddy and bleeding. He had tried to eat some oat-cake that had been offered him, but was unable to swallow.

He continued to be teased with, and to pick or bite at his spring nails.

"I hear steps!" he cried. "They will kill me!"

"Sire, play the man."

Phaon offered him a couple of poniards.

Nero put the point of one to his breast, shrunk and threw it away.

"It is too blunt, it will not enter," he said.

He tried the other and dropped it.

"It is over sharp. It cuts," he said.

At that moment the door opened and Lamia and Epaphroditus entered.

Nero cried out and covered his face:

"Sporus! Phaon! one or both! kill yourselves and show me how to do it."

"To do it!" said Lamia sternly. "That is not difficult. Do you need a sword? Here is one—the sword of Corbulo."

He extended the weapon to the prince, who accepted it with tremulous hand, looking at Lamia with glassy eyes.

"Oh! a moment! I feel sick."

Then Phaon said: "Sire—at once!"

Then Nero, with all power going out of his fingers, pointed the blade to his throat.

"I cannot," he gasped, "my hand is numb."

Immediately, Epaphroditus with his hand full of chain, brought the weighted fist against the haft, and drove the sword into the coward's throat.

He sank back on the bier.

Then Lamia stooped, gathered up the moth-eaten cloak, and threw it over the face of the dying man.

CHAPTER X

UBI FELICITAS?

"Push, my dear Domitia, Push. Of course. What else would you have, but Push?"

"But, sweetest mother, that surely cannot give what I ask."

"Indeed, my child, it does. It occupies all one's energies, it exerts all one's faculties, and it fills the heart."

"But—what do you gain?"

"Gain, child?—everything. The satisfaction of having got further up the ladder; of exciting the envy of your late companions, the admiration of the vulgar, the mistrust of those above you."

"Is that worth having?"

"Of course it is. It is—that very thing you desire, Happiness. It engages all your thoughts, stimulates your abilities. You dress for it; you prepare your table for it, accumulate servants for it, walk, smile, talk, acquire furniture, statuary, bronzes, and so on—for it. It is charming, ravishing. I live for it. I desire nothing better."

"But I do, mother. I do not care for this."

The girl spoke with her eyes on a painting on the wall of the atrium that represented a young maiden running in pursuit of a butterfly. Beneath it were the words "Ubi Felicitas?"

"Because you are young and silly, Domitia. When older and wiser, you will understand the value of Push, and appreciate Position. My dear, properly considered, everything can be made use of for the purpose—even widowhood, dexterously dealt with, becomes a vehicle for Push. It really is vexatious that in Rome there should just now be such broils and effervescence of minds, proclamation of emperors, cutting of throats, that I, poor thing, here in Gabii run a chance of being forgotten. It is too provoking. I really wish that this upsetting of Nero, and setting up of Galba, and defection of Otho, and so on, had been postponed till my year of widowhood were at an end. One gets no chance, and it might have been so effective."

"And when you have obtained that at which you have aimed?"

"Then make that the start for another push."

"And if you fail?"

"Then, my dear, you have the gratification of being able to lay the blame on some one else. You have done your utmost."

"When you have gained what you aimed at, you are not content."

"That is just the beauty of Push. No, always go on to what is beyond."

"Look at that running girl, mother, she chases a butterfly, and when she has caught the lovely insect she crushes it in her hand. The glory of its wings is gone, its life is at an end. What then?"

"She runs after another butterfly."

"And despises and rejects each to which she has attained?"

"Certainly!"

After a pause Longa Duilia said, as she signed to Lucilla the slave to fan her, "That was the one defect in your dear father's character, he had no Push."

"Mother! can you say that after his splendid victories, over the Chauci, over the Parthians, over—"

"I know all about them. They should have served as means, child, not as ends."

"I do not understand."

"Poor simple man, he fought the enemies of Rome and defeated them, because it was, as he said, his duty to his country, to Rome, to do so. But, by Ops and Portumna! that was talking like a child. What might he not have been with those victories? But he couldn't see it. He had it not in him. Some men are born to squint; some have club feet; and your poor dear father had no ambition."

After a pause the lady added: "When I come to consider what he might have done for me, had he possessed Push, it makes my spleen swell. Just consider! What is Galba compared with him? What any of these fellows who have been popping up their heads like carp or trout when the May flies are about? My dear, had your dear father been as complete a man as I am a woman, at this moment I might be Empress."

"That would have contented you."

"It would have been a step in that direction."

"What more could you desire?"

"Why, to be a goddess. Did not the Senate pronounce Poppæa divine, and to be worshipped and invoked, after Nero had kicked her and she died? And that baby of his—it died of fits in teething—that became a goddess also. Nasty little thing! I saw it, it did nothing but dribble and squall, but is a god for all that. My dear Domitia, think! the Divine Duilia! Salus Italiæ, with my temples, my altars, my statues. By the Immortal Twelve, I think I should have tried to cut out Aphrodite, and have been represented rising from the foam. Oh! it would have been too, too lovely.

But there! it makes me mad—all that might have been, and would have been to a certainty, had your dear father listened to me at Antioch. But he had a head." She touched her brow. "Something wrong there—no Push."

"But, dearest mother, this may be an approved motive for such as you and for all nobles. But then—for the artisan, the herdsman, the slave, Push can't be a principle of life to such as they."

"My child, how odd you are! What need we consider them? They may have their own motives, I can't tell; I never was a herdsman nor a slave—never did any useful work in my life. As to a slave, of course Push is a motive—he pushes to gain his freedom."

"And when he has got that?"

"Then he strives to accumulate a fortune."

"And then?"

"Then he will have a statue or a bust of himself sculptured, and when he gets old, erect a splendid mausoleum."

"And so all ends in a handful of dust."

"Of course. What else would you have?—Remember, a splendid mausoleum."

"Yes, enclosing a pot of ashes. That picture teaches a sad truth. Pursue your butterfly: when you have caught it, you find only dust between your fingers."

"Domitia! as the Gods love me! I wish you would refrain from this talk. It is objectionable. It is prematurely oldening you, and what ages you reflects on me—it advances my years. I will listen to no more of this. If you relish it, I do not; go, chatter to the Philosopher Claudius Senecio, he is paid to talk this stuff."

"I will not speak to him. I know beforehand what he will say."

"He will give you excellent advice, he is hired to do it."

"O yes—to bear everything with equanimity. That is the sum and substance of his doctrine. Then not to be too wise about the Gods; to aim to sit on the fulcrum of a see-saw, when I prefer an end of the plank."

"Equanimity! I desire it with my whole soul."

"But why so, mother? It is not running thought, but stagnation."

"Because, my dear, it keeps off wrinkles."

"Mother, you and I will never understand each other."

"As the Gods love me, I sincerely hope not. Send me Plancus, Lucilla. I must scold him so as to soothe my ruffled spirits."

"And, Euphrosyne, go, send the Chaldæan to me in the garden," said the girl.

The slave obeyed and departed.

"Ubi Felicitas? Running, pursuing and finding nothing," said Domitia as she went forth.

The sun was hot. She passed under an arched trellis with vines trained over it; the swelling bunches hung down within.

At intervals in the arcade were openings through which could be seen the still lake, and beyond the beautiful ridges of the limestone Sabine Mountains. The air was musical with the hum of bees.

Domitia paced up and down this walk for some while.

Presently the Magus appeared at the end, under the guidance of the girl Euphrosyne.

He approached, bowing at intervals, till he reached Domitia, when he stood still.

"Ubi Felicitas?" asked she. And when he raised his eyebrows in question, she added in explanation: "There is a picture in the atrium representing a damsel in pursuit of a butterfly, and beneath is the legend I have just quoted. When she catches the butterfly it will not content her. It will be a dead pinch of dust. It is now some months since you spoke on the Artemis, when I asked you a question, and then you were forced to admit that all your science was built up on conjecture, and that there was no certainty underlying it. But a guess is better than nothing, and a guess that carries the moral sense with it in approval, may come near to the truth. I recall all you then said. Do not repeat it, but answer my question, Ubi Felicitas? I asked it of my mother, and she said that it was to be found in Push. If I asked Senecio, he would say in Equanimity. Where say you that it is to be found?"

"The soul of man is a ray out of the Godhead,"answered the Magus, "it is enveloped, depressed, smothered by matter; and the straining of the spirit in man after happiness is the striving of his divine nature to emancipate itself from the thraldom of matter and return to Him from whom the ray emanated."

"Then felicity is to be found—?"

"In the disengagement of the good in man from matter, which presses it down, and which is evil."

"Evil!" exclaimed Domitia, looking through one of the gaps in the arcade, at the lake; on a balustrade above the water stood a dreaming peacock, whilst below it grew bright flowers. Beyond, as clouds, hung the blue Sabine hills.

"The Divine ray," said the girl, "seems rarely to delight in its incorporation in Matter, and to find therein its expression, much as do our thoughts in words. May it not be that Primordial Idea is inarticulate without Matter in which to utter itself?"

"Felicity," continued the Chaldæan, disregarding the objection, "is sought by many in the satisfying of their animal appetites, in pleasing eye and ear and taste and smell. But in all is found the after-taste of satiety that gluts. True happiness is to be sought in teaching the mind to dispense with sensuous delights, and to live in absorption in itself."

"Why, Elymas!" said Domitia. "In fine, you arrive by another method at that Apathy which Senecio the Stoic advocates. I grant you give a reason—which seems to me lame—but it is a reason, whereas he supplies none. But I like not your goal—Apathy is the reverse from Felicity. Leave me."

The Magus retired, mortified at his doctrine being so ill received.

Then Euphrosyne approached timidly.

Domitia, who was in moody thought, looked up. The girl could not venture to speak till invited to do so by her mistress.

"Your lady mother has desired me to announce to you that Lucius Ælius Lamia hath ridden over from Rome."

"I will come presently," said Domitia; "I am just now too troubled in mind. You, child, tell me, where is the physician, Luke?"

"Lady, I do not know; he quitted us on reaching Rome."

"Stay, Euphrosyne. Thine is a cheerful spirit. Where is felicity to be found?"

"My gracious mistress, I find mine in serving thee—in my duty."

"Ah, child! That is the sort of reply my father might have made. In the discharge of what he considered his duty, he was of a wondrous sweet and equable temper. Is it so, that Felicity is only to be found in the discharge of duty? And those torpid flies, the young loafers of our noble families, whose only occupation is to play ball, and whose amusements are vicious; they have it not because none has set them tasks. The ploughman whistles as he drives his team; the vineyard rings with laughter at the gathering of the grapes. The galley-slaves chant as they bend over the oar, and the herdboy pipes as he tends the goats. So each is set a task, and is content in discharge thereof, and each sleeps sweetly at night, when the task is done. But what! is happiness reserved to the bondsman, and not for the master? And only then for the former when the duty imposed is reasonable and honest?—For there is none when such an order comes as to fall on the sword or to open the veins. How about us great ladies? And the noble loafers? No task is set us and them."

"Surely, lady, to all God has given duties!"

"Nay—when, where, how? Look at me, Euphrosyne. When I was a little child here, we had a neighbor, Lentulus. He was a lie-abed, and a sot. He let his servants do as they liked, make love, quarrel, fight, the one lord it over the other, and all idle, because on none was imposed any duty. It was a villainous household, and the estate went to the hammer. It seems to me, Euphrosyne, as if this whole world were the estate of Lentulus on a large scale, where all the servants squabbled, and one by sheer force tyrannizes over the others, and none know why they are placed there, and what is their master's will, and what they have to do. There is no day-table of work. There is either no master over such a household, or he is an Olympian Lentulus."

"But, mistress, is that not impossible?"

"It would seem so, and yet—Where is the Day-Table? Show me that—and, by the Gods! it will be new life to me. I shall know my duty—and see Happiness."

CHAPTER XI

THE VEILS OF ISHTAR

Domitia did not go into the house, as desired, to receive Lamia.

She was well aware that he would come to her into the garden, if she did not present herself within, and she preferred to speak with him away from her mother.

She therefore continued to walk under the vines. She looked up at the sunlight filtering through the broad green flaky shade, with here and there a ray kissing a purple, pendent bunch of grapes.

Then she looked at the dreaming peacock, the sun flashing on its metallic plumage.

No! matter was not evil. Matter, indeed, without life was not even like the statue—for that was a copy of what lived, and failed just in this, that it fell short of life. Domitia felt as though she were touching the edge of a great verity, but had not set her foot upon it. Then she considered what Euphrosyne had said to her, and she to her slave. Wherever the path of duty lay, there violets bloomed and verbena scented the air. Was not life itself, devoid of the knowledge of its purport, and its obligations and its destiny, like matter uninformed by Life? Or if any life entered into it, it was the disintegrating life of decay and decomposition?

She, for her part, had no obligations laid on her. If, however, she were married to Lamia, then at once duties would spring up, and her way would be rosy. Till then her happiness hung in suspense, like that of her mother, during the period of widowhood in which she was expected and required to live in retirement. Out of society, not elbowing and shouldering her way forward—that was a year of blank and of unhappiness to Longa Duilia, in which she found no consolation save in badgering her steward, and in scheming for the future.

Lamia, as Domitia expected he would, came to her under the trellis, and she received him with that dimple in her cheek which gave her expression so much sweetness mingled with pathos,

"Lucius," she said, "you are good to come. My mother is, oh! so dull, and restless withal."

"It is well that she should be away from Rome, my Domitia. I have told her as much. On no account must you leave Gabii. Rome is boiling over, and will scald many fingers. None know who will be up to-morrow, and which down. Galba is dead, almost torn to pieces by those who worshipped him yesterday. Otho is proclaimed by the Senate. Yet there is fresh trouble brewing and threats sound from the provinces. Methinks every general at the head of an army is marching upon Rome to snatch the purple for his own shoulders. Otho has but a poor chance. He can command the prætorians and the household troops—none others. Soldiers that have disbanded themselves and gangs of robbers prowl the streets, waylay men of substance and plunder them, break into houses and strip them of their contents. Murders are frequent. Thus far your palace in the Carinæ is undisturbed."

"Oh, Lucius! my mother has so fretted over that house, as it stands back, and makes no show behind its bank of yews and laurels, and yet those evergreens, I believe, saved it in the fire. She says that the house is unworthy of our dignity."

"You may rejoice that it is so in such times of anarchy. Order in the city is now at an end, none are safe unless attended by armed slaves; and, by the Gods! no man is quite safe even from his own slaves."

"What did my mother say to that?"

"She sighed and said—" there was a twinkle in Lamia's eye, "that she was glad the disturbances were taking place now, as at no time could they have happened so happily, when she was obliged to live in retirement."

"Lucius, what do you think will be the end?"

"That the gods alone can tell. At present the soldiers are masters in the State, and the Senate proclaims whomsoever they set up. Rome is dishonored in the face of the Barbarians."

"What think you, my Lucius,—shall we ask the Chaldee if he can unveil the future?"

"Not of the State, Domitia, that were too dangerous. Women have lost their lives, or been banished on such a charge. No, do not risk it."

"Nay, Lucius, like my mother, the State concerns me only so far as its affairs affect my own silly little interests. But I do want to know something of my future. Elymas is reputed to look into destiny. He hath glimpses beyond the strain of a philosopher's eye. I have offended him by my quips and objections, and would humor him now by asking him to read in the stars, or where he will, what the gods have in store for me."

"I believe not in such vision."

"Nor I greatly, Lucius. Yet I heard say that he had prognosticated evil on the day my dear father set foot in Cenchræa."

"It needed no prophet to foretell that."

"Shall we seek him, Lucius?"

"As you will. I will attend thee. Only, no questions relative to the prince, as to his life, his reign, his health. No questions concerning the State—promise me that."

"It shall be so, Lucius. Come with me to the Temple of Isis. He is there."

The two young people walked to a small shrine or ædiculum at the extremity of a terrace above the lake.

In the colonnade in front of the door was the Magus. He was out of humor, offended at his treatment by Domitia. His sole satisfaction was that Senecio, the Stoic, was placed below him in her estimation.

Now the girl went up to him, with a pretty, winning smile, and said:

"Sir! I fear me greatly that I gave you occasion to think I held your theories cheaply. Indeed it is not so, they are too weighty to be dismissed at once; they take time to digest. There is one thing you may do for me, that I desire of you heartily, and in which I will not controvert your authority. It is said that the stars rule the destinies of men, and that in the far East, on the boundless plains of Mesopotamia, you and your people have learned to read them. I would fain know what the heavens have in store for me."

"Indeed, lady, to consult the stars is a long and painful business, that I will gladly undertake, but it cannot be done hastily. It will require time. There are, however, other ways of reading the future than by the stars. There is Ishtar, whom the Egyptians call Isis, whom thou mayest consult in this temple."

"I am ready."

"That also cannot be undertaken at once. I must even send for my assistant Helena. It is not I who see, save mediately. The goddess has her chosen instrument, and such is Helena. Lady! Ishtar is the Truth, she has no image. She is invisible to us veiled in matter. She hides herself behind seven veils, or rather our eyes are so wrapped about that we cannot see her who is visible only in spirit. Thou knowest that in the Temple floor is a rent, and through that rent the breath of the gods ascends. I will place Helena over that rent, and she will fall into a trance, and if I say certain prayers and use certain invocations, then the veils will fall away, and in pure spiritual essence she will look into the face of Ishtar and read therein the Truth, past, present, and future. Is it your pleasure to consult the goddess?"

"Indeed I do desire it," said Domitia.

"Thou hast no fear?"

"Fear! fear of what?"

"Of the future. It is well for us that the gods hide this from our eyes."

Domitia turned and looked at Lamia.

"No," she said with a smile, "I have no fear for my future."

"That which is anticipated does not always come, but rather that which is unexpected."

"Then when forewarned, one is forearmed."

"If it be thy pleasure, lady, return at sunset. Then Helena shall be here, and I shall have made my preparations."

"That is but an hour hence. Be it so. Come, Lamia. Thou shalt row me on the lake till Elymas call."

"So be it," said Lucius; and as they withdrew, he added, "I like that not. If it pleased the gods to show us what is in store, then they would reveal it to us. I mistrust me, this man is either an impostor or he deals with the spirits of evil."

"Nay, think not so. Why should not the Truth lie behind seven veils, and if so, and we are able, why not pluck away those veils?"

"In good sooth, Domitia, thou hast more daring in thy little soul than have I."

The girl and Lucius Lamia had been so much together in Syria, that they had come to regard each other with the affection of brother and sister. In Greek life the females occupied a separate portion of the house to the males, and did not partake of meals with them. There was no common family life.

Old Roman domestic arrangements had been very different from this. There the wife and mother occupied a place of dignity, with her daughters around her, and sat and span in the atrium, where also the men assembled. She prepared the meals, and partook of them with her husband, and the sisters with their brothers. The only difference between them at table was that the men reclined to eat, whereas the women sat on stools. But this home life, which had been so wholesome and so happy, in the luxury and wealth of the age at the fall of the Commonwealth and the rise of Imperialism, had become an element of demoralization. For the conversation of the men had grown shameless, the exhibitions at banquets of coarse drunkenness, and of dancing girls, and the singing of ribald songs by musicians, had driven away shame from the cheeks of the women, and corrupted the freshness of the children's innocence.

Yet there were, through even the worst periods, households in which the healthy old Roman simplicity and familiarity between the sexes remained, good fathers and mothers who screened their children's eyes from evil sights, devoted husbands and wives full of mutual reverence. Such had been the house of Corbulo, whether in Rome, or in Syria. He had been a strict and honorable soldier, and a strict and honorable father in his family.

Thus it was that Lucius Lamia, and Domitia had seen much of each other, and that affection for each other mingled with respect had grown up naturally and vigorously in their hearts.

And now Lucius was paddling on the glassy tarn. He used but little action. Occasionally he dipped the paddles, then allowed the skiff to glide forward till she ceased to be moving, when again he propelled her with one stroke. He was musing; so also was Domitia.

All at once he roused himself.

"Domitia," said he, "Do you know that there is a rumor about that Nero is not dead, but has fled to the Parthians, and that he will return?"

"You do not say so!" The girl's color died away.

"I do not believe it. It cannot be. The sword of your father would not bite so feebly as to let him live. Yet the tale is circulating. Men are uneasy—expecting something.

"If he be dead and burnt, he cannot return."

"No," said Lucius, "he cannot return from the dead. And yet—there be strange rumors. Among the Christians, I am told, there has risen up a seer, who hath been taken with an ecstasy, and hath beheld wonderful visions. And this is reported, that he saw a beast arising out of the sea, having seven heads, and on each head a golden crown. And one of those heads, the fifth, received a death-wound. Then arose two other heads, and after them the wounded head arose once again and breathed fire and slaughter, and the second state was worse than the first."

"But, Lucius, what can this signify?"

"They say it signifies the Empire of Rome, and that the heads are the princes, and the fifth head, that is wounded as unto death, but not slain, is Nero, and that after two have arisen, then he will return."

Domitia shuddered.

"If he return, Lamia, he will not forget thee. Well, we will ourselves look behind the veils; that is better than hearing through others what some unknown prophet hath said. See, on the shore stands Elymas, calling us."

CHAPTER XII

THE FALL OF THE VEILS

Lucius and Domitia stepped out of the boat; he moored it to the side, and they walked together to the little temple. This was not one to which a college of priests was attached, nor even an ædiculum, with a guardian who had charge of it, to open it on special festivals; it had been erected by the father of Corbulo in deference to the wish of his wife, who had taken it into her head to become a votary of Isis, this having become a fashionable cult. But on her death the doors had been closed, and it had fallen into neglect, till the return of Longa Duilia from the East with the Chaldee Magus from Antioch. It was now fashionable to dabble in sorcery, and a distinguished lady liked to be able to talk of her Magus, to seek his advice, and, at table, air a superficial familiarity with the stars, and the Powers and Æons, the endless genealogies of emanations from the primæval and eternal Light.

Longa had engaged the Magus when at Antioch, but when somewhat summarily sent to Europe by her husband, she had not taken her Chaldæan magician with her. As, however, she had no wish to appear in Rome without him, she had laid it on her husband when he returned to bring the man with him, and if he did not return himself, to despatch the Magus to her.

On her arrival in the villa at Gabii, she had given up the temple of Isis to Elymas, and he had converted it into a place for study.

Before the door hung a heavy curtain, and this Lamia raised to allow Domitia to pass within. The interior would have been wholly dark, but that a brazier with glowing charcoal stood within, and into the fire the magician threw gums, that flamed up and diffused a fragrant smoke.

By the flicker Domitia observed that a bed was laid above a small fissure in the marble floor—a rent caused by earthquake—through which vapor of an intoxicating nature issued.

On this bed lay a woman, or rather a figure that Domitia took to be that of a woman, but it was covered with much drapery that concealed face and hands.

The brazier was near the head, and by it stood Elymas in a tall head-dress, with horns affixed, that met in front. He wore a black garment reaching to the feet.

In the darkness nothing could be seen save his erect figure, and face shining out like a lamp, when he cast resinous drops on the fire, and the motionless couched form of the woman.

Domitia, somewhat frightened, put her hand on the arm of Lamia, to make sure that he was present and could assist her, should need for assistance arise;—that is to say, should her courage fail, or the visions she expected to see prove too alarming.

Then the Magus said:

"As I have told thee, lady, out of the ineffable Light stream rays that are both luminous and life-producing. These rays penetrate to the lowest profundity of matter, and as they pass through the higher atmospheres, gather about them the particles of vapor, and become angels and demons. But other rays passing further down, and assuming grosser envelopes, become men and women, some more animal than others, some with higher spiritual natures than the rest, according as in them matter or spirit dominates. And the rays darting into further depths become the beasts of the field, the fishes of the sea, even the very worm that bores in the soil. As thou knowest, he who stands on a high mountain can see far horizons to right and to left as well as the objects below him. So, to the Eternal, all is visible, the past on one side, the present before Him, and the future on the other side, all in one vision. To Him there is no past, and no present, and no future, for Time is not—all is comprehended in one view. But we, who are below, see only the present, remember the past, and conjecture what is future. If we would see future as well as past, we must rise above matter, mount from our base level to the altitude of spirit. Thence all is clear. But this is not possible to all, only to those elect ones in whom the flesh is subdued, and to it the spirit remains attached only by a fibre. Such is Helena. Through her thou shalt see what thou desirest. Now behold!"

He pointed into the darkness before him, and both Domitia and Lucius saw a spark that grew in intensity and shone like a star.

"That," said Elymas, "is a crystal. It is the lens through which the rays of the Eternal and Immortal Light pass to the soul of Helena, out of Infinite Altitude and Illimitable Space. She is enveloped in seven veils. Now she lieth in a trance, and seeth naught. But I will invoke this Fount of Life and Light and Knowledge, and will gather the rays together into her soul through yonder crystal, and she will see in vision what thou desirest. Seven veils cover her, and seven are the revelations that will be made. I cannot assure thee that all will be future—some may be scenes of the past, for to the All-Seeing, the Eye of Eternity, there is neither past nor future; all is present."

"Well, so be it," said Lamia, "By the past we can judge the future. Let us see things that have been and we can form some notion of what is shown us as future. If the one be incorrect, then the other is untrustworthy."

"Thou shalt behold nothing," said the Magus, "for it is not thou who consultest me, but the lady Domitia Longina."

"How shall I see, and not he who stands beside me?" asked the girl. Her heart fluttered with apprehension.

The sorcerer stooped, and drew from under the covering the right hand of the prostrate woman, and bade Domitia hold it.

She took the hand in hers; it was stiff and cold as that of a corpse, and she shuddered.

"Hold her hand in thine," said Elymas, "and I will invoke the Source of Spirits, and as I withdraw each veil that covers her face, she will see something, and she seeing it, the sense of sight will pass through her hand to thee, and thou wilt see also, inwardly, yet very really. Only let not go her hand, or all will become dark."

Then he went before the crystal, that stood on an altar like a truncated column; and he uttered words rapidly in a strange tongue, then turned, threw a handful of spices upon the coals, and a dense aromatic smoke filled the interior. It dissipated, and Domitia uttered a faint cry.

"What ails thee?" asked Lucius.

Thinking she was frightened, he added—"Let us go forth. This is mere jugglery."

"But I see," she said in tremulous tones.

"What dost thou see?"

"O Lucius! It is the garden at Cenchræa—and my father! O, my father!" she sobbed.

One veil had been withdrawn.

"Enough," said Lucius. "I think naught of this: every one is aware how the noble Cnæus Corbulo came by his death."

"Then see again," said the Magus. He took hold of a second veil that covered the prostrate woman, drew it off, and let it fall on the ground.

Lucius felt the left hand of Domitia contract suddenly on his arm. He looked before him, but saw nothing save the crystal, in which moved lights. It was iridescent as an opal.

Then Domitia exclaimed:

"It was he! the physician Luke—who cut the thong. But for him, we should have run down the Imperial trireme. He did it!"

"What mean you?" asked the young man in surprise.

"Lucius, I see it all—the sea, the vessel on which is Nero carousing;—ourselves—we are running at her. And he has cut the thong, the paddle flies up, and our course is altered."

Then the Magus uttered a few words, and withdrew the third veil.

The young man heard his companion breathing heavily; but she said nothing. He waited awhile and then, stooping to her, asked:

"Seest thou aught?"

"Yes," she answered in a whisper. "Yet not with my bodily eyes, I know not how—but I see—"

"What?"

"The end of Nero. Now thou hast thrown the mantle over his face—enough!"

Then Elymas turned and said:

"Hitherto thou hast beheld that which is past. Sufficeth it? or wilt thou even look into that which is to be?"

"It sufficeth," said Lucius, and would have drawn his companion away. But she held to the hand of the woman on the bed, and said firmly:

"No, my friend. Now I have seen things that are past, I will even look into the future. It was for this I came hither."

And now again did the magician utter prayers, and wave his hands. Thereupon strange lights and changes appeared in the crystal, and it seemed of milky moonlight hue, yet with shoots as of lightning traversing it. All at once the Magus took off the fourth veil and cast it on the marble floor.

Lucius remained motionless, looking at the changing light in the crystal, and feeling the nervous hand of Domitia twitching on his arm. He thought that he heard her laugh, but almost immediately with a cry, she loosed her hand from the unconscious woman on the couch, threw her arms round the neck of Lamia, and sank sobbing on his breast.

It was some time before she was sufficiently recovered to speak, and then was reluctant to disclose what she had seen. Lucius, however, urged her with gentle persuasion, and, clinging to him, between sobs, in whispers she confided:

"Oh, Lucius! I thought—I—I saw that the day had come when you and I—Lucius, when I went to your house and was lifted across the threshold, and then, as I stretched my hands to you and took yours—then, all at once, a red face came up behind—whence I know not—and two long hands thrust us apart. Then I let go—I let go—and—and I saw no more."

"When that day comes, my Domitia, no hands shall divide us, no face be thrust between. Now come forth. You have seen enough."

"Nay, I will look to the end." She took the hand of Helena, into which some flexibility and warmth were returning.

"Art thou willing?" asked the Magus.

She nodded, and the fifth veil fell.

For full five minutes Domitia stood rigid, without moving a muscle, hardly breathing.

Then Lucius said:

"See what a purple light shines out of the crystal. What is thy vision now, Domitia? By the light that beams, it should be right royal."

"It is royal," she said in faint tones. "Lucius! what that Christian prophet spoke, that have I also seen—the beast with seven heads, one wounded to the death, and there cometh up another out of the deadly wound, and—it hath the red face I saw but just now. And it climbeth to a throne and lifteth me up to sit thereon. Away with the vision. It offendeth me. It maketh my blood turn ice cold!"

"Hast thou a desire to see further?" asked the Magus.

"I can see naught worse than this," said Domitia.

A shudder ran through her, and her teeth chattered as with frost.

Then Elymas again waved his hands, and chanted, "Askion, Kataski-on, lix, Tetras, damnameneus,"and raised and cast down the sixth veil.

At once from the crystal a red light shone forth, and suffused the whole cell of the temple with a blood-colored illumination, and by it Lucius could see that there was in it no image present, only a dense black veil behind the altar on which the stone glowed like a carbuncle. He heard the breath pass through the teeth of Domitia, like the hissing of a serpent. He looked at her, her face was terrible, inflamed. The eyes stiffened, the teeth were set, the brow knitted and lowering. Then she said:

"I stand on the beast, and the sword of my father pierces his heart."

Lucius wondered; there was a look of hate, a hideousness in her face, such as he had not conceived it possible so beautiful and sweet a countenance could have assumed.

Then Elymas cast off the last veil.

For a moment all was darkness. The red light in the crystal had expired. In stillness and suspense, not without fear, all waited, all standing save Helena, who had recovered from her trance, and she paused expectant on her couch.

Then a minute spark appeared in the crystal, of the purest white light, that grew, rapidly sending out wave on wave of brilliance, so intense, so splendid, so dazzling, that the magician, unable to endure the effulgence, turned and threw himself into a corner, and wrapped his head about with his mantle. And the medium turned with a cry, as though the light caused her physical pain, buried her face in the pillow, and groped on the floor for the veils to cast over her head to exclude the light.

Lucius, unable to endure the splendor, covered his eyes with his palm.

But Domitia looked at it, and her face grew soft, the scowl went from her brow, and a wondrous tenderness and sorrow came into her eyes; great tears rose and rolled down her cheeks, and glittered like diamonds in the dazzling beam.

Then she said with a sob:

"Ubi lux—ibi Felicitas."

Suddenly an explosion. The orb was shattered into a thousand sparks, and all was black again in the temple—black as deepest night.

Then Lucius caught Domitia to him, put his hand behind him, drew back the curtain, and carried her forth into the calm evening air, and the light of the aurora hanging over the setting sun.

She sobbed, gradually recovered herself, drew a profound sigh, and said:

"Oh, Lucius! where is light, there is felicity!"

CHAPTER XIII

TO ROME!

"Plancus, come hither!"

The lady Longa Duilia was in an easy-chair, and a slave-girl, Lucilla, was engaged in driving away the flies that, perhaps attracted by her cosmetics, came towards the lady.

Summer was over, and winter storms were beginning to bluster, and the flies were dull with cold and only maintained alive by the warmth of the chambers, heated by underground stoves, and with pipes to convey the hot air carried through every wall.

"Plancus, did you hear me speak?"

"I am here, my lady, at your service."

"Really; you have become torpid like the flies. Has the chill made you deaf as well as sluggish?"

"My lady, I can always hear when you speak."

"Do you mean to imply that I shout like a fishwife?"

"I mean not that. But when a harp is played, it sets every thread in every other stringed instrument a-chiming; and so is it with me."

"The simile is wiredrawn. What I want you for is—no, I will have no stroking of your face like a cat!—is to go to Rome and see that the palace is made ready to receive us. The stoves must be well heated, and everything properly aired, The country at best of times is tedious; in winter, intolerable. Besides, I have no right to remain here buried. I must consider—Plancus, why are you scratching? I must consider my daughter. She is in a fit of the blues, and has nothing to say to amuse me. You need not blow like a sea-horse, breathe more evenly and equably;—Plancus, you are becoming unendurable. I must not consider my bereaved feelings, but her welfare, her health. The air or the situation of Gabii does not suit her. Rome is an extraordinarily healthy place in winter. I myself am never better anywhere than I am there. I was pretty well at Antioch; there were military there, and I find the soil and climate salubrious where there are military. Plancus?—as the Gods love me, you have been in the stables. I know it by infallible proofs. Stand at a distance, I insist. And, Plancus! you are not showing off conjuring tricks, that you should fold and unfold your hands. You go to Rome and take such of the family with you as are necessary. I am not going to be mewed up here any longer, because my two years of widowhood are not over. You are making faces at me, positively you are, Plancus. Do, I entreat you, look as if you were not a mountebank mouthing at a crowd."

"I fly, mistress, as though winged at heel like Mercury."

"Much more like Mercury's tortoise. Send me Claudius Senecio. I must know what ails Domitia. She has the vapors."

"I obey," said Plancus,

"Am I much worn, Lucilla?" asked the lady, as soon as her steward had withdrawn. "The laceration of the heart tells on a sensitive nature, and precipitates wrinkles and so on."

"Madam, you bloom as in a second spring."

"A second spring, Lucilla!" exclaimed Longa, sitting bolt upright. "You hussy, how dare you? A second spring, indeed! Why, by the zone of Venus, I am not through my first summer yet."

"You misconceive me, dear lady. When a virgin has been wedded, then come on her the cares of matronhood, the caprices, the ill-humors of her husband—and to some, not without cause, the vexation of his jealousy. But when the Gods have removed him, it sometimes happens that the ravages caused by the annoyances of marriage disappear, and she reverts to the freshness and loveliness of her virginity."

"There is something in what you say; of course it is true only of highly privileged natures, in which is some divine blood. A storm ruffles the surface of the lake. When the storm is past, the lake resumes its placidity and beauty—exactly as it was before. I have noted it a thousand times. Yes, of course it is so. Here comes Senecio; he waddles just like the Hindu nurse I saw at Antioch, laboring about with two fat babies."

The Philosopher approached.

"I will trouble you to come in front of me,"said the widow. "Have you eaten so heavy a meal as to shrink from so much unnecessary exertion? I cannot talk with my neck twisted. The windpipe is not naturally constructed like a thread in a rope. I am returning to Rome."

"To Rome, madam! I do not advise that. The place is in commotion. There have been sad scenes of riot and pillage in the capital."

"As the Gods love me! what care I so long as they do not invade the house in the Carinæ?"

"But there have been also massacres."

"Well, when princes shift about, that is inevitable. They all do it. For my part, I rather like—that is, I don't object to massacres in their proper places and confined to the proper persons."

"Madam, you are secure where you are. Why, there was Galba,—he had not been in Rome seven months before he was killed, and he did not enter the city save over the bodies of seven thousand men, butchered on the Flaminian Way."

"Well! I am not a man. Moreover, I thank the Gods, my house is not on the Flaminian Way, nor is it in the Velabrum, nor the Suburra, nor in the Forum Boarium either. We happen to live in the Carinæ, and I conceive that there have been no massacres and all that sort of thing there."

"No, my dear lady, but when the entire city is disturbed—"

"And here, in Gabii, down to the lizards—dead asleep. Give me massacres rather than stagnation. I shall get back to Rome before the Ides of December, on account of my daughter's health. By the way, will you believe it? She gave away the sword of my dear Corbulo to Lucius Lamia. Just conceive!—how effective that sword would be in my house—in the tablinum, the atrium, anywhere—and how I could point to it, and my feelings!—I can imagine nothing more striking. I have told Lamia to restore it. I would not lose it for a great deal. Well now, come. Any news from the capital?"

"Madam, you are aware that Galba fell, and that Otho threw himself on his sword after a reign of ninety days; and now the new Cæsar Vitellius is menaced. I hear that the East has risen, and that Vespasian has been proclaimed in Syria. The legions in Illyria have also declared for him and are marching into Italy. Egypt has pronounced against Vitellius, and it is but seven months since Otho died by his own hand."

"Vespasian, did you say?" exclaimed the lady. "My good Senecio, he is a sort of cousin, a country cousin, just one of those cousins that can be cultivated into kinship, or dropped out of relationship as circumstances decide. His father was a pottering sort of a man, an auctioneer, and commissioner of drains and dirt and all that sort of thing. A worthy fellow, I dare say; I believe he had a statue erected to him somewhere because he did the scavengering so well. He married above his position, one Vespasia Polla; I have seen and heard of her, a round-faced woman like a pudding; he took her for her blood, but she was only a knight's daughter; and those city knights, as the Gods love me! what a money-grubbing low set they are! His son, Flavius Vespasianus is proclaimed! It is really funny. It is, O Morals! I must laugh. Now, if my good man had but listened to me. But there, I shall become mad.—I don't know how long it is since you have been pecking, or whether you eat all day long? But you have crumbs sticking in your beard. Another time be good enough to comb your beard before approaching me. Tell me, what has given Domitia the dumps?"

"I believe, madam, she has been frightened by that unscrupulous impostor, Elymas, or Ascleparion, or whatever he is called. I do not know particulars, but believe that he pretended to show her the future."

"The future! Delicious! And what did she see?"

"That I cannot say, but she has looked wan ever since, neither smiles nor speaks, but sits, when the sun shines, on the balustrade above the water, looking into it, as in a dream. I hear that she holds converse with none, save her maid, Euphrosyne."

"I wonder what she has seen! Anything concerning me?"

"Madam, that braggart and intriguer is made up of lies. He has frightened her with pretended predictions. If I might advise, I would counsel his expulsion from the house."

"I should like to hear what are the chances for Flavius Vespasian. I think I shall inquire myself. I knew Vespasian once, of course he is vastly my senior. If he be successful, he may get a proconsulship for our Lamia. He! Flavius Vespasian a Cæsar! There is push for you! As the Gods love me, there is nothing like push. I must go to Rome. Positively two years retirement for a widow is unreasonable. In the good old days of the Republic one was thought enough. I would not have the Republic back for anything else, though of course we all talk about Liberty and Cato, and all that sort of thing—it is talk—nothing else. I must go to Rome. Flavius Sabinus is præfect of the city, and he is the elder brother of Vespasian. I might show him some little inconspicuous civilities—give a little cosy, quiet supper. By the way—yes, he is married to an old hunks, I remember. Oh! if his brother gets to the top, he can divorce her. Yes, positively I shall not be able to breathe till I get back to Rome. By the way, draw me up on a couple of tablets some moral philosophizing suitable to widowhood, pepper it well with lines from lyric poets. I will learn it all by heart in my litter, and serve out as occasion offers. I positively must be home before the Ides; why—" with a start of pleasure—"The Ides of December! that is the dedication feast of the temple of Tellus in the Carinæ. There you have it! Devotion to the gods—an excuse for a little supper—a wee little supper—but so good and so nicely turned out."

CHAPTER XIV

A LITTLE SUPPER

Longa Duilia and her entire household had returned to the capital, and were installed in the family mansion in the Carinæ.

Happily, as Corbulo had considered it, this house had escaped in the conflagration of Rome under Nero. This, however, was a matter of some regret to Duilia, who would have preferred to have had it burnt, so that it might have been rebuilt in greater splendor and in newer style.

Nevertheless, although externally dingy, it was a commodious mansion within, and was well furnished, especially with carpets and curtains of Oriental texture, that had been wrought at, or purchased at the bazaars of Antioch and Damascus.

The centre of the house was occupied by the atrium, or hall, open to the sky above the water tank in the midst. On each side at the further end from the entrance extended the "wings" that contained the family portraits enclosed in gilded boxes or shrines, the doors of which were thrown open on festal occasions. In the centre, between the wings was the tablinum, the reception-room of the house, and on the right side of the entrance was the family money-chest, girded with iron.

On the ledge of the water tank before the reception room, smoked a little altar before an image of Larpater, the ancestor and founder of the family, regarded as the tutelary deity of the house.

The penates, the subsidiary household gods, that had formerly been retained in the hall, near the altar—curious, smoked, and badly-shaped dolls, some in rags, some in wood, others in terra cotta—were sometimes consigned to a family chapel, but in the house of the widow of Corbulo, as in many another, they had been relegated to a shelf in the kitchen near the hearth, and a lamp was maintained perpetually burning before them.

In primitive times, when life was simple, the hall had been the common room of the house, in which the wife cooked the meals at the hearth, and where also on seats, father, wife, children and domestics partook together of the common meal. But now all this was altered.

In winter the hall was too cold to be sat in. It was inconvenient to have the cooking done before all eyes. Consequently a separate kitchen and separate dining-rooms were constructed, and the smoking altar and the image by it alone remained in the hall as a reminiscence of the family hearth that once stood there.

It is more difficult to understand the meals and meal times of the old Romans, than the arrangement of their houses.

They rose vastly early in the morning, and took a snack of breakfast of the simplest description, which lasted them till lunch at 10 a. m. But such as were occupied abroad rarely returned home for this meal. At noon they bathed, and then came the great feed of the day, the cœna, which we translate "supper," but which was begun at half-past one in winter and an hour later in summer.

This lasted the entire afternoon, and even on great occasions into the night. Some revellers did not break up till midnight, or even prolonged the orgy to dawn.

It was not till the Goths and Vandals overflowed the classic world, that the supper was postponed until the evening.

The Roman citizen's day was from dawn till noon. Then he had his snooze and his bath, and the remainder of the day was devoted to the mighty meal and to reading, conversation, and amusement.

"I am so pleased to see you," said Longa Duilia, stepping forward to receive the Præfect of Rome, to her little supper.

He was a gray-headed, plain, blunt man, with very ordinary features; he was attended by two lictors, and by his son, Sabinus.

"I thank you, madam, for the courteous invitation."

"I could kill myself with vexation not to have made your acquaintance earlier. You see, for some years I have been at Antioch, with my dearest husband, whose sword—that sword which drank the blood of Germans, Parthians and Armenians—excuse these tears—you see it—suspended yonder. But, as I was saying, we have been from Rome so long, and since my return I have lived in such seclusion, that we have not met—and yet, considering our relationship—"

"My dear lady, I was unaware that I was entitled to such an honor."

"Oh! yes, of course, cousins."

"Cousins!"

"Through Vespasia Polla, your mother. What a sweet creature she was! So distinguished in her manner. She had such an intelligent face, and, as I remember her, the remains of great beauty. Of course I was then quite a mite of a child."

"This is indeed flattering."

"You men have other things to consider beside pedigree. Cousins we certainly are. And how is that sweet lady, your wife? By all accounts as frail as the last autumn leaf on an acacia."

"I am glad to say that, on the contrary, she enjoys rude health."

"You do not say so! What fibs are told! Your son Clemens is not here? I—I have heard, does not go into society, a little peculiar in his views. We are not all made alike. But this, your son Sabinus, is formed like an Apollo. And your daughter Plautilla—so sorry! infected in the same way. Will not go to dinners or shows—ah! well it is her loss. It is a pleasure to reunite family ties. Alas! you know of my irreparable loss. I do not know whether you saw the sword of my darling. He fell on it. Bathed it with his blood. Every night I bedew the sacred blade with my tears. Excuse me—my emotion overcomes me. I would have buried myself at Gabii, clasping the sword to my wounded bosom for the remainder of my shattered life, had it not been for the health of my child. A mother's thoughts are with her offspring. Well, now to table. A widow's fare, only a small supper in a house of mourning—though more than a twelvemonth since the funeral—indeed, two years since my dear one died—on that sword. Oh! I turn away my eyes! The sight of that blade. But, come—that is my daughter. Salute her. A cousin. Give me your hand, Flavius. The table calls us."

The house of a wealthy Roman at this period had not only a summer dining-room, open to the air, but one also for winter, well heated by stoves. Three tables were placed, so as to accommodate nine persons, three at each, leaving the ends of two and an open square in the middle.

Into this hollow the servants ran the "repository," a sort of what-not, on wheels, consisting of a tier of shelves, all laden with dishes; and the guests put forth their hands and selected such meats as they fancied.

Knives they had, but no forks. In place of these latter they were furnished with spoons, having the extremity of the handle turned down as claw or hoof, or sharpened to a point, so as to serve to hold the meat whilst it was being cut. When so employed, the bowl of the spoon was held in the hollow of the hand; but when used as a spoon, then the end was reversed.

A sideboard was piled up with silver and gold plate. In addition in a corner stood a round table with three feet; on which were laid napkins neatly tied up with blue and red bands. These napkins contained trinkets, rings, brooches, comfits, mottoes, and were to be given to the guests along with the dessert. Our presentation of Christmas crackers is a reminiscence of the old Roman custom of making presents to the guests at the close of a banquet.

The males lay at table on couches, with their legs extended behind them, their left elbows reposed on pillows. It was against ancient Roman custom for ladies to recline, but recently some empresses had broken through the rule, and when they set the example of lounging, others followed. Duilia, however, was a stickler in some things, and she some-what affected archaic usages, as a mark of distinction, as a token of the antiquity of the family, whose customs had acquired an almost sacred sanction. Ladies sat on stools.

The couches and seats were sumptuous, inlaid with mother-of-pearl, tortoise-shell and silver, and were covered with Oriental carpets.

Every guest was attended by a slave, bearing an ewer and napkin, so that he might cleanse his fingers directly they became greasy—a necessity of constant recurrence, on account of the absence of proper forks.

A baldachin of embroidered silk was stretched above the table, and the heads of the banqueters. This was done for the purpose of cutting off the draught, as immediately above, in the ceiling, was the lacunar, an opening through which the steam and savor of dinner might escape, and through which, when the canopy was not spread, rose-leaves, violets, a spray of scent, even garlands were scattered over the revellers.

A Roman dinner began, like one in Russia at the present day, with a gustus, a snack of something calculated to stimulate the appetite or to help digestion.

Then came in soft-boiled eggs, the invariable first dish, just as invariably, the meal closed with apples.

With the eggs were served salads and sauer-kraut, cabbage shredded in vinegar, Brussels sprouts boiled with saltpetre to enhance their green, turnips and carrots in mustard and vinegar. Melons were eaten with pepper, salt, and vinegar; artichokes were consumed raw, with oil; mallows and sorrel, olives, mushrooms and truffles were favorite vegetables, and were eaten along with large snails, oysters, sardines, and chopped lizards.

All this was preparatory.

Now entered the repository, groaning under meats and fish. At the same moment a slave produced and handed round a menu card. But before eating, a benediction was pronounced, the household gods were invoked and promised a share of the good things from the table.

It is unnecessary to catalogue the solids and entrées sent up at such a supper. Pork was a favorite dish, and there were fifty ways in which a pig could be served up. Octopus was much relished, as it is to this day in Italy. Wild fowl was stuffed with garlic, mutton with asafœtida, and some meats were not considered in condition till decomposition had begun.

The strong savor produced by those dishes was dissipated by servants holding large fans, and counteracted by the diffusion of aromatic smoke, and the sprinkling of guests and table with essences.

A supper consisted of several courses, but a considerable interval elapsed between each, which interval was filled in with conversation, or enlivened with the antics of buffoons, or with music, or the recitation of poetry.

Nothing in the smallest degree unseemly was allowed in the house of Longa Duilia, at such entertainments.

We read a good deal, in the ancient authors, of the license allowed at such times, but this was not general, certainly was not suffered except in very "fast" houses, and such were attended by none who respected themselves.

The widow knew how to make herself agreeable. Flavius Sabinus, the præfect, was a great talker, and there was a little rivalry between the two as to which should lead the conversation. Domitia hardly spoke, but the guests generally entertained themselves heartily.

Lamia was there, and near his betrothed, but found it difficult to carry on conversation with her. Since the questioning of Ishtar in the Temple at Gabii, she had been haunted by the visions presented to her inner sight, and she was unable to shake off the oppression of spirits and distress of mind, they had caused.

When supper was ended, previous to the dessert, all rose, a grace was said, and again the household gods were invoked.

All were thus standing, in solemn hush, whilst a portion for the deities was being taken away, when the curtain before the door was roughly drawn aside, and a young man ran in—then halted, bewildered by the lights and the company, and hesitated before advancing further.

A faint cry escaped the breast of Domitia; and she staggered back, and caught Lamia convulsively by the wrist.

Then Flavius Sabinus said apologetically to his hostess:

"This youth is my nephew, Titus Flavius Domitianus, the younger son of my brother Vespasian. Pardon his lack of breeding, lady—I bade him find me here, if matters of importance demanded my attention. Excuse me, I pray, if I retire with him and hear what news of weight he bears."

Duilia bowed, and the præfect, leaving his place, went to meet his nephew.

Lamia felt that Domitia was trembling. He looked in her face and it alarmed him. With wide eyes she was staring at the intruder; her lips were slightly parted, every trace of color had deserted them; and between them gleamed her teeth.

Not till the curtain had fallen, and hidden the form of the young man, as he left with his uncle, did she breathe freer.

Then she heaved a long sigh, and said in a faint voice:

"It is he—the eighth crowned head—the fifth come again—the new Nero. O Lamia! Terrible is Fate!"

CHAPTER XV

THE LECTISTERNIUM

"My dear child," said Duilia, "I never did a better stroke of policy than that supper a few evenings ago. It went off quite charmingly, without a hitch. I allowed that good Flavius Sabinus to talk; and he is just one of those men who enjoys himself best where he is given full flow for his twaddle. A good, worthy, commonplace man. I doubt if he has push in him, but he is just so situated now that he must go ahead. The news is most encouraging. Mucianus is on his way to Italy at the head of an army. Primus, with his legions, is approaching; he has beaten the troops sent against him, and has sacked Cremona; there are positively none who hold by Vitellius except his brother in Campania, and his German body-guard. Domitia," the widow dropped her voice, "we can do better than with that milksop Ælius Lamia."

"Mother, I will have no other."

"Then we must push him up into position. But come, my dear, we must show ourselves at the Lectisternia. It will be expected of us, and be setting a good example, and all that sort of thing, and it is positively wicked to mope indoors when we ought to be seen in the streets and the forum. So there, make yourself ready. I am going instantly. I have ordered round the palanquins, and, as you may perceive, I am dressed and my hair done to go out. That supper was quite a success."

The time was now that of the Saturnalia, lasting seven days, beginning on the 17th December with a strange institution, a banquet of the gods. Usually the several gods had their feasts in their own temples and invited others to them, but on certain solemn occasions all banqueted together in public. The distress, the butcheries, the general confusion caused by the setting up and casting down of emperors—three in ten months—and now, eight months after, a fourth tottering; and every change involving massacre, plunder, disturbance of order;—this had moved the priests to decree a solemn lectisternium and supplication for the restoration of tranquillity and the cessation of civil broil.

The banquet was to take place in the forum.

"You shall come in the lectica (palanquin) with me," said Duilia. "It will have quite a pathetic aspect—the widow and the orphan together. Besides, I want some one to talk to. What do you think of Flavius Domitianus? A modest lad, to my mind."

"Shy and clumsy," observed Domitia. "The sight of him is a horror to me."

"My dear child, only a fool will take sprats when he can have whitebait. Look out to better yourself."

"Oh, mother!—what is that?"

"A god going to supper," said the lady. "We shall see plenty of them presently."

That which had attracted her daughter's attention was a bier supported on the shoulders of priests, on which lay a figure dressed handsomely, in the attitude of a man at table, raised on his left elbow that was buried in a pillow, the head erect and the right arm extended, balanced in the air. The body was probably of wood under the drooping drapery, but the face and hands and feet were of wax. In jolting over the pavement, the sleeve had become disarranged, and showed the wooden prop that sustained the waxen right hand. The face was colored, the eyes were of glass, and real hair was affixed to the head; the lower jaw, hung on wires, opened and shut with the jostling. The staring figure swaying on the shoulders of the bearers, had a sufficiently startling effect, sweeping round a corner, wagging its beard, and past the palanquin in which were the ladies.

"A thing like that can't eat," said Domitia.

"Oh, my dear child, no. The gods only sniff at the food. After it has been set before them, it is carried away, and the people scramble for it."

"They are naught but wax and woodwork," said the girl contemptuously.

"My child, how often have I not had to quote to you that text, 'It is not well to be overwise about the gods?' Here we are! What a crowd!"

The forum of Rome, that wondrous basin towered over on one side by the Capitol, inclosed on another by the Palatine, and on the third by the densely packed blocks of houses in the Suburra below the Quirinal, Viminal and Esquiline Hills, was itself crowded with temples and basilicas, yet not then as dense with monuments as later, when the open spaces were further encroached upon by the Antonines.

"Domitia," said Longa Duilia, in her ear, "all things are working out excellently. Vitellius is aware that he has no chance, and has been consulting with our cousin in the Temple of Concord yonder, and they have nearly settled between them that Vespasian is to assume the purple without further opposition. Vitellius will retire to some country villa on a handsome annuity. That will prevent more bloodshed and confiscation, and all that sort of thing. It is always advisable to avoid unpleasantnesses if possible. There, child, there are quite a bevy of gods already at table. See that dear old doll, Summanus, without a head—you know it was struck off by lightning in the time of Pyrrhus. It was of clay, and rolled all the way to the Tiber and plopped in. Since then he has been without a head, the darling!"

"How can he either smell or eat, mother?"

"My child, I don't ask. It is not well to be overwise about the gods. There go the Arval Brothers with the image of Aca Larentia seated—of course not lying. You will see some venerable curiosities, who put in an appearance on days like this so as not to be wholly forgotten."

The sight presented by the forum was indeed strange. A space had been cleared and shut off from the intrusion of the crowd, and there lay and sat the images at tables that were spread with viands. All were either life-size or larger. Some were skilfully modelled, and wore gorgeous clothing, but others were of the rudest moulding in terra cotta, or carved wood, and evidently of very ancient date, of Etruscan workmanship little influenced by Greek art.

Domitia looked on in astonishment. The populace laughed and commented on the images, without the least reverence; and the priests and their assistants laid the dishes before the puppets, then whisked them off and carried them without the barriers. Thereupon ensued a struggle who should get hold of the savory morsels that were being conveyed from the table of the gods; even the vessels used for the viands and for the wine were snatched at and carried away, and the priests offered no resistance.

Domitia was completely transported out of herself by astonishment at the sight. Every now and then the hum of voices spluttered into a burst of laughter at some ribald joke, and then roared up into a hubbub of sound over the trays of meats and wine that were being fought for.

Already the short winter day was closing in, and torches were being brought forth and stood beside the images. Then the tables were cleared and removed.

A trumpet blast sounded, and instantly the barriers were cast down, and the second act of this extraordinary spectacle ensued. This was the supplication. Instantly the temper of the mob changed from scepticism and mockery to enthusiastic devotion, and those pressed forward to kneel and touch the cushions and drapery on which the gods reposed, and to entreat their assistance, whose lips had but recently uttered a scoff.

Nothing so completely differentiates Christian worship from that of Pagan Rome as the congregational character of the former contrasted with the uncongregational nature of the latter. At the present day in Papal Rome the priests may be seen behind glass doors in little chapels annexed to S. Peter's and S. Maria Maggiore saying their offices, indifferent to there being no laity present, indeed, with no provision made that they should assist. This is a legacy of Pagan Rome. The sacrifices, the services in the temples and other sanctuaries, were entirely independent of the people, some performed within closed doors. The only popular religious service was the supplication, which took place but occasionally. Then the public streamed to the images of the gods, uttering fervent prayer, chanting hymns, prostrating themselves before the couches, catching at their bed-coverings, esteeming themselves blessed if they could lay their hands on the sacred pillows. But there was no general consent as to which of the gods and goddesses were most potent. Some cried out that Mother Orbona had helped them, others that Fortuna was a jade and promised but performed nothing. One fanatic, in a transport, shrieked that these gods were good for naught, for his part he trusted only in Consus, whose temple was in ruins, whose altar was buried in earth by the circus of Tarquin. But there were others who swept in a strong current towards the couch of Jupiter and of that of Venus. Another strong current, howling 'Io Saturne! Salve Mater Ops!' made for the images of the Old God of Time and his divine Mate.

Simultaneously came a cross current of vendors of cakes and toys from the Suburra, regardless of the devotion of the people, careful only to sell their goods—for the Saturnalia was a period at which the children were regaled with gingerbread, and treated to dolls of terra cotta, of ivory and of wood. Hawkers selling pistachio nuts, the cones of the edible pine, men with baked chestnuts, others with trays of Pomponian pears and Mattian apples, vociferating and belauding their wares, increased the clamor.

Whilst this was at its height, down from the Palatine by the New Way came the German Imperial Body-Guard, forcing a passage through the mob, their short swords drawn, bellowing imprecations, whirling their blades, striking with the flat of the steel, threatening to cut down such as impeded their progress.

Some vigiles, or city police, came up. There was no love lost between them and the pampered foreigners employed in the palace, and they opposed the household troops. Remonstrances were employed and cast away. Then a German was struck in the face by a pine cone, another tripped, fell, and a hawker with a barrow-load of dolls, in his eagerness to escape, ran his vehicle over the prostrate guardsman. At once the Germans' blood was up, they rushed upon the police, and a fray ensued in which now this side, then that, gained advantage. The populace, densely packed, came in for blows and wounds. When a guardsman fell, and they could lay hold of him, he was dragged away, and almost torn to pieces by eager hands stripping him of his splendid uniform.

The Præfect, who was in the Forum, summoned three cohorts to his aid, to drive back the household troops, and in a moment the trough between the hills was converted into a scene of the wildest confusion, some women screaming that they had lost their children, others crying to the gods to help them. Boys had scrambled up the bases of the statues, and one urchin sat with folded legs on the shoulders of Julius Cæsar, hallooing, and occasionally pelting with nuts where they did not fear retaliation.

The vendors of cakes and toys cursed as their trays were upset, or their barrows clashed. Men fought each other, for no other reason than that the soldiers were engaged, and they were unable to keep their itching hands off each other.

Down a stair from the palace came the Emperor Vitellius, carried on the shoulders of soldiers, while slaves bore flambeaux before him.

He was seen to gesticulate, but in the uproar none heard what he said.

Meanwhile, the priests were endeavoring to remove the gods, and met with the greatest difficulty. Some frantic women clung to the images and refused to allow them to be taken away. Some of the figures had been upset, and the servants of the temples to which they belonged made rings about them with interlaced arms, to protect them from being trampled under foot. Jupiter Capitolinus had been injured and lost his nose.

A priest with the help of a torch, was melting the wax and fastening it on again, whilst the guard of the temple kept off the rabble.

The currents of human beings, driven by diverse passions, jostled, broke across each other, resolved themselves into swirls of living men and women carried off their feet.

The litter of the lady Duilia and her daughter tossed like a boat in a whirlpool, and the widow shrieked with terror.

Then two powerful arms were thrust within the curtains of the palanquin, and the slave Eboracus laid hold of Domitia, and said:—

"There is no safety here. Trust me. I will battle through with you. Come on my arm. Fear not."

"Save me! Me, also!" screamed Duilia, "I shall be thrown out, trodden under foot! O my wig! My wig!"

But Eboracus, regardless of the widow, holding his young mistress on his left arm, with the right armed with a cudgel, which he whirled like a flail, and with which, without compunction he broke down all opposition, drove, battered his way through the throng where most dense, across the currents most violent, and did not stay till he had reached a comparatively unobstructed spot, in one of the narrow lanes between the Fish Market and the Hostilian Court.

CHAPTER XVI

IN THE HOUSE OF THE ACTOR

Hardly had Eboracus conveyed Domitia out of the Forum into a place of safety, than a rush of people down the street threatened to drive him back in the direction whence he had come. The drifting mob, as it cascaded down, cried: "The Prætorians are coming from their camp!"

It was so. Down the hill by the Tiburtine way marched a compact body of soldiery.

The danger was imminent; Eboracus and his young charge were between two masses of military, entangled in a seething mob of frightened people, mostly of the lowest class.

"My lady!" said the slave. "There is but one thing to be done."

He drew her to a door, knocked, and when a voice asked who demanded admittance, answered,

"Open speedily—Paris!"

The door was furtively unbarred and opened sufficiently to admit the slave and Domitia, and then hastily bolted and locked again.

"Excuse me, dear mistress," said Eboracus. "I could do no other. In this insula live the actor Paris and Glyceria. They were both slaves in your household, but were given their freedom by your father, my late master, when he went to the East. They will place themselves at your service, and offer you shelter in their humble dwelling, the first flat on the right."

The house was one of those insulæ, islets of Rome in which great numbers of the lower classes were housed. They consisted in square blocks, built about a court, and ran to the height of seven and even more stories. The several flats were reached by stone stairs that ran from the central yard to the very summit of these barrack-like buildings. They vastly resembled our modern model lodging-houses, with one exception, that they had no exterior windows, or at most only slits looking into the street; doors and windows opened into the central quadrangle. These houses were little towns, occupied by numerous families, each family renting two or more chambers on a flat, and as in a city there are diversities in rank, so was it in these lodging-houses; the most abjectly poor were at the very top, or on the ground floor. The first flat commanded the highest rent, and the price of rooms gradually dwindled, the greater the elevation was. Glass was too great a luxury, far too costly to be employed except by the most wealthy for filling their windows. Even talc was expensive; in its place thin films of agate were sometimes used; but among the poor there was little protection in their dwellings against cold. The doors admitted light and air and cold together, and were always open, except at night, and then a perforation in the wood, or a small window in the wall, too narrow to allow of ingress, served for ventilation.

In a huge block of building like the insula, there were no chimneys. All cooking was done at the hearth in the room that served as kitchen and dining-room, often also as bedroom, and the smoke found its way out at the doorway into the central court.

But, in fact, little cooking of food was done, except the boiling of pulse. The meals of the poor consisted mainly of salads and fruit, with oil in abundance.

Dressed always in wool, in cold weather multiplying their wraps, the Roman citizens felt the cold weather much less than we might suppose possible. In the rain—and in Rome in winter it raineth almost every day—the balconies were crowded, and then the women wove, men tinkered or patched sandals, children romped, boys played marbles and knuckle-bones, and sometimes a minstrel twanged a lyre and the young girls danced to keep themselves warm. There were little braziers, moreover, one on every landing, that were kept alight with charcoal, and here, when the women's fingers were numb, they were thawed, and children baked chestnuts or roasted apples.

Domitia had never been in one of these blocks of habitations of the lower classes before, and she was surprised. The quadrangle was almost like an amphitheatre, with its tiers of seats for spectators; but here, in place of seats, were balconies, and every balcony was alive with women and children. Men were absent; they had gone out to see the commencement of the Saturnalia, and of women there were few compared to the numbers that usually thronged these balconies.

Eboracus conducted his young mistress up the first flight of steps, and at once a rush of children was made to him to ask for toys and cakes. He brushed them aside, and when the mothers saw by the purple edge to her dress that Domitia belonged to a noble family, they called their youngsters away, and saluted her by raising thumb and forefinger united to the lips.

The slave at once conducted Domitia through a doorway into a little chamber, where burnt a fire of olive sticks, and a lamp was suspended, by the light of which she could see that a sick woman lay on a low bed.

Domitia shrank back; but Eboracus said encouragingly:

"Be not afraid, dear young mistress; this is no catching disorder; Glyceria suffers from an accident, and will never be well again. She is the sister of your servant Euphrosyne."

Then, approaching the sick woman, he hastily explained the reason for his taking refuge with his mistress in this humble lodging.

The sick woman turned to Domitia with a sweet smile, and in courteous words entreated her to remain in her chamber so long as was necessary.

"My husband, Paris, the actor, is now out; but he will be home shortly, I trust—unless," her face grew paler with sudden dread, "some ill have befallen him. Yet I think not that can be, he is a quiet, harmless man."

"I thank you," answered Domitia, and took a seat offered her by Eboracus.

She looked attentively at the sick woman's face. She was no longer young, she had at one time been beautiful, she had large, lustrous dark eyes, and dark hair, but pain and weakness had sharpened her features. Yet there was such gentleness, patience, love in her face, a something which to Domitia was so new, a something so new in that old world, that she could not take her eyes off her, wondering what the fascination was.

Glyceria did not speak again, modestly waiting till the lady of rank chose to address her.

Presently Domitia asked:

"Have you been long ill?"

"A year, lady."

"And may I inquire how it came about?"

"Alas! It is a sad story. My little boy—"

"You have a son?"

"I had—"

"I ask your pardon for the interruption; say on."

"My little boy was playing in the street, when a chariot was driven rapidly down the hill, and I saw that he would be under the horses' feet, so I made a dart to save him."

"And then?"

"I was too late to rescue him, and I fell, and the wheel went over me. I have been unable to rise since."

"What! like this for all these months! What say the doctors?"

"Alack, lady! they give me no hope."

"But for how long may this last?"

"I cannot say."

"As the gods love me! if this befell me, I should refuse my food and starve myself to death!"

"I cannot do that."

"What! you lack the resolution?"

"I can bear what is on me laid by God."

"There is no need to endure what can be avoided. I would make short work of it, were this my lot. And your husband?"

"He is here."

Through the door came the actor, a handsome man, of Greek type, with a package in his arms. He would have walked straight to his wife, but had to turn at the door and drive off a clamorous pack of urchins who had pursued him, believing that he was laden with toys.

"There, Glyceria!" he exclaimed joyously; "they are all for you. There is such a riot and disturbance and such a crush in the street, that I had hard work to push through. I misdoubt me some are broken."

"Oh, Paris! do you not observe?"

"What? I see nothing but thy sweet face?"

"Our dear master's daughter, the lady Domitia Longina."

The actor turned sharply, and was covered with confusion at the unexpected sight, and almost let his parcel fall.

Eboracus explained the circumstances. Then Paris expressed his happiness, and the pride he felt in being honored by the visit under his humble ceiling, of the lady, the daughter of the good and beloved master who had given him and Glyceria their freedom.

"Go forth, Eboracus," said Domitia, "and I prithee learn how it has fared with my mother. Bring me word speedily, if thou canst."

When the slave had withdrawn, she addressed Paris and Glyceria.

"I beseech you, suffer me to remain here in quiet, and concern not yourselves about me. I have been alarmed, and this has shaken me. I would fain rest in this seat and not speak. Go on with what ye have to say and do, and consider me not. So will you best please me."

The actor was somewhat constrained at first, but after a little while overcame his reserve. He drew a low table beside his wife's couch, and, stooping on one knee, began to unlade his bundle. He set out a number of terra cotta figures on the table, representing cocks and hens, pigs, horses, cows and men; some infinitely comical; at them Glyceria laughed.

Then, as she put forth a thin white hand to take up one of the quaintest images, Domitia noticed that Paris laid hold of it, and pressed it to his lips.

A lump rose in the girl's throat.

"No," thought she; "if I had one so to love me and consider me, though I were sick and in pain, I would not shorten my days. I would live to enjoy his love."

Then again, falling into further musing, she said to herself:

"In time to come, if it chance that I become ill, will my Lamia be to me as is this actor to his poor wife? Will he think of and care for me? But—and if evil were to befall him, would not I minister to him, care for him night and day, and seek to relieve his sorrow? Would I grow indifferent when he most needed me? Then why think that he should become cold and neglect me? Are women more inclined to be true than men?—Yet see this actor—this Paris. By the Gods! Is Lamia like to be a more ignoble man than a poor freedman that gains his living on the stage?—I should even be happy serving him sick and suffering. Happy in doing my duty."

And still musing, she said on to herself:

"Duty! Yes, I should find content and rest of mind in that; but to what would it all lead? Only to a heap of dust in the end. His light would be extinguished, and then I, having nothing else to live for, would die also—by mine own hand:—there is nothing beyond. It all leads to an ash-heap."

Glyceria, observing the girl's fixed eye, thought it was looking inquiringly at her, and said in her gentle voice that vibrated with the tremulousness given by suffering:

"Ah, lady! the neighbors and their children are very kind. There is more of goodness and piety in the world than you would suppose, seeing men and women only in an amphitheatre. I can do but very little. One boy fetches me water—that is Bibulus, and my Paris has bought him this little horseman—and Torquata, a little girl, daughter of a cobbler, she sweeps the floor; and Dosithea, that is a good widow's child; she does other neighborly acts for me;—and they thrust me on my bed to the side of the hearth, and bring me such things as I need, that I may prepare the meals for my husband. And Claudia, the wife of a seller of nets, she makes my bed for me; but all the shopping is done for me by Paris, and I warrant you, lady, he is quite knowing, and can haggle over a fish or a turnip with a market-woman like any housewife."

"He is very good to you," said Domitia.

Then Paris turned, and, putting his hand on his wife's mouth, said:

"Lady! you can little know what a wife my Glyceria is to me. I had rather for my own sake have her thus than hale as of old. Somehow, sorrow and pain draw hearts together wondrously."

"He is good," said Glyceria, twisting her mouth from his covering hand. "We have had a hard year; on account of the troubles, there has been little desire among the people for the theatre, and he has earned but a trifle. I have cost him much in physicians that have done me no good, yet he never grumbles, he is always cheerful, always tender-hearted and loving."

"Hush, wife!" said Paris. "The lady desires rest. Keep silence."

Then again Domitia fell a-musing, and the player and his wife whispered to each other about the destination of the several toys.

Somehow she had hitherto not thought of the classes of men and women below her station as having like feelings, like longings, like natures to her own. They had been to her as puppets, even as those clay figures ranged on the table, mostly grotesque. Now that great pulse of love that throbs through the world of humanity made itself felt, it was as though scales fell from her eyes, and the puppets became beings of flesh and blood to be considered, capable of happiness and of suffering, of virtue as well as of vice.

"I have a little lamp here—with a fish—the fish on it," said Paris in a whisper. "It is for Luke, the Physician."

"What!" exclaimed Domitia, starting from her reverie, "you know him? We had a talk once, and it was broken off and never concluded. I would hear the end of what he was saying—some day."

CHAPTER XVII

THE SATURNALIA OF 69

Eboracus brushed aside some urchins and girls blocking the door, looking in with eager, twinkling eyes at the strange lady and at the set out of dolls on the table.

There passed whispers and nudges from one to another—but all ceased as the British slave put together his hands as a swimmer and plunged through them.

"Get away you sprats and gudgeons," said he, good-humoredly.

Then entering, he said to Domitia:

"Lady, your mother has reached home in safety. I chanced to run across Amphibolus, sent out in quest of you, and the good-for-naught had turned sulky, because it is the Saturnalia, when, said he, the mistress should do the slave's bidding. 'That can be,' said he, 'but at one time in the year, and should not be forgotten.' And the lanes are clear of rabble. If Paris here will walk on one side of you and I on the other, it will be well. That rascal Amphibolus I bade wait, but not he, said he, 'Io Saturne!'"

"I will attend with joy," announced the actor.

Domitia rose to leave, she tendered thanks to Glyceria and took two steps towards the entrance, halted, turned back, and taking the thin hand of the sick woman in hers, somewhat shyly said:

"I may come again and see you?"

Before Glyceria could reply, so great was her surprise, Domitia was gone.

The streets were nearly empty, they were mere lanes between huge blocks of windowless buildings, towering into the sky, but from the forum could be heard a hubbub of voices, cries, the clash of arms, and anon a cheer.

Presently—"Stand aside!" said Paris, and there swept down the lane a number of young fellows masked and tricked out in ribbons and scraps of tawdry finery.

"I am the king!" shouted one, "Præfect of the guard, arrest those people. Ha! a woman. She shall be my captive and grace my triumph."

Eboracus administered a blow with his fist, planted between the eyes of the youth in pasteboard armor who came towards his young mistress. The blow sent him flying backwards against the king and upset him on the pavement.

A roar of laughter from his mates, and one shouted,

"Hey Tarquinius! thou must e'en fare like the rest, Nero, Galba, Otho—and hem! we know not who else—but down thou art with the others."

"Let us go on," said Paris, and without further attempt at molestation from the revellers they pursued their way.

On reaching the palace inhabited by Longa Duilia, a fresh difficulty arose. Eboracus knocked, but there was no porter at the door to answer. He knocked again and continued to rattle against the panels, till at length the bolt was withdrawn, and Euphrosyne with timid face, and holding a lamp appeared in the entrance.

"Why have you kept us so long waiting?" asked the Briton.

"Eboracus, I could not help myself. It is the Saturnalia, and the slaves will do no menial work. They are carousing in the triclinium and, though they heard the rap well enough, none would rise and respond. Then, for very shame I came, for I thought it might be my dear mistress."

As Domitia crossed the atrium, she heard song and laughter and the click of goblets issue from the dining-room. She hurried by and entered her mother's chamber.

Longa Duilia was in a condition of resentment and irritation.

"You have arrived at last!" said the lady. "I'll have that British slave's hide well basted when the Seven Days are over, for disregarding me and considering your safety alone. Body of Bacchus! This time of the Saturnalia is insufferable. Not a servant will do a stroke of work, nor execute a single order. They are all, forsooth, lords and ladies for seven days, and we must wait on them. Well! if it were not an old custom, I'd get up a procession of all the matrons of Rome to entreat the Senate to abolish the usage."

"Oh, mother dear, how did you escape?"

"My child! it was as bad as that bit of storm we had getting out of the Gulf of Corinth, tossed about in my palanquin I hardly knew whether I were thinking with my head or with my toes. But after a while they got me through. Never, never again will I go gadding after the Gods to their Lectisternia. As the Gods love me! this is a topsy-turvy time indeed. At the Saturnalia no strife is permissible, not a lawsuit, all quarrels are supposed to cease, not even a malefactor may be executed, and there are those precious Immortals with their glass eyes, and extended hands snuffing up the fumes of their dinner, and they allow fighting to go on before them, under their immortal noses, and never interfere! But I don't wonder. There was Summanus, God of the night thunders—and will you believe it, his own head was struck off by the heavenly bolt. Ye Gods! if ye cannot mind your own heads ye are not to be trusted with ours."

The lady was in a condition of towering indignation. She was affronted—she, highborn, with a drop of Julian blood in her, somewhere,—she had been tossed about among the heads and over the shoulders of a dirty, garlic-smelling asafœtida chewing rabble—had been exposed to danger from the swords of the Vigiles on one side, of the Palatine guard on the other. And when finally, she reached home ruffled in garments, her hair in disorder, and her heart beating fast, she found the house in disorder, the slaves in possession keeping high holiday, and disregarding her shrilly uttered, imperiously expressed orders.

"I shall go to bed," said the lady, "I'd lie in bed all these horrible seven days, but that I know no one will bring me my meals. Never mind—when the Saturnalia are over, I shall remember which were insolent and disobliging, and they shall get whippings."

But in the house, on the morrow the condition of affairs was not quite so bad. The servants were alive to the fact that they had liberty for seven days only, and that their mistress had a faculty of remembering and punishing disobedience; not indeed during the holiday period, nor ostensibly because of faults then committed, but by administering double chastisement for light offences committed later.

Some of the slaves, moreover, made no attempt to use their liberty so as to cause inconvenience to their mistress.

But if some sort of order was established within the palace, none reigned without. There civil war raged, at the same time that the citizens observed the festival, and so long as they kept out of the way of the soldiery, it did not much concern them whether the city force or the palace garrison prevailed. Primus, at the head of the Illyrian legions was rapidly advancing on Rome. News had arrived that Spain and Gaul had declared for Vespasian. Britain had renounced allegiance to Vitellius, only Africa still remained faithful.

Next tidings arrived that the army of Vitellius that was at Narnia had surrendered. Thereupon the gross, aged Emperor dressed in black, surrounded by his servants, and carrying his son, still a child, came howling and sobbing from the Palatine through the Forum, to surrender the insignia of Empire into the hands of the Consul, in the Temple of Concord. But the Consul refused to receive them, and then the German guard, having wind of his intention, became clamorous, and cried out for the head of Flavius Sabinus. Vitellius, unable to resign, and incapable of reigning, wandered from one residence to another, asking advice of all his friends as to what he ought to do, but taking none.

Meanwhile the fighting in the streets of Rome had recommenced. Titus Flavius Sabinus, for security escaped into the Capitol, and took with him his sons and daughter, and his nephew Domitian. There he was formally besieged by the Imperial guard; and Sabinus, doubting his ability to hold out long, sent off a despatch to Primus to bid him hasten to his assistance.

"Madam!" exclaimed Eboracus rushing in, "I pray you come on the roof of the house."

"What is the matter? Ye Gods! surely Rome is not on fire again!"

"Madam! The household guard are assaulting the Capitol and have indeed set fire to the houses below, I doubt if the Præfect can hold out till Primus arrives."

Duilia ascended to the flat top of the house. The palace of the family was in the Carinæ, on the slope of the Esquiline hill, hard by the gardens of Nero's Golden House. Being on high ground it commanded the Forum and the Capitol, and looked over the tops of the vulgar insulæ in the dip of the Suburra.

It was the evening of the second day. Heavy clouds had lowered throughout the hours of daylight and the evening had prematurely closed. There had been desultory fighting all day, but as the night approached a determined set was made by the German guard to capture the Capitol, and the citadel of Rome that adjoined it, connected by only a small neck of hill. They knew that Primus was close at hand, and they were determined not to be caught between a foe before and another behind.

The Capitol is a rocky height rising precipitately above the Forum, and enormous substructures had strengthened it and formed a platform on which rose the Temple of Jupiter Capitolinus that stood to Rome almost in the relation that the Temple did to Jerusalem, as the centre of its religious and civil institutions.

It was almost the paladium of the city, the fate of Rome was held to be bound up with its preservation.

And now Domitia and her mother looked on in the gathering darkness at the temple looming out as of gold against the purple black clouds behind, lit with the glare of the flames of the houses below that had been fired by the soldiery.

The roar of conflict came up in waves of sound.

"Really," said Duilia, "Revolutions are only tolerable when seen from a house-top; that is, to cultivated minds—the common rabble like them."

Shrill above the roar came the scream of a whistle, that a boy was blowing as he went down the street.

Suddenly the clamor boiled up into a mighty spout or geyser of noise, and the reason became manifest in another moment. The whole sky was lit by a sheet of flame of golden yellow. The conflagration had caught an oil merchant's stores that were planted against the substructures supporting the temple. Columns, shoots of dazzling light rushed up against the rocks and the walls, recoiled, swept against them again, overleaped them and curled like tongues around the temple.

Instantly every sound ceased. The soldiers sheathed their swords. The citizens held their breath. Nothing for a few minutes was audible, save the mutter of the fire.

"My lady," said Euphrosyne, coming to the roof, and addressing Longa Duilia, "A priest of Jupiter is below, and desires to speak with you."

CHAPTER XVIII

A REFUGEE

"A priest of Jupiter here!" exclaimed Duilia. "When his temple is on fire! Bid him be off—but stay. Who let him in?"

"Lady, the Chaldæan introduced him."

"He had no right to do so. Let him entertain him. I desire to see the end. Run. The roof is on fire—the eagles will be down—or melt away."

"Lady! the Magian commissioned me to assure you that he bears an important communication."

"Say I am engaged."

A minute later, the Chaldæan himself arrived on the housetop and addressed the mistress.

"I cannot attend to your abracadabra," said she, in reply to his request to be heard. "Look there. The Capitol is in flames, the temple of Jupiter Optimus Maximus blazes. I know what he wants—he has come begging. They all beg. I have no money. I am interested in the fire, the Revolution, and all that sort of thing."

"Lady Longa," said Elymas, "There are moments that are turning points in every life. A great chance offers. Take it, or put it away forever."

"You worry me past endurance. What is it? Look! the flames are licking Jupiter in his chariot."

"If you will step aside I will speak. Not here."

Duilia with an impatient toss of her head and shrug of her shoulders, gathered up her garment with one hand, stepped to a distant part of the roof, and said, sulkily—

"Well, what is this about?"

"You know that the Præfect of Rome who supped at your house the other day is besieged in the Capitol."

"Well—this is no news."

"And that for security, lest they should be put to death by Vitellius or the soldiery, he took his children and his nephew there with him."

"So I have been told. That does not concern me. Why did he not take also his fat wife? she would have fed the flames."

"My lady—the Capitol cannot hold out another half hour, and then all within will be butchered."

"Can I help that? They all do it. This sort of thing happens in revolutions invariably. I cannot alter the course of the world."

"But, madam, the son of Vespasian, Flavius Domitianus has escaped through the Tabularium, by a little door into the Forum."

"He might have escaped by turning a somersault over the walls for aught I care."

"His life is in extreme jeopardy. If discovered he will be assassinated, most assuredly."

"Well, that is the way these things go."

"I have brought him hither—disguised as a priest."

"What!"

The lady became rigid, eyes, mouth and nostrils.

"What!"

"He escaped disguised as a priest of Jupiter. As such, with veiled head he has passed unmolested, even through the ranks of the soldiery and people, inclined to tear him to pieces, for they are all on the side of the reigning prince."

"Domitian here! What a fool you are, Elymas. I'll have you tossed off the roof, in punishment. By Hercules! you compromise me. If it be suspected that he is here, I shall have the house ransacked, and all my valuables plundered, and the Gods alone know what may become of me."

"That is true, lady, and you must run the risk."

"I will not," said Duilia, stamping angrily on the concrete of the roof. "Is it not enough to have the house turned upside down with this detestable Saturnalia! Age of Gold indeed! Age of tomfoolery and upside-downedness. If my poor dear man had but done what he ought, there would have been none of these commotions, and I—well—I—I would have put down the Saturnalia."

"Madam, this is all beside the mark. Domitian, the son of Flavius Vespasian, whom the world has saluted Emperor, and sworn to, is under your roof as a suppliant."

"How unfortunate!"

"How fortunate!"

"I cannot see that."

"Then, madam, the clouds of night must have got into your brain. Do you not see that you are running a very slight risk. None suspect that he is in concealment here, as I smuggled him into the house."

"There are my slaves."

"They regard him as a priest escaping from the fire and the siege," said the soothsayer. He continued—"Before morning the Illyrian legions will have arrived in Rome. Do you suppose the German bodyguard can stand against them? What other troops has Vitellius to fall back on? None—he is deserted. His cause is fatally smitten. By to-morrow evening he will be dead, cast down the Gemonian stair. Vespasian will be proclaimed in the Forum. Your risk will be at an end, and you will have obtained the lasting gratitude of the Imperial father, who will do anything you desire, to show his thankfulness to you for having saved the life of his son."

"There is something in that," said Duilia.

"And suppose now that Domitian is here, that you bid your slaves eject him, and he falls into the hands of Vitellius, how will you be regarded by the Flavian family? Do you not suppose that you will be the first to suffer the resentment of the Augustus?"

"There is a good deal in that," said Duilia, to which the Magus said,—

"I have no fear of betrayal from any in the house save Senecio, that owl-like philosopher. He is not like the slaves, he may suspect, and trip me up."

"My good Elymas," interrupted Duilia, "do not concern yourself about him. He is not a man to chew nutshells when he can munch kernels."

"Domitian is in my apartment, will you see him, lady?"

"By all means. I have a notion. Go, fetch Domitia, bring her down there to me."

Then Longa descended to that portion of the mansion where were situated the rooms given up to the soothsayer; they were on one side of a small court, and the philosopher occupied chambers on the other side. Across the water tank in the midst many an altercation had taken place.

Senecio was not there now. He was probably out taking a philosophic view of the internecine strife, and moralizing over the burning of the Capitol.

With a benignant smile and a tear in her eye, Duilia almost ran to Domitian, her two hands extended. She had just looked round the court to make sure she was unobserved and that there was no one within earshot.

"I am so grateful to the Gods," she said, with a tremor in her voice, "that they should allow me the honor and happiness of offering you an asylum. Blood is thicker than water. Though I perish for my advocacy of your dear father—I cannot help it. Cousins must be cousinly. It is with us a family peculiarity—we hang together like a swarm of bees."

The young man cautiously removed his white veil or head-covering, and exposed his face, that was somewhat pale. He had a shy modest appearance, a delicate complexion that flushed and paled at the changes of emotion in his heart. His eyes were a watery gray, large, but he screwed the eyelids together, as though near-sighted. He was fairly well built, but had spindle legs, no calves, and his toes as if cut short.

In manner he was awkward, without ease in his address; owing to the low associates with whom he had consorted, having been kept short of money, and to his lack of acquaintance with the courtesies of the cultured classes.

"I thank you. My life is in danger. I came hither, as my uncle supped here the other day, and I knew something about kinship. I had nowhere else whither to go. I would have been hunted out and murdered had I gone to my uncle—my mother's brother. They would have sought me there first of all."

"You shall stay here till all danger is past. I should esteem myself the vilest of women were I to refuse you my protection at such a time as this. Senecio, my philosopher, is out, gadding about—of course. You shall occupy his room, and I shall give strict orders that he be not admitted. I will not have philosophers careering in and out of my house, at all hours, as pleases them. This is not a rabbit warren, as the Gods love me! But here comes my daughter to unite with me in assurance of welcome and protection."

Domitia had entered, in obedience to the command transmitted by the sorcerer.

There was but one oil lamp on a table in the chamber, and consequently at first she did not discern who was there addressed by her mother. But Duilia stepped aside and allowed the light to flash over the face of Domitian.

The moment the girl saw it, she started back and put her hands to her bosom.

"My dear child," said Longa Duilia, "you will thank the Lares and Penates, that our cousin has taken refuge with us. The Capitol is in flames, the Imperial guards are storming the walls, there is, I fear, no hope for our dear good friend Flavius Sabinus. Poor man, how he enjoyed himself at supper here the other day! We may hope for the best, but not expect impossibilities. Revolutions and all these sorts of things have their natural exits, the sword, the Tullianum and the Gemonian steps—horrible, but inevitable. Domitian has fled to us, disguised as a priest of Jupiter. O my dear, what a nice thing it is that there is so much religion left among the common people that they respected his cloth. Well, here he is, and we must do what we can for him."

"Cast him out," said Domitia hoarsely.

"What, my love?"

"Cast him out—the beast, the crowned beast, the new Nero. The fifth that was and the eighth that will be."

Duilia raised her eyebrows.

"My dear, I don't in the least understand enigmas. I was never clever at them, though my parts are not generally accounted bad."

"Mother, I pray you, I beseech you as you desire my happiness, do not harbor him under your roof. Cast him forth. What ho! Slaves!"

Domitian started and caught the girl by the shoulders.

"You would betray me?"

"I would have you thrust forth into the street."

"To be murdered—torn to pieces by the blood-thirsty mob?"

"It is to save myself."

"Thyself! I do thee no harm."

"Do not attend to her. It is childish, maidenly timidity," said Duilia, frowning at Domitia and shaking her finger at her. "She knows that, to screen you, we run great risks ourselves. We may be denounced—we may.—As the Gods love me! There is no saying what we may be called on to suffer. But I say, perish all the family rather than offend against hospitality."

"Mother," said Domitia. Her face was white as ashes. "Send him forth. If he were not a coward, a mean coward, he would not come here, to the house of two women, and shelter himself behind their skirts. Titus Flavius Domitianus, dost thou call thyself a man?"

He looked furtively at the girl, and muttered something that was unintelligible.

"If thou art a man, go forth, run us not into danger. If thou tarry here—I esteem thee as the basest of men."

"I praise the Gods!" said Longa Duilia, in towering wrath, "she does not command in this house. That do I; and when I say welcome, there you stay, and she shall not gainsay me."

"Mother—to welcome him, is to exile, to destroy me."

"This is rank folly."

"Mother, eject him!"

"I will not. I prithee, Domitian, when your dear father is proclaimed in Rome,—forget this girl's folly, and remember only that I sheltered thee."

"I will remember. I am not one to forget."

"There is no escape," sighed Domitia. "Whom the Gods will destroy—they pursue remorselessly. Well, be it so.—Stay then, coward! I am undone."

CHAPTER XIX

THE END OF VITELLIUS

"I never made a greater mistake in my life,"said Longa Duilia, "and I cannot think how you allowed me to make it."

"What mistake?" asked the Chaldæan.

"The mistake of inviting the uncle in place of the nephew to my little supper. As to that supper, I flatter myself it was perfect—so finished in every detail, as becomes our position; so delicately flavored with reserve, as became my position as a widow; and you recommended me to invite Flavius Sabinus, the Præfect,—and now he has been. That delicate little supper thrown away, and my attentions so nicely adjusted to the circumstances, all that trouble and thought gone for nothing. Do you know that Flavius Sabinus is now in bits? He has been positively hacked to pieces. It is not the supper itself I regret, and my best Falernian wine—but I gave him a gold signet-ring with a cameo, representing Daphne. It had belonged to my dear Corbulo, and was valuable. But I considered it as a means to an end. And now—where is that ring? But for your counsel, I might have invited the nephew."

"Madam, I counselled aright."

"You have the face to say that? Do you not know that Sabinus has had his head struck off, and his body dragged by hooks down the Gemonian stair, and then positively torn to pieces—but there? Who has got hold of the ring? I have lost it—through you. You pretend to read the stars and peer into futurity!"

"Lady, I do see into what is to be, and counsel accordingly."

"Oh, yes! glimpses as of light in a wood through thick foliage. Plenty of obscurity, very little light."

"Madam, consider. Had you not invited the Præfect who has been, you would not have seen the nephew who is, and who came in at the supper to call his uncle away. It was thus he arrived at a knowledge of your house, and your friendly disposition, and thus it was that he was induced to throw himself on your protection."

"There is something in that," observed Duilia. "But how much better had the invitation been sent to Domitian himself."

"On the contrary, that would not have been judicious, therefore I did not recommend it. Had the nephew come here along with his servants, immediately his escape from the Capitol was discovered, and they were tortured to disclose his place of concealment, they would have betrayed this house: but as it has happened they could not suppose he would take refuge here."

"There is a good deal in that," answered Duilia meditatively. "Well, it is only the ring that I regret. If I had but known—something of inconsiderable value but showy would have sufficed. Moreover, I might have done without that dish of British oysters—very expensive, and, as you see, thrown away. Yet! well, I enjoyed them."

"Even that ring is not lost."

"How so?"

"It is on Domitian's finger."

"You really say so?"

"When the Præfect bade his nephew and sons attempt to escape from the Capitol, he recommended the former to engage your protection, and in token of this, he put the ring that you had given him, on his nephew's finger, that he might present it to you—should there be mistrust, in pledge that he came from Flavius Sabinus. I encountered Domitian in the street, I knew him and conducted him to your door, and obtained his admission. There was no necessity for him to show his ring, as I stood sponsor for him."

"You are a good old creature," said Duilia, "I withdraw any offensive expressions I may have used. To gratify you, I will pay that old woman, Senecio, his wage and bid him pack."

"Then, madam, my services shall be amply repaid. The man himself is harmless. Engage him as a clown,—he is consumed with conceit, and so renders himself a laughing-stock. That is all he is qualified to be."

"Go—send me Domitia. She has behaved like a fool."

Shortly after the girl entered the room where was her mother. The latter at once exclaimed:—

"My dear, the ring is not lost. Domitian has it. By the foresight of the Gods, Sabinus removed it from his finger, and confided it to his nephew, before unhappy circumstances arose which might have led to the ring getting into the hands of any Cyrus or Dromo."

"Was it to hear this that you sent for me?" asked Domitia sullenly.

"No, it was not. Your conscience must upbraid you. You have acted in an insensate manner. You have flouted and angered the son of him who in—perhaps half an hour—will be an Augustus, supreme in the state."

"Mother, I do not like him."

"Ye Gods of the Capitol!—confound them, by the way, they are all burnt! O Tellus and Terminus! Do you suppose we are to see and be courteous only to those whom we like? What cared I for that paragon of virtue, Flavius Sabinus, who talked to such an extent that I could not get in a word edgeways. But I gave him a nice little supper—and oysters from Britain, my best Falernian, and that ring of your father's, because I thought he might be useful. And now Titus Flavius Domitianus is our guest—in hiding till matters are settled one way or the other—and you insult him to his face. It is not conduct worthy of your mother. You interfere with my plans."

"What plans?"

"My dear child, Vespasian is old—about sixty I think, and has but two sons, of whom Domitian is the youngest. The elder, Titus Flavius Sabinus Vespasianus has but a daughter. Do you not see? Do you not smell?"

"I do neither, mother."

"More the pity. You sadly take after your father, who had no ambition. Give the old fellow ten years before he becomes a god; the eldest son, if the worst comes, may succeed and be Augustus for another ten, and then,—the second son, Domitian, will be prince. My dear, what opportunities! What gorgeous opportunities!"

"Opportunities for what?"

"For push, my dear, push to the purple. Your dear father, ah, well! We are not all made of the same clay."

"Mother, that is precisely what fills me with dread. He will then be the eighth, for these adventurers of a few months do not count,—the new Nero."

"But consider—the purple. My dear, do you remember how Valeria caught the dictator Sulla. She sat behind him in the theatre, and picked some flue off his toga. He turned round and caught her doing it. 'Sir,' said she, 'I am but endeavoring to get to myself some of the luck that adheres to you!' I could have loved that woman. It was so happy, so neat. That bit of wool drew Sulla and the Dictatorship to her. You, what a blunderer you are. You have offended Domitian, who may some day be greater than was Sulla, when you had it in your power by a word, a look, a dimpled smile, to win him, and with him the purple."

"Mother, I do not covet it. You forget—I am promised to Lucius Ælius Lamia."

"Oh! Lamia! He could be bought off with a proconsulship."

"I do not desire to be separated from him. I love him, and have loved him since we were children together."

"Well, you have done for your chances. If I surmise aright, the young man entertains a great grudge against you."

At that moment Eboracus came in.

"Madam," said he, "the Illyrian legions have entered the city, under Primus, and there is fighting in the streets. The people on the housetops cheer on this side or that, as though they were at a show of gladiators."

"Well—those things happen. We shall know for certain which shall be uppermost, and if fate favors Vitellius—Then, daughter, I shall not scruple to give the young man up."

The condition of the capital was frightful. Vitellius had called in levies from the country to support him, and the prætorian soldiers stood firm. But many men of direction were with the partisans of Vespasian, who advanced steadily over the bodies of the troops opposing them. Fifty thousand persons lost their lives in these eventful days of the Saturnalia.

The legions under Primus succeeded in recapturing the Capitol, which was still smoking, and pushed forward into the Forum.

Meanwhile, Vitellius, in the Palatine palace, a prey to irresolution, had filled himself with wine, and then fled along with his cook and pastrycook to his wife's house on the Aventine. Then deceived by a false report that his troops were successful, he returned to the Palatine, and found it deserted, but a roar of voices rose from the Forum below, and from the Capitol the cries of the legionaries were wafted towards him along with the smoke.

He hastened to collect all the gold he could lay his hands on, stuffed it into his cincture, assumed an old ragged suit, and then again attempted to escape; but now he found every avenue blocked. Filled with terror he crawled into the dog-kennel where the hounds, resenting the intrusion, fell on him and bit his neck and hands and legs. But now Vespasian's soldiery invaded the palace, and a tribune, Julius Placidius, discovering the bloated, bleeding wretch, drew him out by the foot, and he came forth thus, his hands full of dirty straw, and strands adhering to his hair and garments. A howling rabble at once surrounded him, leaping, jeering, throwing mud and stones; a few soldiers succeeded in surrounding him. His hands were bound behind his back, and a rope passed about his neck. Thus he was dragged through the streets an object of insult to the people. Some struck him in the face, some plucked out his hair. In the Forum the rabble were breaking his statues and dragging them about. One ruffian thrust a pike under the unfortunate prince's chin and bade him hold up his head. Then said Vitellius:—

"Thou, who thus addressest me—a tribune thou art, remember I was once thy commander!"

Thereupon a German soldier, desirous of shortening his misery, struck him down with a blow of his sword, and in so doing cut off the ear of the tribune who had insulted the fallen Emperor.

At once the body of the prince, from whom the life was not sped, was dragged to the Gemonian stair, a flight of steps down which the corpses of malefactors were flung, and there he was despatched with daggers.

Longa Duilia had been kept well informed as to all that took place.

No sooner was she assured that Vitellius was dead, than she rushed into the apartment given up to Domitian.

"Salve, Cæsar! As the Gods love me, I am the first to so salute you, son of the Augustus! Oh, I am so happy! And it might have been otherwise, but you they never would have reached save over my body."

CHAPTER XX

CHANGED TACTICS

The anarchy which had lasted from the 11th June, 68, when Nero perished, came to an end on the 20th December, in the ensuing year. In that terrible year of 69, three emperors had died violent deaths, and Rome had been in a condition of disorder on each occasion, and intermittent violence had lasted all the time. Men now drew a long breath, they were disposed to blot out the memory of those eighteen months of misery and national humiliation, as though it had not been, and to reckon the strong Vespasian as prince next after Nero. Indeed, on the morrow of the death of Vitellius, when the Senate assembled and decreed the honors of the former princes, they recited those of the first Cæsars, but ignored the three last who had perished within a twelvemonth, as though they had never been, and were to be forgotten as an evil dream.

That same day also, Domitian received the title of Cæsar, and was made Prince of the Youths, and Præfect of Rome in the place of his uncle, who had been murdered.

That day, also, Mucianus arrived with the Syrian legions, and with plenitude of authority from Vespasian to act in his name.

To Duilia's vast delight Domitian did not forget his obligation to her, but paid frequent visits to her house, and it was a matter of pride to her to have his attendant lictors standing outside her door, as in former days.

When he came, she made a point of summoning her daughter, and requiring her to be present during the interview. But she could not make her speak or compel her to graciousness of manner towards the visitor.

The young prince's eyes watched the girl with question in them, but he addressed all his conversation to the mother.

Longa Duilia did her utmost to disguise her child's incivility, attributed it to shyness, and used all her blandishments to make a visit to her house agreeable to Domitian.

At length, the irksomeness caused by Domitia's irresponsive manner seemed to satisfy the mother that she did more harm than good in enforcing her attendance, and she ceased to require the girl to appear.

Some months passed, and Domitia had not given a thought to Glyceria, and her offer to revisit the sick woman, when, all at once, in a fit of weariness with all things that surrounded her, and a sense of incapacity to find enjoyment anywhere, she started from her languor to bid Eboracus go forth, buy honey-cakes and toys, and accompany her on a visit to the Suburra.

As she was on her way, Domitian came by with his lictors and other attendants. Since his elevation from poverty and insignificance to ease and importance, he had acquired a swagger that made his manner more offensive than before in his phase of cubbishness.

He at once addressed her, for though veiled he recognized her.

"May I attend you? I have at the moment nothing of importance to occupy me."

"I am bound for the Suburra."

"For the Suburra! What can take you into the slums of Rome?"

"I am going to see the wife of Paris, the tragic actor."

"Oh! the wife of the actor, Paris," with a sneer.

"I said so—the wife of Paris the actor," she withdrew her veil and looked him straight in the eyes. He winced.

"And pray—is she a visiting acquaintance of the family?"

"She is our freedwoman. Paris was freed by my father likewise. Are you content? I may add that she has met with an accident and is crippled and confined to her bed."

"Oh!" with a vulgar laugh, "and you are infected with the Christian malady, and go among the sick and starving."

"I know naught of this Christian malady. What is it?"

"We have had the contagion touch us. There is my cousin Clemens, and his wife Domitilla, both taken badly with it. He is a poor, mean-spirited fool. He has been offered excellent situations, with money to be made in them, in bushels, but he refuses—will not swear by the genius of my father, will not offer sacrifice to the Gods. Such thin gruel minds I cannot away with. Were I Augustus, such as would not serve the Commonwealth should be sent to kick their heels in a desert island. These Christians are the enemies of the human race."

"What, because they visit the sick and relieve the poor?"

"The sick are smitten by the Gods and should be left to die. The poor are encumbrances and should be left to rot away. But a man of rank and of family—"

"Flavius Clemens! of what family?"

Domitian bit his lip. The Flavians were of no ancestry; money-lenders, tax-collectors, jobbers in various ways, with no connections save through the mother of Vespasian, and that middle-class only.

"I say that a man who will not serve his country should be pitched out of it."

"About that I have no opinion."

"Clemens was cast to the lions by Nero, but some witchcraft charmed them, and they would not touch him."

Domitia said nothing to this. She was desirous of being rid of her self-imposed escort.

"You must wish me success," said the young prince. "I am off to Germany. There has been revolt there, and I go to subdue it."

"By all means carry with you a pair of shears."

"What mean you?"

"To obtain a crop of golden hair from the German women, wherewith to grace your triumph."

Domitian knitted his brows.

"You have a sharp tongue."

"I need one. It is a woman's sole defence."

"Come, if a cousin, as your mother asserts,—though by the Gods! I know not where the kinship comes in,—wish me well. Such words as yours are of ill-omen."

"I wish confusion and destruction to the worst enemies of Rome," answered Domitia.

"That suffices. I will offer the spoils to you."

"Thank you, I do not yet wear wigs."

He turned away with an expression of irritation.

"You are either silent, or stick pins into me," he muttered.

Domitia continued her course, but as she entered the "Island" in which was the home of Paris, she observed the young Cæsar still in the street, at a corner watching her.

Much annoyed, and with her temper ruffled by this meeting, she ascended the steps to the first story and at once turned towards the apartments of Paris and Glyceria, but had to thread her way among poor people, women weaving and spinning, and children romping and running races.

She was welcomed with pleasure, Glyceria would have raised herself, had she been able; as it was, she could show her respect only by a salutation with the hand, and her pleasure by a smile and a word.

The chamber was fragrant with violets.

Domitia looked round and saw a small marble table on which stood a statuette of a shepherd with panpipes, and a lamb across his shoulders. Violets in a basin stood before the figure.

"Ah! Hermes," said Domitia, and plucking a little bunch of the purple flowers from her bosom she laid it in the bowl with the rest.

"Nay, dear Lady, not Hermes," said Glyceria, "though indeed it was sculptured to represent him—but to me that figure has another meaning. And I hold your offering of the violets as made to Him who to me is the Good Shepherd."[4]

"Whom mean you? Atys?"

"Not Atys."

Domitia was not particularly interested in the matter. She presumed that some foreign cult was followed by Glyceria, and foreign cults at this time swarmed in Rome.

"Do you believe me, Glyceria," said Domitia, "as I came hither, the Cæsar Domitian accompanied me, and said that I must be a Christian to care for the sick and suffering. What are these Christians?"

"I am one," answered the paralyzed woman.

"What! and Paris?"

"Nay, he hovers between two opinions. His business holds him and he will not give that up, he thinks that, were he to do so, he and I might starve. But with the mind I think he is one."

"And what are these Christians?"

"Those who believe in Christ."

"And he?—is that his image?" pointing to the Good Shepherd.

"Oh Lady! it is only so much His image as the words Good Shepherd written in characters are such, they call up a notion and so does that figure. But in our worship we have no images, no sacrifices."

"What is Christianity?"

"That is long to answer, but I may say in two words what it is to me."

"Say on."

"The Daylight of the soul."

"How mean you?"

"I once was in darkness. I knew not why I was set in the world, whither I was going, what I ought to worship, what were my duties, where was right and what was wrong. I had no light, no road, no law. Now I have all."

"So every votary of every new religion says. Where is your guarantee that you are not in delusion?"

---

4   The statuette of the Good Shepherd, of beautiful art, 2d century, in the Lateran Museum. It is an error to suppose in early Christians a complete emancipation from old usages and modes of thought.

"Madam, when the sun rises and there is day, you do not suppose the light, the splendor, the confidence inspired by it is a delusion. You know that you see, and see that you may walk, and act with purpose and direction. The soul has eyes as well as the body. These eyes behold the light and cannot doubt it, by internal conscience that distinguishes between the truth and falsehood. By that internal conscience I am assured that the light is as real as that seen by eyes of flesh."

"I cannot understand you," said Domitia. "Now for other matters—I have made Eboracus bring you some dainties for yourself and presents for the children who are so kind to you. Where is your husband?"

"He is rehearsing. Better times have arrived, and he is now occupied."

"And you see less of him."

"Yes—but we must live. When away from me, I know that in heart he is with me."

"You are sure of that?"

"Yes."

"What, by the conscience that establishes between truth and falsehood?"

"Nay—by trust. We must trust some one and some thing. We trust God, we trust His Revelation, we trust in the goodness there is in mankind."

"There is evil rather than good."

"There is good—but that is oft astray because of the darkness, and does not know its course."

Domitia did not remain long in the Insula. She bade farewell to the wife of the actor and promised to revisit her. The presence of Glyceria refreshed, soothed, sweetened the mind of the girl that was heated, ruffled and soured by contact with so much there was in pagan life that jarred against her noble instincts, by the uncongeniality of her mother, and by the disgust she felt at association with Domitian.

When she arrived at the palace, she heard that her mother had been inquiring after her, and she at once went to her apartments.

Duilia asked where she had been, but did not listen for an answer, or pay attention to what was said, when the reply came.

"What is this I hear?" said Duilia, in a tone of irritation. "Lucilla tells me you have been chatting with Domitian, and in the street too—"

"I had no wish to speak with him. He came after me."

"Oh! he went after you, did he? And pray what had he to say?"

"He is going to Germany to conclude a campaign already fought out and come back and triumph for another man's victories."

"You did not say so to him?"

"Not in so many words."

"My dear, it is true. He is going, and whether he be successful or not, will return wearing the title Germanicus. I shall have a little supper."

"For whom?"

"For whom, do you ask? For him to be sure, to wish him good success on the expedition."

"You will allow me not to be present."

"As you will, perverse girl. My dear," in a confidential tone, "if kittens can't catch rats, cats can."

CHAPTER XXI

THE VIRGIN'S WREATH

"My dear," said Longa Duilia to her daughter, "with wit such as you have, that might be drawn through a needle's eye, it is positively necessary to have you married as quickly as possible. I can no longer bear the responsibility of one so full of waywardness and humors as yourself."

"That, mother, is as Lamia chooses. You know that I can marry only him."

"And I do not ask you to take another. I will get it settled forthwith. I'll see his father by adoption and have the settlements looked to. You are a good match. I presume you are aware of that, and this explains certain poutings and bad temper. Well—reserve them for Lamia, and don't vex me. I wash my hands of you, when that you are married. A camel carries his own hump, but a man his wife's humors."

Domitia was sufficiently acquainted with her mother's elasticity of spirit and fertility of invention to be satisfied that she had a motive for pressing on her marriage, and what that motive was seemed obvious. But it was one that distressed her greatly.

"My dearest mother," she said timidly, "I hope—I mean, since you are so good as not to urge me further to break my engagement with Lamia, that you have not set your mind—I mean your heart—"

"My excellent child," answered Longa Duilia cutting her daughter short, "make no scruple of blurting out what is on your tongue. You allude to Domitian. Well! If you had common sense, you would know that to get on in life, one must fit one's heart with the legs of a grasshopper, so as to be able to skip from an inconvenient, into any suitable position. When a dish of ortolans is set on table, none but a fool will dismiss it untasted to be devoured by the servants in the kitchen!"

"But, mother, he is quite young."

"By the favor of the Gods, Domitia, youths always fall in love with women somewhat older than themselves. The Gods ordered it for their good. If they, I mean the young men—would only follow their—I mean the Gods'—direction, there would be fewer unhappy marriages. For my part, I can't see anything attractive in half-baked girls."

But the thoughts of her own future, and approaching happiness took up the whole of Domitia's brain, and left no space for consideration of her mother's schemes, and their chances of success.

The young prince was away. It was, as had been feared, too late for him to reap laurels in Germany, the revolt had been quelled by Cerealis, but as there was a ferment working in Gaul, it was deemed advisable that Domitian should go thither and overcome the dissatisfied instead of crossing the Alps. He had accordingly changed his route, and had appeared in Lyons.

The marriage between Domitia and Lamia could not take place so speedily as Duilia desired. She was wishful to have it over before the return to Rome of Domitian, so that she might be left a freer hand, and her daughter put out of the way who, she thought, exercised a peculiar fascination over the young prince; but she was unable to decide in her own mind whether what drew his eyes towards Domitia was dislike or love; possibly it was a commingling of resentment at her treatment of him, and admiration for her loveliness.

But hindrances arose. Lamia was absent on his estates in Sicily, where there had been disturbances among the slaves, and till matters were settled there, he could not return.

Then came the month of May in which no marriages might be performed owing to the hauntings of the Lemures, or ghosts of bad men, and such as had not received burial. These, seen in the forms of walking skeletons or bugbears, rioted in that sweetest month of the whole year. Then they obtained opportunities among the incautious to slip into their bodies, and possess them with madness, or to take up their abodes in dwelling-houses and disturb the living occupants by phantom appearances and mysterious sounds.

On three days in the month of May special means were adopted to propitiate or scare away these spectres. On the 9th, 11th, and 13th, at midnight, the master of a house, or, in the event of his death or absence, his widow or wife, walked barefoot before the door to a flowing fountain, where the hands were thrice washed, and then the propitiator of the ghosts returned home, and threw black beans over the shoulder, saying: "These I give to you, and with these beans I ransom myself and mine."

It was supposed that the ghost scrambled for the beans, and so enabled the owner of the house to reach the door before them. There stood the servants beating brazen vessels, pots and pans, shouting, "Out with you! Out with you, ye ghosts!"

At the beginning of June was the cleansing of the Temple of Vesta, and till that was completed, on the 15th, marriages were forbidden.

Consequently the wedding could not take place much before midsummer, and to this Longa Duilia had to submit.

Domitia was content and happy. She had not been so happy since her father's death. Indeed till now she had not been able to shake off the pain she had felt at his loss. For to her, that father was the model of noble manhood, high-minded, full of integrity, strong yet gentle. She had often marvelled at the manner in which he had dealt with her mother, whom she indeed loved but who somewhat rasped her. With his wife he had ever been firm yet forbearing. He allowed her to form her little schemes, but always managed to thwart them when foolish or mischievous, without her perceiving who had put a spoke in the wheel.

Lucius Ælius Lamia she looked upon as formed in her father's school, upon his model. He was modest, honorable, true; a good man to whom she could give her whole heart with full assurance that he would treasure the gift, and that she could trust him to be as true to her as she would be true to him.

Since her father's death, Domitia had felt more than previously the incompatibility of her mind with that of her mother. They had no thoughts, no wishes, no feelings in common. Domitia was a dreamer, speculative, ever with eager mind seeking the things beyond what was known, whereas Duilia had not a thought, a care that were not material. The lady Duilia cared not a rush about philosophy or the theory of emanations. It was to her a matter of complete indifference whether the established paganism was true or false. For she had no apprehension of the importance of Truth. And she had no wish that could not be gratified by money or the acquisition of position.

Now also the haunting horror of those waking dreams that she had seen in the Temple of Isis passed from the heart of the young girl, like the vapors that roll away and disclose the blue heavens and the glorious sun. She had been drifting purposeless; now she saw that she was about to enter on a condition of life in which she would have an object, and would find complete happiness in the pursuit of that object,—in the fulfilment of her duties as housewife to a loved husband, in whom she would find strength, sympathy and love.

And now also, for the first time since the death of Corbulo, she sang as she went about the house, or worked at her bridal dress.

Lamia, on his return from Sicily was surprised to note the change in her appearance. She had been as a beautiful flower bowed by rain and pinched with cold, and now, as in renewed sunshine, she bloomed with expanded petals. Light danced in her blue eyes, and a delicate rose suffused her smooth cheeks. She had stepped back into the childhood out of which she had passed on that terrible day at Cenchræa.

And as he looked at her, her eyes sparkling with love and tears of joy, he thought he had never seen one sweeter and to whom he could so wholly devote himself as to his dear Domitia.

Then arrived the eve of the marriage.

The young girl was in the garden, stooping, picking the flowers of which her virginal crown was to be woven, and singing as she plucked.

Then she came with her lap full of herbs and blossoms to her mother, who said:—

"That is right. None may gather the flowers but the bride. By the way, have you heard? Domitian is back from Gaul. I was rejoiced at the news, and have despatched an invitation to him to attend the wedding."

"Oh, mother! it is a bad omen."

At the mention of the name, the vision of the red face, seen at Gabii between her own and that of Lamia, started up before her, and she let drop the lap of flowers, and they fell at her feet.

"By the Gods! what a silly thing thou art! Quick, gather up the herbs and then go fetch thy dolls and toys of childhood, they must all this evening be offered on the altar of the household gods."

"I have them not, mother."

"Not your dolls!"

"Not one."

"But what have you done with them? I know they were all brought from Antioch."

"Mother, they have been given away."

"Given away! to whom?"

"To Glyceria, the sister of Euphrosyne."

"But what can have induced you to do this?"

"She is paralyzed, and served by little children in the story of the Insula where she lives. I considered that it would amuse her to dress the dolls afresh, and perhaps mend broken limbs, and after that she will distribute them among the little willing children that help her in her infirmity."

"As the Gods love me!" exclaimed Duilia, "Whoever heard before of such madness. Hellebore would not cure it. Verily the more you labor at a hole the greater the hollow. You are a fool, and your folly grows daily greater. You must present your toys of childhood to the Lares, they expect it—it is the custom, it is right."

"But I have none left."

"Mother Ops! what is to be done? Run, Eboracus,—run and buy me half a dozen dolls—dressed if possible. Domitia, you are determined to bring ill-luck on yourself. There is nothing else to be done but for you to spend an hour in playing with the dolls, and then you can present them at the altar, and the Gods will be none the wiser. Between me and you and the pillars of the peristyle, they are bigger fools than us mortals, and easier gulled."

Domitia stooped to collect the fallen flowers.

"What is that?" asked her mother—"Oh! right enough, natrix,[5] that drives away ghosts and nightmare. And that of course is in the virginal wreath, myosotis (Forget-me-not) it dries tears. An Egyptian slave I had—he fell ill, so I exposed him on the isle between the two Bridges— he told me that if one ate the root in the month of Thoth—that is August, one escaped sore eyes for a twelvemonth. That is right also, the scarlet anemone, it betokens the flame of love—and that evergreen its continuance. The centaury—that is the herb of union, it will close a wound so as not to show even a scar—and in marriage, no better symbol than that. What have you here? The lysimachia, that gives harmony and agreement of mind. They say that a plant of it fastened to the pole of a chariot will make the wildest and most impatient horses pull together. And the herb of the Twelve Gods! quite right, always remember the gods, they come in useful. The vervain—of course, it will give you all you will. But, ye Gods of Olympus! What have you done to pluck cypress! My dear Domitia, are you mad? Thyme, mint, if you will—but cypress! the tree of the infernal gods, and—as the Gods love me! let me look at your hands! They are red—what have you plucked—plucked till your hands are dyed—the androsœmum! Oh! Domitia! ill-fated child—look, look at your hands, the juice has stained them, they are dipped in blood."

---

5   Probably *Dictamnus Fraxinella*. For properties of these plants see Pliny, H. N. lib. xxv., xxvi., xxvii.

CHAPTER XXII

QUONIAM TU CAIUS, EGO CAIA!

At the earliest rays of dawn the auguries were taken, not as of old by the flight of birds, but by inspection of the liver and heart of a sheep, that was slaughtered for the purpose by the Aruspices, and this done they came to the palace of Duilia, bearing the skin of the sheep, to announce that the portents were favorable, in fact, were of extraordinarily good promise.

"That is as I hoped," said Longa Duilia, "and that will counteract and bring to naught the disastrous tokens of the wreath. Why, by Venus's girdle, the girl has not been able to get her hands white yet. The stain of that nefast herb is on them still. But—ah! here she comes in her flame-colored veil. By the Body of Bacchus! after all it means no ill, for do not her hands agree in hue with her head-gear?"[6]

Domitia had laid aside her maidenly dress, the toga prætextata woven with horizontal stripes, for the dress of a married woman, the toga recta, with vertical stripes. About her waist was a woollen girdle fastened in a peculiar manner, with the so-called knot of Hercules, that was regarded as a charm against the evil eye, and was also employed in binding up wounds and fractured bones. The girl's dress, as well as a net of red silk threads in which her hair had been tied up on the previous day, had been offered on the altars of the ancestral deities worshipped in the house.

Her hair had been divided that morning, not by a comb, but by the head of a lance, into six tresses that were plaited with colored ribbons. And about her head, beneath the veil, was the virgin's wreath woven out of the flowers she had herself picked—but the ill-omened cypress and the blood distilling androsœmum had been omitted.

And now with pipes and cymbals came the bridegroom attended by all his friends, to fetch the bride home. The house door was decorated with laurels, and incense smoked on the domestic altars, in the vestibule, and in the atrium. The boxes that contained the ancestral wax masks were open, and each face was wreathed about with flowers. Green lines

---

6   Our word *nuptial* comes from the veil wherewith the bride's head was covered.

connecting the boxes united all to one trunk forming a family tree. The household gods were not ignored, lamps burned before them, flowers adorned their heads, and cakes and wine were placed on shelves below them.

Slaves ran to and fro, and ran against each other. Ten witnesses, kinsmen of the bride and bridegroom, assembled to take cognizance of the marriage contract. Two seats were introduced into the hall, and the legs bound together, and over both was spread the skin of the sheep slaughtered that morning for the auspices.

Then bride and bridegroom were seated on these stools, the marriage contract was read aloud, and they received the salutations of their friends. The pronuba, a married female relative united their hands, and that accomplished, the bridegroom rose, and attended by the friends and kinsfolk of both parties, departed for the Temple of Jupiter, where the flamen Dialis offered sacrifice to the gods of marriage, to Jupiter, Juno, Tellus, and the old Latin half-forgotten deities of Picumnus and Pilumnus.

Whilst the sacred sacrifice was being performed, in the house of the bride all was being made ready for the wedding or meal after midday.

The bride was now esteemed to have passed out of the family of her father into that of her husband, his gods would be her gods, his house her house, his name hers. In signification of this the formula was used by her, "Since thou art Caius, I am Caia." At a remote period it would have been "Since thou art Lucius I am Lucia," and she would have lost her name of Domitia. But this was no longer customary, only the liturgical form of surrender was employed.

It was past noon when the procession returned, swelled by more friends and by all well-wishers, and as it entered the house, with a shiver Domitia observed the glowing face and water-blue eyes of the young prince, attended by his lictors. She caught his glance, but he dropped his eyes the moment they encountered hers, and she saw his cheeks pucker, as though with laughter. But she had no time to give thought to him; she was required to acknowledge the felicitations of the visitors, and to entreat them to partake of the hospitality of the hour, and to offer a pinch of incense and a libation to her happiness.

The supper was lengthy—many partook and came in relays, so that the entire afternoon was consumed by it. To the relief of Domitia, the prince Domitian had withdrawn. As each left the table he saluted the bride with the exclamation, Feliciter.

For this long and tedious ceremonial feast, she was allowed to rest on a couch, next to her husband, at the table, in the place of honor.

The meal lasted till evening, and then there ensued a movement.

The household goods of the bride, her spindle and distaff, her chest containing robes, were brought forth, and placed on biers to be conveyed to the new house.

Then Domitia rose, with tears in her eyes, and went to the several chambers she had occupied, to say farewell to the kitchen, to salute the hearth, to the shelf that served as chapel, to bid farewell to the ancestral gods, to the wax forefathers in the hall, then to kiss her mother, finally to turn, kneel and embrace the doorposts of the paternal dwelling, and kiss the threshold from which she parted.

Without, the procession waited. She was gently disengaged from her mother's arms, and to the cries of Talasse! amidst a shower of walnuts thrown among the boys by the bridegroom, the procession started.

Domitia was attended by three lads, one went before carrying a torch, the other two walked, one on each side, carrying spindle and distaff. The torch, according to rule, was of whitethorn wood, and on arrival at the house of the bridegroom would be scrambled for and ripped to pieces by the guests, as every shred was esteemed to carry good luck.

Now rose a burst of song, the so-called Fescennian lays, some old and some new, accompanied by the flutes of musicians and the clash of castanets and cymbals of dancing girls.

The procession descended the hill to the Forum, crowds lining the way and shouting Feliciter!

At a corner there was a little clearing, for there lay a pallet, and on it a sick woman, who had been brought from her dwelling to see the sight. She extended and waved her hand, holding something as Domitia approached, and the bride through her tears noticed her, halted, went towards her, and said:—

"Glyceria! you here to wish me happiness!"

"And to give thee, dear lady, a little present."

She extended to her a small amulet, that Domitia accepted gratefully, and stooping kissed the paralyzed woman on the brow.

An unheard-of thing! unparalleled! A thing she would not have done, had she been in full control over herself—a thing she would not have done, had not her heart brimmed with love for all, at that moment. She, a noble lady, belonging to one of the greatest houses in Rome, kissed a poor actor's wife, an enfranchised slave—and that before all eyes.

About Glyceria was a dense throng of men and women and children, the occupants of the "Island" in which she lived. It was they, who, pitying her sufferings, desirous that she should see the procession, had opened a space before her, and held it open, that none might impede a full view of the marriage train.

And this throng of rude artisans, shoemakers, cordwainers, leather-sellers, hawkers and their wives and children saw this act of Domitia. For a moment they were silent, and then they broke into a roar of "Feliciter! feliciter! the Gods be with thee, dear lady! The Gods protect thee! The Gods shower blessings on thee!"

But Domitia might not tarry; confused, half ashamed of what she had done, half carried off her feet by the thrill of joy that went from the crowd to her, she advanced.

The train descended by the lake of Nero, now occupied by the Colosseum, then ascended the Celian Hill to the house of Lamia.

On reaching his door, the procession spread out, and gave space for the bride to advance.

Modestly, trembling with love, timidity, hope in her heart, she anointed the doorposts with oil and then passed woollen strings round them.

This accomplished, two young men started forward, caught her up, made a seat for her of their hands, and bore her over the threshold, which she might not touch with her feet, lest by accident or nervousness she should stumble, and so her entry into the new house be ill-omened. On being admitted into the habitation of her husband, it was her duty to go to the hearth and make up the fire, then to the fountain and draw water; next to worship the household gods.

The house was pretty. It had been fresh painted, and was bright with color, and sweet with flowers, for every pillar was wreathed and each door garlanded. Numerous lamps illumined the chambers, and in the atrium were reflected in the water tank. The air was vibrating with music, as choirs sang Fescennian songs, and timbrels tinkled and pipes twittered.

Domitia was received by the wife of L. Ælius Lamia, who had adopted Domitia's husband. He was a quiet man, who had no ambition, had taken no offices, and had passed his time in taming birds. He was the son of a better known man, who had been a friend of Horace.

The old woman, gentle in manner, took Domitia by the hand and led her into the tablinum, where was old Lamia, a cripple through gout, and he kissed the girl, patted her hands and spoke an affectionate welcome.

"Claudia and I," said he, "were childless and so we adopted Lucius. He has been a good son to us, and this is a happy day to all three,—to him who has secured the sweetest flower of Rome, and to Claudia and me who obtain so good a daughter. But, ah! we are old and have our humors, I, with my gout, am liable to be peevish. You must bear with our infirmities. You will have a worthy husband, one cut out of the old rock of which were the ancient Romans, and not of the Tiberine mud of which the present generation are moulded."

"Come now," said the old woman, "the guests are about to depart, bid them farewell."

Then she led the young girl back into the atrium.

There stood the Chaldæan, dark, stern, ominous.

Domitia in exuberant joy smiled at him, and said:

"Elymas! You see my happiness. Isis has for once been in error—we, my Lamia and I, are united, and there have been no hands thrust forth to part us."

"My lady," said the astrologer, "the day is not yet over."

"And the auguries were all propitious."

"The promise of the augurs may not jump with thy desire," he replied.

She had no time for more words, as her hand was caught by L. Ælius Lamia, who drew her aside into the lararium or chapel.

"My dearest," he said, "this is a day of trial to thee—but we shall be left undisturbed shortly. The guests depart and the riot will cease."

She looked at him, with eyes that brimmed with tears, and a sob relieved her heart, as she cast herself on his breast and said:—

"Quoniam tu Caius, ego Caia."

CHAPTER XXIII

THE END OF THE DAY

A rumor, none knew from whom it arose, spread rapidly in whispers, sending a quiver of alarm, distress, pity, through the entire wedding party, reaching last of all him most concerned.

None dared breathe in his ear what all feared; but none would separate till it was surely ascertained whether what was surmised was a fact or not.

The slaves knew it and looked wistfully at Lamia.

He was engaged in making trifling presents to the many guests and well-wishers, moving from one to another, attended by slaves with trays piled up with gifts.

Eboracus burst on him, through the throng, forgetting, in his agitation and fear, the diffidence that belonged to his position.

"Sir! Where is the mistress?"

Lamia, without looking at him, or desisting from what he was about, answered:

"Within, being freed from her veil and bridal ornaments."

"Sir! Lucius! she has been stolen from you! she has been carried away."

Lamia stood as one petrified.

"How dare you utter such a jest?"

"It is no jest—she has been conveyed hence. She is not in your house."

Without another word, Lamia flew into the portion of the house to which Domitia had retired.

There all was in confusion. The female slaves were either struck down with terror, or crying out that they were not to blame.

"Where is she?" asked Lamia, hardly realizing that there was actual loss, thinking this was some frolic of his young companions, who on such occasions allowed themselves great licence.

To add to the confusion, a tame magpie with clipped wing, belonging to the gouty old Lamia, got in the way of every one, and screamed when run over; and the elder man roared out reproach and brandished his crutch when the life of his pet was endangered.

Claudia, like a pious woman, had rushed to the lararium to supplicate the assistance of the Gods, especially of Lamius, son of Hercules and Omphale, the reputed half-divine ancestor of the family.

Domitia had disappeared.—How?—none could say. She had been spirited away, one said in this manner, another said in that. One held it as his opinion that she had been carried off by some disbanded Vitellian soldiers who were said to lurk about the suburbs of Rome and commit depredations. Some thought that in maiden shyness she had fled home; some whispered that the Gods had translated her; others that a former lover had suborned the servants to admit him, and that he had conveyed her from her husband's house to his own.

But in what direction had she been taken? There again opinions differed, and tongues gave conflicting accounts. One had seen a litter hurried down the Clivus Scauri. One declared that he had seen a girl running in the direction of Nero's lake, and suggested that this was Domitia who had gone thither to destroy herself. One had noticed suspicious-looking men wrapped in military cloaks lounging about, and these had disappeared—he had even seen the backs of some near the Porta Metrovia. Then one cried out:—

"What else can be expected when such an ill-omened bird is kept in the house, as a magpie?"

Not until all guests, visitors, had been excluded from the house, could anything be learned with certainty, and that was little. During the afternoon, shortly before the arrival of the procession, several male and female slaves had arrived under the direction of a Chaldæan soothsayer, who announced that he had been sent along with them to the house of the bridegroom by the bride's mother, the Lady Duilia, and that they formed a portion of Domitia's attendance, who had been associated with her in her former home, and would be about her person in her new quarters. No suspicion had been roused, and as the Magian spoke with authority, and gave directions, which it was presumed he was commissioned to do, and as old Lamia was crippled with gout and moreover indisposed to attend to such matters, and the old lady was simple to childishness, these strangers were suffered to do much what they pleased; and on the bride retiring to be divested of the flame colored veil, her wreath and other ornaments, had been allowed to take possession of her.

What happened further they did not know. In the excitement of the arrival of visitors nothing had been observed till some of the household servants remarked that the servants of the family of Duilia had left,—that there had been a bustle in the garden court, and that a litter had departed, borne by men who ran under their load. But even then no notion that the bride had been carried off was entertained. For some time no suspicion of mischief arose. When the slaves became aware that their new mistress was no longer in the house, there was first some surprise entertained that she was not seen, then a notion that she might be unwell or over-tired— but the first word that suggested that she had been conveyed away came from without the house, from a guest who inquired casually what lady had left the house, in a litter, borne by trotting porters. Lamia, in violent agitation, at once hurried to the house whence Domitia had come, to ask for an explanation. There he learned nothing satisfactory. No servants had been sent beforehand. Domitia had taken with her two female slaves, but they had attended her in the procession. The sorcerer, it was true, had disappeared and had not returned.

Lamia was obliged to return home, without his anxiety being in any way removed.

On reaching his palace on the Cœlian, he learned something further. In the room in which Domitia had been divested of her bridal ornaments, which lay scattered in disorder, was a crystal cup that contained the dregs of wine, and this wine was drugged with a powerful narcotic. Of this the slave who acted as house-surgeon and physician was certain. He had tasted it and detected the presence of an opiate. Nothing further could be learned, neither whence came the strange slaves nor whither they had gone.

In the mean time a party surrounding a closed litter had passed through the Porta Capena, and was hurrying along the Appian Way.

Directly the city was left, a tall man who directed the convoy called a halt;—then approaching the litter, he drew back the curtains, and said:—

"Asleep! Two of you take her up, lift her, set her on her feet and rouse her."

He was obeyed and a helpless body was removed, sustained between two stout slaves, and made to stand on the causeway.

"Shake her," said the director, who was none other than the Chaldæan. "If she sleep on, she will never wake. Roused and made to walk she must be. We need fear no pursuit. I have left those behind who will spread a false rumor, and send such as think she has been carried away along the wrong road. Make her walk."

The helpless girl—it was Domitia—staggered with drowsiness and stumbled.

"Let me sleep," she murmured.

"It must not be, lady. To let you sleep is to consign you to death. You must be constrained to walk."

"Let me sleep!" she fretfully said.

"If you sleep you die."

"I want to die—only to sleep. I am dead weary."

"Make her move along," said the sorcerer in a low tone, and the slaves who held her up drew her forward. She scarce moved her feet.

"Oh, you are cruel. I want to sleep. An hour! half an hour. For one moment longer!" she pleaded.

Still the bearers drew her forward, they did not lift her so that she need not move her feet. She was constrained to step forward.

"I pray you! I will give you gold. You shall have all my jewels. Lay me down. Let go your hold, and I will lie where I am, and sleep."

"Draw her further.—Hark! here come horses. Aside! behind that tomb!"

The party stole from off the road and secreted itself behind one of the mausoleums that line the sides of the Appian Way.

"Shake her—lest she doze off in your arms," said Elymas, and the slaves obeyed.

Then Domitia began to sob. "Have pity! only for a little while, I am so tired. The day has been so long and so wearying."

"They are passed—mere travellers," said the sorcerer. "Into the road again. Force her to walk."

Then she called, "Lamia—my Lucius! come to me, drive these men away. They will not let me sleep," and she struggled to free herself, and unable to do so by a spasmodic effort, began to sob, and sobbed herself into a half doze.

"She is sleeping. Run with her," called the Magus.

In vain did she weep, entreat, threaten, naught availed, she was forced to advance; now to take a few steps, to rest on her feet, to walk in actuality. The very anger she felt at not being allowed to cast herself down, fold her hands under her head, and drop off into unconsciousness, tended to rouse her.

After about half an hour, her entreaties to be allowed to rest became less frequent, and alternated with inquiries as to where she was, whither she was going, why she was forced to walk, and that at night. Then she ceased altogether to complain of drowsiness, and finding she met with no response to her inquiries as to her destination, she became silent; she was now conscious, but her brain was clouded, perplexed. She could remember nothing that would account for her present position. Whether she were in a dream, laboring under nightmare, she could not tell, and purposely she struck her foot against one of the paving blocks of lava, and by the pain assured herself that she was actually awake.

But where was she?

She looked up. The sky was besprent with stars, a sky limpid, tender, vaporless and vast, out of which the stars throbbed with iridescent light in all the changeful flicker of topaz, emerald and ruby. And the air was full of flying stars, in tens of thousands, they settled on rushes by the roadside in chains of fire, they flashed across the eyes, they settled down on the dress; and out of the cool grass shone the steady lustre of innumerable glow-worms.

The milky way, like an illumined veil, crossed the vault, vaporous, transparent with stars shining through it.

From the black monuments on each side hooted the owls, bats swept by, diving out of night to brush by the passers along the road and plunge back into night, like old forgotten fancies of the dreaming mind, that recur and vanish again, in waking hours. Out of the grass the crickets shrilled, and frogs called with flutelike tones at intervals, whilst others maintained an incessant chatter.

Where was she? What were these great fantastic edifices on each side of the road? They were no houses, for out of none glimmered a light. No occupants stood in the doors, or sang and piped on the threshold. These were no taverns, for no host invited to rest within, and praised his fare. The road was forsaken, still as death, and these mansions were the dwellings of the dead. She knew this now—that she was on one of the roads that led from the gates of Rome, lined with tombs. How she had got there she knew not. Least of all did she know for what reason she was being dragged along it. She had thus trudged for a considerable time; she had ceased to speak. She was occupied with her thoughts. Weary she was, but in too great anguish of mind to be aware how weary she was, till tripping on a stone she fell.

Then a voice said:—

"She is full awake now. There is naught to fear. Let her again mount the litter."

"Elymas!" exclaimed the girl, "I know you, I know your voice. What means this? Whither am I being taken?"

"Madam," said the sorcerer in reply, after a pause, "your own eyes shall answer the question better than my lips, to-morrow."

CHAPTER XXIV

ALBANUM

Sleep-drunk, with clouded brain, eyes that saw as in a dream, feet that moved involuntarily, Domitia descended from the litter and tottered in at a doorway when informed that she had reached her destination.

Where that was she did not care, whose house this was mattered nothing to her in her then condition of weariness.

Female slaves bearing lights received her and directed her steps to a chamber where they would have divested her of her garments and put her to bed, had she not refused their assistance, thrown herself on the couch and in a moment fallen fast asleep.

The slaves looked at each other, whispered, and resolved not to torment by rousing her; they accordingly drew the heavy curtains of the doorway and left her to her slumbers.

But weary though Domitia was, her sleep was not dreamless, the song of a thousand nightingales that made the night musical reached her ears and penetrated the doorways of her troubled brain and wove fantasies; the ever-present sense of fear, not dissipated by slumber, weighed on her and gave sombre color to her dreams; the motion of the palanquin had communicated itself in her fancy, to the bed, and that tossed and swayed under her. Her weary feet seemed stung and burnt as though they had been held too close to the fire. Now she saw Lamia's face, and then it was withdrawn; now her mother seemed to be calling to her from an ever-increasing distance.

Yet troubled though her sleep was, it afforded her brain some rest, and she woke in the morning at a later hour than usual, when by the strip of warm light below the curtains she was made aware that the sun had risen.

She started from sleep, passed her hand across her face, pressed her brows, stepped to the doorway, pushed the curtains aside and looked out into a little atrium, in which plashed a fountain, and where stood boxes of myrtles in full flower, steeping the atmosphere with fragrance.

At once two female servants came to her, bowed low and desired permission to assist in dressing her.

With some hesitation she consented.

"Where am I?" she asked.

"By the lake of Alba," answered a dark-faced servant with hard lustrous eyes, and in a foreign dialect.

"In whose house?"

The slaves looked at each other, and made no reply.

Again she put the question.

"Lady, we are forbidden to say," answered one of the slaves.

"At Alba?" muttered Domitia.

Then, as the woman divested her of her tunic, something fell from her bosom on the mosaic floor. The maid stooped, picked it up and handed it to Domitia, who turned it in her palm and looked at it, at first without comprehension. Then she recollected what this was—the amulet given her by Glyceria. It was a red cornelian fish pierced at one end and a fine gold ring inserted in the hole, so that the stone might be suspended.

Domitia was not in a condition of mind to pay attention to the ornament, but she bade one of the servants thread a piece of silk through the ring that she might wear the amulet about her neck, and then she allowed herself to be conducted to the bath.

With suspicious eyes the girl observed everything. She was obviously in a country villa belonging to some Roman noble, and that villa beside the Alban Lake.

The Ælii Lamiæ had no country-house at this place, of that she was aware. She had heard some of the friends of her mother speak of the beauties of the Alban Lake, and then her mother had lamented that the family estate lay by the Gabian puddle. But she could not recall that any one of them had a villa there.

When she left the bath she walked out of the doorway through the vestibule and stood on the terrace.

Below was the sombre lake, almost circular, with the rolling woods of oak and beech flowing down the slopes to the very water's edge, here and there the green covering interrupted by precipitous crags of tuffa. Yonder was the great ridge on which gleamed white the Temple of Jupiter Latiaris, the central shrine of the Latin races, the great pilgrimage place to which the country people turned in every distress.

She had not previously seen the Alban Lake, although Gabii had been her residence for some months, and that was seated on a low spur of the mountains, in the crater of one of which slept this tranquil and lovely sheet of water. But she knew enough about it by hearsay to be sure that she was not misinformed by the slaves as to where she now was. She certainly was beside that lake, near which once stretched Alba Longa, the cradle of the Roman race—a race of shepherds driven from its first seat by volcanic fires, to settle beside the Tiber on the Palatine Hill.

That road along which she had been conveyed during the night was the great Appian Way. It could have been none other, and that led, as she was aware, along the spurs of the Alban mountains.

She walked the terrace, her brow moist with anxious thought.

Why had she been carried off?

By whom had she been swept as by a hurricane from her husband's side?

A sense of numbness was on her brain still, caused by the shock. To Lucius Lamia her heart had turned with the reverence she had borne to her father, with the sweetness and glow of girlish love for one who would be linked with her by a still nearer tie. She could not realize that she was parted from Lamia finally, irrevocably. She was in a waking dream: a dream of great horror, but yet a dream that would roll away and reality would return. She would wake from it in the arms of her dear husband, looking into his eyes, clinging to his heart, hearing his words soothing her mind, allaying her terrors.

If at this time she could have conceived that to be possible which nevertheless was to take place, she would have run to the lake and plunged into its blue waters.

Singularly enough no thought of the vision in the temple of Isis recurred to her. Possibly she was in too stunned a condition of mind; possibly the effects of the narcotic still hung about her, like the vapors that trail along the landscape after a storm of rain at the break of the weather. No thought of hers connected this outrage with Domitian. This was due to the impression produced in her by conversation with her mother, who, she believed, was designing to secure Domitian for herself.

Moreover, the young prince had never shown her any favor. He had studiously neglected her, that he might address himself to Duilia. He had taunted her, sneered at her, but never spoken to her words that might be construed as a declaration of love. She recalled how she had urged her mother to expel him from the house when he sought refuge there; how she had sought to thrust him forth to certain death, to deny him the rights of hospitality. Such was enough to provoke resentment, not to awaken love. Her mother, on the other hand, had bound him to her by the tie of gratitude, for she had saved him at that time of extreme peril.

Seeing the dark slave girl, Domitia signed to her to approach, and asked:

"Where are some of my family? Is not Euphrosyne here—or Eboracus?"

"Lady—none came with you save the servants of our master."

"And he?"

"Madam, I may not say."

"There is that Magus, Elymas; send him to me."

After some delay the sorcerer appeared, and approached, bowed and stood silent with hands crossed on his breast.

"Elymas," said Domitia, "I require you to enlighten me. What is the meaning of this? Why have I been carried away to Albanum? By whose orders has this been done?"

He bowed again—paused, and then, with obvious uneasiness in his manner replied:—

"Destiny will be fulfilled."

"What mean you? Destiny! some drive it before them as a wheelbarrow, and such seem you to be. Why am I here and not in Lamia's house in Rome?"

"Did you not, lady, behold in vision that which was to be?"

She started, lost color and shivered.

"What mean you?"

"The purple."

"The purple! I desire no purple. You speak enigmatically. You have acted a treacherous part in forwarding this act of violence. I have been snatched from my dear husband's side, the Gods who gave me to him have been outraged, I—I, a member of a noble house, a daughter of Domitius Corbulo, have been treated as though the prey of a party of slave-hunters. What next? Am I to be taken into the market-place, and sold by auction? Or am I carried off by freebooters—to be let go for a price? Name me the captain of this robber band, and the price at which I may be ransomed. I promise it shall be paid. But that condign chastisement be inflicted for this insult, that I will also guarantee. I thank the Gods, Rome is not on the confines of the world, that these deeds can be perpetrated with impunity. We are not at Nizibis or Edessa to be fallen upon by Parthians, or held to ransom by Armenians—"

"Young lady," said the Magian, "your words are high-sounding, but your threats are such as cannot be executed, nor is any price asked for your redemption. When you set your foot on the Clivus Scauri, it is a narrow way, between high walls—and there is no option, you must go on. You cannot turn aside to right or left."

"I can turn back."

"The way is broken up behind. You must go forward."

"Whither?"

"Look!"

A number of male slaves came forth from the villa; they were in white.

"Do you know that livery?" asked the sorcerer.

Then Domitia uttered a cry of despair, and threw herself on the ground. Now she did know where she was, in whose power she was, and how hopeless it was for her to expect to escape.

The white was the Imperial livery.

CHAPTER XXV

BY A RAZOR

Two days passed, and Domitia remained undisturbed. No tidings reached her from Rome, but to her great relief the Cæsar Domitian did not appear. That a meeting with him must take place, she was aware, but in what manner he would address her, that she could not guess; whether he would take occasion to exhibit ignoble revenge for her treatment of him on the night when he sought refuge in her house, or whether he would approach her as a lover. This the sequel could alone disclose. The second alternative was what she mainly dreaded.

On the third day, hearing a bustle in the hall, and conjecturing that some one had arrived, and that the critical moment had come, Domitia waited in her chamber with beating heart, and long-drawn sighs. When the curtains were sharply withdrawn, to her surprise and delight her mother entered, radiant in her best toilette, her face, as far as could be judged through the paint, wreathed with smiles.

"Well!" said she.—"But first a seat. You sly fox! who would have thought it? But there—I am content. I have sent out no invitations to a little supper, there is now no occasion for it, and one does not care to spend—without an expectation of it leading to results. To look at your face no one would have supposed that depth in you—and to play us all such a trick, poor Lamia and me. It would really make a widow of a week old laugh. Don't smother me, my dear, and above all, don't cry—that is to say, if you cry do not let your tears fall on my cheek, you know I am—well—well—it might spoil my complexion."

"Mother," gasped the unhappy girl—"O, how can you speak to me in this manner. You know, you must know, I have been carried away against my will. O mother, Lucius does not suppose that—"

"My dear child, it does not concern me in the least, whether the kitten carried off the rat, or the rat the kitten. Here you are in the rat's hole, and all you have to look to is to eat your rat and not let the rat eat you."

"Oh, mother! mother! take me home with you."

"Domitia, do not be a baby. Of course you cannot return. You have bidden farewell to the household Gods, and renounced the paternal threshold."

"Mother—I have embraced the gate-posts of the Lamiæ."

"But the Gods of that family have been unable or unwilling to retain you, they have resigned you to—I cannot say, in conscience, nobler hands, for the Flavian family—well, we know what we know,—but to more powerful hands, that will not let you go. Besides, my dear, I have no wish to have you home again. When a bird has flown, it has said farewell to the nest, to its cracked eggshells and worms, and must find another."

"Do not be cruel!"

"I am not cruel—but what has happened must be accepted, that is the true philosophy of life, better than all that nonsense declaimed by philosophers."

"Mother! I will not stay here."

"Domitia, here you must stay till somebody comes to take you away. Why! as the Gods love me! I expect yet to hear you proclaimed Augusta, and to have to offer incense and to pour a libation on your altar. Think—what an honor to have your wax head among the ancestors, as a divinity to be worshipped—but no—I am wrong there, you would be in the lararium, or set up in the vestibule, a deified ancestress or member of the family is exalted from the atrium to the temple. I really will go out of my way and have a little supper to honor the occasion. I see it all—we shall before long have a college of Flavian priests, and all the whole bundle of mouldy old usurers, and tax-collectors, and their frowsy womankind will be gods, with temples and a cult, and you, my dear! It makes my mouth water."

"But, mother, why am I carried away?"

"Why! O you jocose little creature, why? because some person I know of has taken a fancy to your monkey ways and baby face."

"I belong to Lamia. I have been married to him."

"Oh! that is easily settled. I thank the Immortals, divorce is easily obtained in Rome—with money, influence in Rome—to the end of time, my dear."

"I do not desire to be divorced—I will not be divorced. I love Lucius and he loves me."

"You are a child—just away from your dolls, and know nothing of life."

"But, mother, there are laws. I will throw myself on the protection of the Senate."

Longa Duilia laughed aloud. "Silly fool! laws bind the subjects and the weak, not princes and the strong. Make your mind up to accept what has happened. It is the work of destiny."

"It is an infamous crime."

"My child, do not use such words, what might be crime among common folk is pleasantry among princes. They all do it. It is their right. It is of no avail your attempting resistance. Domitian has taken a fancy to you—he is young, good-looking, Cæsar, all sorts of honors have been heaped on him, and he has but to put out a rake and comb together all the good in the world. And"—she drew nearer to her daughter,—"he may be Emperor some day. Titus has but one lumpy, ugly girl—no son."

"I care not. I hate him! let me go back to Lamia!"

"That is impossible."

"Not if I will!"

"You cannot. You would be stayed by the servants here."

"But you—cannot you help me? O mother, if you have any love for me! For the sake of my dear, dear father!"

"Even if I would, I could not. Why, there is not a court in Rome, not the Senate even can afford you protection and release. The Flavians are up now."

"I will appeal to Vespasian, to the Emperor!"

"He is in Egypt."

The girl panted and beat her head with her hands.

"Lamia! he shall release me."

"He needs some one to release him."

"How so?"

"He insulted Domitian in the Senate House—all because of you, and is under arrest. For less matters, than what he has done, lives have been lost."

"He will never—no, never!" she could not finish her sentence, her heart was boiling over, and she burst into a paroxysm of sobs.

"The Gods! the Gods help me!" she cried.

"My dear Domitia, you might as well call on the walls to assist you. The Gods! They are just as bad as mortals. You may cry, but they will look between their fingers, accept your prayers and offerings and laugh at you as a fool. Why, as the Gods love me! Does not the family derive from Lamius, and was not he the child of Hercules and Omphale? It was very naughty and shocking, and all that sort of thing—but they all do it, and are not in the least disposed to assist you. On the contrary, they will back up the ravisher."

"Then I have no help—save in myself. I will never be his."

"Be advised by me, you foolish child. When you come under a cherry tree you pluck all the ripe fruit; and what you cannot eat yourself you give to your friends. Do you not perceive that having been fortunate enough to catch the fancy of the young Cæsar, you can use this fancy and make large profit out of it? He is already very freely distributing offices to all his friends and such as most grossly flatter him. What may not you obtain for me! That is if I take a liking for any one and wish to marry him, you must positively obtain the proconsulship of Syria or Egypt for him. And as to Lamia, he can be choked off with a prætorship."

The veil was plucked aside, and Domitian entered.

Longa Duilia rose; not so Domitia Longina.

He stood for a moment looking at the girl.

"Saucy still?" he said.

"Wrathful at this treatment," she answered, with her eyes on the ground, and her hands clasped. "Because I would have denied to you a suppliant, the hospitality of our house, must I, unsoliciting it, be forced to accept yours?"

"Domitia, has your mother informed you what I have designed for you?"

"I should prefer that you concerned yourself with your prætorial duties."

Domitian bit his lip. He had been invested with the office of prætor of the city, but in his overweening conceit deemed it unworthy of him to discharge the duties of the office.

"It is my intent, Domitia, to elevate you into the Flavian family."

"O how gracious!" sneered the girl,—"taken up like Trygdeus."

"Domitia!" exclaimed her mother, then at once perceiving that the allusion was lost on the uneducated prince, she said:—

"Quite so, on the wings of the Bird of Jove."[7]

The young man became crimson. He was convinced that there was some bitter sneer in the words of Domitia, and he was ashamed at his inability to comprehend the allusion.

"What I intend for you," said he, moving from the doorway to where he could observe her face, "what I intend for you is what there is not another woman in Rome who would not give her jewels to obtain."

"Then I pray you address yourself to them. Pay your debts with their subscriptions, and leave me who am content to be disregarded, in the tranquillity I so love—with my husband, Ælius Lamia."

"Lamia!" laughed Domitian. "You are to be divorced from him. Your mother is willing."

---

7   The reference was to the "Peace" of Aristophanes. Trygdeus was carried up to the Gods on the back of a dung-beetle.

"My mother has no more power over me. I am out of the paternal family."

"You will consent yourself."

"Who will make me?"

"That will I. It is easy to rend apart—"

"Any fool can break, not all can bind."

"Domitia, be advised and do not incense me."

"I care not for myself. I have but one wish. Let me go. Take, if you will, what is my property, take that of Lamia, but let us retire together to some little farm and be quiet there, drive us, if you will, out of Italy—but do not separate us."

"You talk at random. Follow me."

He led the way, stood in the entrance, holding back the curtain, and Duilia drew her daughter from her seat.

"Come,—Lamia awaits you," said Domitian.

Then the girl started to her feet.

"He is here! You will be generous,—like a prince!"

"Come with me."

She now followed with beating heart. Her cheeks were flushed, a sparkle was in her eye, her breath came fast through her nostrils, her teeth were set.

Without were many lictors lining the way, filling the court.

He led into that portion of the villa where were the baths and entered the warm room. There Domitia saw at once Lamia, stripped almost to the skin, held by soldiers of the prince's guard, his mouth gagged, and a surgeon standing by with a razor.

She would have sprung to him and thrown her arms around him, had she not been restrained.

"Domitia," said the young Cæsar; "you will see how that to divorce you is in my power, unless you consent to it yourself, and give yourself to me."

Domitia trembled in every limb. She looked with distended eyes at Lamia, who had no power to speak, save with his eyes, and they were fixed on her.

A large marble bath stood near, and both hot and cold water could be turned on into it.

She knew but too well what the threat was. Seneca had so perished under Nero,—by the cutting of the veins he had bled to death.

Petronius, master of the Revels to the same tyrant, had suffered in the same manner, and as his blood flowed he had mocked and hearkened to ribald verses till the power to listen and to flaunt his indifference were at an end.

And now the second Nero, not yet full blown, but giving earnest of what he would be, was threatening Lamia with the same death. It was not a gradual and painless extinction, but a death of great suffering, for it led to agonizing cramps, knotting the muscles, and contracting the limbs. Domitia knew this—she had heard the dying agonies of Seneca and Petronius described,—and she looked with quivering lips and blood-less cheeks on him whom she loved best—on the only one in the world she loved, threatened with the same awful death.

She would do anything short of taking the Cæsar Domitian as her husband in place of him to whom she was bound by the most sacred ties,—anything short of that to save the life of Lamia.

The struggle in her bosom was terrible; her head spun, she tried to speak but could frame no words.

She sought some guidance in Lamia's eyes, but her own swam with tears, and she could not read what he would advise.

"My child," said her mother, "of course it is all very sad, and that sort of thing—but it is and must be so. If a wilful girl will not be brought to reason in any other way—well, it is a pity."

Domitian turned to Domitia.

"His life is in your power," said he. "He has insulted me before the Conscript Fathers, and is under arrest. I have brought him hither—to die. But I give his life to you on the one condition that you allow divorce to be pronounced between you and him, and that in his place you accept me."

Domitia turned her face away.

"So be it," said he. "Surgeon, open his veins."

With a slash of the razor across the arm at the fold, an artery was severed, and the black blood spurted forth.

Uttering a cry of horror, Domitia battled with those who held her, to reach and clasp her husband.

"Cut the other arm," commanded the prince, "then cast him into the bath."

"I yield," gasped Domitia, burying her face in her hands and sinking to her knees.

"Then bind up his wound, and let him go!"

"Destiny must be fulfilled," said Elymas who stood behind. "You were born for the purple."

CHAPTER XXVI

INTERMEZZO

The dramatic composer has this great advantage over the novelist, that when he has to allow for a certain amount of time,—it may be for years—to elapse between the parts of his play, he lowers the curtain, the first or second act is concluded, ices, oranges are taken round in the stalls; the orchestra strikes up an overture, the gentlemen retire to the promenade gallery for a cigar, and the ladies discuss their acquaintances, and the toilette of those in the boxes, after having explored the theatre with their glasses.

At Munich and Bayreuth, at the performance of Wagner's operas, the space allowed between the acts is sufficient for a walk and for a meal. Thus the lapse of time between the parts of a drama is given a real expression, and the minds of those who have followed the first part of the story are prepared to accept a change in the conditions of the performers, such as could be brought about solely by the passage of time.

But a novelist has no such assistance, he is not able to produce such an illusion; even when his story appears in a serial, he is without this advantage, for the movement of his tale, when it is rapid, is artificially delayed by the limitations laid down by the editors of the magazines, and the space allotted to him, and when he does require a pause to allow for the gliding away of a certain number of years, that pause consists of precisely the same number of days as intervened in the serial publication, between chapters in which the action should have been continuous.

The writer must, therefore, throw himself on the indulgence of the reader, and plead to be allowed like a Greek chorus to stand forward and narrate what has taken place, during a period of time concerning which he proposes to pass over without detailed account, before he resumes the thread of his narrative.

When Vespasian was hailed Emperor by the troops he was aged sixty-one, and none supposed that his reign would be long. He associated his eldest son Titus with him in government, but would not allow the younger, Domitian, any power.

When the Emperor reached the capital, he learned the misuse Domitian had made of that which he had arrogated to himself, or which had been granted to him by the Senate, in his father's absence. The old Emperor was vastly displeased at the misconduct of his younger son, and would perhaps have dealt severely with him, had he not been dissuaded from so doing by Titus, who pointed out, that as he himself had no son, in all probability Domitian would at some time succeed to the purple.

The young man, kept in the background, not even allowed the command in any military expedition, carefully watched and restrained from giving vent to his natural disposition, chafed at his enforced inactivity, and at the marked manner in which he was set behind his elder brother, a man who, by the capture of Jerusalem, had gained a name, and had attached the soldiery to him. Domitian was known to the military only by his abortive attempt to pluck the laurels in Germany from the brow of his kinsman Cerealis, for the adornment of his own head.

Domitian was granted none of the titles that indicated association in the Empire. He was not suffered to take part in public affairs. His insolence in neglecting the duties of prætor of the city, as beneath his dignity, was punished in this manner. When Titus celebrated his triumph after the Jewish war, with unusual magnificence, he and his father rode in chariots of state, but Domitian was made to follow on horseback. When Vespasian and his eldest son showed themselves in public, they were carried on thrones, whereas Domitian was made to attend in the rear in a litter.

The envious, ambitious young prince, under this treatment was driven to wear a mask, and he affected a love of literature, and indifference to the affairs of state. Titus, who knew less of him than his father, was deceived, but Vespasian was too well aware of the radically evil heart of his younger son to trust him in any way.

Domitia was unable to escape from compulsary association with this imperial cub. Vespasian was unwilling to undo the past, and have the scandal raked up again, and public attention called to it. The minds of the volatile Romans had forgotten the circumstances and were occupied with new matters of gossip. Domitian married Domitia Longina, and the old Emperor after some consideration concluded that she should remain his wife.

But the relations between her and the prince were strained. She hated him for what he had done, and she made no attempt to affect a liking she did not feel.

Lamia remained unmarried; he had cared for no other woman, and he felt that there was not to be found one who could ever be to him what he had hoped Domitia would have proved.

Once Titus asked him his reason for not marrying.

"Why do you inquire?" said Lamia, with a bitter smile, "do you also wish to carry off my wife?"

On the death of the old Emperor, Titus succeeded without any difficulties being raised. His father had already associated him in the Empire and had gradually transferred the conduct of affairs to his hands.

Hitherto the brothers had lived on very good terms with each other, at all events in appearance, and Domitian had been sufficiently prudent to veil his jealousy of Titus, who had shown himself kindly disposed towards his younger brother.

On the accession of Titus, Domitian hoped to be associated with him in government in the same manner as Titus had been with his father. In this he was disappointed, his disappointment got the better of his prudence, and he declared that his brother had falsified the will of Vespasian, who had divided the power equally between them.

On the first day of his reign, Titus designated Domitian as his successor, but he allowed him no independent power; and the young prince at once involved himself in intrigues and sought to rouse the troops to revolt, and to proclaim him in place of Titus.

The condition of Domitia would have been more intolerable than it was, but that Vespasian, up to his death, retained his younger son about his person, in Rome, and it was but rarely that the prince was able to escape to his villa, at Albanum, where Domitia remained in seclusion. And his visits there were not only few and far between, but also brief.

He was in bad humor when there, at liberty to vent his irritation at the manner in which he was treated by his father, and the behavior towards him of Domitia was not calculated to dispel his vapors.

A considerable change had come over her face. The expression had altered; it had been full of sweetness, and the muscles had been flexible. Now it was hard-set and stern.

Domitian cursed her for the fascination she still exercised over him. It was perhaps her unyielding temper, her openly expressed scorn, and her biting sarcasms which stung him to maintain his grip on her, knowing that this was to her torture. Yet her beauty exercised over him a hold from which he could not escape. His feelings towards her were a mixture of passionate admiration and savage resentment. From every one else he met with adulation, or at least respect, from her neither. His will was a law to a legion of sycophants, to her it was something she seemed to find a pleasure in defying.

Domitia nursed her resentment, and this soured her nature and reflected itself in her features.

In the long Chiaramonte Gallery of the Vatican Museum is an exquisite and uninjured bust of Domitia Longina as a girl; the face is one that holds the passer-by, it is so sweet, so beautiful, so full of a glorious soul.

In the Florence Gallery is one of the same woman after Domitian had snatched her away from Lamia, and hidden her in his Alban villa. Lovely the face is still, but the beautiful soul has lost its light, the softness has gone out of the face, and the shadow of a darkened life broods over it.

At Albanum the solitary Domitia had the satisfaction of being attended by her servant Euphrosyne, and the faithful Eboracus was also allowed to be there as her minister.

She occasionally visited her mother in Rome, but the chasm between them widened. Duilia could not understand her daughter's refusal to accept the inevitable and failure to lay hold of her opportunities, and, as she termed it, "eat her rat." The older Duilia grew, the less inclined she was to acknowledge her age, and the more frivolous and scheming she became. She was never weary of weaving little webs of mystery and of contriving plans; and the initiating of all these was a supper. She was well off, liked ostentation, yet was withal of a frugal mind, and never ordered costly dishes, or broached her best wine without calculation that they would lead to valuable results.

It was possible that Vespasian might have interfered in favor of Domitia, had he been made to understand how strongly she disliked the union, but Domitia herself was never able to obtain an interview with the aged Emperor, and Duilia took pains to assure him that the marriage had been contracted entirely with her approval, that the union with Lamia had been entered on without feeling on either side, in obedience to an expressed wish of Corbulo before his death, and that her daughter was quite content to be released.

The period was not one in which the personal feelings of a girl were counted as deserving of much thought, certainly not of being considered by an Emperor, and Vespasian took no steps to relieve Domitia. Titus was better aware of the facts, and had some notion of the wrench it had been to the young married people, but he was not desirous of having the matter reopened. It would not conduce to the credit of the Flavian house, and that was in his eyes a matter of paramount consideration—as the process of deification of the Flavians had already begun.

BOOK II

CHAPTER I

AN APPEAL

"What can I do for thee, Domitia?" asked Titus, who was pacing the room; he halted before the young wife of his brother, who was kneeling on the mosaic floor.

She had taken advantage of her introduction into the Imperial palace to make an appeal to Titus, now Emperor. She had not been allowed to appear there during the reign of Vespasian.

Titus was a tall, solidly built man, with the neck of a bull; he had the same vulgarity of aspect that characterized both his father and brother, and which was also conspicuous in his daughter Julia. The whole Flavian family looked, what it was, of ignoble origin,—there was none of the splendid beauty that belonged to Augustus, and to the Claudian family that succeeded. Their features were fleshy and coarse, their movements without grace, their address without dignity.

If they attempted to be gracious, they spoiled the graciousness by clumsiness in the act; if they did a generous thing, it carried its shadow of meanness trailing behind it.

Titus had not borne a good character before his elevation to the purple. He had indulged in coarse vices, had shown himself callous toward human suffering. Yet there was in his muddy nature a spark of good feeling, a desire to do what was right, a rough sense of justice and much family affection.

It was a disappointment to him that he had but one child, a daughter, a gaunt, stupid girl, big-boned, amiable and ugly.

He knew that Domitian, his younger brother, would in all probability succeed him, but he also was childless. Next to him, the nearest of male kin, were the sons of that Flavius Sabinus, who had been butchered by the Vitellians, and their names were Sabinus and Clemens.

The former was much liked by the people, he was an upright grave man. The second was regarded with distrust, as a Christian. It was not the fact of his following a strange religion that gave offence. To that Romans were supremely indifferent, but that which they could not understand and allow was a man withdrawing himself from the public service, the noblest avocation of a man, because he scrupled to worship the image of the Emperor, and to swear by his genius. They regarded this as a mere excuse to cover inertness of character, and ignobility of mind.

For the like reason, Christians could not attend public banquets or go to private entertainments as the homage done to the gods, and the idolatrous offerings associated with them, stood in their way. The profession of Christianity, accordingly, not only debarred from the public service, but interfered with social amenities. Such withdrawal from public social life the Romans could not understand, and they attributed this conduct to a morbid hatred entertained by the Christians for their fellow-men.

The public shows were either brutal or licentious. The Christians equally refused to be present at the gladiatorial combats and at the coarse theatrical representations of broad comedy and low buffoonery. This also was considered as indicative of a gloomy and unamiable spirit.

There were indeed heathen men who loathed the frightful butchery in the arena, such was the Emperor Tiberius,—and Pliny in his letters shows us that to some men of his time they were disgusting, but nevertheless they attended these exhibitions, as a public duty, and contented themselves with expressing objection to them privately. The objection was founded on taste, not principle, and therefore called for no public expression of reprobation.

Clemens was quite out of the question as a successor. If he was too full of scruple to take a prætorship, he was certainly unfit to be an emperor. Not so Flavius Sabinus his elder brother. Him accordingly, Domitian looked upon with jealousy.

"What can I do for thee?" again asked Titus, and his heavy face assumed a kindly expression; "my child, I know that thou hast had trouble and art mated to a fellow with a gloomy, uncertain humor; but what has been done cannot be undone—"

"Pardon me," interrupted Domitia, "it is that I desire; let me be separated from him. I never, never desired to leave my true husband, Lamia, I was snatched away by violence—let me go back."

"What! to Lamia! That will hardly do. Would he have thee?"

"Tainted by union with Domitian, perhaps not!"exclaimed Domitia fiercely. "Right indeed—he would not."

"Nay, nay," said Titus, his brow clouding, "such a word as that is impious, and in another would be treason. Domitia, you have a bitter tongue. I have heard my brother say as much. But I cannot think that Lamia would dare to receive thee again after having been the wife of a Flavian prince."

Domitia's lip curled, but she said nothing. These upstart Flavians made a brag of their consequence.

"Then," said she, "let me go to my old home at Gabii. I have lived in seclusion enough at Albanum to find Gabii in the current of life—and my mother and her many friends will come there anon. Let me go. Let there be a divorce—and I will go home and paddle on the lake and pick flowers and seek to be heard of no more."

"It would not do for you and Lamia to be married again. It would be a political error; it might be dangerous to us Flavians."

"I should have supposed, in your brand-new divinity that a poor mouse like myself could not have scratched away any of the newly-laid-on gold leaf."

"Domitia," said Titus, who had resumed his walk, "be careful how you let that tongue act—it is a file, it has already removed some of the gilding."

A smile broke out on his face at first inclined to darken.

"There! There!" said he, laughing; "I am not a fool. I know well enough what we were, as I feel what we have become. Caligula threw mud, the mud of Rome, into the lap of my grandfather, because he had not seen to the efficient scouring of the streets. It was ominous—the soil of Rome has been taken away from the divine race of Julius—and has been cast into the lap of us money-lenders, pettyfogging attorneys of Reate. Well! the Gods willed it, Domitia—it is necessary for us to make a display."

"Push, as my mother would say."

"Well—push—as you will it. But, understand, Domitia, though I am not ignorant of all this, I don't like to have it thrown in my teeth; and my brother is more sensitive to this than myself. Domitia, I will do this for you. I will send for him, and see if I can induce him to part from you. I mistrust me,"—Titus smiled, looked at Domitia, with one finger stroked her cheek, and said,—"By the Gods! I do not wonder at it. I would be torn by wild horses myself rather than abandon you, had I been so for-tunate—"

"Sire, so wicked—"

"Well, well! you must excuse Domitian. Love, they say, rules even the Gods, and is stronger than wine to turn men's heads."

He clapped his hands. A slave appeared. "Send hither the Cæsar," he ordered. The slave bowed and withdrew.

Domitian entered next moment. He must have been waiting in an adjoining apartment.

"Come hither, brother," said Titus. "I have a suppliant at my feet, and what suppose you has been her petition?"

Domitian looked down. He had a pouting disdainful lip, a dogged brow, and eyes in which never did a sparkle flash; but his face flushed readily, not with modesty, but shyness or anger.

"Brother," said Domitian, "I know well enough at what she drives. From the moment, the first moment I knew her, she has treated me to quip and jibe and has sought to keep me at a distance. I know not whether she use a love-philtre so as to hold me? I know not if it be her very treatment of me which makes me love her the more. Love her! It is but the turning of a hair whether I love or hate her most. I know what is her petition without being told, and I say—I refuse consent."

"Listen to what I have to propose," said Titus, "and do not blurt out your family quarrels before I speak about them. It is not I only, but all Rome, that knows that your life together is not that of Venus's doves. It is unpleasant to me, it detracts from the dignity of the Flavian family"—he glanced aside at his sister-in-law, and his lips quivered, "that this cat-and-dog existence should become the gossip of every noble house, and a matter of tittle-tattle in every wine-shop. Make an end to it and repudiate her."

Domitian kept his eyes on the floor. Domitia looked at him for his answer with eagerness. He turned on her with a vulgar laugh and said:—

"Vixen! I see thee—naught would give thee greater joy than for me to assent. I should see thee skip for gladness of heart, as I have never seen thee move thy little feet since thou hast been with me! I should hear thee laugh—and I have heard no sound save flout from thee as yet. I should see a sun dance in thine eyes, that perpetually lower or are veiled in tears. Is it not so?"—He paused and looked at her with truculence in his face—"and therefore, for that alone, I will not consent."

"Listen further to me, Domitian," said Titus; "I have a proposition to make. Separate from Domitia, send her back—"

"What, into the arms of Lamia?"

"No, to Gabii. She shall be guarded there, she shall not remarry Lamia."

"I shall take good heed to that."

"Hear me out, Domitian. I have but one child, Julia. The voice of the people has proclaimed itself well pleased with our house. We have given to Rome peace and prosperity at home, and victory abroad. I believe that there are few who regard me unfavorably. But it is not so with thee. Thy folly, thy disorders, thy violence, before our father came to Rome, have not been forgotten or forgiven, and Senate and people look on thee with mistrust. I will give thee Julia to wife. It is true she is thy niece—but since Claudius took Agrippina—"

"Thanks, Titus, I have no appetite for mushrooms."[8]

"Tut! you know Julia, a good-hearted jade."

"I will not consent," said Domitian surlily.

"Hear me out, brother, before making thy decision. If thou wilt not take Julia, then I shall give her to another—"

"To whom?" asked Domitian looking up. He at once perceived that a danger to himself lurked behind this proposal. The husband of Julia might contest his claims to the throne, should the popularity of Titus grow with years, and his own decline.

"I shall give her to our cousin, Flavius Sabinus."

Domitian was silent, and moved his hands and feet uneasily.

Looking furtively out of the corners of his eyes, he saw a flash of hope in those of Domitia.

He held up his head, and looking with leaden eyes at his brother, said:—

"Still I refuse."

"The consequences—have you considered them?"

Domitian turned about, and made a tiger-like leap at Domitia and catching her by her shoulders said:—

"I hate her. I will risk all, rather than let her go free."

---

8   The allusion was to the death of Claudius attributed to poisoned mushrooms administered to him by his wife-niece Agrippina.

CHAPTER II

THE FISH

Domitian had been accorded by his brother a portion of the palace of Tiberius on the Palatine Hill, that was crowded with imperial residences; and Domitia had been brought there from Albanum.

She was one day on the terrace. The hilltop was too much encumbered with buildings to afford much space for gardens, but there were platforms on which grew cypresses, and about the balustrades roses twined and poured over in curtains of flower. Citrons and oleanders also stood in tubs, and against the walls glistened the burnished leaves of the pomegranate; the scarlet flowers bloomed in spring and the warm fruit ripened till it burst in the hot autumn.

Domitia, seated beside the balustrade, looked over mighty Rome, the teeming forum, roofs with gilded tiles of bronze, lay below her, flashing in the sun, and beyond on the Capitol, white as snow, but glinting with gold, was the newly completed temple of Jupiter, rebuilt in greater splendor than before since the disastrous fire.

The hum of the city came up to her as the murmur of a sea, not a troubled one, but a sea of a thousand wavelets trifling with the pebbles of a beach, and dancing in and out among the teeth of a reef; a hum not unlike that of the bees—but somewhat louder, and pitched on a lower note.

Domitia paid no attention to the scene, nor to the sounds, she was engaged with her jewel-box, that she had brought forth into the sun, in order that she might count over her treasures.

At a respectful distance sat Euphrosyne spinning.

Domitia had some Syrian filagree gold work in her hand—it formed a decoration for the head, to be fastened by two pins; the heads were those of owls with opals for eyes.

She laid it aside and looked at her rings and brooches. There was one of the latter, a cameo given her by her mother, of coral of two hues, a Medusa's head, a beautiful work of art. Then she took up a necklace of British pearls from the Severn, she twisted it about her arm and lovely were the pure pearls against her delicate flesh,—like the dainty tints on the rose and white coral of the brooch she had laid aside.

She replaced the chain, and took up a cornelian fish.

"Euphrosyne," said Domitia, "come hither! observe this fish. Thy sister gave it me the day I was married, but alack! it brought me no luck. Think you it is an omen of ill? But Glyceria would not have given me one such."

"Nay, lady, the fish brings the greatest happiness."

"What is its meaning? It is a strange symbol. It must have some purport."

The slave hesitated about answering.

Then, hearing steps on the pavement, and looking round, Domitia called—"Thou! Elymas! who pretendest to know all things, answer me this, I have an amulet—a fish—what doth it portend?"

"What?—the murex? That gives the imperial purple."

"Bah! It is no murex, not a sea snail but a fish. What is the signification?"

"Lady, to one so high, ever-increasing happiness."

"Away! you are all wrong. Happiness is not where you deem it. False thou art, false to thy creed. Thou speak of a divine ray in every man and woman! an emanation from the Father of Light, quivering, battling, straining to escape out of its earthly envelope and soar to its source!— thou speak of this, and in all thy doings and devisings seekest what is sordid and dark!"

The gloomy man folded his cloak about him, and looking at her from under his penthouse brows answered:—

"Thou launchest forth against me without reason. Knowest thou what is a comet? It is a star that circles about the sun and from it drinks in all the illumination it can absorb, like as the thirsty soil in summer sucks in the falling rain, or the fields the outflow of the Alban Lake; then it flies away into space, and as it flies it sheds its effulgence, becoming ever more dim till it reaches infinite darkness and is there black in the midst of absolute nigritude. Then it turns and comes back to replenish its urn."

"Nay," said Domitia, "that can never be. When all light is gone, then all desire for return goes likewise. I know that in myself—I—I am such a comet. When I was a child I longed, I hungered for the light, and in my days of adolescence it was the same, only stronger—it was as a famine. I was the poor comet sweeping up towards my sun; but where my sun was, that—in the vast abyss of infinity—I knew not. I sought and found not, I sought and shed my glory, till there was but a faint glimmer left in me; and now—now all light is extinguished, and with it desire to know, to love, to be happy, to return."

"Madam, you, as the comet, are reaching your apogee, your extreme limit; you must shed all your light before you can return to the source of light."

"What! is that your philosophy? The Father of Light sends forth his ray to expire in utter darkness, predestined this ray of light to extinction. If so—then He is not good. And yet," she sighed, "it is so. I am such. In blackness of night. Look you, Elymas, when I was a child, I laughed and danced; I cannot dance, I can but force a laugh now. I once loved the flowers and the butterflies; I love them no more. My light is gone. The faculty of enjoyment is gone with it. Do I want to return? To what? To the source of light that launched me into this misery? No, not into that cold and cruel fate. Let me go on my inky way, I have no more light to lose—I look only to go out as a fallen star and leave nothing behind me."

"What! when a great future is before you?"

"What future? you have none to offer me that I value. Away with your hints concerning the purple—it is the sable of mourning to me."

She panted. The tears came into her eyes.

"It is you who have wrecked my life—you—you. It was you who devised that crime—when I was snatched away from the only man I loved—the only man with whom I could have been happy—whom I—" she turned aside and hid her face. Then recovering herself, but with a cheek glistening with tears, she said: "I admit it, I love still, and ever shall love. And he loves me. He has taken none to wife, for he thinks on me. There, could darkness be deeper than my now condition? And you did it, you betrayed me into the hands—" she had sufficient self-control not to say to whom, before this man and her slave.

"Lady, it is not I, but Destiny."

"And you, with your tortuous ways, work to ends that you desire, and excuse it by saying, It is Destiny."

"What, discussing the lore of emanations, little woman?" asked the Emperor, coming suddenly up.

Elymas stood back and assumed a deferential attitude. Titus waved him to withdraw, and was obeyed. Then he took Domitia by the hand.

"A philosopher, are you?"

"No, I ask questions, but get no answers that content me."

"Ah! you asked a favor of me the other day and spiced it with a sneer—your jibes hit me."

"I meant not to give pain."

"I have come to you touching this very matter. I am not sure, child, that the scandal is not greater so long as you and Domitian remain linked together, and pulling opposite ways, than if you were parted. Your quarrels are now the talk of Rome, and many a cutting jest is put into your pretty mouth at our expense; invented by others, attributed to you."

"You will have us divorced!" her breath came quick and short.

"Listen to what I propose. Domitia, I am not well. I have this accursed Roman fever on me."

"Sire, I mark suffering in your face."

"It has been vexing me for some days, and it is my intent to leave Rome and be free from business and take my cure at Cutiliæ—our old estate in the Sabine country. Perhaps the air, the waters of the old home, the nest of our divine family—" his mouth twitched, but there was a sad expression in his face—"they may do me good. It is something, Domitia, to stand on the soil that was turned by one's forbears, when they bent as humble farmers over the plough. They were honest men and happy; and when one is down at heart, there is naught like home—the old home where are the bones of one's ancestors, though they may have been yeomen, and one a commissioner, and another an usurer, and so on. They were honest men. Aye! the rate-collector, he was an honest man. Here all is false, and unreal, and—Domitia—I feel that I want to stand on the soil where my worthy, humble, dear old people worked and worshipped, and laid them down to die."

"You are downcast indeed," said Domitia.

"And because downcast, I have been brooding over your troubles, little sister-in-law. Come! I did something for your poor Lamia,—I made him consul, and I will do more. Can you be patient and tarry till my strength is restored? I shall return from my family farm in rude health, I trust, and by the Gods! the first matter I will then take in hand will be yours. I know what my brother is. By Jupiter Capitolinus! if Rome should ever have him as its prince, it will weep tears of blood. I know his savage humor and his sullen mind. No, Domitia, you cannot be happy with him. A cruel wrong was done you, and when I return from Cutiliæ I will right it. You shall be separated!"

She threw herself at his feet.

He smiled, and withdrawing from her clasp, said:—

"I will do more than that for your very good friend, in whom you still take such a lively interest. I shall find means to advance him to some foreign post—he knows Antioch, I will give him the proconsulship of Syria and Cilicia, and so move him away from Rome. And then—" he took a turn, looked smilingly at Domitia, and said,—"I do not see that you need mope at Gabii. You know Antioch; you were there for some years. It is, I believe, not well for a governor to take his wife with him; she has the credit of being a very horse-leech to the province. But I can trust thee, little woman! There, no thanks, I seek mine own interest, and to protect our divine images and the new gilding from the rasp of that tongue. That is the true motive of my making this offer. Do not thank me. On my return from Cutiliæ you may reckon on me."

Then hastily brushing away her thanks, and evading her arms, extended to clasp him, he walked from the terrace.

"Euphrosyne!" cried Domitia, "did you hear! The comet has reached its extreme limit, it is turning—it is drawing to the light—to hope. Happiness is near—ah!"

In her excitement she had struck her jewel-case that stood on the marble balustrade, and sent it, with all its costly contents, flying down the precipice into the thronged lanes at the back of the forum in a glittering rain.

"Ye Gods!" gasped Domitia, "the omen! O ye Gods! the bad omen."

"Lady," said Euphrosyne, "all is not lost"

"What remains? Ah! the Fish!"

"Yes, mistress dear, when all else is lost, remember the Fish."

CHAPTER III

IN THE "INSULA"

"Now, for a while I am as one who has cast off a nightmare," said Domitia to herself. "He is away—why he has attended Titus to the Sabine land I know not, unless the Emperor could not trust him in Rome—or may be, in his goodness he has done it to relieve me of his presence. I will go see my mother."

Domitia ordered her litter and bearers. She had no trinkets to put on, save the fish of cornelian. Her mother liked to see her tricked out, and usually when Domitia paid her a visit she adorned herself to please the old lady,—now she could not assume jewelry as she had lost all her articles of precious stones and metal. So she hung the cornelian amulet about her neck.

When a Roman lady went forth in palanquin, it was in some state. Before her went two heralds in livery, to clear the way and announce her coming at the houses where she purposed calling, then she had six bearers, and attendants of her own sex, carrying her scent bottles, kerchiefs, fans, and whatever she might think it possible she would require.

Domitia was impatient of display, but it had been imposed on her by the Emperor. "The Flavians," said he smiling, "must make a show in public."

A Roman lady was at this period expected to wear yellow hair, if she would be in the fashion. Under the Flavians, it was a compliment to the reigning princes to affect this color. It was true that the word flavus meant anything in color, from mud upwards to what might be termed yellow by courtesy. It was employed as descriptive of the Tiber, that was of the dingiest of drabs, and of the Campagna when every particle of vegetation was burnt up on it, and the tone was that of the dust-heaps. But now that the parsnip-haired Flavians were divine and all-powerful, the adjective was employed to describe the harvest field and gold. Ladies talked of their hair as "flavan" when it had been dyed with saffron and dusted with gold. Not to have yellow hair was expressive of disaffection to the dynasty—so every lady who would be in the fashion, and every husband who wanted office, first bleached and then dyed their hair, and as hair was occasionally thin, they employed vast masses of padding and borrowed coils from German "fraus" to make the utmost show of their loyalty to the august house of the divine Flavii.

Domitia dared not be out of fashion, and she was constrained to submit to having her chestnut hair dredged with gold-dust before she went forth on her visit. For her, conspicuously to wear her hair in its natural color would at once have provoked animadversion, and been interpreted as a publication, in most defiant manner, of the domestic discord that was a topic of gossip in the saloons of Rome.

When she had entered her palanquin, she gave her orders and was carried lightly down the sloping road into the Forum. This was crossed, and then, drawing back the curtains of her litter, she said:—

"Eboracus, tell the fellows not to go at once to the Carinæ. I have a fancy to see the wife of Paris the actor, in the Insula of Castor and Pollux."

She was playing with the fish suspended on her bosom, as she was being conveyed down the hill, and the thought had come to her that she had not seen Glyceria for a long time, and that now was a good occasion as her husband—whom these visits annoyed, and who had in fact forbidden them—was absent from Rome.

The porters at once entered the narrow, tortuous lanes, where the lofty blocks of buildings cut off all sun and made twilight in midday.

As Domitia stepped out of her litter, she saw coming down the street, a man much in the company of Domitian, for whom she entertained a particular dislike. He was a very dark man, and blind; his face was pointed, and his nose long; he ran with projecting head, turning his sharp nose from side to side, like a dog after game. His name was Valerius Messalinus.

One of his slaves whispered something into his ear, and he twisted about his head, and then came trotting in the direction of the litter of Domitia.

"Quick," said she, "I must go in; I will not speak with that man. If he asks for me, say I am out—out of the litter."

She at once entered the block of lodgings, and impatiently waved back her heralds, who would have ascended the stairs before her and pompously announced her arrival.

Taking Euphrosyne along with her, Domitia made her way towards the apartments of the crippled woman. But already the news had spread that men in the imperial livery had entered the building, and there was a rush to the balustrade to see them.

When Domitia reached the first landing, she saw that the women and children, and such men as were there, had ranged themselves on either side, to give her passage, every face was smiling, and lit with pleasure, the men raised their forefingers and thumbs to their mouths, and the women and children strove to catch her hand, or kneeling to touch, raise and kiss the hem of her dress.

If, at one time it had caused surprise that she a rich lady, should enter a common haunt of the poor, it was now a matter of more than surprise, of admiration and delight—to welcome the sister-in-law of the Emperor, one who it was whispered would some day be herself Empress, Augusta, and an object of religious worship.

This sort of welcome always went to the heart of Domitia, and gave her a choke in the throat.

The great people never regarded the poor, save as nuisances. An emperor had said of the populace that it was a wolf he held by the ears. And it was wolf-like because brutally treated, pampered as to food given without pay, supplied with scenes of bloodshed, also without cost, in the arena, every encouragement to work taken from it, every demoralizing, barbarizing influence employed to degrade it.

The great people were supremely indifferent to the sufferings of the small, provided no hospitals for the poor who were sick, no orphanages for the homeless children—let them die—and the faster the better,—that was one wish of the great;—then shall we be alone on the earth with our slaves.

Had these poor people hopes, ambitions, cares, sorrows? Did they love their wives, and hold to their hearts their cubs of children? Did they have any desire that their children should grow up to be good men and virtuous women? Oh, no! such rabble were not of one blood with the rich. They had no fine feelings, they were like the beasts; they were without human souls; and so, when the poor died their bodies were rammed down wells contrived to contain a thousand corpses at a time, and then heaped over with a little earth.

But Domitia had learned that it was not as supposed. Amidst the falsity, barbarity of heart, and coarseness of mind of such as were of the noble Roman order,—the cultured, the rich, the philosophic—there was no sincerity, no truth. She felt happier and better after one of these visits to the Insula in the Suburra as though her lungs had inhaled a purer atmosphere. To the smiles and kisses and blessings lavished on her, she answered with kindly courtesy—and then stepped into the room of the paralyzed woman. Glyceria was as much a cripple as when first visited. She was more wasted—some time had passed—but she hardly seemed older, only more beautiful in her purity, a diaphanous lamp of mother-of-pearl through which shone a supernatural light.

Domitia drew a deep sigh.

"Glyceria," she said, "when I come here, it is to me like seeing a glimpse of blue sky after a day of rain, or—like the scent of violets that came on me the first time I visited you."

"And when you, lady, come to me, it is as though a sunbeam shone into my dark chamber."

"Nay, nay—no flattery from thee, or I shall hate thee. I get that till it cloys. But tell me now, times have been better, and why has not Paris moved into superior quarters? Surely he is in better employ and pay than of old."

"It is so, but only to a small degree," answered the actor's wife. "Paris performs in the grand old dramas in Greek only; in those of Æschylus and Eurypides and Sophocles, he is a tragic actor,—and—" the poor woman smiled, "perhaps home troubles have taken the laughter out of him. He is a sad bungler in comedy. Now the taste of Rome is not for the masterpieces of the ancients. The people clamor to see an elephant dance on a tight-rope, and a man crucified who pours forth blood enough to swamp the stage—the Laureolus! that is the piece to bring down the house. Or some bit of buffoonery and indecency. To that the people crowd. However, we live; I hang as a log about my Paris's neck, but thank God, he loves his log and would not be rid of it, so I am content."

"But if you will suffer me to assist you," said Domitia.

Glyceria shook her head. "No, dear lady, do not take it ill if I refuse your kind offer, made, not for the first time. I am very happy here, very— with these dear kind people about me, running in and out all the day, of- fering their gracious good wishes, lending their ready help. On my word, lady! I do believe that they would all be in tears and feel it as a slight if I were to go; and for myself, I could never be happy away from them."

Domitia stood up and went to the door. Her heart swelled in her bo- som.

"None but the poor know," said the cripple, "how kind, how tender the poor are to one another. Poverty is a brotherhood—we are all of one blood, and one heart."

"And I—" said the great lady, looking out on the balcony with its swarm of people, some busy, some idle, most merry—"And I—" said she, dreamily—"I love the poor."

"Then," said a low firm voice, "thou art not far from the Kingdom of Heaven."

She turned and started.

She recollected him, that stately man with deep, soft eyes. Luke, the Physician.

"I am not surprised," he added, "if you be His disciple," and he touched the cornelian fish.

It was not strange that in this splendid lady with golden hair he did not recognize the timid, crushed girl with auburn locks, he had seen on the Artemis.

But the recollection of that night came back with a rush like a tidal wave, over Domitia, and she threw forth the question, "Why did you cut the thong?"

He did not comprehend her. She saw it, and added, "You do not recollect me. Do you not recall when we nearly ran down the galley of that monster Nero? On that night, we would have sent him to the bottom of the sea, but for you,—you spoiled it all; you cut the thong of the rudder. Why did you prevent us from doing it?"

"Because," answered the physician, "It is written, Vengeance is mine, I will repay, saith the Lord. It was not for you to do it. You were not called to be the minister of His sentence."

"I understand you not."

"My daughter—"

"Hold!" said Domitia, rearing herself up. "Dost thou know to whom thou addressest thyself? I—I thy daughter? I am Domitia Longina, daughter of the great Corbulo, and—" but she would not add, "wife of the Cæsar Domitian."

"Well, lady," said Luke, "forgive me. I thought, seeing that sign on thy breast, and hearing thee say that thou didst love the poor, that thou wast one whom, whatever thy rank and wealth and position I might so address, not indeed as one of the Brethren, but as a hearer and a seeker—enough—I was mistaken."

"What means this fish?" asked Domitia, her wounded pride oozing away at once. "I pray you forgive me. I spoke hastily."

"The fish," said he—

But before he could offer any explanation, Paris appeared, his face expressive of alarm; he had seen the servants in the imperial white below, and knew therefore whom to find in his wife's lodgings.

He hastily saluted her and said:—

"Lady! I beseech thee to go at once. Something has occurred most grave. Return immediately to the palace."

"What is it? Tell me."

"Madam, I dare not name it, lest it be untrue. To speak of it if untrue were to be guilty of High Treason."

"High Treason!" gasped Domitia. She knew what such a charge entailed.

"The Cæsar Domitian has passed at full gallop through the streets, his attendants behind him."

"Whither has he gone?"

"To the Prætorian barracks."

"Ye Gods!"spoke Domitia, she could not raise her voice above a whisper. "Then the worst has happened. My light is out once more."

CHAPTER IV

ANOTHER APPEAL

On reaching the street, Domitia saw at once that the aspect of the populace was changed. Instead of the busy hum of trade, the calls of hucksters, the laugh of the mirthful, a stillness had come on every one; no face smiled, no voice was raised, scarcely any person moved.

Those who had been bustling here and there stood motionless, trade had ceased. A sudden frost had arrested the flow of life and reduced all its manifestations to the lowest term. Such as had been running about collected in clusters, and conversed in whispers. Blank faces looked at Domitia as she entered her litter, with awed respect.

"Eboracus! What is the meaning of this?" asked the lady.

"Madam, I know not. None will confide what they seem to know or to suspect."

"Go forward," said she, "I will visit my mother in the Carinæ. She will know everything."

In another moment her train was in movement, and as she passed along, all bowed and saluted with their hands; they had done as much previously, but without the earnestness that was now observable. In the heart of Domitia was as it were a blade of ice transpiercing it. She was in deadly alarm lest her surmise should prove true.

She would not draw the curtains of her litter, but looked at everything in the streets, and saw that all were in the same condition of stupefaction.

On reaching the entrance to the palace occupied by her mother, Domitia noticed another palanquin and attendants.

"The Vestal Abbess, Cornelia, is with the Lady Duilia," said Eboracus.

"I will go in!—I know her well, and esteem her," said Domitia.

She passed the vestibule, traversed the Atrium and entered the Tablinum. But Longa Duilia was not there. A slave coming up, said that she had entered with the Great Mother into a private apartment, where she might not be disturbed.

"Well! I am no stranger. Lead the way."

In another instant she was ushered into her mother's presence, and at once Duilia bowed to her with profound respect.

"Mother—what does this mean?"

"Here is the Lady Abbess, Cornelia, let me present her to your Highness."

"Mother—I salute the Lady Cornelia—what is this that has cast a shadow over Rome and frightened the people as with an eclipse?"

"My dear, of course you have heard. It may be only rumor and yet,—he was suffering when he left Rome."

"Ye Gods! do not say so! Mother, withdraw your words of bad omen. Naught has befallen him! It was but a slight fever."

"So we esteemed it, but—"

"But, mother—" Domitia panted.

"The news are weighty, and concern you vastly, my daughter."

"It is too horrible for me to think. Surely, surely, mother, it is false."

"Hearken, my dear,—Lady Cornelia, come also to the top of the house. It is a fine situation for seeing and hearing, and out of all reach of eavesdroppers. I hear shouts, I hear horns blowing. Come—speedily! let us to the house-top."

Laying hold of Domitia and the Vestal Superior by the wrists, she drew them with her to the roof.

The silence that had fallen on Rome had passed away, the town was now resonant with horns and trumpets pealing from the Prætorian camp, with the shouting of many voices from the same quarter. In the streets, messengers were running, armed with knotted sticks, and were hammering at the doors of Senators to summon them to an extraordinary meeting. The clash of arms resounded, so also the tramp of feet, as the city police marched in the direction of the Palatine. Here and there rose loud cries, but what they signified could not be judged.

In another moment Eboracus came out on the housetop, and hastening to his mistress, said:—

"Madam, the Augustus—Titus, has been. The Cæsar Domitian is proclaimed Emperor by the troops. The vigiles are hastening in cohorts to swear allegiance."

"I congratulate you—I congratulate you with all my heart!" exclaimed Longa Duilia, throwing her arms round her daughter. "I have reached the summit of my ambition. I vow a kid to Febronia for her opportune—ahem!—but who would have thought the Roman fever would have been so speedy in bringing us luck. Run, Eboracus, summon the housekeeper; order the ancestral masks to be exposed, all the boxes opened, dust the noses with the feather brush; let the lares be garlanded. Tell Paulina to bring out the best incense, not the cheapest this time, and I vow I will throw a double pinch on the altar of the household gods. Who would have thought it! I—I, mother to an empress. I would dance on the house-top, but that my wig is not properly pinned, and might come off. I must, I positively must embrace you again, Domitia; and you too, Cornelia, I am so happy!—As the Gods love me! Wig pinned or not, I must dance."

"Let us go down," said Domitia in a hard tone.

"Come down, by all means," acquiesced her mother. "I must see that the Gods be properly thanked. I stepped this morning out of bed left leg foremost.[9] I knew some happiness would come to me to-day. As the Gods love me! I'll give a little supper. Domitia! whom shall I invite? None of your second-class men now. There!—I thought as much; my wig has come off. Never mind! no men can see me, and women don't count."

On reaching the private apartment of the lady, Domitia said:—

"Mother—a word."

She was white, save that a flame was kindled on each cheek-bone and her eyes scintillated like burning coals.

"Well, my dear, I am all ears—even to my toes."

"Mother, he murdered him. I know it—I feared there was mischief meant, when Domitian attended him to Cutiliæ and took Elymas with him. It was not fever that—"

"My dear, don't bother your head about these matters. They all do it. We women, I thank the Gods, are outside of politics. But—well—well, you must not say such things, not even think them. It is all for the best in the best of worlds. I never had the smallest wish to see behind the scenes. Always eat your meat cooked and spiced, and don't ask to see it as it comes from the shambles. If you are quite positive, then I won't throw away the kid on Febronia. It is of no use wasting money on a goddess who really has not helped."

"Mother," said Domitia, her whole frame quivering with excitement; "I am sure of it. Did not the Augustus give his daughter Julia to Flavius Sabinus? I know that Domitian was alarmed at that. I saw it in his looks, I heard it in his voice; his movements of hand and foot proclaimed it. He feared a rival. He feared what the will of Titus might be—whom he might name as his successor. Mark me, my mother; the first to fall will be Flavius Sabinus."

"Hist! the word is of bad omen."

"It was of bad omen to Sabinus and to Titus alike when Julia was given to her cousin."

---

9   The left was lucky with the Romans, the reverse with the Greeks.

"Well, my dear," said Longa Duilia, "I do not see that we need concern ourselves about politics. You see,—every night, stars drop out of the heavens; the firmament is overcrowded, and those stars that are firmest planted elbow out the weakest. It is their way in heaven, and what other can you expect on earth? Of course, it were much to be desired—and all that sort of thing; but we did not make the world, neither do we rule it. All eggs in a nest do not hatch out, some addle."

"Mother, I will not go back to him."

"Folly! you cannot do other."

"I will not. My condition was bad enough before, it will be worse now."

"Domitia, set your mind at rest. I have no doubt that there have been little unpleasantnesses. Man and wife do not always agree. Your poor father would not be ruled by me. If he had—ah me!—Things would have been very different in Rome. But he suffered for his obstinacy. You must be content to take things as you find them. Most certainly it would be better in every way if peacocks had eyes on both sides of their tails, but as they have not, only very silly peacocks turn about and expose the eyeless side. Make the best of matrimony. It is not many marriages are like young walnuts, that you can peel off the bitter and eat only the sweet. In most, the skin adheres so tightly that you have to take the sweet with the gall, and be content that there is any sweet at all."

"I shall go away. I will not return to the palace."

"Go whither? the world belongs to Domitian. There is not a corner where you can hide. There are officials, and when not officials—spies. I have no doubt that the fish in that tank put up their heads and wish they were butterflies to soar above the roof and get away and sport among the flowers, instead of going interminably about the impluvium. But, my dear, they can't do it, so they acquiesce in tank existence. Yours is the finest and best lot in the world,—and you would surrender it! From being a lioness you would decline to be a house cat!"

Domitia turned abruptly away, tears of anger and disappointment were in her eyes.

She said in a muffled voice:—

"Lady Cornelia, will you come with me?"

"I am at your service," answered the Vestal.

The ladies departed together, and at the portal each entered her own litter.

"To the Atrium Vestæ," said Domitia.

Her retinue started, and a moment after followed that of the Vestal Cornelia.

The streets were full of excited multitudes, currents running up one side, down another, meeting, coming to a standstill, clotting, and choking the thoroughfares, then breaking up and flowing again.

If it had not been for the liveries of the two heralds, the palanquin of Domitia could not have got through, but when it was observed whose litter and servants were endeavoring to make way, the crowd readily divided, and every obstacle gave way immediately. But the Vestal Superior needed not that the Cæsar's wife should open the road for her. As much respect was accorded to her as to Domitia.

Both trains, the one following immediately after the other, entered and traversed the Forum, passed the Temple of Julius, and at the south extremity reached the Atrium of the Vestal Virgins, a long building without a window, communicating with the outer world by a single door.

At this door Domitia descended from her litter, and awaited the Abbess.

Cornelia also stepped from her litter. She was a tall and stately lady of forty years, who had once been beautiful, but whose charms were faded. She smiled—

"You will pay me a visit, as you go your way? that is a gracious favor."

"A lengthy visit," said Domitia.

"Time will never seem long in your sweet society," answered the Vestal and taking Domitia's hand led her up the steps to the platform.

No sooner was Domitia there, than she ran to the altar of the Goddess on which burned the perpetual fire, within a domed Temple, and clasped it. Cornelia had followed her, and looked at her with surprise.

"I claim the protection of the Goddess," said Domitia. "I will not return to the palace! I will be free from him."

Cornelia became grave.

"If your Goddess has any might, any grace, she will protect me. Do you fear? Have you lost your rights? I claim them."

"Be it so," said the Abbess. "None have appealed to the Goddess in vain, none taken sanctuary with her, who have been rejected. She will maintain your cause."

CHAPTER V

ATRIUM VESTÆ

When the Romans were a pastoral people at Alba, then it was the duty of the young girls to attend to the common hearth and keep the fire ever burning. To obtain fresh fire was not always possible, and at the best of times not easy.

Fire was esteemed sacred, being so mysterious, and so indispensable, and reverence was made to the domestic hearth (hestia) as the altar of the Fire goddess.

When the Roman settlement was made on the banks of the Tiber, one hut of a circular form was constituted the central hearth, and provision was made that thence every household should obtain its fire. This hut became the Temple of Hestia or Vesta, and certain girls were set apart to watch the fire that it should never become extinguished.

This was the origin of the institution of the Vestal Virgins, an institution which lasted from the founding of Rome in B. C. 753, to the disestablishment of Paganism, and the expulsion of the last Vestal, in A. D. 394, nearly eleven hundred and fifty years.

No girl under six or above ten years of age was admissible as priestess of the sacred fire, and but six damsels were allowed,—their term of service was thirty years, after which the Vestal was free to return home and to marry. The eldest of the Vestals was termed Maxima, and she acted as superior or abbess over the community.

They enjoyed great possessions and privileges and were shown the most extraordinary respect. Seats of honor were accorded to the Vestals in the theatres, the amphitheatre and the circus.

The Vestals had other duties to perform beside that of maintaining the perpetual fire. They preserved the palladia of Rome, those mysterious articles on which the prosperity, nay, the very existence of the city was thought to depend. What these were was never known. The last Vestal carried them away and concealed them. With her death the secret was lost. Moreover, they took charge of the wills of great men, emperors and nobles, and in times of civil war they mediated between the conflicting parties.

Cornelia gently detached the hands of Domitia from the altar of Vesta, and led her within the college of the Vestals, the only door to which opened on the platform on which stood the Temple.

On entering, she found herself in an oblong court surrounded on all four sides by a cloister, the prototype of those to be in later days erected in the several convents and abbeys, and collegiate buildings of Christendom. In the open space in the midst was the circular treasury of the palladia, at one end was the well whence the virgins drew their water. The cloister was composed of marble columns, and sustained an upper gallery, also open to the court but roofed over and the roof supported on columns of red marble.

Between the columns below and above stood statues of the Superiors, who had merited commemoration. There was no garden, the place for walking was the cloister.

Cornelia conducted Domitia into the reception-chamber, and kissing her said:—

"Under the protection of the Goddess you are safe."

"I trust I in no way endanger your safety."

"Mine!" Cornelia laughed. "There is none above me save the supreme pontiff, and so long as I do no wrong, no one can molest me. But tell me—what wilt thou do?"

"In the first place send out and bid my servants return home; and if they ask when to come for me, answer, when I send for them."

"That is easily done," said the Abbess. She clapped her hands and a slave girl answered and received this commission.

"Now," said she, "now we come to the real difficulty. Here you are, but here you cannot tarry for long. For six days we may accord sanctuary, but for no more. After that we must deliver over the person who has taken refuge with us if required."

"I have for some time considered what might be done. I have been so miserable, so degraded, so impatient, that I have racked my brain how to escape, and I see but one course. When we were at Cenchræa, my mother and I, we were in the house of a Greek client of our family, who was very kind to us, and his wife loved me well. If I could escape thither in disguise, then I think he would be able to secrete me, there are none so astute as are the Greeks, and who so love to outwit their masters."

"But how is this possible?"

"That I know not—only let me get away from Rome, then trust my craft to enable me to evade pursuit. Let it be given out that I am here in fulfilment of a vow, then no suspicion will be roused, and I can take my measures."

"It is not possible," said Cornelia in some alarm. "Have you considered what your mother said? the Augustus is all-seeing and all-powerful, and has his hand everywhere."

"Get me out of Italy, and I shall be safe. I will not return to the Palatine. If my life was hateful to me before, what will it be made now? Then he had some fear of his father and of his brother, now he has none to fear."

The Vestal said, "Let me have time to think this over—and yet, it doth not seem to me feasible."

"Get me but a beggar's suit, and walnut juice, that I may stain my face and hands and arms. I will wash all this gold-dust from my hair—and I warrant you none will know me, with a staff and a wallet, I will go forth, right willingly. I will not return to him."

"That is impossible. You—with your beauty—your nobility—"

"My nobility is of no account with me now."

"You think so, and so it may be whilst untouched, but I am certain the least ruffle would make your pride flash out."

Domitia remembered her resentment at the physician's apparent familiarity.

"Well—my beauty will be disguised."

"That nothing can conceal."

"Oh! do not speak thus, or I shall mistrust you, as I mistrust every one else—except my slave Euphrosyne, and Eboracus, and Glyceria the actor's wife. These seem to me the only true persons in the world. I would cast myself on them, but two are slaves and the other is paralyzed. Consider now, Cornelia, do you not understand how that one may reach a condition of mind or soul, call it which you will, when we become desperate. One must make an effort to break away into a new and free and better life, or succumb and become bad, and dead to all that is noble and true and good, hard of heart, callous to right and wrong. I am at that point. I know, if I were to return to him, and to be Empress of the Roman world, that I should have but one thing to live for—the pride of my place and the blazoning of my position; and to all that which lies deep within me, bleeding, crying out, hungering, and with dry lips—dead."

"My dear lady, you were never made for what you are forced to become."

"Then, why do the Gods thrust me on to a throne that I hate, tie me to a man that I loathe, surround me with a splendor that I despise. Tell me why? O Vesta! immaculate Goddess! how I would that I had been as one of thy consecrated virgins, to spend my days in this sweet house, and pure, peaceful cloister! Do you see? I must away. I am lost to all good—if I remain. I must away! it is my soul that speaks, that spreads its hands to thee, Cornelia! save me!"

She threw herself on her knees and extended her arms to the Vestal Abbess, caught her dress and kissed it.

Cornelia was deeply moved,

"I beseech you, rise," she said, lifting the kneeling suppliant, clasping her in her arms, and caressing her as a child.

"Hearken to me, Domitia, I can think but of one person that can assist us; that is my cousin Celer. He is a good man, and whatever I desire, he will strive to execute as a sacred duty. Yet the risk is great."

"I pray you!—I pray you get him to assist me to escape."

"He must furnish you with attendants. It will not be secure for you to be accompanied by any of your own servants. They might be traced. Celer has got a villa. Stay, I will go forth at once and see him. He can give counsel. Do nothing till my return."

The Vestal Great-Mother left, and Domitia was glad to be alone.

The habitation of the Vestals was wonderfully peaceful, in the midst of busy, seething Rome, and in the centre of its greatest movement. As already said, it had no windows, and but one door that opened on the outer world. It drew all its air, all its light, from the patch of sky over the central court. Figures of Vestals glided about like spirits, and the white statues stood ghostlike on their pedestals.

But to be without flowers, without a peristyle commanding a landscape of garden and lake and trees and mountains! That was terrible. It would have been an unendurable life, but that the Vestal college was possessed of country seats, to which some of the elder of the sisterhood were allowed occasionally to go and take with them some one or two of the novices.

Although there were no flowers in the quadrangle, there was abundance of birds. In and out among the variegated marbles, perching on balustrades, fluttering among the statues, were numerous pigeons, as marbled in tint as the sculptured stonework, and looking like animated pieces of the same; and a tame flamingo in gorgeous plumage basked himself, then strutted, and on seeing a Vestal approach hopped towards her. When, moreover, the same maiden drew water from the well, the pigeons came down like a fall of snow about her, clustering round the bucket to obtain a dip and a drink.

Several hours passed. At length the Abbess returned. She at once sought Domitia, who rose on her entry. Cornelia took both her hands within her own and said:—

"We women are fools, that is what Celer said, when I told him your plan. As he at once pointed out, it is impossible for you to lie hid anywhere in Italy—and impossible to escape from it, unknown to the Augustus. Any one endeavoring to assist you to escape would lose his life, most assuredly. 'I cannot sell smoke to a clown,' said he bluntly—he is a plain man—'I will not put out a finger to assist in such an attempt, which would bring ruin on us all. But,' he said, 'this may be done; let the Lady Domitia retire to one of her own villas, in the country, and commit the matter to the Vestals. Your entreaty is powerful, and if attended by two of the sisters—or perhaps better alone, for this is not a matter to be made public—go to the prince, and plead in the lady's name, that thou feelest unequal to the weight of duties that will now fall on the Augusta, and that thy health is feeble and thou needest repose and country air—then he may yield his consent, at least to a temporary retreat.' But my kinsman Celer advised nothing beyond this. In very truth, nothing else can be done. Most men's noses are crooked,—he said—and he is a blunt man—and those who have straight ones do not like to follow them. But in your case, Lady Domitia, there is practically no other way."

"Then I will to Gabii," said Domitia with a sigh. "If he will force me back—there is the lake."

Then, said Cornelia, "Dost thou know that blind-man Messalinus?"

"Full well—he hangs on to the Cæsar Domitian, like a leech."

"Since thou didst enter the house of us Vestals, he hath been up and down the Via Nova and the Sacred Way, never letting this place out of his eye—blind though he be. Some say he scents as doth a dog, and that is why he works his head about from side to side snuffing the wind. When I went forth he detached two of his slaves to follow—and they went as far as myself and stood watching outside the door of the knight Celer, and when I came forth they were still there, and when I returned to the Atrium of Vesta, I found Messalinus peering with his sightless eyes round the corner. But, I trow, he sees through his servants' eyes."

"He is a bird of ill omen," said Domitia, "a vulture scenting his prey."

CHAPTER VI

FOR THE PEOPLE

Domitia was at Gabii. Cornelia, the Vestal Great Mother had sent her thither in her own litter, and attended by her own servants, but with the assistance of the knight Celer, who had gone before to Gabii to make preparations.

Gabii had none of the natural beauties of Albanum, but Domitia cared little for that. It was a seat that had belonged to her father and here his ashes reposed. The villa was by no means splendid; but then—nor had been that of Albanum when she was first carried thither. Domitian had bought it immediately after the proclamation of his father, and it had then been a modest, but very charming country residence. Since then, he had lavished vast sums upon it, and had converted it into a palace, without having really improved it thereby. To Albanum he had become greatly attached; to it he retired in his moody fits, when resentful of his treatment by his father, envious of his brother, and suspicious of his first cousin Sabinus. There he had vented his spleen in harassing his masons, bullying his slaves, and in sticking pins through flies.

But if Gabii was less beautiful and less sumptuous, it had the immeasurable advantage of not being occupied by Domitian. There, for a while, Domitia was free from his hateful society, his endearments and his insults, alike odious to her.

And she enjoyed the rest; she found real soothing to her sore heart in wandering about the garden, and by the lake, and visiting familiar nooks.

Only into the temple of Isis she did not penetrate, the recollection of the vision there seen was too painful to be revived.

On the third day after she had been in the Gabian villa, Celer came out from Rome. He was a plain middle-aged man with a bald head, and a short brusque manner, but such a man as Domitia felt she could trust.

He informed her that Cornelia had been before the Augustus and had entreated him to allow his wife to absent herself from the palace, and from his company. She had made the plea that Domitia Longina was out of health, overstrained by the hurry of exciting events, and that she needed complete rest.

"But I demand more than that," said she.

"Madam, more than that, my cousin, the Great Mother, dared not ask. The prince was in a rough mood, he was highly incensed at your having withdrawn without his leave, and he saw behind Cornelia's words the real signification. He behaved to her with great ill-humor, and would give no answer one way or the other—and that means that here you are to remain, till it is his pleasure to recall you."

"And may that never be," sighed Domitia.

"The Augustus is moreover much engaged at present."

"What has he been doing? But stay—tell me now—is there news concerning Sabinus?"

"Ah lady! he has been."

"I knew it would be so. On what charge?"

"The Augustus was incensed against him, because under the god Vespasian he had put his servant in the white livery, when Flavius Sabinus was elected to serve as consul for the ensuing year. Unhappily, the herald in announcing his election gave him the title of Emperor in place of consul, through a mere slip of the tongue. But it was made an occasion of delation. Messalinus snapped at the opportunity, and at once the noble Sabinus was found guilty of High Treason, and sentenced to death."

"And what has become of Julia, daughter of the god Titus, the wife of Sabinus?"

"She has been brought by the Augustus to the Palatine."

Next day, the slave Euphrosyne arrived. She had been sent for by Domitia, and was allowed to go to her mistress. She also brought news.

The town was in agitation. It was rumored that the Emperor was about to divorce Domitia, and to marry his niece.

"It would be welcome to me were this to take place," said Domitia. "Come, now, Euphrosyne, bring me spindle and distaff, I will be as a spinster of old."

So days passed, occasionally tidings came from Rome, but these were uncertain rumors. Domitia was enjoying absolute peace and freedom from annoyance in the country. And she had in Euphrosyne one with whom she talked with pleasure, for the girl had much to say that showed novelty, springing out of a mind very different in texture from that usual among slaves.

"It is a delight to me to be still. Child!—I can well think it, after a toilsome and discouraging life, it is pleasant to fold the hands, lay the head on the sod, and go to sleep, without a wish to further keep awake."

"Yes, when there is a prospect of waking again."

"But even without that, is life so pleasant that one would incline to renew it? Not I for one."

Domitia looked up at the fresco of the Quest of Pleasure, and said—
"Once I wondered at that picture yonder, and that all pleasure attained
should resolve itself into a sense of disappointment. It is quite true that
we pursue the butterfly, after we have ceased to value it, but that is because we must pursue something, not that we value that which is attained
or to be attained."

"Ah, lady, we must pursue something. That is in our nature—it is a
necessity."

"It is so; and what else is there to follow after except pleasure?"

"There is knowledge."

"Knowledge! the froth-whipping of philosophers, the smoke clouds
raised by the magicians, the dreams and fancies of astronomers—pshaw!
I have no stomach for such knowledge. No! I want nothing but to be left
alone, to dream away my remainder of life."

"No, lady, that would not content you. You must seek. We are made to
be seekers, as the bird is made to fly, and the fish to swim."

"If we do not seek one thing, we seek another, and in every one,
find—what the pinched butterfly is—dust."

"No, mistress, not if we seek the truth. The knowledge of the truth,
the Summum Bonum."

"But where, how are we to seek it?"

"In God," answered the slave.

"The Gods! of them we know only idle tales, and in place of the tales,
when taken away, there remains but guesswork. There again—the pinch
of dust."

"Lady, if we are created to seek, as the fish to swim, there must be an
element in which to pursue our quest, an end to attain. That is inevitable,
unless we be made by a freakish malevolent power that plants in us desire that can feed only on dust, ever, ever dust. No, that cannot be, the
soul runs because it sees its goal—"

"And that?—"

A bustle, and in a moment, in sailed Longa Duilia, very much painted,
very yellow in hair, and with saffron eyelashes and brows.

"Little fool!" said the mother. "Come, let me embrace thee, yet gently
lest you crumple me, and be cautious of thy kisses, lest thou take off
the bloom of my cheek. Thou art ever boisterous in thy demonstrations.
There, give me a seat, I must put up my feet. As the Gods love me! what
a hole this Gabii is! How dingy, how dirty, how shabby it all looks! As
the Gods—but how art thou? some say ill, some say sulky, some say

turned adrift. As the Gods love me! that last is a lie, and I can swear it. The Augustus distills with love, like a dripping honeycomb. You must positively come back with me. I have come—not alone. Messalinus is with me—a charming man—but blind, blind as a beetle."

"What, that fourfolder!"[10]

"Now, now, no slang! I detest it, it is vulgar. Besides, they all do it, and what all do can't be wrong. One must live, and the world is so contrived that one lives upon another; consequently, it must be right."

"Well have the Egyptians represented the God who made men as a beetle—blind, and this world as a pellet of dung rolled about blindly by him."

"My dear, I am not a philosopher and never wish to be one. Come, we have brought the Imperial retinue for taking you back."

"Whither? To your house in the Carinæ?"

"Oh, my Domitia! How ridiculous! Of course you go to the Palatine, to your proper place. My dear, you will be proclaimed Augusta, and receive worship as a divinity. The Senate are only pausing to adjudge you a goddess, to know whether the Emperor intends to repudiate you or no. It is absolutely necessary that you come back with me."

"My godhead is determined by the question whether I be divorced or not!" exclaimed Domitia contemptuously. "I cannot go with you, mother."

"Then," said Duilia, looking carefully about, "that jade, big-boned and ugly as a mule—you know to whom I refer, will get the upper hand, and your nose will be broken."

"Mother, I ask but to be left alone."

"I will not suffer it. By my maternal authority—"

"Alas, mother! I have passed out of that—I did so at my marriage."

"Well then, in your own interest."

"If I consider that I remain here."

"Avaunt nonsense! Your position, your opportunities! Just think! There is cousin Cnæus must be given a help up. He is a fool—but that don't matter, you must get him a proconsulship. Then there is Fulvia, you must exert yourself to find her a wealthy husband. As the Gods love me! you can push up all your father's family, and mine to boot. Come, get the girls to dress you becomingly and make haste."

"I cannot go."

"You must. The Augustus wills it."

"And if I refuse?"

---

10   Informers were so termed, because they obtained a quarter of the goods of such as they denounced and who were condemned. The Latin word is *quadruplator*.

"You cannot refuse."

"I do so now."

"My dear, by the Good Event! you shall come. You can no more re-fuse him than you can Destiny."

"Let him send his lictors and lead me to death."

"Lead you to—how can you talk such rubbish? You must come. This is how the matter stands. There has been a good deal of disturbance in Rome. As the Gods love me! I do not know why it is, but the people like thee vastly, and the rumor has got about that thou wast about to be repudiated, and that raw-boned filly taken in your place. First there were murmurings, then pasquinades affixed to the statues of the august Domitian. Then bands of rioters passed under his windows howling out mocking songs and blasphemies against his majesty, and next they clus-tered in knots, and that Insula of Castor and Pollux is a nest of insubordi-nation. In fact, return you must to quiet men's minds. You know what a disturbance in Rome is, we have gone through several. By Jupiter! I shall never forget the rocking I went through that night of the Lectisternium. These sort of things are only unobjectionable when seen from a distance. But they leave a taste of blood behind them. When the riot is over, then come proscription; the delators have a fine time of it, and the rich and noble are made to suffer."

"But, mother, let Julia do what she will, I care not."

"Rome does. The Roman rabble will not have it so. You have been familiar with the base and vile multitude. Can't think how you could do it! However, it has succeeded this time and turned out a good move, for the people are clamorous for your return. The Augustus is but recently proclaimed and allegiance is still fresh—and I believe his cousin Ursus has been at him to have you back so as to humor the public."

"Yet, if I refuse to gratify him."

"Then, my dear, of course, it will be a pity, and all that sort of thing; but they all do it, and it must be right. The Augustus would prefer not to use severity—but if severe he must be, he will put down this disturbance with a hand of iron. He bears no actor's sword, the blade of which is innocuous. I will call in Messalinus. He will tell you more."

She clapped her hands; in obedience to her order a slave went outside the villa, and presently returned with the blind man.

He entered, working his sharp nose about, and then made a cringing bow towards the wall—not knowing where stood Domitia.

"Catullus Messalinus," said Duilia, "have the goodness to inform my daughter of the intentions of the Augustus relative to the rabble in the Insula of Castor and Pollux, whence all the agitation proceeds."

"Madam," said the blind informer, "my god-like prince has already given command to clear the streets by means of the prætorian swords. As to that herd in the block of Castor and Pollux, they are reserved for condign punishment, unless my dear lady return at once. They will all—men, women and children, be driven into the circus. There are a pair of British war chariots, with scythes affixed to the axles, and the green drivers will be commanded to hustle round the ring at full speed among this rebellious rabble, to trample them down, and mow them as barley with the scythes—till not one remains alive as a seed of disaffection. What I say is—if a thing has to be done, do it thoroughly. It is true kindness in the end. Of course some must suffer, and one may praise the Gods that in this case it is only the common people."

"The common people," gasped Domitia.

Her eyes were glazed with horror. She saw the Insula, its crowds of busy, kindly, happy people, so good to one another, so affectionate to Glyceria, so grateful to her for visiting among them. And it was she, she by winning their love who was bringing this punishment upon them. In their blind, foolish way, they had misconceived her flight, and in their blind and stupid way, had resented an imaginary wrong offered to her, and because of their generous championship—they must suffer.

With bursting heart, and with a scalding rush of tears over her cheeks, Domitia extended her hand to her mother:—

"I go back," she said, "My people! my poor people, my dear people! It must be so.—For their sake—pro populo."

CHAPTER VII

"THE BLUES HAVE IT!"

On her return to Rome and the palace, Domitia did not see the Emperor, but he sent her notice to be prepared to appear with him in public at the opening of the Circensian Games that he gave to the people in honor of his accession to the principate. This was to take place on the morrow. The games began at an early hour and lasted all day, with an interruption for the cena or supper at two o'clock.

The Circus was close under the Palatine Hill and occupied the valley between it and the Aventine. The site has now been taken possession of for gas-works.

It was a long structure, with one end like a horseshoe, the other was straight, or rather diagonal, a contrivance to enable horses and chariots when starting abreast to have equal lengths to run, which would not have been the case had the end been drawn straight across the circus.

This end was dignified with two towers, with a central gate between them and four arched doors on each side closed with ornamental wooden gates.

The seats of the spectators rose in tiers on all sides, except that of the straight side, where above the great entrance was the seat of the director of the sports. On one side of the Circus near the winning post was the imperial box.

Down the middle of the course ran a wall with statues planted on it, but at each end was a peculiar structure; that near the winning post sustaining seven white balls like eggs, that at the other extremity supporting as many bronze dolphins.

Each race consisted of seven circuits of the course, and a servant of the management at each end attended to the number of rounds made, and as each concluded, an egg was removed at one end, and a dolphin turned round at the other.

There was a separate entrance, with waiting-room for the prince and his party. Domitia with her train arrived first, and remained in the waiting-room till his arrival.

She was dressed in blue, with gold woven into the garment, and her hair was tied up with blue. She looked very lovely, slender and delicate in color, with large earnest indigo eyes, the darkest blue points about her. The sadness of her expression could not be dissipated by forced smiles.

In the waiting-chamber she could hear the mutter of voices in the circus; all Rome would be there. As she had descended from the Palatine she had seen scarce a soul in the forum or the streets, save watchmen and beggars.

Now pealed the trumpets, and next moment the prince, attended by his lictors, and with his niece Julia at his side, entered. He scowled at Domitia, and beckoned her to approach, then, without another word he went out of the door into the Imperial box. Hitherto it had been customary for the Empress to sit with the Vestal Virgins. But Nero had broken this rule and Domitian, the more to emphasize his reconciliation with Domitia, so as to please the people, followed the example of Nero.

Domitia entered and moved to the seat on his right; Julia, that on his left. Behind them poured a glittering retinue of lictors and soldiers, officers of the guard, and officials of the city and chamberlains. At once the whole concourse stood, and thundering cheers with clapping of hands rose from the circus. The Emperor made a hasty, ungracious sign of acknowledgment and took his seat.

The applause, however, did not die away, it broke out afresh, in spurts of enthusiasm, and the name of the Empress was audible—whereupon the cheers were prolonged with immense vehemence.

Domitian heard it. His brow darkened and his face flushed blood-red. He made a signal with his hand, at once three priests attended by men bearing pick and shovel entered the course, and directed their way to the end of the dividing wall or spine; there they threw up the soil, till a buried altar was reached, on which at once burning coals were placed, and all the concourse rose whilst incense and a libation and prayers were offered to the God Consus.

That ended, the fire was extinguished by the earth being thrown over it. Again the altar was buried, and the soil stamped above it.

This ceremony was hardly complete before the great central gates were thrown open, to a peal of trumpets, and heralds entered to proclaim the opening of the sports given by the Emperor, the Cæsar Domitian, the Augustus, son of the God Vespasian, high priest, holder of the tribunician power, consul, perpetual Censor, and father of his country; sports given for the pleasure of his well-beloved, the citizens of Rome, senators, knights, and people generally, and of such strangers as might at the time be in Rome, the centre of the world.

Again rose a roar of approbation, men stood up, stamped, jumped on their seats, and clapped their hands.

Then through the Triumphal Gate came the Circensian procession. This was properly a ceremonial of the 13th September; but in honor of the proclamation of the accession of Domitian to the throne, and to his giving the shows at his own charge, it was now again produced.

First came boys on horseback and on foot, gayly clothed, and immediately behind them the jockeys and runners who were to take part in the games. The racers were divided into four classes, each wearing the color of one season of the year. Green stood for spring, red for summer, blue for autumn, and white for winter. The riders and drivers were dressed according to the class to which they belonged. The chariots were drawn by four horses abreast, and each furnished with an outrider in the same colors, armed with a whip. At once cries rose from all sides, for every jockey and every horse was known by name, some cheered the drivers, some shouted the names of the horses, some proposed bets and others booked such as they had made.

Then came huntsmen with hounds, armed with lances, and behind them dancing soldiers, who clashed shields and swords in rhythm, accompanying their dance with choric song.

Next entered a set of men dressed in sheep's and goats' skins, and with fluttering ribbons, and lastly images of the gods on biers. The "pomp," though a quaint and pretty sight, was looked on with some impatience, as wanting in novelty, and as but a prelude to the more exciting races.

The procession having made the circuit of the arena, retired, and with great rapidity the first four racing chariots were got into their caveæ, the vaults on the right side of the entrance with four doors opening on to the circus.

And now a chalked line was rapidly stretched across the course in front of the gates. A trumpet sounded, the gates were thrown open and the four chariots issued forth and were drawn up abreast behind the line, and lots cast to determine their positions.

Then Domitian stretching forth his hand, threw a white napkin into the arena, the white cord fell, and instantly the chariots started.

The spectators swayed and quivered, shouted and roared, women waved their veils, men clashed potsherds; some yelled out bets, and one or two from behind stumbled forward and fell among the occupants of the benches in front.

At the further end, where the circus described a horseshoe, a gallery of wood projected over the heads of those on the lower stages, to accommodate still more spectators; and these hammering on the boards with feet and fists greatly increased the din.

The roar of voices rolled like a wave along the right side of the circus, then broke into a billow at the curved end, and then surged down to the further extremity, again to swell and run and revolve, as an egg was dismounted, and a dolphin turned.

At each end of the spine, detached from it, were three obelisks, or conical masses of stone, sculptured like clipped yew trees. These were the Metæ.

Attending every charioteer was, as already said, an outrider in his colors, to lash the horses, and to assist in case of accident. Moreover, boys stood about with pitchers of water, to dash over the axles of the wheels when they became heated, or to wash away blood stains, should there be an accident.

Domitia sat watching the race, at first with inattention. Yet the general excitement was irresistible, it caught and carried her out of herself, and the color mounted into her ivory cheek.

The Emperor paid no attention to her, he studiously avoided speaking to her, and addressed his conversation to Julia alone—who was constrained to be present notwithstanding that the execution of her husband had taken place but a few days previously. But her heavy face gave no indication of acute sorrow. It was due to her position and relationship to the prince to be there, and when he commanded her attendance, it did not occur to her to show opposition.

The keenest rivalry existed between the parties of the circus, at a time when political partisanship was dangerous except to the sycophants of the regnant prince, all faction feeling was concentrated on the colors of the race-course. Caligula had championed the green, so had Nero, who had even strewn the course with green sand when he himself, in a green suit, had driven on it. And now Domitian accepted the green as the color that it comported with the dignity of his parvenu dynasty to favor. It was also generally preferred to the other, at any rate in the betting, because it was known that the Imperial favorites were allowed to win the majority of the races.

Yet the jockeys and horses and chariots belonged to different and rival companies, and were hired by the givers of games. It was not in the interest of the other colors to be beaten too frequently. They therefore arranged among themselves how many and which races were, as a matter of course, to be won by the green, and the rest of the races were open to be fairly contested. But the public generally were not let into the secret; though indeed the secret was usually sold to a few book-makers.

Hah! down went the red. In turning the metæ at the further end, the wheel had caught in that of the white, throwing the latter out, but not upsetting the chariot, whereas the car of the red jockey overturned, one horse went down, sprang up again, and would have dragged the driver along, had he not dextrously whipped a curved knife out of his girdle and cut the reins. This was necessary, as the reins of all four horses were thrown over the shoulder and wrapped round the body. Consequently a fall was certain to be fatal unless the driver had time and presence of mind at once to shear through the leathers.

"He is out! the red is out!" roared the mob. Then, "The white! the white is lagging—he cannot catch up!—the red did for him? Out of the way! Out ye two! ye cumber the course."

The white struggled on, driver and outrider lashed the steeds, they strained every muscle, but there was no recovering from the loss of time caused by the lock of wheels, and on reaching the doors on the right, which were at once swung open, both chariots retreated into the caveæ, amidst the groans of such as had bets on their favor.

"It lies now between green and blue!" was the general shout. "On with the Panfaracus!" "Nay! hit the off horse, he sulks, Euprepes!" "Well done, Nereus! Pull well, Auster! Brave horses! brave greens! greens for ever! The Gods befriend the greens!"

Then some one looking in the direction of the imperial box noticed Domitia in her blue habit, with her blue eyes wide distended, and the blue ribbons in her hair. Suddenly in a clear voice he cried,—

"The blue! the blue! It is the color of the Augusta! The blue! Sabaste! I swear by her divinity! I invoke her aid! The blue will win."

Like an electric shock there went a throb through the vast concourse— there were nearly three hundred thousand persons present. At once there rose a roar, it was loud, thrilling, imperious:—

"The blue! It shall win! The color of the Augusta! of the divine Augusta, the friend of the Roman people! The blue! the blue! we will have the blue!"

The drivers lashed furiously, the outriders swung themselves in their saddles to beat the horses. But the gallant steeds needed no scourging, they were as keen in their rivalry as were their drivers and their supporters.

"The last egg! the last dolphin! Again! the green is ahead!" a groan broken by only a few cheers. Wonderful! In the sudden contagion even those who had betted on the green, cheered the rival color.

"Who was that cried out for the blue?" asked Domitian, turning sharply about. "Find him, cast him to the dogs to be torn."[11]

His kinsman Ursus whispered in his ear,—

"It is the actor Paris. Yet do nothing now. It would be inauspicious."

11   On another occasion, a show of gladiators, this savage order was actually given and carried out under the eyes of Domitian.

The command was grudgingly withdrawn.

A gasp—stillness, the extreme meta had been turned; then a restless, quivering sound, men, women, too agitated to shout, held their breath, but muttered and moved their feet—the blue! the blue gains; nay! the green is forging ahead—Ha! Ha! at the last moment in swung the blue, across the white line, one stride ahead of the green.

Then there rolled up a thunder of applause.

"The blue! the dear blue! the blue of the Augusta has it! Ye Gods be praised! I vow a pig to Eppona! The blue has it. All hail to the Augusta! to heaven's blue!"

Domitian turned with a look of hate at his wife, and whispered:—

Nevertheless she shall come in second.

CHAPTER VIII

THE LOWER STOOL

"Come now!" said the Emperor, rising from his seat; "it is time that we should eat. My lady Longina, may it please you to sup with us?"

There was a malevolent glance in his pale watery eye. But Domitia did not see it, she looked at him as little as might be.

She rose at once. So also did Julia, the daughter of Titus, and the Emperor and his train left the circus; but as they withdrew there rose ringing cheers, the people standing on their benches and applauding— not the Cæsar, the Augustus, the Imperator—but her, Domitia, the blue. The people's own true blue. He heard it, and ground his teeth—his face waxed red as blood. Domitia heard it, and her heart filled and her eyes brimmed with tears.

Then Domitian turned and looked at her savagely, as a dog might look at another against which it was meditating an onslaught, and said:—

"Remove that blue—I hate it, and come to the banquet." Then with an ugly leer—"I have sent for the actor to amuse you."

"What actor?"

"Paris, madam, the inimitable, the admired Paris, that he may recite from Greek plays to our pleasure. These Greek tragedians are at a discount. Our people do not care for the dismals. But they are wrong, do not estimate true art. You do that really! You like tragedy! and tragedy you shall have, I warrant you."

The blood mounted to the brow of Domitia at the sneers and covert insinuations. Paris! what was Paris to her? what but the struggling husband of Glyceria? Was it impossible for her to do a kind act, to give expansion to her heart, without misinterpretation, without the certainty of incurring outrage?

She withdrew to her apartments and changed her dress, from the blue to white with purple stripe and fringes. Then she entered the triclinium where the meal was spread.

Domitian was already there, together with Julia, Messalinus, Ursus, and some other friends. The Emperor, standing apart from the latter, said with a sneer to Domitia,—

"So you have shed your blue—a cloud has passed over the azure! That is well. And now, madam, I granted you the first place at the games, in the circus, to humor the people; but in my palace it shall be as I will, not as they. Julia shall take the precedence, and she shall occupy the first position at table, and everywhere. She is the daughter of the God Titus, granddaughter of the God Vespasian-"

"And great grand-daughter of the Commissioner of Nuisances."

"Silence," roared Domitian, "she has the sacred Flavian blood, she is of Divine race, and shall sit by me, recline by me, in the position of honor, and you occupy a stool at my feet. Julia and I will have a lectister-nium of the Gods! Am not I divine?—and she divine?"

"Certainly," answered Domitia, "she is the daughter of a victor who has triumphed, I the wife of a man who will filch laurels from his gener-als, and himself has never seen a battle."

Domitian clenched his teeth and hands, and glared at her.

"I wish to the Gods I could find it in my heart to have thee strangled, thou demon cat."

"I can understand that, having let out the divine blood of the Flavii from the throat of your cousin Sabinus, you would stoop to me."

"What—what—what is this?" exclaimed Messalinus, thrusting his pointed face in the direction of the prince and Domitia; he scented an altercation.

As for her—she wondered at herself, having the courage to defy the Lord of the World. She could not keep down the disgust, the hatred she felt for the man who had wrecked her life, it must out, and she valued not her life sufficiently to deny herself the gratification of throwing off her mind the taunts that rose in it, and lodged on her tongue.

Domitian signed to table—Julia, with a flutter of clumsy timidity, shrank from the place of honor, and looked hesitatingly at her sister-in-law, who without a word seated herself on the stool indicated by the Em-peror. There was no vulgar pride, no ambition in the daughter of Titus.

The guests looked at each other, as Julia was forced by the command of her uncle to recline on the couch properly belonging to his wife, and whispered to each other.

"What, what? Who is where?" asked the ferret-faced Messalinus. "What has been done? Here, Lycus," to a slave, who always attended him, "Tell me, what has been done. In my ear, quick, I burn to know."

Something was communicated in an undertone, and Messalinus broke into a cackle, that he quickly smothered—

"That is admirable, great and god-like is our prince! As a Jew physi-cian said to me, he sets down one and setteth up another, at his pleasure.

That is divine caprice. The Gods alone can act without having to account for what they do. I like it—vastly."

And now at once the sycophant herd began to pay their addresses to Julia, and to neglect Domitia. The former was overloaded with flattery, her every word was repeated, passed on from one to another, as though oracular. Domitian, conspicuously and purposely ignored his wife made to sit at his feet; and raising himself on the left elbow upon his pulvinar, or cushion of gold brocade, talked with his niece, who also reclined instead of sitting.

Domitia remained silent with lowered eyes, carnations flowered in her cheeks. She made no attempt to speak; eat she could not. She felt the slight. Her pride was cut to the quick. The humiliation, before such as Messalinus was numbing. She would have endured being ordered to execution, she would have arranged her hair with alacrity, for the bowstring that would have finished her troubles, but this outrage before members of the court, before the imperial slaves,—and the knowledge that it would be the talk on the morrow of Roman society, covered her with confusion, and filled her soul with wrath, for she had pride—not a little.

Ursus, a kinsman of the Emperor, an elderly man, of good character and upright walk, was near her. He alone seemed to feel the indignity put upon the Empress. His eyes, full of pity, rested on her, and he waited an opportunity to speak to her unheard by others. Then he said, turning his head towards Domitia,—

"Lady, recall the fable of the oak and the bulrush. Humor the prince and you can do with him what you will. Believe me, and I speak sincerely,—he loves you still, loves you madly—but you repel him and that offends his pride. All things are his, in earth,—I may almost say in heaven—and he cannot endure that one frail woman's heart should alone be denied him."

"There are certain waters," answered Domitia, "that turn to stone whatever is exposed to them—even a bird's feather. It is as though I had been subjected to this treatment. My heart is petrified."

"Not so, dear lady, it beats at the present moment with anger. It can also beat with love."

"Never towards him who has maltreated me."

"By the Gods! forbear. I am endangered by listening to such words."

"What—what—what is Ursus saying?" asked Messalinus, who caught a word or two. "He is beside the Augusta—what did he say—and in a low tone also. No treason hatching at the table of our Divine Lord, I trust."[12]

"Here come the jesters and the mimes," said Ursus, "and may the god of Laughter provide such matter for mirth as will satisfy Catullus Messalinus."

"Then it must be a tragedy," said another guest, "for to our blind friend here, naught is jocose unless to some other it be painful."

"We have all our gifts," said Messalinus, smirking.

Then entered some acrobats who went through evolutions, casting knives and catching them, forming human pyramids, ladders, wheels, balancing poles on their chins whilst a boy went through contortions at the top.

But there was no novelty in the exhibition. The Emperor wearied of it, and ordered the performers to withdraw.

Next appeared mimes, who performed low buffoonery in gesture and dialogue, interspersed with snatches of song, that were so offensive to decency that Domitia, who had never seen and heard anything of the kind at her mother's house, sprang to her feet with flaming cheeks, brow and bosom, and made a motion to leave. She knew it—this disgusting performance had been commanded by the prince, for the purpose of humiliating her. She would go. But Domitian, whose malignant glance was on her, saw her purpose and called out,—

"It is my will, Domitia, that you remain in your seat. The cream of the entertainment has yet to come."

Ursus put his hand to her garment and gently drew her down on her seat.

"Endure it," he whispered, "it will soon be over."

"It is the worst outrage of all," said she with heaving breast, and the blood so surged into her eyes and ears that she could see and hear no more.

Indeed, she was hardly conscious when the buffoons withdrew, her eyes rested on the marble floor, strewn with the remains of the feast.[13] But suddenly she started from the dream, or the stupefaction into which she had fallen, by hearing the voice of Paris, the tragic actor.

---

12   The titles of lord and god were given to Domitian by his flatterers, and accepted and used by him, as of right.

13   There are mosaic pavements at Rome representing a floor after a dinner, with crawfish heads, oyster shells, nuts, picked bones, flower leaves, strewn about.

She looked up sharply, and saw him, a tall, handsome man, of Greek profile, and with curly dark hair. He was clad in a long mantle, and wore the buskins. Behind him were minor performers, to take a part in dialogue, or to chant a chorus.

"Lord and Augustus, what is it your pleasure that we represent in your presence?" asked the actor.

"Repeat the speech of Œdipus Coloneus to Theseus towards the close of the drama. That, I mean, which begins, 'O son of Ægeus, I will teach the things that are in store.'"

Paris bowed, and drawing himself up, closing his eyes to represent the blindness of the old king he personated, and with hands extended began:

> *"O son of Ægeus, I will teach the things that are in store.*
> *Myself unguided, straightway go, ye follow, I before.*
> *The spot where I am doomed to die—That spot will I reveal.*
> *But on your lips, I pray you set, to that a holy seal."*

"Do you mark, Domitia?" called the Emperor with bantering tone.

"I have looked under the table, sire, to see whether, like your kinsman Calvisius, you keep there a prompter who has read Eurypides."[14]

Some of the guests hardly controlled their laughter. The deficiency in the education of Domitian was well known.

"Go on, fellow," ordered he surlily. "Skip some lines—it is tedious, draw to the end."

Paris resumed:—

> *"Now let me to that place repair; an impulse from on high,*
> *A sacred impulse carries me to where I'm doomed to die.*
> *O daughter! I must show the way—aye, I, myself, the guide,*
> *To you who hitherto did lead, or clave unto my side.*
> *Nay! touch me not, but suffer me, myself to find the road*
> *That leadeth to the silent tomb, and to the dark abode.*
> *O Hermes! guardian of the soul that fleeteth from this breast!*
> *O Goddess of the darkest night—Give to thy weary rest!*
> *O light! beloved, glorious light! that once did fill these eyes.*
> *Now I embrace thy sacred beams, then turn where shadow lies.*
> *O dearest friends, when well with you, and with this land, recall*
> *Me, as about my bowed head Death's purple shadows fall."*

---

14   Calvisius Sabinus, a rich and ignorant man, made one of his slaves learn Homer by heart, another Hesiod and others the nine Greek lyric poets. When he gave a dinner, he concealed them under the table to prompt him with quotations.

Then the chorus, in rhythmic dance sang:—

"If it be meet—O Goddess thou, unseen whom all men dread,
If it be meet—O awful King who rulest o'er the dead,
Be pitiful unto this man, a stranger in the land,
And gently, without pain acute, conduct him by the hand
From out the world of light into the Stygian deeps below,
Remember how that ever here, he suffered want and woe!
Ye polished iron gates unclose, and as ye backward roll,
Let not the rav'nous monster leap and lacerate the soul.
And then on son of Tartarus advance with pity sweet,
The fluttering, frightened, parted soul, approaching gently
greet!"

"Enough," said Domitian, and waved his hand. "How likest thou that, Domitia?"

"Methinks, sire, the words are ominous. Suffer me I pray thee to retire—for I am not well."

As she rose, she looked at Paris. Their eyes met, and at once a horror—a premonition of evil fell on her, and turned her blood to ice.

He raised his hand to his lips and said in a low tone as she passed him:—

"Morituri te salutant."

"I' faith it is an excellent jest!" said Messalinus—"I relish it vastly."

CHAPTER IX

GLYCERIA

Domitia returned to her apartments, quivering like an aspen in a light air; but no sooner was she there, than she summoned Eboracus, and said to him:—

"Be speedy. Follow Paris, and protect him. There is evil planned against him. Fly—lest you be too late."

The slave departed at once.

Domitia paced the room, in an agony of mind, now shivering with cold, then with face burning. But it was not the humiliations to which she had been subjected that so affected her,—it was fear of what she suspected was meditated against the actor, and through him against Glyceria.

A cold sweat broke out on her brow, and icy tears formed on her long eyelashes. It seemed to her that for her to show favor to any one, was to bring destruction on that person. And hatred towards the Emperor became in her heart more intense and bitter.

She could think of nothing else but the danger that menaced Paris. She went out on the terrace, and the wind blowing over her moist brow chilled her; she drew her mantle more closely around her, and re-entered the palace. Already night was falling, for the days were becoming short.

Her heart cried out for something to which to cling, for some one to whom to appeal against the overwhelming evil and tyranny that prevailed.

Was there no power in earth above the Cæsar? There was none. No power in heaven? She could not tell; all there was dark and doubtful. There was a Nemesis—but slow of step, and only overtaking the evil-doer when too late to prevent the misery he wrought, sometimes so lagging as not to catch him at all, and so blind as often to strike the innocent in place of the guilty. No cry of the sufferer could reach this torpid Nemesis and rouse her to quicker action. She was a deity bungling, deaf and blind.

Again she tramped up and down the room. She could endure to have no one with her. She sent all her servants away.

But the air within was stifling. She could not breathe, the ceiling came down on her head, and again she went forth.

Now she could hear voices below in the Sacred Way. She could see lights, coming from several quarters, and drawing together to one point where they formed a cluster, and from this point rose a wail—the wail of the dead.

She wiped her brow. She was sick at heart, and again went within, and found Eboracus there, cast down and silent.

"Speak," she said hoarsely.

"It was too late. He had been stabbed in the back, whilst leaving the palace, and a pupil was assassinated at the same time, because somewhat resembling him."

Domitia stood cold as marble. She covered her mouth for a moment with her right hand, and then in a hard voice said:—

"Inform Euphrosyne. I cannot."

Then she turned away, went to her bed-chamber, and was seen of none again that night. Several of her female slaves sought admission to undress her, but were somewhat roughly dismissed.

In that long night, Domitia felt as one drowning in a dark sea. She stretched out her hands to lay hold of something—to stay her up, and found nothing. She had nothing to look forward to, no shore to which she might attain by swimming, nothing to care for, nothing to cling to. There was no light above, only the unsympathetic stars that looked down on the evil there was, the wrong that was done, and cared not. The pulsation of their light was not quickened by sense of injustice, they did not veil their rays so as to hide from them the horrors committed on earth. There was no light below, save the reflection of the same passionless eyes of heaven.

She felt as though she were still capable of the sense of pain, but not of being sensible to pleasure.

The faculty of being happy was gone from her forever, and life presented to her a prospect of nothing better than gray tracts of monotonous existence, seamed with earthquake chasms of suffering.

Next day she rose white and self-restrained, she summoned to her Euphrosyne, but did not look at her tear-reddened eyes.

"Euphrosyne," said she, "I bid you go, and take with you Eboracus, I place you both wholly at the disposal of your sister—and bid her spare no cost, but give to him who has been, a splendid funeral at my expense. Here is money. And—" she paused a moment to obtain mastery over herself, as her emotion threatened to get the upper hand—"and, Euphrosyne, tell Glyceria that I shall go to see her later. Not for a few days, not till the first agony of her grief is over; but go I will—for go I must—and I pray the Gods I may not be a cause of fresh evil. O, Euphrosyne, does she curse me?"

"Glyceria curses none, dear mistress, least of all you. Do not doubt, she will welcome you when you do her the honor of a visit."

"If she were to curse me, I feel as if I should be glad—glad, too, if the curse fell heavy on my head—but you know—she knows—I meant to do well, to be kind—to—but go your way—I can speak no more. Tell Glyceria not to curse me—no—I could not bear that—not a curse from her."

Euphrosyne saw by her mistress's manner, by her contradictory words, how deeply she was moved, how great was her suffering. She stooped, took up the hem of her garment, and kissed the purple fringe. Then sobbing, withdrew.

That day tidings came to Domitia to render her pain more acute.

The kindly, sympathetic people in the insula of Castor and Pollux, in poetic, picturesque fashion had come with baskets of violets and late roses, and had strewn with the flowers the spot stained with the blood of Paris.

This was reported to the Emperor, and he sent his guards down the street to disperse the people, and in doing this, they employed their swords, wounding several and killing two or three, of whom one was a child.

Three days later, Domitia ordered her litter and attendants that she might go to the Insula in the Suburra.

She had said nothing of her intentions, or probably Domitian would have heard of them—she was surrounded by spies who reported in his ear whatever she did—and he would have forbidden the visit.

Only when the Forum had been crossed, did she instruct the bearers as to the object of her excursion.

On entering the block of lodgings and ascending the stairs Domitia was received with respect but with some restraint. The people did not press about her with enthusiasm as before; they knew that it was through her that evil had overtaken them, and they dreaded her visit as inauspicious.

Yet there was no look of resentment in any face, only timorous glances, and reverential bows, and salutations with the hand to the lips. The poor folk knew full well that it was through no ill-will on her part that Paris and his pupil, and some of their own party had fallen.

It was already bruited about that Julia daughter of Titus was honored in the palace, and advanced above Domitia, the Empress. Some said that Domitian would repudiate his wife, that he might marry his niece, and that he waited only till the months of mourning for her husband were passed, so as not to produce a scandal. Others said that he would not repudiate Domitia, but treat her as Nero had treated Octavia, trump up false charges against her and then put her to death.

Already Domitia was regarded as unlucky, and on the matter of luck attaching to or deserting certain persons, the Roman populace were vastly superstitious.

And now, although these poor creatures loved the beautiful woman of imperial rank who deigned to come among them, and care for one of their most broken and bruised members, yet they feared for themselves, lest her presence should again draw disaster upon them.

Domitia was conscious rather than observant of this as she passed along the gallery to the apartment of Glyceria.

At the door to the poor woman's lodgings she knocked, and in response to a call, opened and entered. She waved her attendants to remain without and suffer none to enter.

Then she approached the bed of the sick woman, hastily, and threw herself on her knees beside it.

"Glyceria," she said, "can you forgive me?"

The crippled woman took the hands of Domitia and covered them with kisses, whilst her tears flowed over them.

This was more than the Empress could bear. She disengaged her hands, threw her arms about the widow, and burst into convulsive weeping.

"Nay, nay!" said Glyceria, "do not give way. It was not thy doing."

"But you fear me," sobbed Domitia, "they do so—they without. Not one touched, not one kissed me. They think me of evil omen."

"There is nothing unlucky. Everything falls out as God wills; and whatever comes, if we bow under His hand, He will give sweetness and grace."

"You say this! You who have lost everything!"

"Oh, no! lady," then the cripple touched the cornelian fish. "This remains."

"It is a charm that has brought no luck."

"It is no charm. It is a symbol—and to you dark. To me full of light and joy in believing."

"I cannot understand."

"No—that I know full well. But to one who does, there is comfort in every sorrow, a rainbow in every cloud, roses to every thorn."

"Glyceria," said Domitia, and she reared herself upon her knees, and took hold of both the poor woman's hands; so that the two, with tear-stained cheeks, looked each other full in the face. "My Glyceria! wilt thou grant me one favor?"

"I will give thee, lady, anything that thou canst ask. I should be ungrateful to deny thee ought."

"It is a great matter, a sharp wrench I ask of thee," said the daughter of Corbulo.

"I will do all that I can," replied the widow.

"Then come with me to the palace. Here you have none to care for you, none to earn a livelihood for you,—I want you there."

Glyceria hesitated.

"Do you fear?"

"I fear nothing for myself."

"Nor I," said Domitia. "Oh, Glyceria, I am the most miserable woman on earth. I thought I could not be more unhappy than I was—then come—I will not speak of it,—thy loss—caused unwillingly by me, because I came here—and that has broken my heart. I have done the cruellest hurt to the one I loved best. I am most miserable—most miserable." She covered her face, sank on the bed and wept.

The widow of the player endeavored to soothe her with soft words and caresses.

Then again Domitia spoke. "I have no one, I have nothing to look to, I am as one dead, and the only life in me is hate, that bites and writhes as a serpent."

"And that thou must lay hold of and strangle as did Hercules."

"I cannot, and I will not."

"That will bring thee only greater suffering."

"I cannot suffer more."

"It is against the will of God."

"But how know we His will?"

"It has been revealed."

Again Domitia threw her arms about the sick woman, she pressed her wet cheek to her tear-moistened face, and said:—

"Come with me, and tell me all thou knowest—and about the Fish. Come with me, and give me a little happiness, that I may think of thee, comfort thee, read to thee, talk with thee—I care for no other woman. And Euphrosyne, thy sister, she is with me, and I will keep thee as the apple of mine eye."

"Oh, lady! this is too great!"

"What? anon thou wouldst deny me naught, and now refusest me this."

"In God's name so be it," said Glyceria. "But when?"

"Now. I will have no delay, see—" she went to the door and spoke with her slaves. "They shall bear thee in my litter, at once. Euphrosyne shall tarry here and collect thy little trifles, and the good Eboracus, he shall bear them to thy new home. O Glyceria! For once I see a sunbeam."

Never could the dwellers in the Insula have dreamt of beholding that which this day they saw. The actor's crippled widow lifted by imperial slaves and placed in the litter of the Empress, the Augusta, to whom divine honors had been accorded. And, further, they saw the cripple borne away, down the lane of the Suburra in which was their block of lodgings, and the Empress walked by the side, holding the hand of the patient who lay within.

They did not shout, they uttered no sound indicative of approval, no applause. They held their breaths, they laid their hands on their mouths, they looked each other in the eyes—and wondered what this marvel might portend. A waft of a new life had entered into the evil world, whence it came, they knew not, what it would effect, that also they could not conceive—whom it would touch, how transform, all was hid from their eyes.

CHAPTER X

THE ACCURSED FIELD

No notice was taken by Domitian of the presence in the palace of the murdered actor's widow. It concerned him in no way, and he allowed the unfortunate woman to remain there, under the care of his wife, and without making any protest.

Domitia found an interest and a delight in the society of the paralyzed woman, so simple in mind, gentle in thought, always cheerful, ever serene, who lived in an atmosphere of love and harbored no resentments.

She marvelled at what she saw, but it was to her an unattainable condition. Her own affections were seared, and a gnawing hate against the man who had blighted her life, and to whom she was tied, ever consumed her.

She was like a dead plant in the midst of spring vegetation. It looks down on the beautiful life about its feet, but itself puts forth no buds, shows no signs of mounting sap.

Every now and then Glyceria approached the topic of the Fish, and the mysteries involved in the symbol, but would not disclose them, for she saw that Domitia, however miserable she felt, however hopeless, was not in a frame of mind to receive and welcome the interpretation. For in her, the one dominating passion was hate—a desire to have her wrongs revenged, and a chafing at her powerlessness to do anything to revenge them.

Her treatment by Domitian was capricious. At one time he neglected her; then he went sometimes out of his way to offer her a slight; at others he made real efforts to heal the breach between them, and to show her that he loved her still.

But he met with not merely a frosty but a contemptuous reception, that sent him away, his vanity hurt, and his blood in a ferment.

In her indifference to life, she was able to brave him without fear, and he knew that if he ordered her to execution she would hail death as a welcome means of escape from association with himself.

His blundering and brutal tyranny was no match for her keen wit cutting into him, and maddening him. He revenged himself by a coarse insult or by a side blow at her friends. She was without ambition. Many a woman would have endured his treatment without repining, for the sake of the splendor with which she could surround herself, and the towering position which she occupied. But neither had any attraction for Domitia. The one thing she did desire, to be left alone in retirement, in the country, that he could not, he would not accord her.

Usually, when he was in his splendid villa at Albanum, she elected to remain in Rome, and when he came to the palace on the Palatine, if permitted, she escaped to Albanum; but he would not always suffer this.

Thus a wretched life was dragged on, and the heart of Domitia became harder every day. It would have become as adamant but for the presence of Glyceria, whom the Empress sincerely loved, and who exercised a subtle, softening and purifying influence on the princess.

Glyceria saw how the Empress suffered, and she pitied her, saw how hopeless the conditions were for improvement; she saw also what was hidden to other eyes, that circumstances were closing round and drawing towards a crisis.

Beyond a certain point Glyceria could effect nothing, once only did she dare to suggest that the Augusta should assume a gentler demeanor towards the sovereign of the world, but she was at once cut back with the words:—

"There, Glyceria, I allow no interference. He has wronged me past endurance. I can never forgive. I have but one hope, I make but one prayer—and that for revenge."

When Domitian was at Albanum, the Empress enjoyed greater freedom. She was not compelled when she went out, to journey in state; and she could make excursions into the country as she pleased. The absence of gardens on the Palatine and the throng of servants and officers made it an almost intolerable residence to her, beautiful as the situation was, and splendid as were the edifices on it. Nor was this all. Domitian had not rested content with the palaces already erected and crowding the summit of the rock,—those of Augustus, of Tiberius, and of Caligula, he must build one himself, and to find material, he tore down the golden house of Nero.

But the construction of his palace served still further to reduce the privacy of the Palatine, for it was thronged with masons, carpenters and plasterers. Indeed the Palatine hill-top was almost as crowded and as noisy as was the Forum below.

From this, then, Domitia was glad to escape to a little villa on the Via Nomentana, on a height above the Anio, commanding a view of the Sacred Mount.

On one occasion, when Domitian was away at Albanum, she had been at this modest retreat, where she was surrounded by a few servants, and to which she had conveyed Glyceria, to enjoy the pure air and rest of the country.

But she was obliged to return to Rome; and with a small retinue, and without heralds preceding her, she started, and in the morning arrived at the Porta Collina. Then Eboracus, coming to the side of the litter, said:—

"Lady, there is a great crowd, and the street is full to choking. What is your good pleasure? shall we announce who you are, and command a passage?"

"Nay," answered the princess, "my good Eboracus, let us draw aside, and the swarm will pass, then we can go our way unconcerned. I am in no precipitate haste, and, in faith, every minute I am outside Rome, the better satisfied am I."

"But, madam, it is an ill spot, we are opposite the Accursed Field."

"That matters not. It is but for a brief while. Go forward, Eboracus, and inquire what this crowd signifies. Methinks the people are marvellously still. I hear no shout, not even a murmur."

"There be priests leading the way."

"It is some religious rite. Run forward, Eboracus, and make inquiries. That boy bears an inverted torch."

The sight was extraordinary. A procession of priests was advancing in silence, and an enormous crowd followed through the gate, pouring forth like water from a sluice, yet without a word spoken. The only sound was that of the tramp of feet.

The place where Domitia had halted was just outside the Collina gateway, where was the wall of Servius Tullius and in its moat, thirty feet deep, but dry, out of which rose the wall of massive blocks to another thirty above the level of the ground.

This ditch was a pestilential refuse place into which the carcasses of beasts, foul rags, sometimes even the bodies of men, and all the unmentionable filth of a great city were cast. So foul was the spot, so unwholesome the exhalations that no habitations were near it, and the wide open space before the wall went by the designation of the Accursed Field.

And now, through the gateway came a covered hearse, and at each corner walked a youth in mourning garb, one bearing a lamp and oil, another milk in a brass vessel, a third water, and a fourth bread. Now, and now only, with a shudder of horror, did Domitia suspect what was about to take place. She saw how that as the crowd deployed, it thickened about one portion of the bank of the ditch, and she saw also the battlements above crowded with the faces of men and women leaning over to look down into the dyke. And there, at one spot in the fosse stood three men. Instinctively Domitia knew who they were—the executioner and his assistants.

But who was to be put to death—and on what charge, and by what means?

Now the hearse was slowly brought to the edge of the moat and the curtains were raised.

Then Domitia saw how that within, prostrate, lay a woman, bound hand and foot to the posts by leather straps, with her face covered, and her mouth muffled that her cries might not be heard.

She saw the attendants of the priests untie the thongs and the unfortunate woman was raised to a sitting posture, yet still her face was veiled, and her hands were held by servants of the pontiff. Now one by one the attendants descended into the moat bearing the lamp and the bread and milk, and each handed what he had borne in the procession to the executioner, who gave each article as received to one of his deputies; and the man immediately disappeared with it.

Domitia's heart beat furiously, she put forth her head to look, and discovered a hole at the base of the wall, and through this hole she discerned the twinkling light of the lamp as it passed within, then it was lost. The bread followed, the milk and the water, all conveyed into some underground cellar.

And now the chief pontiff present plucked the veil from the face of the victim, and with a gasp—she could not cry out, the power was taken from her—the Empress recognized Cornelia.

She made an effort to escape from her litter, and fly to her friend with outstretched arms, but Eboracus, who with white face had returned, caught and restrained her.

"Madam," he said in a low tone, vibrating with emotion, "I pray you, for the sake of the Gods—do nothing rash. Stay where you are. No power—not that of the Sacred Twelve can save her."

"Ye Gods! But what has she done?"

"She has been accused of breach of her vows, and condemned by the Augustus, as Chief Priest—" in a lower tone, hardly above a whisper, "unheard in her defence."

"I must go to her."

"You must not. Nothing can save her. Pray for a speedy death."

With glazed eyes, with a surging in her ears, and throbbing in the temples—as in some paralyzing nightmare—Domitia looked on.

And now the gag was removed, and with dignity the Great Mother of the Vestals descended from the bier. She stood, tall and with nobility in her aspect, and looked round on the crowd, then down into the moat, at the black hole under the roots of the wall.

"Citizens, by the sacred fire of Vesta, I swear I am innocent of the charge laid against me, and for which I am sentenced. No witnesses have been called. I have not been suffered to offer any defence. I knew not, citizens, until I was told that I was sentenced, that any accusation had been trumped up against me. Thou, O Eternal God—above all lights in the firmament, Thou, O Sovereign Justice that holdest true balances—I invoke Thee—I summon the Chief Pontiff who has sentenced me, before your just thrones, to answer for what is done unto me this day. I summon him for midnight three days hence."

Then the deputy of the Chief Pontiff, who presided at the execution, Domitian being absent at Albanum (he being Pontifex Maximus), raised his arms to heaven in silent prayer.

His prayer ended, he extended his hand to Cornelia, but she refusing his help, unaided descended into the fosse.

The vast concourse was as though turned to stone by a magician's wand—so immovable was it and so hushed. Some swallows swept screaming along the moat, and their shrill cries sent a shudder through the entire concourse, wrought to such a tension, that even the note of the birds was an intolerable addition.

The Vestal reached the mouth of the pit—the ends of a ladder could be seen at the threshold of this opening. It was evident that the opening gave access to a vault of some depth.

Beside it were stones from the wall piled up, and mortar. As soon as the Abbess reached the opening, she turned, and again declared her innocence. "The Emperor," said she in clear, firm tones, "has adjudged me guilty, knowing that my prayers have obtained for him victory, triumph and an immortal name. I repeat my summons. I bid him answer before the throne on high, at midnight, three days hence."

Then she looked steadily at the blue sky—then up at the sun,—to take a last view of light. With calmness, with fortitude, she turned, and entering the opening began to disappear, descending the ladder.

In so doing her veil caught in one of the ends of the side poles of the ladder. She must have reascended a step or two, for her hand was visible disengaging the white veil, and then—hand and veil disappeared.

Immediately stones were caught up, trowels and mortar seized, and with incredible celerity the opening was walled up. The pontiff applied his leaden seal.

"Be speedy! Remove her! Run—" shouted Eboracus, for his mistress had fallen back in the litter in a dead faint,—"At once—to the Palace!"

CHAPTER XI

AGAIN: THE SWORD OF CORBULO

Eboracus was able to open a way for the litter through the crowd, now clustered on the bank of the dyke, watching as the workmen threw down earth and stones, and buried deep that portion of the wall in which was the vault where the unhappy Abbess Cornelia was buried alive. And now the populace broke forth in sighs and tears, and in murmurings low expressed at the injustice committed in sentencing a woman without allowing her to know that she had been accused, and of saying a word in her own defence. Some of the crowd was drifting back into Rome, and by entering this current, the train of Domitia travelled along.

Eboracus returned from the head of the litter repeatedly to the side, to look within and ascertain whether his mistress were recovering. At the first fountain he stopped the convoy and obtained for her water to bathe her face, and at a little tavern, he procured strong Campanian wine, which he entreated her to sip, so as to nerve her.

As the litter approached the Forum, the crowd again coagulated and at last remained completely stationary. Again the street was blocked.

Eboracus went forward and forced his way through, that he might ascertain the cause, and whether the block was temporary and would speedily cease. He came back in great agitation, and said hastily to his mistress:—

"Lady, you cannot proceed. Suffer me to recommend that you go to the Carinæ and tarry there—with your lady mother for a while, till your strength is restored, and till the streets be more open."

"Eboracus—what is going on? tell me."

"Madam, there is something being transacted in the comitium that causes all the approaches to be packed with people. We might make a circuit—but, lady! I think if you would deign to repose for an hour at your mother's house, after what you have suffered, it would be advisable."

"Tell me what is taking place in the comitium."

"I should prefer, lady, not to be asked."

"But I have asked."

"Then, dear mistress, do not require of me to make answer."

"Answer truly. Tell me no lie. What is it?"

He hesitated. Then Domitia said:—

"Look at my hand, it is firm, it does not tremble. Nothing that I hear can be worse than what I have seen."

"Lady—your strength has already failed."

"And now I have gathered my resolution together, and can bear anything. I adjure you, by your duty to me—answer me, what is taking place in the comitium, what is it that causes the streets leading thereto to be impassable."

"If I must reply—"

"If you do not, I will have you scourged."

"Nay, lady, that is not like thee. It is not fear that will make me speak, but because I know that if I do not, the information can be got from another."

"Well—what is it?"

"The knight Celer, on the same charge as that which lost the Great Mother Cornelia, is being whipped to death with the scorpion."[15]

"By the same orders? To my mother's in the Carinæ."

Hastily Domitia drew the curtains of her litter, and was seen no more, spoke no more till she reached the door of Longa Duilia.

Here she descended and entered the house.

"My dear Domitia! my august daughter! What a pleasure! What an honor!"

The lady Duilia started up to embrace the Empress.

Domitia received the kiss coldly, and sank silent on a stool.

Her mother looked at her with surprise. Domitia was waxen white, her eyes with dark rings about them, and unnaturally large and bright. The color had left her lips and these were leaden in hue.

Domitia did not speak, did not move. She remained for some moments like a statue.

"As the Gods love me!" exclaimed her mother after a long pause, "you are not going to be ill, surely—nothing dangerous, nothing likely to end unhappily. Ye Gods! and I have so much I want you to do for me. Tell me, I entreat you. Hide nothing from me. You are suffering. Where is it? What is it? Shall I send for a doctor?"

"Mother, no doctor can cure me. It is here,"Domitia pressed her hands to her heart—"and here," to her temples. "I am the most miserable, the most unfortunate of women."

"Ye Gods! He has divorced you?"

"No, mother. I would that he had."

---

15   A scourge of leather thongs and nails knotted in them.

"Then what is the matter? Have you eaten what disagrees with you? As the Gods love me! you should not come out such a figure. Who was your face-dresser to-day? she ought to be crucified! Not a particle of paint—white as ivory. Intolerable—and it has given me such a turn."

Domitia made no reply.

"But what is it? What has made you look like Parian marble?"

"The Great Mother Cornelia—" Domitia could say no more, a lump rose in her throat and choked her. Then all at once she began to shiver as though frost-stricken and her teeth chattered.

"I have an essence—you must take that," said the lady Duilia. "My dear, I know all about that. An estimable lady. I mean she was so till the Augustus decreed otherwise. I am sorry, and all that—but you know—well, these things do happen and must, and I dare be bound that some are glad, as it makes an opening for another needy girl, of good family of course. What is one person's loss is another's gain. The world is so and we can't alter it, and a good thing, I say, that it is so."

"Mother—she was innocent."

"Well, well, we know all about that. Of course it was all nonsense what was charged against her, that we quite understand. It would never have done for the real truth to have been advertised."

"And what was the truth?"

"My dear Domitia! How can you ask such a silly, infantile question? It was your doing, you must understand that. You threw yourself on her protection, embraced the altar of Vesta, and Cornelia with the assistance of Celer did what she could to further your object in leaving Rome. If people will do donkey-like things they must get a stick across their backs. It is so, and always will be so in this world, and we cannot make it otherwise."

"I thought so. I was sure it was so," said Domitia gravely. There was an infinity of sadness, of despair in her tone. "Mother, I bring misfortune upon all with whom I have to do."

"Ye Gods! not on me! I hope to be preserved from that! Do not speak such unlucky words—they are of bad omen."

"I cannot help it, mother, it is true. I am the most unfortunate of women myself—"

"You speak rank folly. Ye Gods forgive me! saying such a thing to one who is herself divine. But, it is so—you are positively the most fortunate of women. What more do you desire? You are the Augusta, the people swear by your genius and fortune."

"By my fortune! Alack poor souls!"

"And is it not a piece of good fortune to be raised so high that there is none above you?"

"My fortune! The Gods know—if they know anything—that I would gladly exchange my lot with that of a poor woman in a cottage who spins and sings, or of a girl among the mountains who keeps goats and is defended by a boisterous dog. Mother, listen to me. I have brought misfortune on Lucius Lamia, I have caused the death of that harmless actor Paris, I have been the occasion of Cornelia being—buried alive—watching the expiring of the one lamp. Ye Gods! Ye Gods! I shall go mad—and of Celer also.—He—"

She held her face, rocked herself on the seat and sobbed as if her heart would break.

"Yes," said the old lady, roused to anger at her daughter's lack of appreciation of the splendor of her position. "Yes, child, and mischief you will work on every one, if you continue in the same course. Do men say that the Augustus is morose? Who made him so?—you by your behavior. Do they say that he is severe in his judgments? Who has hardened him and made him cruel?—You—who have dried up all the springs of tenderness in his breast. He was not so at first. If he be what men think—it is your work. You with your stinging words goaded him to madness and as he cannot or will not beat you, as you deserve, he deals the blows on some one else. Of course he cuts away such as you regard and love—because they obtain that to which he has a right, but which you deny him."

"He—he—a right!"

Domitia started up, anger, resentment, hatred flared in her eyes, stiffened the muscles of her whole face, made her hair bristle above her brow.

"He a right, mother! he who tore me away from my dear Lamia, to whom I had given my whole heart, to whom I had been united by your sanction and our union blessed by the Gods! He who violated hospitality, the most sacred rights that belong to a house, who repaid your kindness in saving his life—when he was hunted like a wolf, by breaking and destroying, by trampling under his accursed heel, the brittle, innocent heart of the daughter of her who had protected him! No, mother, I owed him no love. I have never given him any, because he never had a right to any. Mother—this must have an end."

She sank into silence that continued for some while.

Duilia did not speak. She did not desire another such explosion, lest the slaves should hear and betray what had been said. Presently, however, she whispered coaxingly:—

"My dear Domitia, you are overwrought. You have eaten something that has affected your temper. I find gherkins always disagree with me. There, go and take a little ginger in white wine, and sleep it off."

Domitia rose, stiffly, as though all her joints were wooden.

"Yes, mother, I will go. But there is one thing I desire of thee. I have long coveted it, as a remembrancer of my father—may I take it?"

"Anything—anything you like."

Domitia went to the wall and took down the sword of Corbulo, there suspended.

"It is this, mother. I need it."

Then she departed.

"That sword—ah!" said Duilia. "It has been a little overdone. I have caught my guests exchanging winks when I alluded to it, and dropped a tear. O by all means she shall have it. It has ceased to be of use to me."

CHAPTER XII

THE TABLETS

Elymas the sorcerer stood bowing before Domitia, his hands crossed upon his breast.

She looked scrutinizingly into his dark face, but could read nothing there. He remained immovable and silent before her, awaiting the announcement of her will.

"I have sent for thee," she said. "How long, I would know, before the sixth veil falls?"

"Lady and Augusta," answered the Magian, "remember that when thou lookest out upon the Sabine Mountains, on one day all is so distinct that thou wouldst suppose a walk of an hour would bring thee to them. On the morrow, the range is so faint and so remote, that thou wouldst consider it must require days of travel to attain their roots. It is so with the Future. We look into its distance and behold forms—but whether near or far we know not. This only do we say with confidence, that we are aware of their succession, but not of their nearness or remoteness."

"What! and the stars, will they not help thee?"

"There is at this time an ominous conjuncture of planets."

"I pray thee, spare me the details, and tell me that which they portend."

"Is it thine own future, Augusta, thou desirest to look into?"

"Elymas, my story has been unfolded—to what an extent it has been managed by such as thyself, that I cannot judge. But of a certainty it was thou who didst contrive that I was carried away from my husband's house. Then what followed, the Gods know how far thou wast in it, but I have heard it said that the God Titus would not have had his mortal thread cut short but that, when in fever, thou didst persuade him to a bath in snow water. It is very easy to predict what will be, when with our hands we mould the future. And now—I care not whether thou makest or predictest what is to be—but an end there must be, and that a speedy one—for thine own safety hangs thereon."

"How so, lady?"

"The Augustus has been greatly alarmed of late at sinister omens and prophesies; and he attributes them to thee. Perhaps," with a scornful intonation, "he also is aware that fulfilment is assured before a prophesy is given out."

The Magus remained motionless, but his face became pale.

"I know, because at supper with his intimates, Messala and Regulus and Carus, he swore by the Gods he would have you cast to savage dogs, and he would make an example of such as filled men's minds with expectation of evil."

"Lady—"

But Domitia interrupted him. "Thou thinkest that I say this to alarm thee and bend thee to my will. If the Augustus has his spies that watch and repeat to him whatsoever I do, whomsoever I see, almost every word I say—shall not I also have a watch put upon him? Even now, Magus, that I have sent for thee, and that thou art closely consulted by me this has been carried to his ears, and as he knows how I esteem him, he will think this interview bodes him no good."

"When, Lady Augusta, was this said?"

"The Emperor is this day returned from Albanum, and the threat was made but yesterday. Who can say but that the order has already been given for thy arrest, and for the gathering together of the dogs that are to rend thee."

The man became alarmed and moved uneasily.

"Magus," said Domitia, "I cannot save thee, thine own wits must do that. Find it written in the stars that thy life is so bound up with that of the Cæsar, that the death of one is the extinction of the other; or that thou holdest so potent a charm that if thou wilt thou canst employ it for his destruction. It is not for me to point out how thou mayest twist out of his grasp—thou art a very eel for slipperiness, and a serpent for contrivance. What I desire to know is—How much longer is this tyranny to last, and how long am I to suffer?"

Then the magician looked round the room, to make sure that he was unobserved; he raised the curtain at the door to see that none listened outside, and satisfied that he was neither observed nor overheard, he pointed to a clepsydra.

This was an ingenious, but to our minds a clumsy, contrivance for measuring time. It consisted of a silver ball, with a covered opening at the top, through which the interior could be replenished. About the base of the globe were minute perforations through which the liquid that was placed in the vessel slowly oozed, and oozing ran together into a drop at the bottom which fell at intervals into the bucket of a tiny wheel.

When the bucket was full, the wheel revolved and decanted the liquid whilst presenting another bucket to the distilling drops.

At each movement of the wheel a connection with it gave motion to the hand of a statuette of Saturn, who with his scythe indicated a number on an arc of metal. The numbers ranged from one to twelve, and the contrivance answered for half the twenty-four hours.

"Lady," said the Magus, "before Saturn has pointed to the twelfth hour—"

Steps were heard, approaching the room, along the mosaic-laid passage, and next moment, the curtain was snatched aside, and Domitian, his face blazing with anger, entered the apartment of his wife.

"So?" said he, "you are in league with astrologers and magicians against me! But, by the Gods! I can protect myself."

He clapped his hands, and some of the guard appeared in the doorway.

"Remove him," said the Emperor. "I have given orders concerning him already. Hey! Magus! knowest thou what will be thy doom, thou who pretendest to read the fate of men in the stars?"

"Augustus," answered the necromancer, "I have read that I should be rent by wild dogs."

"Sayest thou so? Then by Jupiter! I will make thy forecast come to naught. Go, Eulogius!—it is my command that he be at once, mark you, this very night, burned alive. We will see whether his prophecies come true. Here is my order."

Domitian plucked a packet of tablets from his bosom, bound together with a string, drew forth one, and wrote hastily on it, then pressed his seal on the wax that covered the slab and handed it to the officer.

Then the guard surrounded the astrologer, and led him away.

Domitian waved his hand.

"Every one out of earshot," ordered he, and he walked to the window and looked forth.

It was already night; to the south the sky was quivering with lightning, summer flashes, without thunder.

"A storm, a storm is coming on," said the Emperor; "there'll be storms everywhere, and lightning falling on all sides—portents they say. So be it! as the sword of heaven smites, so does mine. But it falls not on me, but on my enemies. Domitia," said he, leaving the window, "there has been a conspiracy entered into against my life, and the fools thought to set up Clemens—he, that weakling, that coward; but I have sent him to his death, and those who were associated with him, the sentence is gone forth against them also."

"I marvel only that any in Rome are suffered to live."

"Minerva gives me wisdom—to defend myself."

"Any wild beast can employ teeth and claws."

"Domitia," he came close to her, "I am the most lonely of men. I have no friends; my kinsmen either have been, or hate me; my friends are the most despicable of flatterers, who would betray their own parents to save their own throats; I use them, but I scorn them. You know not what it is to be alone!"

"I! I have been alone ever since you tore me from Lamia."

"Lamia!" he ground his teeth; "still Lamia! But by the Gods! not for long. And you—you my wife whom I have loved, for whom I would have done anything—you are against me; you take counsel with a Chaldæan how long I have to live; the Senate, the nobles hate me, and by Jupiter, they have good cause, for I cut them with a scythe like ripe wheat. That was a good lesson of Tarquin to his son Sextus to nip off the heads of the tallest poppies. And the people—you have been currying favor with them—against me; the soldiers alone love me, because I have doubled their pay; let another offer to treble it and, to a man, they will desert me. By the Immortals! it is terrible to be alone—and to be plotted against, even by one's wife."

He walked the room, flourishing his tablets, then halted in front of the clepsydra.

"What said that star-gazer about the twelfth hour?" he asked. "Walls have ears, nothing is said that does not reach me. So, old Saturn, with thy scythe, dost thou threaten? Then I defy thee—ha! I saw the storm was coming up over Rome."

A long-drawn growl of thunder muttered through the passages of the palace.

"I saw no flash," said the prince, "yet lightning falls somewhere, maybe to kindle the pyre on which that sorcerer will burn; I care not. Fire of heaven fall and strike where and whom thou wilt!"

He went again to the window and looked forth. The air was still and close. The sky was enveloped in vapor and not a star could be seen. A continuous quiver of electric light ran along the horizon. Then the heavens seemed to be rent asunder and a blaze of lightning shot forth, blinding to the eyes.

Domitian turned away, and laid the tablets on the marble sideboard as he pressed his hands to his eyeballs.

"By the Gods!" he exclaimed a moment later, "here comes the rain; it descends in cataracts; it falls with a roar."

He paced the room, halted, stood in front of the clepsydra and looked at the dropping water. The water had been reddened, and it seemed like blood sweated out of the silver globe. At that moment the wheel revolved, and sent a crimson gush into the receiver. With a jerk Saturn raised his scythe and indicated the hour ten.

The Emperor turned away, and came in front of Domitia.

"None have ever loved me," he said bitterly, "how then can it be expected that I shall love any? my father disliked me, my brother distrusted me—and you—my wife, have ever hated me. I need not ask the cause of that. It is Lamia, always Lamia. Because he has never married you think he still harbors love for you; and you—you hate me because of him. It is hard to be a prince, and to be alone. If I hear a play—I think I catch allusions to me; if it be a comedy—there is a jest aimed at me; if a tragedy, it expresses what men wish may befall me. If I read a historian, he declaims on the glories of a commonwealth before these men, these Cæsars became tyrants, and as for your philosophers—away with them, they are wind-bags, but the wind is poisonous, it is malarious to me. When I am at the circus, because I back green—you, the entire hoop of spectators cheer, bet on the blue—to show me that they hate me. At the Amphitheatre, if I favor the big shields, then every one else is for the small targets. A prince is ever the most solitary of men. If you had protested that you loved me, had fondled me, I would have held you in suspicion, mistrusted your every word and look and gesture. Perhaps it is because that you have never given me good word, gentle look, and gesture of respect that I feel you are true—cruelly true, and I have loved you as the only true person I know. Now answer me—you asked after my death?"

"Yes," answered Domitia.

"I knew it."

"And," said she, in cold, hard tones, looking straight into his agitated, twitching countenance, "I bear to you a message."

"From whom?"

"From Cornelia, the Great Mother."

"Well, and what—" he stopped, some one approached the door. "What would you have?"

The mime Latinus appeared.

"Well—speak."

"Sire, the rain extinguished the pyre, before that the astrologer was much burnt; then the dogs fell on him, as he was unbound, and they tore him and he is dead."

"Ye Gods!" gasped Domitian, putting up his hand. "His word has come true after all."

Domitia signed to the actor to withdraw.

"You have not heard the message of Cornelia."

He did not speak.

"She has summoned you, the Augustus, the Chief Pontiff, the unjust Judge, to answer before the All-righteous Supreme Justice, above—before the scythe points to Twelve."

Domitian answered not a word, he threw his mantle about his face and left the room.

He had left his tablets on the table.

CHAPTER XIII

THE HOUR OF TWELVE

For some moments Domitia remained without stirring. But then, roused by a glare of lightning, succeeded by a crash so loud as to shake the palace, she saw in the white blaze the tablets of the Emperor lying on the table.

At once, aware of the importance of what she had secured, she seized them, and went to the lamp to open them.

They consisted of thin citron-wood boards, framed and hinged on one side, the surfaces within covered with a film of wax, on which notes were inscribed with a stile or iron pen. There were stray leaves that served for correspondence, orders and so forth, but what Domitia now held was a diptych, that is to say, two leaves hinged, like a book-cover, which had included loose sheets and were bound together by strings.

She at once opened the diptych, and saw on the first page:—

"To be executed immediately:—
In the Tullianum, by strangulation,
   Lucius Ælius Lamia Plautius Ælianus.
To be torn by dogs:—
   The Chaldæan Elymas, otherwise called Ascletarion."

On the second leaf:

"To be executed on the morrow:—
By decapitation:
   Petronius Secundus, Præfect of the Prætorium.
   Norbanus, likewise Præfect of the Prætorium.
By strangling, in the Tullianum:
   Parthenius and Sigerius, Chamberlains of the Palace.
To be bled to death:
   Stephanus: steward to my niece Domitilla.
   Entellus: Secretary *a libellis*."

The words applying to Lamia acted on her as a blow against her heart. She staggered to a stool, sank on it and struggled for breath.

But the urgency of the danger allowed no delay—she rallied her strength immediately, flew from the room and summoned Eboracus.

To him, breathless, she said: "Fly—summon me at once Stephanus the steward, Petronius and Norbanus, præfects, and the chamberlains Parthenius and Sigerius. Bid them come to me at once—not make a moment's delay."

She sank again on the stool and put her hands to her temples and pressed them.

The lightning continued to flare and the thunder to roll. There ensued a turmoil, and a sound of voices crying; then a rush of feet. Euphrosyne entered with startled mien—"My mistress! The bolt of heaven has fallen on the Palatine, and the chamber of the Augustus has been struck. The Temple of the Flavians is on fire, and is burning in despite of the rain."

The chamberlain, Parthenius, entered.

"Augusta!" said he, "the lightning has struck that part of the palace occupied by Cæsar. He must have his apartment for the night on this side."

"That is well," answered Domitia. "Parthenius, have you received my message from Eboracus?"

"No, lady."

"Then read this," she extended to him the wax tablets.

The chamberlain turned ash gray and trembled.

"Parthenius," said Domitia, "it is no vain augury that lightning has struck the Temple of the Flavians, and driven Cæsar from his apartments. Let his place of rest be to-night in the room adjoining this—and—if he wakes—" she looked at the clepsydra, as at that moment with a click the wheel turned and Saturn moved his scythe—"there is but an hour in which the fate of more than yourself, of Lamia—of Entellus must be decided. Take the tablets."

Scarce had she spoken, before quick steps were heard, and in a moment Domitian entered.

Parthenius hastily concealed the tablets by throwing a fold of his garment over the hand that held them. "Sire," said he, "I have come to announce that thy chamber must be on this side."

"Go thy way," said Domitian roughly, "see to it that I have a bed brought at once. Hast heard, Domitia, the fire has fallen!"

"Sire," said Parthenius, "I haste to obey and pray the Gods that in spite of thunder and lightning you may sleep sound and not wake."

The Emperor walked to the clepsydra, and laughed scornfully. "The bolt of Jove has missed me," said he. "The red-handed One made a mistake. I am wont to be in bed at this hour—by good luck, this night I was not. He has levelled his bolt at my pillow and burnt that—I am escaped scot-free. Now I have no further fear."

"The temple of your divine family is in flames."

"What care I? I will rebuild it—the majesty, the divinity of the Flavians resides not in stones and marble—it is incorporate in Me. I may have been in danger for a moment. Now I snap my fingers in the face of that blunderer Jove, who burnt a hole in my pillow instead of transfixing my head. And yon old Chronos—" he made a sign of contempt towards scythed Time, "I defy thee and thy bucket of blood. Twelve o'clock! In spite of Jove's bolt, and the summons of Cornelia—I shall be asleep by that hour."

"I pray the Gods it may be so."

Then Domitian went out precipitately. His defiant attitude, his daring talk did not serve to disguise the alarm which he felt. Suddenly, after having left the room he turned, came back and said, "Domitia! What sword is that? What need has a woman with a sword?"

He pointed to that of Corbulo, suspended against the wall.

He went to it and took it down.

"Leave it," said she harshly. "It is that on which my father fell. It is stained likewise with the blood of Nero."

He held it by the scabbard. She caught the handle and, as he turned, drew forth the blade.

At the same moment he heard steps in the passage approaching the door, and without noticing that he held but the sheath, or else purposing to demand the weapon itself later, when the interruption was over, he walked towards the entrance uttering an expression of impatience, holding the empty scabbard in his right hand.

In the doorway stood Stephanus, a freedman, the steward of Flavia Domitilla, wife, or rather widow of Clemens, whom Domitian had recently put to death. Domitilla had been exiled, and the Emperor had appropriated to his own use the estates of his kinsman.

"Why camest thou hither?" asked the prince roughly. "I shall have enough to say to thee on the morrow because of thy embezzlements."

"Augustus! I am innocent."

"A thief, a vile purloiner, a blood-sucking leech, that has fattened as do all thy kind on thy masters. Go thy way—I want thee not here."

And striding towards him, with Corbulo's scabbard he struck the freedman across the face.

Stephanus uttered a cry of rage and pain, and instantly smote at the Emperor with a dagger he had held concealed in his sleeve.

"What, hound! You dare! You shall be flayed alive! Ho! to my aid!"

Stephanus threw himself on the Emperor.

Then Domitia stepped between the struggling men and the doorway, and with one hand drew together the curtains so as to muffle the cries.

"To my aid! to my aid!" called Domitian, as the powerful steward grappled him, and struck his dagger into the thigh of the prince.

"To my aid! Ho, a sword!" shouted the Emperor, and he grasped the weapon of the steward but so that, holding the blade with his hand, the weapon cut it across and the blood streamed forth.

He now made an effort to reach the doorway; and the steward, holding him, strove to wrench away the dagger and inflict a mortal wound. But Domitian, aware of his object, with his bleeding hand retained his grasp of the blade.

All at once, the Emperor let go his hold, and seizing the steward by the head drove his thumbs into his eyes.

Stephanus instantly dropped the dagger in his attempt to save himself from being blinded.

The two men twisted and writhed in grapple with each other. The freedman was a powerful man—it was for this reason he had been sent to despatch the prince. But Domitian was battling for his life. Though his legs were thin and out of proportion to his body, he was a strong man—he had ever maintained his vigor by exercise of the muscles and had never weakened himself by excess in eating and drinking.

By a happy turn he flung Stephanus, but clasped by him fell with him on the floor.

And now the two men rolled and tossed in a tangled mass together. Their snorts and gasps and the bestial growl of rage filled the room.

"Quick! Domitia—the sword! At once—the sword—the sword!" said the Emperor. He spoke in gulps and gasps.

He had Stephanus under him; his knee was on his chest and his hand, the gashed left hand flowing with blood, contracted the prostrate man's throat.

"Domitia! the sword!"

But she stood, stern, cold, without stirring a step, and she folded the sword of her father to her breast, with her arms crossed over it.

"Because of Paris—No!"

"The sword! be speedy. I will finish him!"

"Because of Cornelia—No!"

"Domitia—help!"

"Because of Lucius Lamia—No!"

She went to the curtains, drew them apart, and called down the passage to Norbanus.

The two Prætorian præfects were there with the chamberlains—but they were ill able to restrain the guard who suspected that their prince and Emperor was in danger and scented treachery.

Instantly a rush was made. Some of the soldiers, with the præfect Norbanus, came on running, whilst the other, Petronius Secundus, endeavored by his authority to restrain the rest.

But from the other end of the passage came gladiators running, hastily brought together by Parthenius.

For a moment there was a jam in the doorway, a burly gladiator and a soldier of the guard were wedged together, each endeavoring to hold the other back and force himself in.

Meanwhile Petronius continued to exhort his soldiers to stand back, and Parthenius to promise rewards to the gladiators who pressed on. The tumult became terrible. Men came to blows without, there was a running together of slaves and freedmen—of frightened women and pages from all sides. Some had leaped from their beds, roused from sleep, and were not clothed. Some bore lamps—but again certain others attempted to extinguish the lights. Some cried "Treason!" Others "Away with the monster!" Some called out "Nerva is the Emperor!" others "Domitian is the Augustus!"

Then the gladiator at the door, by dint of elbowing, forced his way within, but he was unarmed.

Next moment the Prætorian guardsman held back by the gladiator entered and struck at Stephanus, dealing a frightful blow.

Relieved by this assistance, Domitian staggered to his feet and glared about him. He was too much out of breath to speak, and in at the door came others pressing, some crying one thing, some another.

Then Domitia unfolded her arms, and taking the sword of Corbulo in her right hand, extended it to the gladiator and said—"Make an end."

The man snatched at the haft; and with a blow drove the blade into the breast of the Emperor.

Still the prince remained standing, and stretched forth his hands gropingly for a weapon.

Parmenas leaped at him, and with a knife struck him in the throat.

Then he reeled; in another moment he was surrounded, blows from all sides were rained on him. Again the sword of Corbulo was lifted and again smote, and he fell as a heap on the body of Stephanus.

For a moment there was stillness.

Then in that hush sounded a click and a gush. The bucket of the clepsydra had discharged, and with a jerk Saturn raised his scythe and pointed to the hour of midnight.

"He has answered his summons before the seat of Divine Justice!" said Domitia.

She stooped and plucked the signet ring from the finger of the murdered prince.

CHAPTER XIV

IN THE TULLIANUM

No sooner had Domitia got the signet from the finger of the dead Emperor, than she hastened from the room, trembling, almost blind as to her course, but armed with more than her natural strength to force her way through those who filled the passage.

Parmenas was now there, and he cleared a way for her, and in a loud voice forbade any of the slaves to leave the palace; Petronius at the same time gave orders to the soldiers of the guard to remain where they were, keeping watch that none left to spread the tidings, until Cocceius Nerva had been communicated with, and the Senate had been summoned.

Domitia, however, made her way from among the excited and alarmed throng, and finding some of her own slaves, bade them bring Eboracus to her.

"I am here, lady," answered the Briton.

"Then quick—with me. Not a moment is to be lost. Light a torch and lead the way."

"Whither, mistress?"

"To the Tullianum."

He stared at her in amazement.

"Quick—a life, a precious life is at stake. Not a minute must we delay or it will be too late."

"I am ready, lady."

He snatched a torch from an attendant, and advanced towards a postern gate that communicated with a flight of steps leading to the Forum. It was employed almost wholly by the servants and was used for communication between the kitchen and the markets.

"Shall we take any one else with us?" asked Eboracus. He answered himself—"Yes—here is Euphrosyne. She shall attend, and a boy shall carry the link. At night—and on such a night, I must have both arms at my disposal."

Domitia said nothing. She was eager to be on her way, was impatient of the smallest delay. Euphrosyne came up, and obeyed a sign from the Briton. He caught a scullion who was rubbing his sleepy eyes, and wondering what had caused the commotion, and had roused him from his bed. Eboracus thrust the torch into his hand and opened the door for the Empress.

Domitia stepped out to the head of the stairs. The rain had ceased, but the steps were running with water. The eaves dripped. The shrubs were laden with rain, they stooped their boughs and shed a load of moisture on the soil, then raised their leaves again, once more to accumulate the wet, and again to stoop and shower it down. Runnels conveying water from the roof were flowing as streams, noisily: the ground covered with pools, reflected the torch; as also every gleam from the retiring storm. Still in the distance thunder muttered, but it was a grumble of discontent at having failed to achieve all it had been sent to execute.

On such a night few would be abroad, except the patrols of the Vigiles and them there would be no difficulty in passing as the watchword was known to Eboracus, the word which allowed those only who could say it to traverse the streets at night in the respectable portions of the city. But there were no lamps, not even the feeble glimmer of a lantern slung in the midst of the street. Notwithstanding all the civilization of ancient Rome the art of lighting the thoroughfares at night was unknown. Such as were constrained to walk abroad after dark were attended by slaves bearing torches.

The streets of Rome had for long been of bad repute for the brawls and murders committed in them at night. Tipsy youths and rufflers had assaulted honest men, and should a woman be out after dark, she was certain of insult. Nero himself had distinguished himself in such vulgar performances. But under the Flavian princes much had been done to establish order and to ensure protection to life and purse of such as were out after dark, so that now, except in the slums, a citizen could visit his friends, a doctor his patients, by night, without fear of molestation.

And of all portions of Rome, the Forum with its splendid monuments, its rich temples, especially that of Saturn, that contained the city treasures, was most patrolled and therefore the safest. Eboracus had little expectation that his mistress would meet with rudeness or encounter danger, the rain must have swept the street of all idlers.

The long flight of steps was descended with caution, as they were slippery with rain, indeed with more caution than Domitia approved, so impatient was she to reach the object of her journey. The distance was not great. She had but to traverse the upper end of the Forum.

That at which she aimed was the prison of Rome. It lay at the foot of the Capitoline Hill, and consisted of an ancient well or subterranean chamber in which flowed a small spring. Above this was the prison, consisting of a series of cells that rose in stages to a considerable height,

against the rock, the chambers being in part scooped out of the trav-
estine. From the top of the hill ran a set of steps called the Gemonian
stair, and it was customary for State prisoners who had been condemned
to death, after execution to be cast from the upper chamber of the Tullianum down the stairs; whence with hooks the corpses were dragged
across the Forum and then flung into the Tiber.

To the house of the jailer, Domitia with her attendants made her
way. She had been stopped once in crossing the Forum, but the watch
recognized her, and saluted with respect, though with an expression of
astonishment on his countenance at seeing Cæsar's wife abroad at such a
time of the night, in such weather and with such scant attendance.

On reaching the jailer's door, Eboracus knocked. No answer was
given. He knocked again and louder, and continued knocking, till at
length a gruff voice from within called to know who was without, and
what was wanted.

"Open—in the name of the Augustus," said the British slave; and at
once the keeper of the prison let down the bars and withdrew the bolts
and chains, then carrying a lamp, peered out at those who demanded
admittance.

Then Domitia stood forward.

"You have a prisoner here—Lucius Ælius Lamia?"

"Yes."

"You must lead me to him."

The jailer appeared disconcerted, he held his lamp aloft and eyed the
woman who spake. He did not know her, his light was feeble, and as it
happened, he had seen little of the Empress.

"You do not know me," said Domitia. "Know you this ring?"

The prison-keeper held the flame of his lamp to the signet, and made
the usual sign of respect and recognition.

"You are required to lead me within," said Domitia.

The jailer at once stood aside, and suffered the Empress and her attendants to enter. Then he barred and bolted the door again.

"And now," said Domitia, impatient at the leisurely proceeding of the
man, "lead me to him."

Without another word he went forward, holding his lamp down that
those who followed might see the steps and not stumble at them.

"This way," said he, "and bow your heads, the entrance is low; but
most of them that pass this way have to hold their heads still lower
when they are taken out. Look at these stones—great blocks built by the
Kings—by Servius Tullus, they say. By Hercules! this is not a tavern
where men tarry long, nor do they relish our fare. One thing I must say

in our favor, we make no charge for our hospitality." Thus the jailer muttered as he went along.

"Look there—on your right—there is the cell where Simon Bar Gioras, the Jew, was strangled—he who was the last to maintain the struggle against the God Titus, in defence of Jerusalem; and see—" he threw open a door. "Here is the Bath of Mamertius in which Jugurtha was starved, all in blackness of darkness and soaking in ice-cold water. What! Impatient—do you not care to see the sights and hear my gossip? Well, well—but I have pretty things to show. I have a shankbone of Appius Claudius, who committed suicide in yon cell, and a garment of Sejanus, and the very bowstring wherewith—I am going on as fast as may be. See! we have had Christians here also. There was another Jew, Simon Petrus by name, he was in this cell, and I have the chain whereby he was bound, and I sell the links to the followers of the Nazarene," he began to cackle. "By Hercules! the chain is long enough. They come for more links than there would be, were the chain to reach across the Tiber. But any bit of old iron will serve, and they are not particular—take any scrap and pay in silver. I am going as fast as may be. I am not young. Fast enough I warrant. He is in no hurry—not Lamia. He can wait. All the same to him whether we reach him now or an hour hence."

Then Domitia, whose brow was beaded with cold sweat, like the stones of the vault that ran with moisture, laid hold of the prison-keeper's arm and said:—"Tell me—is he—" she could not say the word, her heart beat so furiously, and everything swam before her eyes.

"Aye, aye, you shall see for yourself. Come from the Augustus to satisfy him that we do our work properly, I trow. I have not much strength in these old-hands, but my two sons are lusty—and say the word—they will bend your back and snap the spine, smite and shear off your head like a pumpkin under a scythe, twist, and the life is throttled out of you. Here—here we are. Go in and see for yourself that we are good workmen."

He threw open a door and raised his lamp.

A low vaulted chamber was faintly illumined by the flame, the torch held by Eboracus was behind Domitia and the jailer; he had taken it from the link boy at the prison door. He and Euphrosyne attended their mistress, the boy was left without.

The old prison-keeper stood on one side.

"The order came yesterday," said he, "and we are not slack in the execution."

Domitia saw the figure of a man lying on the stone floor. She started forward—

"He sleeps!"

"I warrant you—right soundly."

She uttered a smothered cry.

"Put down the lamp!"

She turned and faced the jailer. "Leave me alone with him. I will wake him. I know he but sleeps."

The man hesitated.

Then Eboracus pressed forward and laid hold of the jailer and whispered—"Go without, it is the Augusta!"

The keeper of the prison started, raised his hand to his lips, bowed, set the lamp on the moist floor and drew back.

"Without! Without all!" ordered Domitia.

Then Eboracus pulled the jailer out of the cell. Euphrosyne stood doubtful whether to remain with her mistress or obey—but an impatient sign from the Empress drove her forth, and the British slave closed the door.

"He is dead," said the jailer. "Did the Augustus desire to withdraw the order? His signet has arrived too late. The prisoner has been throttled by my sons."

The old man and the two slaves remained for some quarter of an hour in the passage almost smothered by the smoke emitted by the torch.

From within they heard a voice—at intervals, now raised in weeping, then uttering low soothing tones, then raised in a cry as the conclamatio of hired wailers for the dead, calling on Lamia by name to return, to return, to leave the Shadowland and come back into light.

And then—a laugh.

A laugh so weird, so horrible, so unexpected, that with a thrust, without scruple, Eboracus threw open the door.

On the stone pavement sat Domitia, her hair dishevelled, and on her lap the head of the dead man. She was wiping his brow with her veil, stooping, kissing his lips, weeping, then laughing again—then pointing to purple letters, crossed L's woven into his tunic.

Eboracus saw it all—her reason was gone.

CHAPTER XV

DRAWING TO THE LIGHT

In the old home of Gabii, under the tender care of Euphrosyne and in the soothing company of Glyceria, little by little, stage by stage, Domitia recovered.

There was a horrible past to which no reference might be made. The true British slave, Eboracus, was ever at hand to help—when needed. Never a day, never half a day, but his honest face appeared at the door to inquire after his dear lady, and as her senses came flickering back, it was he to whom she clung to take her in his arms into the trellised walk, or when stronger to lead her where she could pick violets for Glyceria, and to pile about the feet of the little statue of the Good Shepherd. He took her a row on the lake and let her fish—he found nests of young birds and brought them to her; and all at once disclosed great powers of story-telling; he told marvellous British tales as to a little child, of the ploughing of Hu Cadarn, of Ceridwen and her cauldron. And he would sing—he fashioned himself a harp, of British shape, and sang as he accompanied himself, but his ballads were all in the Celtic tongue that Domitia could not understand—nevertheless it soothed and pleased her to listen to his music.

Longa Duilia did not visit her often. She made formal duty calls at long intervals, and as Domitia became better, these visits grew proportionately fewer.

Duilia, as she herself said, was not created to be a nurse. She knew that some were fitted by nature to attend to the sick, and all that sort of thing—but it was not her gift. Society was her sphere in which she floated and which she adorned, but she was distraught and drooping in a sick-room. She wished she had the faculty—and all that sort of thing—but all women were not cast in the same mould, run out of the same metal—and, my dear, parenthetically—some are of lead, others of Corinthian brass—and which are which it is not for me to say—she thanked the Gods it was so.

Nor did the visits and efforts to amuse, of Duilia, avail anything towards Domitia's cure. On the contrary, she was always worse after her mother had been with her. The old lady ripped up ill-healed sores, harped on old associations, could not check her tongue from scolding.

"My poor dear child—I never made a greater blunder in my life—I, too, who have the pedigree at my finger's ends—as to fancy that there was any connection with those Flavians. My dear! yellow hair is quite out of fashion now, quite out. Look at mine, a raven's wing is not darker. It was through Vespasia Polla—I thought we were related—stupid that I was—it was the Vipsanians we were allied to, not those low and beggarly Vespasians. As the Gods love me, I believe Polla's father was an army contractor. But I have made it all right. I have smudged out the line I had added to the family tree, and as for the wax heads of those Flavians, I have had them melted up. Will you believe it—I had the mask of Domitian run into a pot and that stupid Lucilla did not put a cover on it, and the rats have eaten it—eaten all the wax. I hope it has clogged their stomachs and given them indigestion. They doubtless thought it was dripping. But I really have made a most surprising discovery. I find there was an alliance with the Cocceii—most respectable family, very ancient, admirable men all—and so there is a sort of cousinship with the present admirable prince. His brother Aulus—rather old perhaps—but an estimable man—is—well—may be—in a word, I intend to give a little supper—a dainty affair—all in the best style—so sorry you can't be there, my dear Domitia—but of course absolutely impossible. Your state of health and all that sort of thing. Don't be surprised if you hear—but there, there—he is rather old though, for one who is only just turning off the very bloom of life and beauty."

After such a visit and such talk the mind of Domitia was troubled for several days. She became timid, alarmed at the least noise, and distraught. But then the poor crippled woman succeeded in comforting and laying her troubles, and the painful expression faded from her face. It became placid, but always with a sadness that was inseparable from the eyes, and a tremulousness of the lips, as though a very little—a rough word or two—would dissolve her into tears.

With the spring, the growing light, the increasing warmth, the bursting life in plant and insect, she began to amend more steadily, and relapses became fewer.

One sweet spring day, when Glyceria had been carried forth into the garden, and Domitia sat on the turf near her with purple anemones in her lap, that she was binding into a garland, the paralyzed woman was startled by hearing Domitia suddenly speak of the past.

She spoke, and continued weaving the flowers, "My Glyceria, I intend this for the little temple of my father. It is all I can do for him—to give flowers where his ashes lie—but it does not content me. There were two whom I loved and looked up to as the best of men, and both are gone—gone to dust: my own dearest father, and my lover, my husband, Lamia. I cannot bear to think of them as heaps of ashes or as wandering ghosts. When that thought comes over me, I seem to be as one drowning, and then darkness is before my eyes. I cannot cry—I smother."

"Why should you think of them as wandering ghosts or as heaps of dust?"

"I know that they are dust—I suppose they are shadows. But of anything else, all is guess-work, we know nothing—and that is so horrible. I love two only—have loved two only—and they are no more than shadows. No, no! I mean not that." She flung her arms about Glyceria, and laid her cheek against that of the sick woman. "No, I do love you, and I love Euphrosyne and I love Eboracus. But I mean—I mean in a different manner. One was my father, and the other my husband. It is so terribly sad to think they are lost to me like yesterday or last summer."

"They are not lost. You will see them again."

"See my father! See my Lamia!"

"Yes—I know it will be so."

"O, Glyceria, do not say such things. You make my heart jump. How can it be? They have been."

"They are and will be. Death is swallowed up in Life."

"That is impossible. Death is death and nothing more."

Then Glyceria took the hand of Domitia, and looking into her eyes, said solemnly: "Dost thou remember having asked me about the Fish?"

"Yes—this amulet," answered the noble lady, and she detached the cornelian from her throat, and held it in the hand not engaged by Glyceria. "Yes—I recollect—there was some mystery, but what was it?"

"The Fish is a symbol, as I said once before, and it is no amulet."

"Of what is it the symbol?"

"Of One who died—who tasted of the bitterness of the parting of soul and body, and who went into the region of Shadows and returned—the soul to the body, and rose from the dead, and by the virtue of His resurrection gives power to all who believe in Him to rise in like manner."

"And he could tell about what the ghosts do—how they wander?"

"I cannot say that. There would be no comfort in that. He rose to give us joy and to rob death of its terrors."

"But what has this to do with the Fish?"

"You know what the word Fish is in Greek."

"Very well."

"Take each letter of that word, and each letter is the first of words that contain the very substance of the Christian belief—Jesus Christ, the Son of God, the Saviour."

Domitia looked at the little cornelian fish; she could not understand.

"I believe that one could die and wake again. I have fainted and come round. And he might say what was in the spirit world into which he had been—but the region of ghosts is very dreary, very sad."

"Nay, He can do more. As He rose, He can raise us to new life, and He will do it, for He is God. He made us, and He will recall us from death."

"What—my father! Lucius! I shall see them again—not as shadows, but as they were—?"

"Not so—not as they were, mortal; but raised to an immortal life."

"I shall kiss my darling father—put my arms around my Lucius from whom I have been parted so long, and so cruelly, and who has been so—so true to me."

Then Domitia burst into tears.

Glyceria stroked her hand.

"There—you see how joyous is our hope. Death is nothing—it is only a good-bye for a bit to meet again."

"O, Glyceria! O, if I could see them—O Glyceria! O, you should not have said this if it be not true. My heart will break. O, if it might be so! if I could! but once only—for a moment—"

"Nay, that would not suffice; forever, never to be separated; no more tears, no more death."

"O, Glyceria—not another word—I cannot bear it. My heart is over full. Another time. My head, my head! O, if it might—it could be!"

Next day Glyceria saw by the red eyes of Domitia that she had slept little and had wept much. She did not turn the conversation to the same topic; she wisely waited for the noble lady to begin on it herself, and she judged that she would take some time to consider what had been spoken about and to digest it.

And in fact Domitia made no further allusion to the matter for some days. But after about a week, when alone with the paralyzed woman, she said to her abruptly: "You have never been in Syria?"

"No, dear lady."

"I have—and I have been on the confines of the desert and looked away, as far as the eye could reach, and have seen nothing but sand and barren rock. Behind me a rose-garden, syringas, myrtle and citron trees, and murmuring streams, before me—no green leaf, only death. It is to me, as I stand now and look back on my life as if it were that barren desert; and the fearful thing is—I dare not turn and look the other way, for it is into impenetrable night. But no, my life is not all desolation, there are just two green spots in it where the date palms stand and there are wells—my childhood, when I sat on my father's knee and cuddled into his arms; and once again, when I was recovering from the loss of him and was basking in the joy of my love for Lucius Lamia. All the rest—" she made a gesture of despair—"Death."

"Dearest lady! I would like to turn you about and show you that where you think only blackness reigns, lies a beautiful garden, a paradise, and One at the gate who beckons and says, Come unto Me, all you that labor and are heavy laden, and I will give you rest."

"Ah! but that may be all fancy and dream work like the promises of the Magi, and the mysteries of Isis."

Glyceria got no further than this. Domitia was disposed to talk with her on her hope, and on the Christian belief, but always with reserve and some mistrust.

There were old prejudices to be overcome, there was the consciousness that the promises so largely made by the votaries of the many cults from East and South who came to Rome were unfulfilled, and this made her unable to place confidence in the new religion held by slaves and ignorant people, however alluring it might seem.

Among the very few who came to Gabii during her illness and convalescence, was Flavia Domitilla, the widow of Flavius Clemens, who had been put to death by Domitian. Domitilla had been banished, but returned immediately on the death of the tyrant. She had suffered as had Domitia. In her manner and address there was something so gentle and assuring, that the poor ex-empress, in the troubled condition of her brain, was drawn to her, and after her visits felt better. She knew, or rather supposed, that Domitilla was a Christian. Her husband had been one, and had suffered for his faith.

It was with real pleasure that she ran to welcome her one morning, when the steward entered and announced: "The Lady Flavia Domitilla."

CHAPTER XVI

AN ECSTASY

"I have come, dear Domitia, with a petition,"said the widow of Flavius Clemens. "And it is one you will wound me if you refuse."

"But who would wound so gentle a breast?"answered Domitia, kissing her visitor. "He must be heartless who draws a bow against a dove."

"Hearken first to what I ask. I am bold—but my very feebleness inspires me with audacity."

"What is it, then?"

"That you come with me to my villa for a little change of scene, air and society. It will do you good."

"And I cannot refuse. It is like your sweet spirit to desire nothing save what is kindly intended and does good to others."

"As you have assented so graciously, I will push my advance a little further and say—Return with me to-day. Let us travel together. If you will—I have a double litter—and we can chatter as two magpies together."

"Magpies bring sorrow."

"Nay, two—mirth—we have cast our sorrows behind us. You said I was a dove, so be it—a pair of doves, perhaps wounded, lamed—but we coo into each other's ear, and lay our aching hearts together and so obtain solace."

"I will refuse you nothing," said Domitia, again kissing her visitor.

Accordingly, a couple of hours later the two ladies started, Domitia taking with her some attendants, but travelling, as was proposed, in the large litter of Domitilla.

This latter lady was, as already mentioned, the widow of Clemens, one of the two sons of Flavius Sabinus, præfect of the city, who had held the Capitol against the Prætorians of Vitellius and had been murdered but a few hours before Rome was entered by the troops that favored his brother Vespasian. On that occasion his sons had escaped, and the elder was married to Julia, daughter of Titus, but had been put to death by Domitian. The younger brother, Clemens, a quiet, inoffensive man, who took no part in public affairs, had been executed as well, shortly before Domitian himself perished.

And now Flavia Domitilla lived quietly on her estate not far from the Ardeatine Gate of Rome.

"How!" said Flavia, suddenly, as she espied the little cornelian suspended on the bosom of Domitia, "you have the Fish!"

"Yes, Glyceria gave it me—long ago."

"Do you know what it means?"

"Glyceria told me—but it is a dream, a beautiful fancy, nothing more. There is no evidence."

"Domitia, you have not sought for it."

"My cousin, Rome is full of religions. Some say the truth is in Sabazius, some in Isis, some in the stars, some in Mithras—a new importation—and some will go back to the old Gods of our Latin ancestors. But one and another all are naught."

"How know you that?"

"By the spirit that is within me. It can discern between what is true and false. Not that which promises best is the most real."

"You are right, Domitia—that is truest and most real which meets and satisfies the seeking, aching heart."

"And where is that?"

"Where you have not sought for it."

"If I were sure I would seek. But I am weary of disillusionings and disappointments."

"Well—will you hear?"

"I am not sure. I have met with too many disappointments to desire another."

Nothing further was said on this topic till the villa was reached. Domitia showed that she did not desire to have it pursued.

As Flavia alighted from her litter, a young man approached, handed her something and asked for an answer.

The widow of Clemens opened a tied diptych and read some words written therein.

She seemed disconcerted and doubtful. She looked questioningly at Domitia, and then asked leave of the latter to say a word in private to Euphrosyne. Leave was granted and a whispered communication passed between them.

Again Flavia looked inquiringly at Domitia, and it was with considerable hesitation that she signed to the young man to approach, and said:—"Be it so. The Collect shall be here."

That evening before she and her guest parted for the night, Flavia took Domitia by the hand and said:—"You are right—the faculty of determination is seated in every breast. Inquire and choose."

A few days passed, and then the hostess became uneasy. Evidently she had something that she desired to say, but was afraid of broaching the subject.

At length, abruptly, she began on it.

"Domitia, I show you the utmost confidence. I must tell you something. You know how that the Christians have been persecuted under—I mean of late, and how we have suffered. My dear husband shed his blood for the cause, and he was but one among many. Now there is a respite granted, but how long it will last we know not. The laws against us stand unrepealed and any one who wishes us ill can set them in motion for our destruction."

"You do not think, Cousin—"

"Nay, hear me out, Domitia. You saw a young man approach me as we arrived here. He is what we term a deacon, and he came to announce that, if I saw fit, the Church would assemble in my house next first day of the week, that is the day after the Jewish Sabbath. It is customary with us to assemble together for prayer on that day, early, before dawn, sometimes in one house, then in another, so as to escape observation. And now, on the morrow—this assembly, which we term the Collect, will take place. Do thou tarry in thy chamber, and thou shalt be summoned when all have dispersed."

"Nay, I would see and hear what takes place."

"That may not be, Domitia, that is only for the initiated."

"But why secrecy if there be naught of which to be ashamed?"

"Our Master said, Give not that which is holy unto dogs, neither cast ye your pearls before swine. Tell me, Domitia, how would you endure were your father made a mock of, his sayings and acts parodied on the stage, and turned into a matter of low buffoonery?"

Domitia's brow flamed and her eyes flashed.

"I see your answer in your face. So with our Great Master. His mysteries are holy, and we would preserve them from outrage. Now you understand why you cannot be present."

"But I would not mock."

"It is our rule, to avoid the chance of profanity."

"As you will."

"There is one thing more," said Flavia. "You will not be angry if I have sent to have poor Glyceria brought here. Owing to her infirmity she has not been able to be present at a gathering of the Church for a long time, and nothing could give her greater consolation and happiness."

"I am willing for anything that can cheer her,"answered Domitia; then in a tone of vexation, "So—a freedwoman, and Euphrosyne, a slave, will be admitted where I am shut out—I, who was Empress—"

"Do not be offended. Is it not so in every sodality, that the members of the Club alone attend the gatherings of the Club."

"You are a Club then?"

"We are the worshippers of God."[16]

Domitia was silent, then Flavia started up. "I hear them—they have come with Glyceria. I must see that she be cared for. The long journey to that frail and broken frame will have exhausted her slender powers."

"And I will go, too"—with a tinge of jealousy in her manner. Domitia little liked that another should interest herself about the poor woman, and should stand to her in a more intimate relation than herself.

On going forth, all feeling of envy disappeared at once before a sense of alarm.

An accident had occurred on the way. Owing to some fault in the paving of the road, one of the bearers had stumbled and, in falling, the litter had been thrown down and the woman within injured.

Domitia saw by the ashen face and the green hue about the mouth and temples that Glyceria was in great pain. But her eyes were bright and sought her at once and a world of love flowed out of them, she put forth her thin hand to lay hold of the great lady. Domitia at once flashed into anger. "This comes of bringing her here. Had she been left at Gabii it would never have happened. Where is the fellow who threw her down?—Flavia! have him whipped with the scorpion."

Glyceria caught her hand. "It was an accident. He was not in fault. I am happy. It is the will of God—that is everything to me."

"You suffer."

The paralyzed woman could not speak more. She was being lifted out of the litter, and fainted as she was moved. She was conveyed, in a condition of unconsciousness, to the room she was to occupy, a room opening out of the same corridor as that given up to Domitia.

The family physician was summoned; he gave little hopes of the poor woman recovering from the shock, her natural strength and recuperative power had long ago been exhausted.

---

16   The Roman benefit Clubs were under the invocation of some god or goddess, and the members were called Cultores Apollinis, or Jovi, as the case might be.

All that evening Domitia remained silent, apparently in ill humor, or great distress, and Flavia Domitilla was unable to get many words from her.

She retired early to rest, but could not sleep. Before going to her bed, she had visited the sick woman, and she convinced herself with her own eyes that the flame of the lamp of life was flickering to extinction.

Domitia loved the actor's widow with all the passion of her stormy heart; and the thought of losing her was to her unendurable.

The night was still, balmy, and the heavens star-besprent. She looked from the corridor at the lights above, and then dropped the curtains over her door. She threw herself on her cushions, but her thoughts turned and tossed in her head.

She pressed her knuckles to her eyeballs to close her eyes, but could not force on sleep.

It was to her as though every person whom she loved was taken from her; till she had no one left to whom her heart could cling.

"I vow a pig to Æsculapius!" she said, "if he will recover her!" and then impatiently turned to the wall. "What can Æsculapius do? Whom has he succored at any time? He is but a name." To whom could she cry? What god of Olympus would stoop to care for—even to look at an actor's widow, a poor Greek freedwoman.

The gods! They revelled and drank Ambrosia; made love and deceived the simple, and lied and showed themselves to be arrant knaves. They were greedy of sacrifices, they accepted all that was given—but they gave nothing in return. Their ears were open to flattery, not to prayer. They were gods for the merry and rich, not for the miserable and poor.

She thought she heard hasty steps in the passage, then voices. "And He! the God of Glyceria—why had not He saved her from this fall? Was He as powerless, as regardless, of His votaries as those of Olympus?" Yes—something was the matter—there was a stir in the house—at that hour—at dead of night—Domitia's heart bounded. Was Glyceria passing away?

She threw a mantle about her, and barefooted as she was, ran forth into the gallery.

She saw at the further end a light at the door of the sick room, and sounds issued thence.

Instantly she flew thither, plucked aside the curtain, and stood in the doorway, arrested by the sight.

Euphrosyne was seated on the bed, and had raised her sister in her arms; the sick woman rested against her in a sitting posture; Flavia Domitilla was there as well. Directly she saw Domitia she signed to her to approach.

But Glyceria!—she was at once transfigured. Her face seemed to shine with a supernatural light—it had acquired a loveliness and transparency as of an angel—her eyes were upraised and fixed as in a trance, and her arms were outspread. She seemed not to weigh on Euphrosyne, but to be raised and sustained by supernatural power.

The joy, the rapture in that sublimated countenance were beyond description. She saw, she knew, she felt none of those things that usually meet the senses. And yet Domitia, Flavia, were convinced that those illumined happy eyes looked on some One—were gazing into a light to themselves unseen.

From her lips poured rapturous prayer.

"I see Thee! Thou—the joy of my heart, my hope and my portion forever! Thee whom I have loved and longed for! I hold Thee—I clasp Thy feet! O give her to me—the dear mistress! Take me, take me to Thyself—but ere I go—by Thy wounded hands—by Thy thorn-crowned head—by Thy pierced side—bring her to the light! To the light! To the light!" And suddenly—with an instantaneous eclipse the illumination died off from her face, the tension was over, the arms, the entire body sank heavily against the bosom of Euphrosyne, the eyes closed; she heaved a long sigh, but a smile lingered about her lips.

Awed, not daring to draw nearer, unwilling to go back, Domitia stood looking. Neither did Flavia Domitilla stir.

After a little while, however, the latter signed to Domitia to depart, and made as though she also would go.

"She sleeps," she said.

Then Glyceria's bright eyes opened, and she said:—

"Not till after the Collect—at that I must be—bear me down—then only—"

CHAPTER XVII

HAIL, GLADSOME LIGHT!

Before the day began to break, from various quarters came men and women, in twos and threes to the house of Flavia Domitilla.

The visitor to Rome may see the very spot where stood her house and garden. For this good woman converted the latter into a place of sepulture for the Christians, and the catacomb that bears her name is one of the most interesting of those about Rome. Not only so, but the ruins of her villa remain, on the farm of Tor Marancia, or the Ardeatine Way. Here lived the widow of the martyr Clemens, with her sister-in-law, Plautilla, and her niece, of the same name as herself, all three holy women, serving God and ministering to the necessities of the poor.

The Collect, or assembly of the Faithful, was to take place in the atrium or hall of the villa. Domitilla had only Christian slaves with her in her country residence, and could trust them.

In the large mansions of the Roman nobility there were grand reception halls, called basilicas, with rows of pillars down the sides dividing them into a nave and aisles, with an apse, or bema as it was termed, at the end, in which the master of the house sat to receive his visitors. Here he and his clients, his parasites and friends walked, talked, declaimed, listened to readings, when the weather was wet or cold. At a later period, when the nobility became Christian, many of them gave up their basilicas to be converted into churches, and such is the origin of several churches of Rome. They never were, as some have erroneously supposed, halls of justice—they were, as described, the halls attached to the great Roman palaces.

But at the time I am speaking of, no such surrenders had been made. The great families had not been converted, only here and there, at rare intervals, some of their members had embraced the Gospel. But smaller people had become Christian, and these did temporarily give up the more public portion of the house, the atrium and tablinum for Christian worship. It was dangerous to thus assemble, and it would have been infinitely more dangerous had the assemblies taken place always at the same house. Accordingly it was contrived to vary the place of meeting and to give secret notice to the faithful where the gathering would be on the ensuing Lord's day.

The danger of these Collects was further reduced by their being held sometimes in the churches underground in the catacombs, or in the cellæ near the tombs; and these gatherings passed uncommented on, as it was customary for the pagans to meet for a solemn banquet in the decorated chambers attached to their places of interment on the anniversaries of the death of their friends.

The various guilds also had their meeting for the transaction of business, a sacred meal, and a sacrifice to the gods, and the early Christians were able so to copy the customs of the guilds or sodalities, as to carry on their worship undetected by the authorities, who supposed their assemblies were mere guild gatherings.

The hour was so early that lights were necessary, and lamps were suspended in the tablinum, which was raised a couple of steps above the floor of the hall.

Round the arc of the chamber, which was semi-circular, seats had been arranged, and in the centre against the wall one of more dignity than the rest, covered with white linen. In the midst of the tablinum at the top of the two steps was a table, and on one side a desk on legs.

Great care was taken at the door to admit none but such as could give the sign that they were Christians. The ostiarius or porter in the early Church held a very important office, on his discretion much of the safety of the Church depended. He had to use the utmost caution lest a spy should slip in.

The hall rapidly filled.

Before the steps into the apse lay Glyceria on a sort of bier, her hands folded, and her earnest eyes upraised! She had been gently, carefully conveyed thither, to be for the last time united in worship with the Church on earth, before she passed into the Church beyond.

On each side of the tablinum were curtains, that could be easily and rapidly drawn along a rod and so close the apse.

In the atrium itself there were few lights. They were not needed, day would soon break.

In the tablinum, against the wall, sat the presbyters with Clement, the bishop, in the centre. He was an old man, with a gentle face, full of love. He had been a freedman of the Flavians, and it was out of respect to them that he had taken the name of Clement, which was one of those in use in their family.

At his side, on the right hand, was one far more aged than he—one we have seen before, Luke the Physician and Evangelist.

Now one with a pair of clappers gave a signal and all rose who had been seated.

A deacon standing at the top of the step said:—"Let us pray for the Emperor."

Whereupon all the congregation responded as with a single voice: "Lord, have mercy."

Then Clement, the Bishop, prayed:—"We beseech Thee, O Father, to look down upon the Emperor and to strengthen him against his foes, and to illumine his mind that he may rule in Justice, and be Thou his defence and strong tower."

Thereupon the deacon called again:—"Let us pray for the magistrates." To which the people responded in the same manner, and the Bishop prayed in few terse words for the magistrates. In precisely similar manner was prayer made for the bishops and clergy, for all the faithful, for those in chains, working in mines, for the sick and the sorrowful, for the widows and orphans; it was as though a flood of all-embracing charity flowed forth.

Then the intercessions ended, Luke came to the desk, and a deacon brought the roll of the Law and unfolded it before him, and another held aloft a torch.

He read as follows:—"This commandment which I command thee this day, it is not hidden from thee neither is it far off.... But the word is very nigh thee in thy heart and in thy mouth, that thou mayest do it. See, I have set before thee life and good, and death and evil.... I call heaven and earth to record this day that I have set before you life and death, blessing and cursing; therefore choose life ... that thou mayest love the Lord thy God, and that thou mayest obey His voice, and that thou mayest cleave unto Him."

Then the Evangelist closed the roll and returned it to the deacon, and he spake some words of exhortation thereon.

Next came another deacon and unfolded the roll of the Prophets; and Luke read:—"The Spirit of the Lord God is upon me; because the Lord hath anointed me to preach good tidings unto the meek; He hath sent me to bind up the broken-hearted, to proclaim liberty to the captives, and the opening of the prison to them that are bound. To proclaim the acceptable year of the Lord, and the day of vengeance of our God; to comfort all that mourn.... To give to them that mourn beauty for ashes, the oil of joy for mourning, the garment of praise for the spirit of heaviness; that they might be called Trees of Righteousness, the Planting of the Lord, that He might be glorified."

Then again Luke spoke a few simple words and declared how that the prophecy of old was fulfilled in Christ who was the healer of all sick souls, and the strengthener of all who were feeble, the restorer of the halt, the comforter of all that mourn, and the planter in the field of the Church of such as would grow up plants of righteousness to bear their fruit in due season.

And when he ceased, the congregation sang a psalm: "Praise the Lord, O my soul: and all that is within me praise His holy name."

In the first age of the Church the liturgical service grew out of that of the synagogue. As in the latter there were the two lessons from Law and Prophet, so was there in the Church, but after the Psalm there were added to these, two more lessons, one from an Epistle by an Apostle and one from a Gospel.

At the time of our narrative the service was in process of formation and was not yet formed; and the sequence of Epistle and Gospel had not as yet been established. However, now Luke stood forward and said:—

"Beloved, we have a letter written by the Blessed John—the Disciple that Jesus loved, and therefrom I will read a few words."

Then he unfolded a short roll and read as follows:—

"Behold what manner of love the Father hath bestowed upon us, that we should be called the sons of God! therefore the world knoweth us not, because it knew Him not. Beloved, now are we the sons of God; and it doth not yet appear what we shall be; but we know that, when He shall appear, we shall be like Him, for we shall see Him as He is. And every man that hath this hope in him purifieth himself, even as he is pure."

He ceased, for a strange sound reached the ears of all—a sound that swelled and rose and then fell away and became all but inaudible.

Once again he began to read—and again this sound was heard.

"This is the message that ye heard from the beginning, that we should love one another."

Again he ceased, and looked round, and listened. For once more this strange wailing sound arose.

But as it declined, he resumed his reading.

"Marvel not, my brethren, if the world hate you. We know that we have passed from death unto life, because we love the brethren."

He was constrained to cease.

Then at a signal, two deacons went in the direction of the sound. And the whole congregation was hushed. But Glyceria, on her bed, lifted her hands and her eyes shone with expectation.

Presently the deacons returned:—"A woman—a weeping woman in a dark room."

Then Luke descended from the bema, and attended by them went in the direction of the voice, and came, where crouching, concealed,

Domitia lay on the ground, sobbing as if her heart would break—they could not stay her—they did not try—they waited.

And presently she raised her face, streaming with tears, and said—"The light! the glorious light!"

And the sun rose over the roof, and shone down into the atrium, on the face of Glyceria.

Then Flavia Domitilla stooped over her, laid her hand on her eyes and said:—"In the Joy of thy Lord, Face to Face!"